He twi   one closed, b   . An odor bur   ee a filthy green miasma.   and I obeyed, looking through eyes tearing from the stench. Even so, I saw the corpse of my Uncle Reinhart, whom I knew only from his portrait in the gallery. The putrescent features still bore a resemblance to the painting, though the eyes had long ago fallen in, and much of the flesh had liquified.

"This is death, Victor," said my father.

Ravenloft is a netherworld of evil, a place of darkness that can be reached from any world—escape is a different matter entirely. The unlucky who stumble into the Dark Domains find themselves trapped in lands filled with vampires, werebeasts, zombies, and worse.

Each novel in the series is a complete story in itself, revealing the chilling tales of the beleaguered heroes and powerful evil lords who populate the Dark Domains.

Ravenloft BOOKS

Vampire of the Mists
Christie Golden

Knight of the Black Rose
James Lowder

Dance of the Dead
Christie Golden

Heart of Midnight
J. Robert King

Tapestry of Dark Souls
Elaine Bergstrom

Carnival of Fear
J. Robert King

I, Strahd
P. N. Elrod

The Enemy Within
Christie Golden

Mordenheim
Chet Williamson

Tales of Ravenloft
Edited by Brian Thomsen
Forthcoming

The Screaming Tower
James Lowder
Forthcoming

BOOKS

Mordenheim

Chet Williamson

This one's for Colin.

MORDENHEIM

First Printing: May 1994
Printed in the United States of America
Library of Congress Catalog Card Number: 93-61465

9 8 7 6 5 4 3 2 1

ISBN: 1-56076-852-5

TSR, Inc.
P.O. Box 756
Lake Geneva, WI 53147
United States of America

TSR Ltd.
120 Church End, Cherry Hinton
Cambridge CB1 3LB
United Kingdom

ONE

Even from several miles away, the castle dominated the landscape. It loomed on the horizon like the head of a beast crawling out of the sea, peering over the top of the cliff for victims.

Hilda Von Karlsfeld leaned forward, all the better to see out the window of the coach. "Is that it, do you suppose?" she asked her fiance, Friedrich Kreutzer. He edged forward as well, happy for the chance to draw nearer to his love. An old man dressed in rough tweeds sat across from them and paid them no mind, looking down at the floor of the coach where his gaze had rested ever since they had left Rivalis.

"Schloss Mordenheim?" Friedrich peered through the mist that seemed a permanent part of Lamordia's weather, whatever the season. "It may be." He turned to the elderly passenger. "Is that Castle Mordenheim, do you know?"

The man looked up with eyes only, glanced out the window, then peered back down at the floor. He spat out the words, "It is."

"Are you from Ludendorf?" Friedrich asked, referring to their destination only a few miles away.

"I am."

"Then do you know Doctor Mordenheim?"

"Mordenheim? Never met him, praise the gods, but I know *of* him—a *monster* he is. A monster worse than the fiend he created!"

Friedrich and Hilda looked at each other uneasily.
"A monster?" Hilda said. "Then the things we have
heard . . ."

"They're all true," the old man said. "And worse
besides. There's not an evil thing credited to Victor
Mordenheim that is a lie. And if it is, 'tis only because
he hasn't yet thought of doing it."

Though they pressed him, the man said little more.
"Ask them when you get to Ludendorf. They know.
They *all* know. . . ." He then sank into a deep silence
from which he would not be raised. No one spoke again
until the coach stopped in the market square of the little
town of Ludendorf.

It was midafternoon, but no sun shone on the few
stall keepers hardy enough to set out their wares.
Autumn was nearly done, and an early winter was
wrapping its bony fingers about the country. The con-
trast between this strange land and Friedrich and
Hilda's native Darkon was all too easily seen. What
might be only a drizzle in Darkon would be a blizzard in
the neighboring domain of Lamordia.

Friedrich and Hilda stepped from the coach as two
men scurried out from the Black Bear Inn and began
hauling down their luggage. "Into the inn, squire?"
asked the first man, a round and jolly sort.

"No, thank you. Just off the street will be fine." Friedrich tipped them, though he could ill afford to, then
looked at his watch, the last remnant of the small inher-
itance his father had left him. "We have an hour. Shall
we keep warm inside?"

Hilda nodded, and arm in arm they entered the inn.
Mostly men sat inside, and the majority of those were at
the short bar that served ale and wine. Friedrich and
Hilda sat at a table near the fire and ordered tea, which
a thin, sallow woman brought to them. It was weak but

hot, and they sipped it thankfully.

"Not staying here then, are you?" the woman asked.

"No, we're being met," Friedrich said.

"Met? By whom?"

The woman displayed no shame in her curiosity, and the couple glanced at each other, wondering whether they should tell, particularly after the reaction of the man in the coach. Then Hilda shrugged. "We're going to Schloss Mordenheim."

The woman's pale skin grew even paler, and she made a gesture to ward off evil. "Mordenheim?" she said huskily. "And what's your business with him?"

Friedrich bridled at her boldness. "Well, that's *our* business, isn't it?"

The woman looked over toward the bar. "Otto!" she called, and a huge man whose bare head resembled a fleshy cannonball came to the table. "They're going out to see the doctor at the castle, and they say it's *their* business why."

Otto did not look at all cheered by this news. "It's our business too," he growled in a voice that seemed to rattle the cups in the saucers. "When the bodies of our daughters and wives and mothers disappear, it becomes our business fast."

"Bodies . . . ?" said Hilda. "Surely you don't mean—"

"I mean corpse robbin', missy. Stealin' the newly dead from morgues and graves and even deathbeds. Maybe even helping them along, for all we know. But only women. And we know why." Otto nodded his massive head sagely.

Hilda tried desperately not to evince her distaste for the odor of onions and cheap wine that issued from Otto's mouth. "Why, then?" she asked.

The old woman snorted. "To make a mate for his creature, that's why. *Everybody* knows that. But so far nothing he's done has worked. Otherwise there'd be a horde of the monster's brood overrunning Lamordia."

"As it is," Otto observed, "one's bad enough."

"One?" said Friedrich. "What do you mean?"

"He means *Adam,*" the woman said.

"We heard," said Friedrich delicately, "that Mordenheim had successfully created life in dead tissue."

"Life? A walking dead man is what he made—a monster with no goodness and no pity for nothing. He roams the country doing what he will."

"Well, why hasn't anyone done anything?" asked Hilda. "If Mordenheim is committing crimes, why isn't he arrested? And why isn't this . . . Adam you mentioned captured?"

"Oh, as if it's that easy!" the old woman said. "When the monster don't want to be found, there ain't nobody as can find him. And as for arresting Mordenheim, that old fool Baron Von Aubrecker tells us the doctor has to be caught in the act for any charges to be brought against him."

"Sure," said Otto scornfully. "The baron's safe up there in his own castle, but us common folk are prey to both Mordenheim and his monster." The man's eyes narrowed so that they almost disappeared. "And what've *you* two got to do with him?"

"We're . . . scholars," Friedrich answered. "The doctor simply wants to consult us on a few points."

"And what're you scholars *of?*" Otto asked.

Friedrich began to answer, but Hilda leapt adroitly into the conversational gap. "Metaphysics. Spiritual philosophy."

"That have aught to do with raising the dead?" Otto's intonation implied that he would not be pleased with a positive answer.

"Oh, no," Hilda said. "From the doctor's letter to us, I assume he intends to give up his unholy ways and turn to philosophy for consolation."

For a moment, Otto and the old woman looked as if they didn't know what to say. Then the old woman nodded. "Well," she said thoughtfully, "that's better than raising the dead, I suppose." Then she and Otto turned back to the bar.

"What did you tell them that for?" Friedrich whispered.

"To keep us from being run out of town," Hilda said with an uncomfortable smile. "Can you imagine their reaction if we had said we were practitioners of necromancy and spirit transference?"

"Well, we're hardly practitioners. We've never raised a single spirit. Not yet anyway."

"All right then—we're students. Either way, our field of study would have been sure to dismay them." She sipped her tea and shook her head. "But not as much as these rumors about Doctor Mordenheim dismay me."

"We've heard such rumors before, back in Darkon."

"Yes, but rumors at a distance are easier to dismiss. This is practically Mordenheim's backyard. Do you really think he has created a being from dead flesh? And that he wants us to help him create another?"

"Mordenheim is a scientist," Friedrich reflected. "In his letter to us, his rational outlook showed through. Even while he practically begged us to aid him, he still seemed fairly skeptical about our abilities."

"He seemed downright rude, if you ask me," said Hilda. She sighed. "But I guess his skepticism was justified. The term *charlatans* describes us better than *necromancers.*"

"It's not for want of trying, Hilda. We've *seen* it, if not done it, so we *know* that the dead can rise and that one spirit can be put into another's body."

"Yes," said Hilda, thinking back with dull horror to that night in the graveyard when their mentor had finally demonstrated the practice to them—but died a few weeks later, having fallen victim to the chill night air. "A pity old Von Schreck couldn't turn his arts on himself—"

"And finish the lessons we had already paid for."

Hilda nodded. How ironic, she thought, that the man who had called himself the "Master of the Graveyard" should have met his death by catching a cold in one. And in that very graveyard his corpse had been buried.

Graveyards. She sighed and took another sip of the warming tea, seeing pictures of her past in its swirling steam. So much of her life had taken place in graveyards.

That was, after all, where she and Friedrich had first met. . . .

 **TWO**

Hilda Von Karlsfeld shuddered deliciously. The moment and the place were perfect. She had never felt so alive, so vibrant, so . . . frightened.

The Graymoor Cemetery was, as she had heard, the eeriest of all the many cemeteries of Il Aluk. And here she was. Alone. At midnight. If ever she would be blessed with inspiration for her work, it was here.

She stood just within the front gate. The broad avenue before her seemed like a path through a jungle. Rank vegetation clawed at the walkway, and ancient stones heaved up on either side. Many of the monuments were sunken, showing just the tips of their obelisks, like the fingers of drowning men reaching desperately from the sea of choking weeds.

Oh, yes, this was *splendid!* She could see it now, writing scenes in her head as she picked her way around the sickly plants and the chunks of gray stone that had surrendered their purpose and fallen from the tops of memorials. Ermentrude, her heroine, comes to the graveyard in the dead of night to meet her lover Raoul, since they know that they will not be seen there, as everyone fears Grosz, the lich who haunts the graveyard. And Ermentrude arrives there before Raoul, and finds herself alone, and the thoughts that flit through her mind . . .

Well, how better to create those thoughts than to

experience them firsthand? It was much the same way that Mrs. Felicia Henry, Hilda's favorite writer of action-filled romances, had braved the dangers of spots where kobolds and goblins and ghouls freely roamed in order to get just the right flavor for the books Hilda had read from youth to womanhood.

As Hilda walked through the vast necropolis, she began to feel her excitement slowly transforming itself into something not unlike real fear. Had Mrs. Henry, she wondered, gone to all these places alone? Or had she taken, perhaps, some strong companion or a wizard armed with spells?

Well, it hardly mattered, did it? Hilda Von Karlsfeld went alone, and would reap a more colorful account for her boldness.

She had neither candle nor torch, and felt she was all the better for the lack of one, since a light would have only drawn attention to her—if there were anything living here to see. Besides, a waning, nearly full moon was shining down, bathing the cemetery in a pale glow. She would not have considered coming when the moon was totally full for fear of the occasional lycanthrope, a person who turned into a ravenous beast when the moon shone its brightest. There were enough creatures in Darkon already.

On she walked, keeping to the main path through the graveyard and hoping to come out at the other end. Several times she was startled by what she took to be people—or worse—standing perfectly still among the weeds, but every time, the figures turned out to be nothing but funeral statuary, and she breathed a quiet sigh of relief.

At the far end of the cemetery was the Great Circle, a vast, round structure with tombs on both its inner and outer edges. Within the circle was a large open space peppered with other gravestones. Hilda decided to enter the area, observe it in the moonlight, and then leave this place of mold and death. And quickly, too.

But as she drew closer to the circle, she thought she could see a dim light coming through the apertures that gave entry to the inner tombs. At first she thought she would retreat and leave the way she had come in, but then decided that the undergrowth was high enough here that she would not be noticed if she trod quietly.

She made her way to one of the arches, where she stood for a moment, gathering the courage to go farther. Dimly there came to her the sound of a voice, deep and cavernous, from within the Great Circle. There was a regularity to the words, as though the speaker were chanting, and she shuffled nearer in spite of her fear, making her way from one tombstone to the next. She had heard rumors of necromancers working their ghastly spells in Graymoor Cemetery, but had also heard that such spells were only efficacious during the dark of the moon.

Whether or not the moon was right, Hilda wanted desperately to see what was happening. She wondered if she would see anything like the hideous ceremonies that Mrs. Henry had detailed in *The Sorcerer and the Succubus*. Perhaps she could even write down some of the words so as to make her own writings more realistic.

Hilda burrowed in the reticule that hung from her sash. From it, she withdrew a pencil and several sheets of folded foolscap, then summoned the necessary grit to look around the tombstone behind which she hid.

At last she could see the speaker, and she was only initially disappointed. He was an old man with a long white beard and a face crosshatched with deep fissures. But these were the only concessions to tradition his appearance made.

He did not have the majestic height that most wizards, fictional at least, were able to claim, and was in fact rather portly. Instead of wearing a wizardly robe and hat decorated with arcane symbols of his calling, the old man wore a rather shabby coat with patches on the sleeves, and a soft, floppy hat dedicated more to comfort than to ritual.

At least his voice was deep and commanding, and his props seemed authentic. Two thick, black candles, giving off a greasy smoke that could only be the product of corpse-fat, stood on either side of him. In his stubby-fingered hands he held a book that appeared to be suitably antiquated. On the ground before him, a patch of weeds had been hacked away to reveal the bare earth beneath, and in it were scrawled various magical symbols. A tall staff that may have made the designs leaned against a time-blackened gravestone, and Hilda was thrilled to see that the staff's headpiece was a yellowed skull.

This was far more than she had dared hope for, and, she thought, it was relatively safe as well. She could watch unobserved, and even if she was seen, the odds were that she could outrun the old man.

Unless . . .

Unless the wizard was not alone.

As quickly as the thought came to her, she looked around and saw a living face only a foot away from her own.

To her credit, she did not scream, but she could not help releasing a sharp cry of surprise that could be easily heard. It was partly muffled, however, by the exclamation barked out by the other party, also startled.

It took her only a second to see that no monster accosted her here, but a young man, very alive and decidedly nonmonstrous in appearance. From the expression on his face and from the way in which the two youths turned their heads in tandem back toward the wizard, she received the unmistakable sensation that he was an interloper in the ceremony just as surely as she.

The wizard, by this time, was looking up from his book in their general direction, a displeased look on his round, wrinkled face. Frowning, his lined visage resembled a street map of Il Aluk. "Who's there?" he cried.

Hilda and the young man looked at each other again, and an unspoken agreement to *remain* unspoken passed between them.

"All right, all right, come out now, or I'll blast you with a spell that will make your prying eyes drip from their sockets like so much coney stew! I *mean* it! Come on out! And *now!*"

They looked at each other sheepishly, then rose like twin wraiths from behind their respective monuments to show themselves to the old man.

"Two snoopers, eh? All right, don't be shy, come on into the light. You've already ruined my ceremony, so let's see what you look like!"

As they shuffled toward the wizard, Hilda felt the overwhelming urge to take the young man's hand—to seek the comfort two guilty children could find in each other. She reached out and was not surprised to find his hand reaching toward hers as well.

"You know each other, I see," said the wizard slyly.

Hilda and the young man traded glances, then looked at their hands and separated them gingerly. "Not really," said the young man.

"We've . . . just met," said Hilda.

"Well then, perhaps you'd care to introduce yourselves to me as well," said the old man.

"Oh, we haven't . . . been introduced," said the young man, very flustered.

The wizard covered his eyes with his hand, as if he could not believe the absurdity of what was interrupting his solemn ritual. "Under the circumstances, let's not stand on ceremony." He looked at his scrawled symbols and sighed. "Though that's precisely what I was *trying* to do." He shot a glance at the man. "Your name, sir, and quickly!"

"Kreutzer," he said so fast that Hilda feared his tongue would tangle. "Friedrich Kreutzer."

The mage turned his ferocious glare on Hilda, who said, "Hilda Von Karlsfeld!" as though she were answering an examination question in school.

"And I," said the old man, "am Herman Von Schreck. But you undoubtedly know that since you were here to spy on me. Now who sent you? Azarian? Gustavus Grimm? Izodius the Elder? The Younger? *Which?*"

Friedrich stood in front of Hilda as if to protect her, but it annoyed her, and she edged from behind him. "Sir," he said, "on my honor, I have been sent by no wizard. I was here on my own, heard your chanting, and decided to investigate, and that's all."

"Our tales are very similar," said Hilda. "We were startled when we happened to confront each other, and . . . well, you heard us."

"And you expect me to believe that?" asked Von Schreck. "Perhaps you'd care to explain what you were doing here in the first place. A midnight stroll, perhaps, in the most haunted cemetery of Il Aluk?"

Friedrich cleared his throat. "I came here," he said, "for . . . atmosphere."

"Atmosphere?" Von Schreck said in disbelief.

"I am a poet. Perhaps you have read my *Quatrains of Loss.*"

"And perhaps not," said Von Schreck. "And you, my dear?"

"I write as well . . . or am trying to. Romances. In

particular, I was working on a scene set in a graveyard at midnight." She turned to Friedrich. "You are a writer? And published as well?"

He smiled crookedly. "*Self*-published. I could only afford to have fifty copies done."

"Pardon me," said Von Schreck. "Could we save the meeting of the Il Aluk Literary Society for later? You expect me to believe both of you? With the same story?"

Friedrich tossed his hands in the air. "I'm a poet and a secretary, what else can I tell you? Do I look like a sorcerer's apprentice to you?"

Von Schreck frowned again. "No." Then he smiled for the first time. "But perhaps you *should* be."

"I beg your pardon?"

"And you, my dear. What is your trade? Do you live in your parents' home?"

"My parents are both dead," said Hilda. "I tutor the daughters of Herr Gimpfel."

Von Schreck nodded. "I know the good burgher well. We have . . . crossed paths in the past. I cannot imagine that sanctimonious sheepshank approving of your literary endeavors, however."

"He . . . does not. He knows nothing of it."

Von Schreck crossed his fat arms over his chest. "So. Let me see if I have this right. A governess and a secretary. Both longing for more romantic and thrilling experiences, and endeavoring to find them secondhand through writing. Would you call that accurate?"

Hilda and Friedrich looked at each other again, then turned back to Von Schreck and nodded.

"Then," said the old mage, "why not make those dreams reality? Why not become sorcerer's apprentices?" He gestured at the tools of his profession. "You were entranced by all this, weren't you? And you would have been even more entranced if you had seen what was to transpire next. Each of you came here alone, which proves your courage, and from at least one of you—you, miss—I feel a great deal of psychic ability. Am I wrong?"

He was not. Ever since she was little, Hilda had known all too well what those around her were thinking, if not the specifics, at least the generalities. And she could often tell when she was being lied to. "You are right," she said.

"And you should know," replied Von Schreck. "As for you, young man, you may not be terribly gifted, but you have the drive, I believe. The desire to make your life poetry rather than poetry your life, yes? Beside the secrets of the human heart, you wish to learn those of the *in*human heart as well, along with the secrets of the spheres, and what lies beyond the grave. You wish to know what all true poets seek, yes?"

"Uh, *yes,* I suppose I do."

"And I can teach you. I—and my book." He held it up so that they could see the worm-eaten leather of its binding. "But there is . . . a *price.*"

Though Hilda's mouth was too dry to swallow, she heard Friedrich gulp. "You mean," he said, "our spirits?"

"No, I mean fifty kroner from each of you for a full course of study. I may be able to summon spirits from the vasty deep, but I have to buy victuals just like anyone else." It was a singularly unromantic but realistic price to pay, and Hilda was greatly relieved to hear it.

Von Schreck gathered his belongings and led Hilda and Friedrich from the graveyard to his home, a fair sized cottage, where an old and nearly deaf servant brought them tea while Von Schreck talked long into the morning about such subjects as their course of study and the conditions of their tuition.

He constantly stressed the exciting and romantic aspects of the science and art of sorcery, as well as touching on the more practical fact that a good wizard is always in demand.

"Treasures to find, secrets of the dead to reveal, revenants to lay, great houses to cast haunts out of—the list is endless."

"Then," said Friedrich casually but pointedly, "why share your knowledge with us, if all these wonders and treasures can be yours alone?"

Von Schreck scowled at him. "Look at me, boy. How old do you think me to be?"

"Seventy, perhaps?"

"I am one hundred and twenty years old. I cannot, nor do I wish to, live much longer. It would be nice to pass my secrets down to someone with a motivation other than making money. You wouldn't *believe* the fools who clamor at my door, begging me to teach them. And if you decide, when your learning is completed, that you wish to use sorcery as a literary fountain more than a life's practice, well, so be it. You shall have color, experience, and research in abundance. Enough to fill your blank pages for the rest of your lives. Well, what say you?"

They left early that morning after tentatively agreeing to Von Schreck's proposal. On their walk to Herr Gimpfel's estate, Hilda and Friedrich discovered that they had much in common—a love of literature, fascination with the weird and outre, and a desire for pastoral rather than urban scenes.

Their relationship began that day, and their attachment to each other grew slowly and surely into the love that led to their betrothal.

They met every week at Von Schreck's cottage, bringing him whatever amounts they could save from their meager earnings, until several months later he declared their tuition paid in full and promised them that now they should begin their education in earnest.

The old man was true to his word. Whereas before he had only lectured and theorized, he now took them "into the field," out to deserted houses and crumbling castles, long forsaken charnel pits and forgotten grave-yards. There he conjured up gheists and specters and, on a particularly horrifying night, a grave elemental, a huge and hideous creature seemingly formed out of dead men's bones, rotted chunks of coffins, and the earth of the graveyard itself. To Hilda and Friedrich's terror and to Von Schreck's annoyance, the elemental would not be laid to rest until the wizard allowed it to shatter what was left of a stone temple that adjoined the graveyard. Only then did the monstrous being sink back into the earth from whence it had come.

"Let this teach you a lesson," Von Schreck told them on their way home. "Never lose your concentration. My mind wandered for just an instant, and see what hap-pened?" They had indeed, and would never forget it.

They had learned much from the old man, and learned even more in the months that followed. Those days were made doubly enjoyable by Herr Gimpfel's hiring of Friedrich as his new secretary. Hilda and Friedrich had become betrothed by this time, and when an opening occurred for Gimpfel's estate secretary, Hilda told the sanctimonious burgher that she had heard of a qualified and experienced man who could more than adequately fill the position. Friedrich acquit-ted himself well at the interview, and soon they were living under the same large roof.

They were, however, fastidious about keeping their love for one another a secret, since Gimpfel looked askance on any affection between his servants and employees. The only times the two lovers met were on the nights when both sneaked away from the estate to attend Von Schreck's arcane lessons.

Their discovery by Gimpfel was not the sole tragedy

of that one particular night, but it was the most immediate. A stable servant who had set his eye on Hilda had seen the two of them stealing away from the estate and jealously reported it to Gimpfel, who, even with his vast bulk, was swift enough to follow them to the estate's entrance. There he saw Hilda and Friedrich climb into a coach driven by Von Schreck's ancient servant.

Inside the coach, meanwhile, the couple were surprised to find not only their mentor, but a middle-aged man and a younger woman, whom Von Schreck introduced as Herr Meyer and his daughter.

Von Schreck explained that tonight Hilda and Friedrich would see something very special, the transference of a spirit from a dead woman into a living body. "Herr Meyer has a problem," Von Schreck told them. "His wife was killed in an accident several weeks ago. She controlled all the finances of the house, since Herr Meyer, well . . ."

"I drink too much," the thin, red-nosed man confided.

"At any rate, though," Von Schreck went on, "Herr Meyer and his daughter have been unable, try as they might, to discover where Frau Meyer hid their money, which includes all their savings. So tonight we will go to the graveyard in which Frau Meyer is buried, disinter her, and discover the secret that she took with her to her grave."

Herr Meyer shook his head admiringly. "You make it sound so simple."

"Let me assure you, it is not. Nor will it be simple for you or your daughter. Yet if you do as I say, it shall be safe enough for us all."

That night spent in the little graveyard miles from Il Aluk had been the most shocking night of Hilda's life. While she and Meyer's daughter held torches, Friedrich and Meyer dug in the nearly frozen earth of the new grave, and Von Schreck traced esoteric designs in the red dirt. Mist hung heavily in the air, catching the torchlight and twisting it like tormented phantoms.

Aside from the sound of the spades biting into the dirt, the only other noise was the hacking cough of the wizard. It came often and so persistently that Hilda feared for his health in the freezing night air, but he waved away her concerns and kept copying the symbols with his staff.

"It takes more than a little cough to slow the Master of the Graveyard," he growled, then coughed for a full minute without stopping.

By the time he had finished writing his symbols, the group heard a jarring sound that made Hilda clench her teeth. It was the crunch of the shovel blades striking the wood of the coffin. In another few minutes, the rough-hewn box lay on the ground, placed carefully according to Von Schreck's directions.

Friedrich slid the blade of the shovel beneath the coffin lid and pried upward until the nails shrieked their way out of the hard wood. The lid fell onto the ground, and Frau Meyer, already well decayed and fissured by the ravenous worms, lay exposed to the torchlight.

Von Schreck took the torch from Meyer's daughter, knelt, lit his corpse-fat candles, then plunged the torch into the pile of dirt to extinguish it. Hilda did the same. Then the wizard directed Meyer's daughter to lie on the ground next to her mother's coffin, facing him.

"On the bare ground?" asked the girl. These were the first words she had spoken.

"This is a spirit-shifting," said Von Schreck, "not a picnic. Lie *down*." She did as she was told. "Now close your eyes and think of nothing." Hilda heard him add under his breath. "That shouldn't be too hard. . . ."

He turned to where Friedrich and Hilda stood watching, arm in arm. "The proper words are in the book. I know this spell quite well, so I needn't cast it from the page. As I have told you before, if you do not have the spells memorized, one use of a spell will wipe it clean from your book until it is recopied. So . . ."

Von Schreck started to chant then, and the girl on the ground instantly stopped shivering. Her eyes closed, and she seemed at perfect peace.

In several more minutes, during which Von Schreck's voice thickened but he managed not to cough, the corpse of the dead wife began to glow with a cold blue radiance. The light was trapped by the mists so that there appeared to be a gleaming, blue glass lid over Frau Meyer's crude coffin. Von Schreck's words ceased, and the glow lifted itself from Frau Meyer and migrated as what must have been the spirit transmigrated a few feet from the body to hover above the perfectly still form of the dead woman's daughter. Then it flowed down and over the girl so that her body now gave off the same eerie light.

"Gerthe Meyer, sit you up," Von Schreck intoned, and the daughter, bathed in the blue light, sat up as easily as though someone had gently pushed her upright, with no need to use her own muscles at all.

"Open your eyes and look on your master." The eyes opened, and Hilda felt herself tense. There was indeed someone else in the girl's body. The eyes were far older, and Hilda knew that they had looked on things that would drive the living mad.

"I compel you to tell us," Von Schreck went on, "under pain of your spirit wandering aimlessly through all eternity, where the money is that belongs to your family."

The girl's mouth opened, and a cracked and hollow voice came from the dark opening. "Within the dry spring behind the house. The left side. Behind a loose stone. Now release me, I beg you."

Von Schreck turned to Hilda. "Has she spoken true?"

Hilda nodded. Anguish and fear seemed to pour from the dead woman's spirit into Hilda's own. Even without the exercises Von Schreck had been giving her to heighten her sensitivity, she would have believed the dead woman implicitly. What torment, Hilda wondered, could the spirit be feeling at having been ripped from the grave or the afterlife? It must have been terrible indeed, beyond the imaginings of human torture.

"Then," said Von Schreck, "I dismiss you, and abjure you to—"

But the dismissal was startlingly interrupted by a shouted "*Ha!*" an exclamation that both Hilda and Friedrich knew all too well. It was the unmistakable voice of Herr Gimpfel, who stood several yards away with his hulking coachman.

"I . . . I abjure you to return to your—" Von Schreck went gamely on, but his voice shook, and a hacking cough escaped his throat, choking off the words.

"So *this* is where I find you!" Gimpfel went on. "In the middle of a graveyard at the dead of night with the most disreputable of the sorcerous breed! Magicians! As if there's not enough evil in this land!"

"Sir," said Friedrich, "please! Allow Herr Von Schreck to finish his ceremony! Interrupting could be—"

Hilda didn't know whether her fiance was planning to say *dangerous* or *fatal,* since Gimpfel burst in again. "And there's no telling what *else* the two of you may have been up to together! I shan't have such goings on in my household. You are dismissed! Both of you! Your things will be thrown out into the road, and you may pick them up when you return!" So saying, he and the coachman stormed back into the darkness from which they had stealthily come.

"Sir, are you all right?" Friedrich asked Von Schreck,

who seemed to be seriously trying to cough up his tattered lungs.

Von Schreck held up his hands. "Don't touch me! It would destroy them both. . . ." His words fell away into the gulf of another wracking fit.

When it was over, he took several deep breaths, and in the silence Hilda heard a high keening sound, and saw that it came from Meyer's daughter, whose eyes were wide and ablaze with pain and terror.

"I *abjure* you," Von Schreck spat out with a gobbet of blood, "to return to your grave to rest among the shades of the dead until I should call you up again!" And with those words, the old man collapsed.

At the same instant, the possessed girl fell backward. The blue aura swooped over to the dead woman, settled upon her corpse, and fell into it, vanishing like a bird returned to its nest.

Hilda and Friedrich dashed to the side of their fallen teacher, Friedrich taking off his cloak and putting it around the old man. " 'Tis done," he rasped out, blood trickling off his lower lip. "Take me home and let them rebury their dead themselves."

They helped him to his feet and walked him toward the coach. The servant, who had been sleeping on the box and so had not heard the approach of Gimpfel, helped them lift Von Schreck onto the seat. Suddenly the old wizard raised his head as if he had just been stung.

"What is it, sir?" asked Hilda.

"The *fee*. . . ." Von Schreck said. "Don't forget the *fee*."

He would not permit them to leave until Friedrich pressed the promised fifty kroner from Meyer into his hand.

He died two weeks later, babbling ceremonial words in foreign tongues. Hilda and Friedrich and the old servant were at his side. "He was sick," the servant said over and over. "I told him not to go out on so cold a night, but he never listened, never listened to me. . . ."

Following the old man's death, Friedrich and Hilda returned to the cheap inn where they had rented two mean rooms after gathering their belongings from in front of Gimpfel's estate. They took with them only Von Schreck's book, which he had handed to them in his final moments of lucidity. "I want you to have it," he had said. "There is no one else. . . ." He left the thought unfinished.

Now Hilda and Friedrich had only their personal belongings, forty kroner between them, no immediate hopes for employment, and their nearly shattered dreams of someday marrying and buying a small freehold of their own. But there was one thing more that came to them before their money for lodging ran out.

It was a letter they received several months after the wizard's death, when both had nearly given up in their attempts to find positions. It read:

> To Friedrich Kreutzer and Hilda Von Karlsfeld:
> I recently wrote to Herman Von Schreck, but have been informed by his servant that he has died. The servant, having read my letter, was made aware of what services I desired from his master, and has informed me that the two of you were his final students, so it is to you that I now turn.
> I wish to undertake an experiment in the transference of spirit, and since my studies have all been in the realm of the rational and tangible, I find myself requiring someone versed in these mythical "arts." I must confess my doubts as to the efficacy of what is referred to as magic, but as my other efforts have not as yet borne fruit, I am willing to experiment with what I

have always thought of as a fool's business.

I hope my frankness does not offend, but perhaps money may take the place of tact. Should you come to Schloss Mordenheim to assist me, I shall pay you five thousand kroner for your efforts, regardless of the outcome. Should the experiment prove successful, ten thousand kroner shall be yours.

If you are desirous to participate in this experiment, inform me as quickly as possible when your coach will reach Ludendorf, and I will arrange to have you brought from there to Schloss Mordenheim.

I await your prompt reply.

Victor Mordenheim

It was like an offer from the gods. Even five thousand kroner would let them buy a little place of their own with a garden in which to grow their own food and little rooms in which Friedrich could write his poetry and Hilda could pen her thrilling romances, which had never been supplanted by the grim and frightening realities of sorcery.

Of course there was the danger that Mordenheim would see them as the amateurs they really were. But perhaps not. After all, they had had a good teacher, and they did have Von Schreck's book of spells. There was no reason they could think of that the incantations should not work equally well for them, as long as they made the proper preparations and recited the words correctly.

And so they took what remained of their money and purchased two tickets on the first coach to Ludendorf, from whence they would be taken to Schloss Mordenheim.

There, in an unknown castle in a strange land, they would have to prove that they were indeed the wizards they were supposed to be.

 **THREE**

The door of the Black Bear Inn boomed open, and the harsh Lamordian wind blew in, stirring Hilda from her reminiscent reverie. At first she thought that a bogey of some sort stood in the doorway, the outside light casting a shimmering glow around its twisted silhouette. But as the figure stepped into the inn and all talk ceased, she saw that it was only a man—if a strange one—holding a coachman's whip.

He was between four and five feet tall, but he looked shorter; his back was bent as if he toted a heavy sack. Hilda quickly saw, however, that it was not a sack, but a growth of some kind that he had probably been cursed with since birth. His age was indeterminate, for he had the angelic face of a child, wide eyed and seamless, oddly anachronistic on that old man's body. Perhaps he felt the same, for his beautiful face was nearly hidden by a slouch hat pulled low over his forehead.

He broke the silence with a high, piping voice that asked if Herr Kreutzer and Fraulein Von Karlsfeld were present, and when they identified themselves, he told them that he was there to take them to Schloss Mordenheim. The rest of the folk in the inn watched with cold, hard eyes, but said nothing as Friedrich paid for the tea, took Hilda's hand, and followed the man outside.

"What shall we call you?" Friedrich asked.

The little man picked up all their luggage at once, lumbered over to a coach that had once been elegant but was now badly weathered, and threw it onto the top as easily as if he were tossing pillows. "You can call me Horg," he said, opening the door for them, "for that's my name."

As Friedrich and Hilda got into the coach and sat upon the tattered velvet seats, they saw the citizens of Ludendorf leave the inn and stand watching them.

"Careful for her, boy," said Otto from the inn door. "Be careful for her, if not for yourself. 'Tisn't men he wants, leastwise not anymore."

Friedrich took Hilda's hand in his, and nodded his thanks toward Otto, then looked into his fiancee's eyes as the coach started to move.

They left the main road several miles outside of town, then headed toward the castle. Darkness was beginning to fall like a dark glove over the land, and soon, Friedrich knew, the fingers of night would close entirely, shutting out the light. The road to the castle was far bumpier than that from Rivalis to Ludendorf, and Hilda feared for the safety of their luggage. Friedrich called up to the little coachman, who shouted back, "It's there, and there it'll stay." Neither his tone nor his manner assuaged their fears.

Soon, approaching the castle through the mists, they were able to see it more clearly. It was not huge—more a manor house than an actual castle, though it was built of heavy gray stones that looked as though they could withstand a cannonade.

From the front, Schloss Mordenheim appeared symmetrical, save for a watchtower on the right that overlooked the Sea of Sorrows, and whose peaked slate top Friedrich judged to be nearly a hundred feet above the ground—perhaps twice that above the sea.

Horg stopped the coach at the bottom of a short,

broad flight of stairs that led to a solid iron gate. He
vaulted from the box, grabbed their baggage, and told
them to follow him. The rusty iron gate screeched in
protest as he pushed it open. He waited until Friedrich
and Hilda had passed through, then pushed it closed
again, securing it as if he expected to be followed.

Now that mist and distance no longer softened their
view of the castle, they could see that it was in a dreadful state of dilapidation. Many of the cobblestones that
paved the courtyard in which they stood were askew,
making walking treacherous. The water in the nearby
fountain was covered with a layer of withered leaves that
looked almost alive as it drifted and pulsated in the
wind, occasionally parting to reveal the filthy, brackish
liquid beneath. The windows in the two wings that
flanked them and in the larger part of the castle ahead
of them were coated with grime so thick that no light
shone from within, if indeed there were any.

Just as this thought occurred to Friedrich, he looked
upward to the right and saw what appeared to be an arc
light flashing in one of the windows. It sparked for just
an instant, then went out, leaving a sullen yellow glow
behind it. He nudged Hilda, but she had already seen it.

Horg turned back toward them and impatiently said,
"Come, come, 'tis too cold out here to tarry," then
added under his breath, "though not much warmer
within."

He led them through the main door and into what
had once been a great dining hall. There, he set down
their luggage and lit a lantern, whose light barely
touched the highest reaches of the vaulted ceiling,
where cobwebs festooned smoke-grimed rafters. The
floor was thick with dust, and the woven tapestries that
decorated the walls had rotted from the bottom up and
hung in tatters where mice had nibbled away pieces for
their nests.

Hilda ran her finger along the arm of a heavy wooden chair that sat against the wall and found it coated with a gray layer of dust and mildew. The sea seemed to encroach on the entire castle, so that she breathed dampness even within its walls, and Hilda found herself wishing desperately for the cheeriness of a fire.

At the far end of the room, they could just make out the bottom steps of a staircase, and it was from that general direction that they now heard a loud, dull, booming sound, as of a great door ponderously closing. Both Friedrich and Hilda jumped slightly, but Horg remained unruffled. "The master," he said quietly.

They heard Mordenheim's footsteps long before they saw him. When he did appear, he seemed a ghost, merely an illuminated head high above them in the darkness, his candle lighting his white face, which was turned toward them as he walked across a balcony they could not see. At last he reached the stairway, and the ghostly head began to descend, growing larger with every step.

Hilda held her breath until he spoke, though she was sure that what she beheld was not a phantasm. Even so, with his first word she gasped despite herself—hearing her own name issue from the thin, pale lips of this man who seemed as lifeless as his castle.

"Hilda Von Karlsfeld," he said, and his voice was like dry leaves blowing over stones, "and Friedrich Kreutzer, I presume. I am Mordenheim." When he stopped at the bottom of the staircase, thirty feet still separated them. He made no effort to come closer.

"Good evening, Doctor," Friedrich said, and Hilda greeted him as well.

"I trust you did not have too unpleasant a journey," the doctor said, "for there seem to be no pleasant ones in Lamordia." He did not wait for a response. "I must apologize for the condition of my home. Horg is my only remaining servant, and he is hard pressed to care for a place this size. Therefore, cleanliness must suffer, although you should find your quarters tidy enough. Horg is, however, an adequate cook, and while he prepares our dinner, I would like you to follow me. Take candles from the table there if you like, for the way is dark."

He turned and started back up the steps. Friedrich and Hilda grabbed candles from where he had pointed, lit them, and followed quickly.

"Forgive me for not crossing the room to meet you," Mordenheim said as he walked, "but I dislike unnecessary exertion."

"You have been ili?" asked Friedrich.

"No. I merely wish to conserve all my energies for my ongoing work. It is to see this . . . unfinished work that I am taking you now."

They reached the top of the stairs and turned to the right. "You may think this a bit abrupt, and undoubtedly you expected social amenities when you first arrived—a nourishing glass of wine, a warm fire, pleasant conversation. But I find—and have always found—such things to be extraneous to the true needs of life. I have been forced to replace the niceties of the ballroom with the harsh realities of my workplace. For in society I was bound by the vision that haunted me and the riddle whose answer I must find or . . ." He stopped walking and smiled a deep, sad smile. "I must find it. And that is why I have called you here."

The balcony ended, and they passed through a small door into a short hall. "I thought it best to show you the case immediately, for you have undoubtedly heard all sorts of lies and slander concerning me in that ignorant little town of Ludendorf, and perhaps even in your native Darkon." He paused again and eyed them meaningfully. "Have you not?"

"Rumors," Friedrich said. "Certainly as absurd as you suggest."

"We heard," said Hilda with more courage than she felt, "that you were building a . . . a wife for the monster you have created."

"Monster?" Mordenheim said, as though the word were foreign to him.

"Yes. A creature called Adam."

Mordenheim stared into the flame of the candle he held. "A *man* called Adam," he said, then walked on.

At the end of the hall they came to a staircase, which they ascended. Mordenheim stopped at a heavy wooden door that blocked their way. "The villagers are wrong," he said. "I am not trying to build a wife for Adam. What I am trying to do . . . what I have been trying to do for years now . . . is to simply bring my own wife back to me." So saying, he opened the door.

 **FOUR**

At the same instant, both Hilda and Friedrich saw the woman on the table. She heard his sharp intake of breath, and she stumbled for a moment, taken aback by the sight. But she regained her balance immediately, furious at herself for the sudden weakness. She had seen worse than this.

Still, it was a dreadful sight. The thing on the table was scarcely recognizable as a woman. She seemed rather a crudely preserved mummy dredged up from some ineffably ancient bog. A pristine white sheet, shockingly out of place in this castle of dust and shadows, covered most of her torso, but the flesh of her head, neck, arms, and legs was the texture and shade of worn and weathered leather.

Mordenheim spoke, and his matter-of-fact tone seemed blasphemous, like someone laughing in a tomb. "Her hair is still blond, you see, what is left of it. It stopped growing and so never became discolored. The same cannot, unfortunately, be said of the flesh." He stepped closer and lit a lantern on a workbench. "Come, see her. She is harmless, I assure you."

Hand in hand, Hilda and Friedrich walked to the table where the woman lay. Both were startled to see that the brown and wrinkled eyelids were open, the eyes visible beneath. The eyeballs looked rippled, and a small needle pierced the white of each. The ends of the needles were connected to rubber tubes that led to a liquid-filled bladder operated by a mechanical pump.

"Her eyes were once the deepest blue," Mordenheim said wistfully, "and so they shall be again. I keep them lubricated with a saline solution. The other hoses you see—the two in the sides of the skull, the pair in the nostrils, and those running beneath the sheet—all force fluids to circulate throughout her body . . . brain, lungs, internal organs, any part that needs lubrication.

"The large tube in the mouth is a feeder tube leading directly to the stomach. The one in the hollow of her left arm drains her blood into a machine of my own invention, which cleanses and nourishes it and returns it to her body through the tube in her right arm." When he looked up at them, his face was beaming. "Is she not wondrous, my Elise?"

"She . . ." Friedrich cleared his throat. "She is alive?"

"Look closely." Mordenheim beckoned them to lean over the body, which they did reluctantly, and saw that the thin chest was rising and falling, but with only a third of the speed of a normal person's chest, and with far less power.

"Touch her," Mordenheim said in a voice that brooked no refusal. Friedrich did as he was told, though he was unable to repress the shudder that went through him as his fingertips came into contact with the parchmentlike skin.

"She's . . . she's warm," Friedrich said, then looked at Hilda. "She really is alive."

Hilda, not to be outdone in courage by her fiance, unhesitatingly pressed the flesh of the woman's arm, and gritted her teeth so that she would not flinch. It was not as bad as she had expected, like touching a leathern sack that had been sitting by the stove.

Mordenheim crossed the laboratory to a small wooden chair, the seat of which was clean and smooth. He now he sat down wearily and steepled his long fingers.

He seemed less ghostly now. Perhaps it was the light, Hilda thought, now finding herself at greater leisure to observe him closely. Seated, he seemed less dominating, for he was a tall man and had towered over both her and Friedrich as they had passed down the halls and up the stairs. She guessed that he was in his late forties, though he may have aged prematurely. His hair, sweeping back from his high forehead in a leonine fashion, was heavily grayed, with just a few streaks of the original brown still in evidence.

His figure was extremely thin, but his movements had been economical and elegant, so Hilda suspected a tough wiriness underneath. The elegance did not extend, however, to his clothing. He wore a shabby laboratory coat whose whiteness had dulled to a dingy gray and was spotted here and there with brownish stains. His trousers and shoes were nothing more than functional, and the shirt visible beneath his lab coat was equally undistinguished.

It was in Mordenheim's face, however, that authority and aristocracy reigned. The aquiline nose and firm jaw were those of a man accustomed to being obeyed, and the blue eyes, though weary and cradled by dark pouches, were nonetheless piercing. And though Hilda watched him closely, she did not see him blink.

The muscles of his jaw occasionally twitched tensely, and the years had not left him unscathed. There was a long scar on his forehead, a paler stripe against his pale skin. She saw too that his left earlobe was missing, as well as the tip of his left ring finger, which he had folded around the side of his other hand.

"You have deduced, I assume," Mordenheim said, seeming to watch both of them at once, "exactly why I have asked you to come here."

"I . . . suppose," Friedrich hazarded, "that it has

something to do with your wife?"

"Indeed it does."

"You wish us to, shall I say . . . animate her?"

"No, young man. I wish you to do far more than that with her. I have no desire for her walking and moving in the form she now has. But what I treasured of Elise is there still. I want you to help me find that vitality and make it live again . . . in a new vessel."

Mordenheim suddenly shot to his feet, making both of them jump. "But first the needs of our own bodies must be satisfied. Horg should have dinner prepared by now, and afterward I shall tell you my tale from the beginning. Come."

Mordenheim led them back the way they had come, through the castle's great hall, and then into the left wing, where they had entered. He stopped in front of two doors that stood side by side in the hall.

"You may wish to wash off the dust of the road before dinner. Horg has put your luggage in this room, Fraulein Von Karlsfeld, and yours in this one, Herr Kreutzer. We shall consider dinner dress informal. I shall see you in one half hour in the small dining room across the great hall, in the east wing."

He stood and waited like a chaperon until they had each gone into the appointed room. Hilda sat for a moment on the small bed, which, she was happy to see, was made with clean enough linen, and she listened as Mordenheim's footsteps retreated down the hall. Then her thoughts turned to the serious matter before them, the living corpse up in the laboratory, and Mordenheim's somber, almost threatening demeanor. What had he meant about a "new vessel?" Another body? And did he mean hers? He had looked at her closely when they first met. Perhaps . . .

She dismissed the horrid thought. He had examined Friedrich in the same close way, probably to decide if they were really what they claimed to be. Well, they seemed to have fooled him so far, and perhaps they could do whatever it was he wanted after all. She hoped so, for a man like Mordenheim would not be forgiving. She started to prepare for dinner and tried to shake off the thought of a disappointed Mordenheim.

*   *   *   *   *

Dinner was far more hospitable than Hilda and Friedrich had imagined. The small dining room was relatively clean, and the smell of dampness and mildew that permeated the air in the rest of the castle was partly dispelled by a roaring fire on the hearth.

Horg had done himself proud with the victuals. There was a fish chowder to start with, then a large haunch of venison surrounded by potatoes, carrots, and onions in a hearty sauce. A concoction of dried fruits and cream made up the dessert.

Horg served a dry red G'Hennan wine with the main course, and a sweet Borcan wine with cheese after dessert. Friedrich had studied the amber liquid dubiously, having heard wild stories of Borcan drinks transforming into deadly poison after crossing the domain's border, but Mordenheim assured them that the wine was quite safe to drink.

"It has been said—probably by someone who spent his entire life behind a desk—that it is the touch of danger that makes life taste sweetest." So saying, Mordenheim drained his own glass to the dregs. He licked his lips, then nodded. "You see, I am perfectly fine. And filled. I usually eat very little, but I make an exception when guests come to call."

"Do you have guests here often?" Friedrich asked, delicately sipping his wine.

The muscles in Mordenheim's jaw twitched, and he

clenched his teeth for a moment until they stopped. "You are the first . . . *guests* I have had in many years." He sat back in his chair, rested his head against the high back, and closed his eyes.

"It is very good to have people here . . . people with curiosity about matters of life and death and creation." He opened his eyes and looked at Horg, who was piling soiled dishes atop one another. "Horg, leave us now. And return only if I ring for you."

The servant nodded and left the room with his burden. "He's a good servant," Mordenheim said, "but not quick of mind. He is obedient, however, and there is much to be said for that. I believe Horg would do anything for me," he mused, looking at the door through which Horg had passed. "Anything."

"You told us," Friedrich said, "that you would relate your tale tonight. I'm sure I can speak for Hilda as well when I say that we are most anxious to hear it."

"We are indeed, Doctor," said Hilda. "Your wife's state is quite extraordinary, and—"

"My wife's state is *unique*," Mordenheim interrupted.

"And . . . amazing." Hilda sipped her wine to keep him from seeing the red that sprang to her cheeks. "As Friedrich said, we are both anxious to hear about what brought her to . . . to this state."

"To this horror, don't you mean?" Mordenheim said. "For she is a thing of horror to you—I know that. As she would be to anyone who never knew what she once was." He sighed deeply. "Very well then. I shall tell you all. I shall tell you how it was, how Elise and I came to this place, this time, this . . . horror. The tale is long, but it must be told.

"It all started a long, long time ago, what seems an eternity . . ."

 **FIVE**

. . . My curiosity in matters of life and death began
when I was very young. I was only five years old when
my mother died, but I recall it all so vividly that it seems
like yesterday.

She was taken ill, by what malady I never knew, and
my father never would tell me. I suspect the cause of
her illness was some unwholesome activity of my
father's. I imagine she contracted the disease from him;
though wealthy and respected, he frequently engaged
in social intercourse with far less reputable people when
his business took him away from home.

Whatever the reason and whether my father was
partly responsible or not, she died, and I, of course,
grieved. She was my *mother,* the sun and moon and
stars to me. While my father treated me harshly, she
was ever tender, ever vigilant to my needs, comforting
me when I fell and scraped a knee, kissing away my
childish cares. And, as I had no brothers or sisters, she
was my only friend.

Her body was lying in state in the parlor, and late
that night after I thought everyone else would be
asleep, I crept down to be with her one final time before
she was interred the next day. There was no fear in me
at all. She was my mother, and she had never hurt me.
I simply wished to know what had happened to her.

Candles flanked her casket, the upper half of which

was open. Her hair was elegantly coiffured, and her face was beautifully made up—by her maids, I suppose. Her eyes were closed, and she looked as though she were gently sleeping. I did not understand death then, you see. I had no idea of its finality, for my father had told me only that my mother was very sick, then that she was dead.

So I watched her for a long time, thinking that death must mean not moving, not opening your eyes or letting your chest rise and fall with your breaths. And after a while, I wanted her to wake up, to acknowledge my presence. I said, "Mother," softly, then louder, but not too loud, fearing that the others in the house would hear me. Finally I touched her. And then I knew that death must mean coldness as well.

I thought that if I could only get her to open her eyes she might stop pretending to be asleep. So I pressed her eyelid up.

I did not expect to see that orb as I did—grayish, and shot with flecks of red. I did not expect my small finger to sink into its rotting softness.

I did not expect to scream.

But scream I did, jerking my hand away so quickly that droplets of fluid spattered me. Terrified, I stood there, wiping them away from my nightshirt, gasping in horror, knowing that there was something more to death than just coldness of flesh and closed eyes. And then I felt my father's steely fingers grasp my shoulder.

"You little beast," he growled. "What have you *done?*"

I told him that I was sorry, that I had wondered what being dead meant, and that was why I had come downstairs.

He laughed harshly, then said, "Wondering about death, eh? Well, I'll show you what death is, son. . . ."

He bundled me up in a coat, threw on a cloak himself,

grasped a lantern, and dragged me outside to the
stables, where he awoke a groom and had him saddle a
horse. Then he threw me onto the saddle, leapt up
behind me, and spurred the steed down the lane, across
a field, and toward the cemetery where lay the tombs
and graves of Mordenheims going back tens of genera-
tions.

The land lay bright under the moon, so the horse neither staggered nor slowed, and soon we were at the
gate of the graveyard. My father leapt down and
plucked me off the saddle as easily as if I had been a
ripe apple. He threw open the gate and dragged me into
the place.

To me, it was just a piece of ground with upright
stones and several small stone houses without windows. It had nothing to do with the dead. But then my
father took me to the largest of the tombs, withdrew a
heavy ring of keys from the folds of his cloak, and
opened a massive iron door that led within. He tugged
me in after him, and I beheld what, to me then, was a
horrid sight.

Along the sides of the tomb, in several tiers, were
wooden coffins. Several of them had been eaten
through by the years, insects, and rodents, and through
the splintered holes I could see skulls and bones still
partially clothed in decayed rags. My father led me to
one of the tiers and pushed my head toward a wide gap
through which a skull grinned out at me.

"That is your grandfather, boy, and that is *death*.
There is no longer flesh on those bones, or a brain in
that skull. All that was alive is gone, fled, *dead*. Dead
forever, with no hope of return. And *here* . . ."

He twisted me around to face another casket, this
one closed, but he pushed the lid open with his free
hand. An odor burst upon me that was so solid I could
almost see a filthy green miasma. "Behold!" my father

ordered, and I obeyed, looking through eyes tearing from the stench. Even so, I saw the corpse of my Uncle Reinhart, whom I knew only from his portrait in the gallery. The putrescent features still bore a resemblance to the painting, though the eyes had long ago fallen in, and much of the flesh had liquified.

"This is death, Victor," said my father, and then took me to the back wall of the tomb, where he raised the latch of a recessed door that had not been open for many years, if the crumbling of caked rust from its edges was any indication.

"And this," he said as he thrust the lantern into the blackness with one hand and held me in the doorway with the other.

The light was too bright; what was inside should have remained in the dark forever. It was a charnel pit, filled with a mad conglomeration of bones, skulls, and fragments of coffins. The pit was ten feet across, and was densely packed with human remains. The surface was a good twenty feet below us, and I have no idea of how much deeper it went, of how many crumbling relics of mortality lay beneath the topmost, visible layer.

"*This* is death." My father's voice boomed, echoing so that one would have thought the pit descended to the very foundations of the world. "Forever and eternal. This is what all life becomes." Then he hauled me out, slammed the door shut, and stared into my face, my eyes only inches from his own. "Are you content now?" he asked me in a dangerously low voice. "Do you know now what death is?"

I was so terrified I could only nod my head yes. My trembling and tearful reaction must have mollified my father, as he said nothing more, only turned and walked out of the tomb. Needless to say, I followed close behind.

But on the ride home, and later, lying awake in my

bed long into that night and for many nights to come, the thought began to rise in me that man *should not die,* that, despite my angry father's view of things, death could *not* be the goal of all life. Death, as embodied in that pit of bones, my uncle's rotting corpse, and particularly in my dear mother's stillness and decay, was a *negation* of life, a blasphemy against everything that man has striven to become.

Of course, my five-year-old mind did not put it in those terms, but the kernel of the thought was the same. It was the spark that lit the blaze that has guided me my entire life, like the blaze that spread from cell to cell in my son, my creation . . . my nemesis.

But I yet anticipate my greatest—and so far only—glory. Back then I knew only that if I had had the power, the *knowledge,* my mother—the only being that I truly loved—would not have died. I would have restored her to life. It was too late for her now, but it would not be too late for others whom I should love.

For even then, I knew that I would love again. One day as Mother and I sat together under the linden trees, she had told me that someday I would love a woman who was then only a girl. Mother said that I would love this woman even more deeply than I loved her, and would be happier with her by far. I recalled those words of my mother, and I swore to myself that I would not let happen to this future love what had happened to my mother.

This woman I would love would not die. I would keep her alive, and we would be happy forever. Alive forever, not dead. We would not become those lifeless, yellow-white sticks that my father had shown me on that night of ultimate horror, that night when I realized how what we think of as the gods cheat men through death.

So my life's work was chosen, my fate was sealed.

Above all things I desired knowledge, the knowledge

of what made creatures live, and not what made them die. I had no wish to study diseases, except insofar as disease processes could lead me toward my goal. There were too many diseases, so many that one could not hope to find a cure for even a few, let alone for all.

No, I wished to find a cure for the greatest plague of all, death itself. I wanted nothing less than to restore life and warmth to dead tissue, to bring the spirit back into the empty shell and make it rise and walk again.

I began humbly enough by examining everything that I could of life, by reading works far beyond the comprehension of children my age. Eventually, by constant repetition and the insistence of my young will, I began to perceive what the scientist-authors were saying, and eventually I began to understand.

It took years, of course, and while I was puzzling out these strange words and driving my tutors to distraction with my incessant questions, I investigated the twin riddles of life and death as best a child could. I began by spying on the doctor who had tended my mother during her final illness.

His name was Doctor Horst, and he was called to my father's estate whenever any of the family or servants were ailing. A few weeks short of my sixth birthday, Gunter, a stableboy, began suffering from intense pains in his abdomen. When Klaus, the head groom, questioned him, Gunter confessed that he had swallowed a horseshoe nail when another of the boys had bet him a week's wages that he could not. After Klaus clouted the other lad, he had him ride as fast as he could for the doctor, being fearful that the ride into Neufurchtenberg could kill Gunter in his current condition.

The doctor arrived near dusk and was taken into the room above the stable where Gunter lay. Of course, he closed the door behind himself and Klaus, who would assist him, but when the other stableboy told me that they were going to "cut his insides open," as he put it, I knew that I had to see what would transpire. At least one of the mysteries of the human organism would be revealed to me.

There was a tall oak tree that grew next to the stable. The stableboys called it the Dead Man's Tree because a footman bested in love had hung himself from one of its branches many years before. The story was that the body could often be seen just after sunset, dangling from its rope, its eyes open and bulging. The rope would supposedly twist so that the eyes of the apparition could follow the one unlucky enough to see it. But that is all the motion it was reputed to make. Even when a strong wind was blowing, the corpse would neither sway nor swing, just turn slowly.

I had heard this legend only a short time before, and avoided the tree as much as possible. Though even then a materialist, I was enough of a child to think it foolhardy to tempt fate. It was not long before that grudging semi-belief in the supernatural would leave me completely, but at that time the tree chilled my blood. However, it was necessary for me to conquer my fear of it, since one of its topmost limbs overlooked the boy Gunter's window at the top of the stable.

I shivered in every limb as I approached the massive oak, not for fear of my father's punishment if he caught me spying, for he was in a distant town on business, but for fear of seeing the revenant of the suicidal footman and his dead eyes. The sun had just sunk beneath the horizon, and the darkness under the tree seemed almost alive, waiting for a little boy to begin climbing the branches before it revealed its dread secret to him.

But my burning curiosity was stronger than my chilling fear, and, making sure I was not observed, I dashed under the tree, sprang to the first branch, and began to pull myself upward in the dying light of dusk. I climbed under the most adverse of conditions, my eyes partially closed so as to avoid the chance of my gaze meeting the ghost's.

But soon I was forced to open my eyes wider as the climb grew more treacherous, and the hard ground farther away. I heard Frau Dorfmann, who was in charge when my father was away, call my name, but I ignored her.

After another few minutes of rigorous ascent, I found myself on the limb I had sought, and slithered farther out upon it until I could see into the lantern-lit room where Doctor Horst was working on Gunter.

I had arrived in the nick of time. Klaus was just setting down a large glass that I now assume had been filled with liquor meant to stupefy the boy. It had not done its work; he still thrashed about with pain. The doctor and the groom lashed him down to his cot so that he could not move his arms and legs, and then Klaus held the boy's torso steady while Doctor Horst made his next incision just above the crop.

Gunter screamed so loudly that I nearly fell from the branch, but managed to hang on. I was shocked. I had never seen blood in that quantity before, only the small amounts visible when I'd accidentally scratched or cut myself. From what I beheld here, there seemed to be pints, quarts, gallons inside a person, and I imagined each human as a veritable wineskin filled with blood, and wondered why we did not slosh as we walked.

Then the screams stopped abruptly, and Gunter lay still. I thought that perhaps he had died, but the doctor continued to work, and I realized later that the boy had mercifully passed out from the pain. The silence made it easier to watch what took place, and for the first time I beheld the wonder of the human body, the inner workings of life itself.

In truth, all I saw was an incision, the edges of the

flesh, the fatty layer beneath, and the wall of the crop, but it was glorious to me. These strangely textured things were life in all its marvel, and I clung to the branch, gazed through the window, and marveled at the exquisite beauty of it, of these tissues and organs and fluids working beneath our skins to make us live and see and feel.

I had forgotten the footman's ghost, forgotten even the surgeon's purpose in opening Gunter's body. All I saw in that exposed blood and tissue was truth and knowledge and beauty.

When Doctor Horst's forceps drew out the bloody horseshoe nail, it was almost anticlimactic, after what his scalpel had exposed to my view. I continued to watch, however, as he sutured up the riven tissues, hiding the inner secrets from my eager and excited sight.

Then, after several minutes more, the greatest miracle occurred. The body that had been pierced, cut, and sewn up again trembled—moved; the eyes flickered open, and life was restored. The vision shook me to my core.

And shook me right out of the tree.

The sight had so intoxicated me that I seemed to lose all physical sensation. My grasp on the branch had involuntarily loosened, and down I plummeted, jouncing from limb to limb, trying to regain my hold, but finding it impossible in the darkness. I was moving laterally as well as vertically, the limbs tossing me closer and closer to the stable building, the brick wall, the open stable door.

At last there were no more branches to cushion my fall, and I plunged into thin air, arms and legs flailing, until my head struck the sharp corner of the door. The impact stunned me so that I barely felt my body land heavily on the hard cobbles. I lay there for a moment, then tried to get up but could not. Just then Doctor

Horst came through the stable doorway, cursed softly, and knelt by my side.

"First one, now another," he said, and told me not to move. He asked me some questions, and I must have answered them to his satisfaction of my well-being, for he told me to get up and to come inside the house. He held a bandage on my forehead as we walked, for I was bleeding profusely from the cut I had gotten when I hit the edge of the door.

Frau Dorfmann nearly fainted at the sight of her wounded charge, but I was still invigorated by what I had seen through the dusty stable window. I scarcely felt any pain at the site of the wound, though my body was stiff and sore from its descent through the branches and landing on the stones.

"Get some schnapps," Doctor Horst ordered Frau Dorfmann. "I must sew this up." Then he looked down at me. "Can you be a brave boy?"

I looked at him with fire in my young eyes. "No schnapps," I said. "I want to see it. In a mirror."

Doctor Horst was puzzled at first. "You mean the cut?"

I shook my head. "I mean the sewing."

The doctor's eyes widened. "You wish to . . . see?"

I wished to see indeed. I wished to see far more than my own flesh stitched up, but I would take what was offered.

At my insistence the doctor took me to a mirror, where, my senses undulled by drink, I watched intently as he sutured my wound closed. It hurt damnably, but I gritted my teeth and watched as Doctor Horst carefully cleansed the cut and ever so gently (I *was* the young master, after all!) joined the two torn edges together with surgeon's twine, piercing the flesh again and again, then finally securing the whole deftly in a small knot. I still bear the scar. I wear it proudly. It was my first honor, the first badge of my dedication to mankind.

When my father came home, I told him what I had told Frau Dorfmann and the doctor, that I had fallen from the tree while trying to retrieve one of our cats from a high limb. I was punished, but not as much I would have been had I told the truth. When the story got out, I was much admired by the stableboys for having the courage to climb Dead Man's Tree after sundown, a feat none of them had ever dared.

It was not long before I strove to emulate Doctor Horst and the other medical and scientific explorers of whom I read. I started by dissecting the humblest of creatures, insects and earthworms, making sure that my studies were unobserved, especially by my father. After his reaction to my curiosity about my mother's corpse, I would take no further chances by sharing my confidences with him. Despite his seeming materialism, I looked on him as one who would have burned the greatest scientific scholars of past times as witches.

Invertebrates, however, did not give me even the rudimentary knowledge I required. Their organic complexity was interesting per se, but they lacked the characteristics that warm-blooded creatures seemed to possess, and by the time I was seven I developed a foolproof trap to capture birds alive. Sparrows and wrens, though plentiful, were too small for my purposes, and so I usually released them. Grackles were larger, and I never let one of them go. But best of all were crows, with large, meaty bodies filled with things to discover and explore and experiment with.

Birds were the first creatures with which I performed living experiments, since they were relatively easy to secure by means of their wings and were easily silenced —though most of my experiments were done far away from the house, in a small cavern I had discovered in the deep woods. This cavern became my private chapel of scientific worship. It was there that I kept the fruits of many of my experiments in earthen jars filled with a crude preservative that I had developed from kitchen stuffs, having no access to formaldehyde.

In another few years I had learned all I could from avians, so I turned to small mammals, harder to trap than birds, but infinitely more enlightening to work upon. The woods were filled with animals, but my traps mostly netted chipmunks, squirrels, and coneys. The coneys were the most suitable, since they were far larger than chipmunks and more tractable than squirrels, whose ferocious dispositions and sharp teeth made experimenting on them more dangerous than illuminating, as the countless scars on my fingers will attest.

The disadvantage of the coneys, however, was their screaming. Nothing shrieks louder than a rabbit in pain, and those of Mordenheimwald were no exception. Though there was no chance of anyone other than myself hearing them, I developed a swift and simple surgical procedure to silence the coneys, thus saving my ears and a large portion of my sanity.

Besides dissecting the creatures, I experimented with removing the organs, then replacing them where they had been before, making carefully detailed anatomical sketches. I attempted to sew the various viscera back into place, using needles and strong thread stolen from Frau Dorfmann's sewing basket. She was so absent-minded that she never missed a thing, always blaming herself for misplacing yet another spool.

I would also saw off legs and paws and reattach them, fusing the bone before suturing muscles and skin. I remember the joy I felt when restoring a coney's head to its body, having successfully fused the verte-brae beforehand.

Once I came upon a stag that had been wounded by

a hunter's arrow and was near death. Though it was too heavy for me to drag back to my cavern, I quickly fetched my implements and did a rapid dissection, sketching and taking notes frantically all the while before it expired.

My behavior may seem rather heartless for a child, but I was, as I say, driven by something far more important than kindness to dumb animals. I never received pleasure from their pain, and I would have drugged them had I had the capacity. But wine was closely guarded by my father's cellar master, and the other liquor was kept locked up in cupboards to which my father had the only key.

My greatest desire indeed was to work on insensible animal subjects, for the mental and physical trauma that my probings necessitated often killed the beast before I had successfully traced the living nerve or blood vessel or cord back to its source. I needed my subjects to live longer, and drugging them would have provided that benefit.

If there was one thing I learned in those early and butcherlike experiments, however, it was the idea of holism, that the body was a single functioning machine. The fact that it was made up of many parts was incontestable, but the primary impression I received was that those parts, every single one of them, had to be working together to provide life to the whole.

The greatest illustration of that concept—and its *reversal*—that I saw in my youth was one spring day when I found the body of a bear deep in the woods. It had been dead for several days, and the limbs were quite stiff. Flies buzzed around it and had begun to lay their eggs within. Despite the desiccated condition of the carcass, I had never examined a bear before, and began to dissect it.

I found a huge growth amidst the intestines—rank,

black, and odorous—and I noticed that whatever vile condition this tumor caused had spread to the surrounding organs and tissues, discoloring and decaying them. This *thing* that grew inside the creature had killed it by spreading throughout the body. This much was clear.

So if one part of the body malfunctioned, it could be the start of a process by which the entire body could eventually become devoid of life. Later I would learn that if even one *cell* turned rebel, it could bring death to the whole.

Therefore, why could not the spark of life in one previously dead cell be the start of a process that could bring life to *all* cells, and ultimately to the whole organism itself?

It was this thought, as yet only roughly formed, that would be my guidon throughout my life and bring me to the creation of life, evil and reprehensible as that life may have turned out to be.

My father still had no suspicion of what acts I was engaged in, and merely thought that I was romping in the woods with a sling or a bow and arrows, which I frequently took with me as camouflage when I went on my scientific forays. The only thing that disturbed him was that I never seemed to kill anything with my weapons, so from time to time I would take home the undissected corpse of a coney or squirrel to show him. He seemed happy and proud of me whenever I did that, so I did not do it often.

He finally became aware that my interest in wildlife was far from that of Nimrod when I attempted to examine his hunting dog, Dora. She was his prime hunter, and had given whelp once before to six pups that became great hunters all, and that he had given as gifts to some of the other landholders of the county.

She had become pregnant again, and the thought of

life actually growing inside her electrified me. I hovered near her, patting her growing abdomen whenever my father was not watching, marveling at the fact that there were small pups within. And I knew that I had to see them, to see life created within the womb, as I wished to sustain, and later to create, life outside it.

Fortunately for me, or so I thought, Dora loved wine. After a hunt, when my father would have in his cronies for a feast and drinking, he would give Dora a small dish of red wine, which she would lap up with pleasure. He let her have no more, but that was enough, for within minutes after imbibing it, she would walk tipsily, much to the amusement of the men. She would then frolic like a puppy for a short time, her happy face grinning, then stagger over to the fireplace, collapse, and go to sleep.

One night, when Dora was well along in her pregnancy, my father was feeling rather ill due to gorging on fresh venison at dinner, and retired early, leaving me with a book in front of the fire. My father's usual bottle of after-dinner port was open on the sideboard, but both it and the glass were untouched. The servants had gone to their own beds, except for the one who solicitously aided my ailing father in his bedchamber.

Dora lay snoring at my feet, the wine sat on the sideboard, and the rest of the house was abed. Conditions would never be better.

I stood up, took a decorative serving bowl from atop a cupboard where it was displayed, and filled it with port. It held half the bottle, an amount far more than Dora had ever drunk before. I set it down on the hearth next to her, nuzzled her until she woke, dipped a finger in the port, and held it under her nose. "Here, girl," I said. "Nice wine . . ."

She needed no cajoling, but was on her feet and at the bowl, slurping down the sticky-sweet liquid as fast as her tongue could lap it into her mouth. At this proof of her gluttony, I grinned as widely as the dog did when she looked up at me, licking her chops so as to capture any stray droplets that might have clung to her jaws. I knelt, emptied the remainder of the bottle into the bowl, and watched Dora drink it down as avidly as she had the first portion.

This fortified wine was much stronger than the red wine she was used to, and no frolicsome mood came upon her. Instead, she simply took one or two trembling steps, then rolled over onto her side, gave a single wet snore, and closed her eyes.

For a moment I was afraid I had killed her, but I saw her flanks rising and falling with her breath, and breathed a sigh of relief myself. Then I ran to my bedroom to get my instruments.

I had made scalpels by grinding down the blades of small knives, then honing them to razor sharpness. My clamps were pilfered from the estate carpenter's shop. But they had been fine for my purposes until now, as had Frau Dorfmann's needles and thread. Though I had never incised and then sutured a subject that lived, I always felt it was because of the trauma of working without drugs. Dora, I felt, had a good chance of survival.

In retrospect, it was a foolish and dangerously stupid thought. The dog would certainly have died, had I been able to accomplish my end. It was my frenzy to *see*, however, that drove me on, not logic. After I had gotten my tools, I picked up the dog and carried her into the kitchen. There I laid her on the oilcloth spread on the table where the cook prepared our food.

I cleaned the instruments carefully, and palpated Dora's abdomen until I thought I could actually feel the pups. Then, taking up my scalpel, I pressed it against the dog's flesh, and made a light, tentative cut.

I should have shaken the dog first to make sure that she was sleeping. But I did not, and the animal instantly woke with a howl, and just as speedily ripped through the air with her jaws agape.

I twisted my head away to protect my eyes, but the fangs tore into the side of my head and closed firmly on my ear. I lunged backward, but felt the pain hammering through my head and a gush of blood pouring down my neck.

The dog fell back onto the table panting, as I lurched away from her, my hand held to my bleeding ear. I could feel the lobe dangling from just a thin strand of flesh, and desperately put it back, as if holding it against the rest of my ear could make it all one piece again.

The kitchen door banged open, and I saw my white-faced father standing there, his robe thrown over his sleeping gown. When Dora saw him, her tail began to wag, and she attempted to stand up, but her claws only slid on the oilcloth. She smiled her dog smile at him, my blood on her mouth, and then she seemed to become aware of the small cut in her abdomen, and twisted her body so that she could lick it.

My father looked at the dog, the blood-tinged scalpel lying on the floor, and at me, blood running down over my knuckles as I clamped my chewed ear together.

Frau Dorfmann appeared behind my father, and she gasped as she saw my condition. "Bandage his head," my father told her. "Then bring him outside. We'll ride to Doctor Horst's." He turned and left without another word.

Frau Dorfmann, rendered half sick by the sight of my dangling lobe, was nonetheless able to put a clean cloth on the wound, winding strips of ribbon around my head to hold it in place, so that I could barely see. Then she hurried me outside, where my father, mounted on his horse, held the reins of mine.

I climbed on, and we spurred toward Neufurchten-berg. I could just hear my father's voice above the thud-ding hooves of the galloping horses. "Is Dora hurt?" he said.

"No, sir," I shouted, then added more truthfully, "she's just very drunk, and has a . . . small cut on her stomach."

"What were you trying to do?"

"I . . . I wanted to look inside . . . see the pups."

"Little doctor, eh?" I could not tell from his voice whether he was angry or not.

"Yes, sir. I'm sorry, Father."

He said no more. When we arrived in Neufurchten-berg, we had to hammer on the doctor's door to rouse him from sleep, but he ushered us into his dispensary and unwrapped the binding from my head while my father told him that a dog had done it.

"Nasty," said Doctor Horst. "But I think I can stitch it up so that there will be just a small scar. The blood vessels, you see, have kept the lobe nourished, and—"

"Take it off," my father said.

The doctor looked at him oddly. "Pardon, sir?"

"Take it off."

I shivered at the coldness of his tone as much as I did the actual words and what they implied for me.

"Remove the lobe. It will be a beneficial reminder to Victor of the foolhardiness of too much curiosity."

"But, good sir . . ." said Doctor Horst.

"And," my father went on, as if the doctor had not spoken, "its absence will also encourage him to leave surgery to the surgeons."

The comment enraged me. My father's smugness seemed to imply that I was not and never would be a surgeon, while all the time I knew that I had performed dozens, nay, hundreds of examinations upon birds and animals, and I would continue in my chosen work whether my father stood in my way or not. If all the gods were to suddenly attain reality, take shape and bar my way, even they could not stop me.

Furious, I stood up from the examining chair. I would show him who was and would be a surgeon. I stepped to the doctor's table and plucked up a scalpel from the array of instruments there. I think the doctor thought that I meant to use it upon my father, for he said, "No, boy! He is your father!"

I looked up at him with all the courage my ten-year-old heart could muster, then smiled. "And it is *my* ear."

So saying, I grasped the lobe with my left hand, and with the right severed in a single stroke the flap of skin that held it to me.

The pain was short-lived but intense. Still, I did not cry out. Tears surged to my eyes as wetly as the new blood from my severed ear. Biting back my pain, I laid the scalpel back on the table, and let the doctor see to the bleeding. My father only looked dazedly at me, his mouth open in disbelief at what I had done.

"Poor boy," Doctor Horst crooned as he worked. "Poor, poor boy."

"It's not much of a loss," I said, wishing that my voice would stop shaking. "The lobe of the ear has no practical function, after all."

The doctor cleaned and stitched my wounded ear the same as he had patched my forehead a few years before, and I sat there patiently, making no sound, looking at my father as he looked at me. And in his aspect, I descried a new respect for me, an admiration given almost against his will. It was the same kind of look he wore when I had hauled home my "hunting" trophies, but now it was more sincere and deeply felt.

And I realized that I had impressed him by doing what I did. I had somehow become a man in his eyes by cutting my own flesh, inflicting pain upon myself as an empty gesture of what I believed in. But empty or not, the gesture had made him look at me far differently than before.

We rode home slowly, our horses trotting the same path they had galloped before, and after a time my father spoke to me, and the tone of voice was not the usual demeaning one he used with me, but rather one I had heard him use with his friends and colleagues. He was speaking to me as though I were his equal.

"When I called you a 'little doctor,'" he said, "was I right? Was it for medical knowledge you wished to . . . examine the hound?"

"Yes, sir, it was. Medical and scientific."

"You have . . . done this sort of thing before? With other animals?"

"I have, sir."

"Why did you not tell me of it?"

"I did not think you would approve, sir."

He rode for a while before he answered. "The specifics, perhaps not. But I do approve of courage. Of dedication. Of passion toward a goal. Tell me, what do you know of medicine, science . . . anatomy?"

For the rest of the ride I poured out my heart and my knowledge. I did not speak of my mother's death or my desire to preserve, sustain, and even create life—those were still wild dreams and would sound like wild dreams even from grown men, scholars well versed in the medical arts.

But I did let my father know the extent of my private studies, my examinations, and my experimentation. When he asked if my tutor had been encouraging me in these subjects, I answered truthfully that the pedant knew nothing of it other than what he might have deduced from my preference for the scientific rather than the philosophical or literary.

"We must make him aware of it then," said my father. "If this is what you wish, what you are dedicated to, then you must concentrate on it and immerse yourself in it."

I must confess that I was amazed by my father's attitude. I had expected to be severely punished, particularly after the incident of the earlobe, but instead he was taking me and my concerns seriously for the first time in my life.

I brought up what I knew would be a delicate subject. "Father, I know that you had in mind that I should take control of your business and the estate when I grew to manhood. If you still wish this, I can—"

But he cut me off. "Put it out of your mind. A disinterested businessman is a bad businessman. The estate will be yours when I die, and you may do with it as you will—turn it into a sanitarium, or a hospital, or . . ." He mused a moment. "Or a great college of medicine. I have but one request."

"Yes, sir?"

I could sense his smile, even in the darkness. "Just don't do any more operations on Dora!"

And we laughed together for the first time that I could recall.

 **SIX**

From that time on, I got on well with my father. He never had any idea of my true goal, for he died just before I left the university. He became insistent that my tutor concentrate my studies on medicine and science, and he did so. So until I was sixteen I had specimens aplenty to work on and assuage my curiosity with.

I no longer had to set snares to trap the subjects myself. That task fell to Horg, who was then a youth several years my junior, the son of one of the gardeners, not a bright fellow, but obedient. I was often amazed at the ease with which he brought me the animals I needed.

My tutor was often appalled by my experiments, but he was well paid, and so remained quiet. Only once did he complain to my father about a certain project of mine involving two calves and the head of a heifer, but my father, after examining the laboratory, merely called the tutor squeamish, and told the man not to bother him again with trifles.

By the time I went to the university when I was sixteen, I knew as much as many of the professors, most of whom were put off by my advanced knowledge, but some few of whom encouraged me. There for the first time I got to work with human bodies—cadavers, of course. Even though they had not the spark of life, I found them endlessly fascinating. I would stay in the dissecting rooms long after the appointed time, literally unraveling the mysteries of the human organism, always with a view to gaining the knowledge I would need to do the great work that lay ahead of me.

Often my professors or their assistants would have to order me out, so enrapt was I by the maps of flesh and blood that lay before me. Indeed, I considered myself a cartographer of the human spirit, preparing myself to guide mankind on a voyage to immortality.

It was not long before my lust for knowledge surpassed the ability of my teachers to convey new wisdom to me. I began charting my own course, reading the works of scholars and scientists whom the learned men of the university had long forgotten or dismissed as dreamers and fools.

But I quickly came to believe that those dreams could be made reality, that the spark of genius I felt within me could ignite the flame of life in dead tissue, though I knew not yet how it could be accomplished. I only knew that I would do it.

Though my firm dedication pleased my father, it displeased the staid purveyors of dead lessons at the university, and it was not long before I was threatened with expulsion, not only for going far beyond what was expected of me in the realm of research, but also for my disrespect for the required metaphysics and philosophy courses. All the tired musings of the philosophers seemed to me flat and useless, a total waste of time. I found that *how* man lived—the mechanics of life and its survival—dwarfed in importance the purely theoretical questions of *why* he lived, and I was quick to say so in front of the entire class.

Eventually I tempered my criticism and learned to feed back on paper the mindless mental meanderings the doddering old idiots wanted to hear. I had realized, nearly too late, that I needed to remain in the university to receive my doctoral degree. And without that degree,

I should be unable to proceed with my studies.

So I treated metaphysics as a necessary evil, receiving top grades nevertheless. I meanwhile continued to concentrate wholeheartedly on my main interests, science and medicine, especially the triumvirate of chemistry, physics, and biology, for it was by a combination of these three fields that I would achieve my desire.

I accomplished in five years what took most students eight, though I would have finished sooner had it not been for my time-consuming independent studies. I received my degree of Doctor of Medicine when I was twenty-one years of age. It was just a few months before my graduation that I made the acquaintance of Fraulein Elise Von Brandthofen.

Elise was the daughter of Doctor Henrik Von Brandthofen, who was my professor of biologic chemistry at the university. He was one of the few teachers who honored me for my knowledge rather than disparaged me as a know-it-all, and we formed a convivial friendship. At no time, though, did I inform him of my motivation for such a surfeit of knowledge.

He invited me to his house for dinner on a cold January night, but that night was made warm by the presence of Elise, who greeted me at the door. She was more than beautiful. She was breathtaking, her blond hair glowing in the light of dozens of candles, her satin gown caressing her lithe, athletic body. And her smile!

No woman had ever smiled at me like that before, and none have since. It made her entire face light up like a beacon and made me realize for the first time that there were things other than the smell of formaldehyde, scalpels, and cadavers.

I had made myself a monk for the sake of knowledge, never joining my fellow students on their sojourns in taverns or gaming houses, where slatternly females would try to divorce them from the contents of their purses. I suppose one might say I had saved myself for the right woman, when she came along, and, that night, come along she did.

I was delighted to learn over dinner that her pretty face did not mask a stupid mind, for she spoke far more often of things chemical in nature than she did of the fashions and gossip of the time. Although as a woman her formal schooling was limited, she had entreated her father to teach her the principles of science and had quite an affinity for it. She was far better grounded in chemical knowledge than were many of my classmates, and our conversation made the dinner flash by at lightning speed.

I suspected that her father might have me in mind as a suitor, for he was discerning enough to see that I had a miraculous future ahead of me. Miracles, however, are not always to be desired. It would have been better for him and his daughter if he had turned me out of that house, forbidding me to ever see his child again. But that night, with the wine flowing, the fire warm, the food delicious, and the first buds of love beginning to sprout, the future looked as bright as the present, and none of us knew what horrors it would hold.

Doctor Von Brandthofen had me to dinner every week from that time on, and my relationship with Elise blossomed. We talked together, laughed together, and began to go for walks once the first warm days of spring commenced.

At the end of winter, I received word that my father had died. The night I learned of it, I went to the Von Brandthofen house seeking sympathy. I found it there in the comforting arms of Elise, and as we held each other, I knew that there would be no other woman in the world for me. That evening, I asked her if she would be my bride after my graduation, and, to my great joy, she agreed.

After my father's funeral, I asked Doctor Von Brandt-hofen for his consent, which he gave wholeheartedly, and Elise and I became Dr. and Mrs. Victor Morden-heim on the twenty-third day of June, beginning a life of love that has not yet ended and, whether for good or ill, will not end in the foreseeable future.

On our honeymoon, a wonderful week spent touring the mountains, Elise confessed to me that she had been the cause of my being invited to dinner that first evening. Her father had told her of a brilliant young student in his class, and when he added that she would also find the student pleasant to look upon, she gave poor Doctor Von Brandthofen no rest until he finally extended to me the invitation. I was delighted by this revelation, and kissed my dear Elise until she blushed.

After our honeymoon, the realities of life took command, and I spent most of what remained of the year dealing with my father's estate and holdings. I sold most of it outright, converting it to cash. There was plenty on which to retire the more aged of my father's servants, and to stake the younger ones until they could find positions elsewhere.

I retained one servant only, and that was Horg, the boy who captured my animal subjects for me. And he has remained with me through all these years, all these trials and tribulations. Even now he greets—or more often turns away—visitors at my door. As is very noticeable, he has a humped back. It was far worse years ago, but I was able to perform some surgery on it and removed a good deal of the tissue. I would have excised more, but the threat of damage to his internal organs stopped me. I would hate to lose Horg. He does things that no one else could do . . . or possibly *would* do. He is my loyal right hand. I believe he would die for me should I ever ask him.

By the spring of the following year, my father's business was dispensed with, and I found myself a very wealthy young doctor. I bought a large house in the town of Leidenheim and went into practice as a hospital surgeon there while continuing my private studies. The hospital would, I felt, give me access to both living patients and dead subjects. Where better to continue learning the mysteries of life and death than in a hospital, where births, deaths, illnesses, and recoveries are the norm?

But I soon found that the other surgeons, though inured to human suffering, had little patience for and even less understanding of what I was slowly trying to achieve. They found my studies rather unwholesome.

Still, they put up with my nocturnal activities, for it is not boasting to say that I was the finest surgeon the hospital possessed, and those in charge were willing to turn a blind eye to my experiments in order that the hospital benefit from my lifesaving abilities.

Deaths occurred, of course, though I must say that I always labored mightily to save my patients. My desire for subjects was not so great that I ever helped usher them through the door of death. My goal was the preservation of life, and although in my often unnecessary "autopsies" I might have treated the cadavers with less than pristine decorum, I always saved what lives I could.

I worked in the hospital for two years, spending the days saving lives, the nights trying to puzzle out what made tissue live at all, and how to bequeath life to it. I explored the puzzles of the human body with the precision and patience of a watchmaker. It was work in miniature, tracing and understanding the minutest, seemingly least important parts of the machine that was man, but knowing that everything was important, contributed toward the whole, and could not be ignored.

Even though I labored incessantly, I still made it a point to spend two nights a week with my lovely bride, whose patience knew no bounds. Never did she chide me for staying at the hospital too long, and always arose when I entered the house, even if it were long after midnight, and poured me a glass of wine and rubbed my shoulders to relax my muscles from tediously bending over bloodstained tables.

Like all young married couples, we dearly wanted to be parents, Elise perhaps more than I. But alas, it was not to be, as we quickly discovered. Elise could not conceive a child, a conclusion borne out by the examination of a colleague of mine. Her sorrow at this news was overwhelming, and it cast a pall on our formerly happy house. How ironic it was that I of all men, who wished only to create and preserve life, could not create a son of my own flesh.

Very well then, I thought. I shall make a son out of other flesh, but he shall still be mine, for *I* shall give him life. And at length I told Elise of my dreams, not only of preserving life where none should be, but of creating life in what was dead tissue. At first, she looked at me oddly, but then seemed to share my enthusiasm, saying, "You are so wise, Victor, that I would not put anything beyond you."

These words gave me great encouragement, and I have heard them hundreds, nay, thousands of times since, calling them up from my memory whenever a problem presented itself as so vast that I feared I might not be able to overcome it. Yet I always did, my dear Elise's sweet words giving me the courage and determination to press on.

So we lived with our grief of childlessness, and I continued to labor to find a way in which we might be childless no longer, and that mankind need never again fear the specter of death, which ultimately carries away *all* children born into this world, whether at the age of eight or eighty.

At the end of my second year at the hospital, however, something occurred that made it necessary for me to change my venue. The other doctors had been growing less comfortable with my investigations, but the final straw came one night when I was working over the corpse of a patient who had died earlier that day.

Doctor Schuldt, the supervisor of surgeons, entered and was rather upset by what he saw. The procedure may have looked brutal, but it was absolutely necessary for the current track of research I was following. I suppose it did not help matters that the expired subject was Doctor Schuldt's mother-in-law. I myself was so startled at being disturbed when I thought everyone else had gone, that I pressed down too hard on the surgical saw I was using, and cut off the tip of my left ring finger. It was a foolish thing to do, and it demonstrates the nervous state under which I then worked.

When Doctor Schuldt saw what I had done to myself and what I was doing to my subject, he grew ill, and hurried out of the room, lest he empty his stomach amidst an already gruesome scene of carnage. After I stanched the blood of my severed finger and wrapped it thoroughly, I tried to explain to him that it was all in the name of scientific progress. He replied that even fiends would quail at such blasphemous practices on a human body, and he ordered me to clear everything out of my tiny dispensary that very night and never to return to the hospital.

I agreed, but asked if he would be willing to reattach my severed fingertip to my finger while the tissue was still alive and capable of regeneration. He merely sneered and said that I should keep the wound as a grisly souvenir of this grim night. Now that I think of it, he and my father had a somewhat similar sense of justice. Nevertheless, I was unable to operate on myself with one hand, and the piece of finger withered quickly.

I threw it away, wearily accepting my newest self-produced deformity.

Of course I appealed to the hospital board for reinstatement, explaining the procedure in full detail, but my own words condemned me, as Doctor Schuldt had not told the board precisely what I was doing when he ordered my dismissal. When the old fools heard from my own lips what I had done, they were so outraged that several of them suggested bringing criminal charges against me, but were dissuaded by the others, who argued that the public exposure would bring everlasting shame to the hospital.

So, under a cloud, I left the hospital and Leidenheim as well. In truth, I was not sorry to go. I had begun to grow tired of prying and disapproving eyes. As much of my time was spent in covering up my experiments as was in performing them, and my fear of discovery by those unsympathetic to me had greatly shaken my concentration.

Elise was ready to go wherever I suggested, dear girl that she is. Or rather was, and will be again—I swear it.

We remained in our house until I found the place in which we now reside. I decided that I wished a spot far from prying eyes, but one that would nevertheless be near a source of experimental subjects. I found it in Schloss Helmreich.

The castle is five miles from Ludendorf, the nearest town of any size, and when I first saw it I knew it would be ideal for my purposes. Remote, perched between land and sea as is man between life and death, it is surrounded as well on the east by a number of small freeholds, each with its own family cemetery. Ships crash frequently on the rocks, and much flotsam and jetsam are washed ashore, including newly drowned bodies. There could not have been a better place.

The last of the Helmreichs had died, so I christened

the castle Schloss Mordenheim. Elise and I, as well as Horg and a small retinue of servants, moved in during the autumn of '05, and I began in earnest my great work. I did not realize then how many years longer it would take, and what it would take out of my life as well.

But even if I had, I could not have stopped. It was my destiny, a destiny of my own making, for I had no truck with the gods of men. For I thought that if man could be his own creator, of what use were the gods? And, as I learned later to my great grief, what need were the gods if man can damn himself, as well?

So I worked through months, years, with Elise the only bright spot in my weary days. From time to time I allowed her to talk me into brief vacations, when we would return to the mountains where we had spent our honeymoon and relive those ardent times. But before too long, my thoughts would stray back to my work, and I would champ at the bit to be back in my self-imposed harness of scientific labor. Elise, to her eternal credit, never complained when my need to work demanded that we cut our holidays short and return to Schloss Mordenheim.

Within a year of our arrival at the castle, I had begun to synthesize my observations to the point where I was experimenting with restoring life to dead animal cells. It took several years alone to achieve that—to reawaken life in a single dead cell. Through long analysis, examination, and recreation of the tremendously complex electrochemical alterations that occur in the cell's tiniest particle, I was able to concoct a fluid that would stimulate the cell back to life. It took me more than five years to do this.

Once I had accomplished it, the greatest of all challenges still lay ahead. There was no conceivable way for me to inject each and every cell In a living organism, for I would still be working when the sun finally burned itself out and the world grew dark and cold.

The trick, rather, would be to create a chain reaction with that first spark, so that the life would go leaping from cell to cell, organ to organ, heart to brain to limbs, from the core of the most important source of life to the end of every living hair on the head.

To find this secret took me five more years. I worked with animals first, both living and dead, and then with the corpses of men. Horg and I would take newly buried bodies from the nearby family cemeteries, filling in the graves so carefully that no one could ever tell we had been there. Often bodies would be washed up after shipwrecks, and instead of returning them to their families, I made their deaths a sacrifice to save the lives of others. And, when all else failed, there were men in Ludendorf who, for a price, could supply what was needed. I never asked where they got the bodies. They told me they stole them from hospices and graveyards, and I never wished to disbelieve them.

At any rate, I had enough subjects upon which to experiment. But the unpleasant methods of acquisition, the rumors—often true—that began to run rampant among the people of Ludendorf, and even the mutterings of the servants began to wear on Elise's nerves. At last I thought it would be best if she went to stay with her cousins in Neufurchtenberg until I had finished what I had no choice but to do.

She was reluctant to go, but when I told her that it would not only be best for her peace of mind, but also for my concentration, she agreed, willing to leave my presence only for the sake of my work. Little did we know that the separation would last for years, relieved only by our bimonthly visits to each other for a day or two at a time, and occasional meetings in one of the inns of Ludendorf. It was hard on her, but it was the only way for me to accomplish my goal.

And ever so slowly the promised prize drew nearer, an edifice of science erected on a framework of corpses and severed limbs held together by spiderlike strands of nerve tissue and blood vessels. Each day brought a new speck of knowledge, every month saw new wisdom, and so the years passed by.

And then one day, I felt ready. It was as if all the years and every tiny bit of information I had gleaned had been rungs on a ladder, lifting me higher and higher, until at last I could see the amazing, bright, and magical land over the wall behind which I and all of mankind had been imprisoned. I knew then that I could accomplish my dream of creating life.

Horg and I, and the legion of resurrection men and brigands to whom I had access, worked unceasingly, gathering the seeds of flesh from which my greatest flower of life would bloom. I thought it best to make everything larger than normal, as the increased size made the near-microscopic work of connection, grafting, and fusion slightly easier.

While the proper parts were being collected, I did preliminary work with mammals and found that the early decay of the tissues was not a boundary to revivification, for the process I had developed actually reversed the decay; the tissue appeared perfectly healthy under my microscopes.

The revived animals, however, were less than docile. A few of them escaped while I was examining them or when Horg was taking them in or out of their cages. In the winter, we were able to catch them before they left the castle, but in the summer, when windows were opened, they leapt out, often falling fifty feet or more, but landing unharmed and scurrying away. I suppose there are still a few at large in the countryside, since every now and then I hear rumors of a hunter killing a beast that bears the marks of my handiwork. After all, a creature half rabbit and half wolverine can hardly have been created by nature itself.

As the individual pieces began to come to me, I would attach them in the procedure only I have full knowledge of, the method that would let life flow from one to the other swiftly and ceaselessly. I then chilled them in a natural ice cave in the side of the sea cliff until the next section should come in. I added skin to skin, fused bone to bone and muscle to muscle to make my creation more than a man. He would be a super-man, whose existence would promise health and immortality to *all* men.

Other, weaker men might have begun to pray at this point, but I had not come all this way by the sweat of my own brow and the labor of my own mind to revert to superstition. Only by accepting that which could be proved had I come this far. Did any being other than myself guide my way? How could I believe such a thing?

I admit that it would have been easy to succumb, particularly in light of the mists that began to gather around the castle as the night of creation approached. I had never seen anything quite so eerie. They seemed like long, tenuous fingers longing to enwrap the castle in their clutches. I laughed at these fancies, however, and continued to work.

Soon all was accomplished save for the head. The corpses brought to me up until then had all had heads that were unacceptable for one reason or another—a massive brain tumor that surely would have hampered the thought processes of my creation, an injury that had crushed the skull, blind eyes, or even such a minor problem as faulty channels of the ear. Whatever the impediment to perfection, it was enough to prevent me from completing my work.

In vain we searched for the perfect head, and ulti-mately I decided to construct one myself. The difficulty was extreme, but at length it was finished, and attached to the rest of the body.

As I completed the surgery, a storm began to brew outside the castle, and the sun slowly sank into the sea. At long last I was ready to give my creation life.

 **SEVEN**

That night was perhaps the most vile the countryside had ever known. The mists parted just enough for the sky to spit down hard, pelting drops of rain, making the dirt leap wherever they struck. Vast peals of thunder shook the sky and earth, slashes of lightning ripped the heavens and blinded any eyes daring enough to behold their fury, and clouds shaped like pustulant growths on long-dead corpses loomed overhead. It was, I thought, the perfect night for my endeavors.

I would certainly have no visitors, I told myself, for on such a night no one would dare venture out. The cowardly farmers would be huddling close to their fires, wood hissing with the bitter rain that shot down the chimneys. And in Ludendorf the streets would be bare, everyone having run indoors. At sea, the ships would trim their sails, but many seamen were nonetheless swept over the side, for the next day Horg found bloated corpses washed up beneath the cliffs of Schloss Mordenheim.

The winds and waters assailed the stones of the castle like fists battering a door. I heard the sound not as nature's fury, but instead as the knock of opportunity, a natural phenomenon fortuitously timed for my purposes, a storm that would provide a force powerful enough to send my elixir of life surging through the cells of my creation so quickly as to be practically instantaneous.

I called for Horg, and together we descended a long stairway that led from the deepest cellar of the castle down into the heart of the cliff to the ice cave where my creation lay waiting for reanimation. We trembled, I only from excitement and Horg only from cold; we had both seen enough of graveyards and cadavers to inure us to any fear of the dead. We managed to secure the body to a lightweight gurney, which we then hauled up the steps by means of a counterweight.

Once in the cellar, we wheeled the gurney into a large dumbwaiter that climbed upward from the cellar to the kitchen, and then higher into the laboratory itself. Above, we could hear the sizzle of electricity as lightning frequently struck the metal rod I had placed atop the watchtower, two hundred feet above the sea.

I filled the veins and arteries of the being with fresh blood, injecting it directly into the chambers of the heart. Then I stimulated the chest with vibrations to settle the blood throughout the body. Finally we wheeled the creature out onto the terrace between the laboratory and my personal quarters.

The wind threatened to tear us from our flat perch, and we bowed our heads against it as we worked. The danger of being struck by lightning was very real; Horg cowered as a white-hot bolt slammed into the lightning rod above us, and he dropped to the slate surface, his hands over his head.

Over the scream of the wind, I shouted to him to get up, for I certainly would not sacrifice all those years of work because a coward was afraid of a storm. Then he said something that made me laugh.

"But, Doctor," he sniveled, looking up over his crossed arms, "it's as if the gods themselves roar!"

I could taste burgeoning life in the rain that spattered my open mouth as I told him that these "gods" were nothing but the vicissitudes of weather, and that there were no gods, only man and his knowledge, who could do *anything* that gods could do.

At my words, the fury of the storm increased, but while others would have interpreted it as the rage of supernatural beings, I viewed it as raw nature acknowledging my credo of rationality. Then I set an example for Horg by walking firmly to the cables that would lead the lightning to my creation, grasping them, and moving back toward the table that held the creature.

Just then a blue-white blaze of fire that seemed a mile long skittered down from the sky and wrapped around the lightning rod. But I only laughed again, for I knew that the cables would not translate the power until I had thrown the switch. I had nothing to fear from the lightning or from the pantheon of false gods!

My courage brought Horg to his feet, and he helped me attach the cables to the metallic table on which my serendipitous being waited for life. When that was done, I went back into my laboratory, filled a hypodermic needle with the rejuvenative fluid that had taken me so many years to develop, and walked back out into the jaws of the storm.

There I surveyed my creature, naked to the rain, observed the lines of sutures that held the myriad parts together, and thought that I had never seen anything half as awesome.

Pride welled up in me as I cried to the storm, "Behold him! Arms stronger than Hercules'! Legs swifter than Hermes'! A face more handsome than Apollo's!" Overwhelmed by the moment, I turned toward Horg, my rain-wet face gleaming with joy. "*This,* Horg, is a true god!"

And with that, I lifted my face toward the heavens. The full moon was nothing but a nimbus of light at the edge of the sea, but it illuminated the sky just enough so that I could see clouds darker than the darkness merging overhead. There was a faint line of lightning, an anticipatory rumble that would have seemed a warning to the superstitious. I knew it was time.

I called to Horg to see to the switch, and he scurried over to the massive lever and pulled it toward him, opening the lines of power from the storm to my creation. And immediately a searing shaft of lightning began high above, so that I could actually see it reaching toward the lightning rod.

Without a moment's hesitation, I thrust the needle into the hollow just below the creature's heart and plunged the elixir home, then leapt back as the blinding streak of lightning embraced the rod, flashed through the wires, and hurled its full power directly into the corpse on the table, making it rise and buck.

The straps that held it to the table smoked and slowly burned and separated. The electricity made every portion of the body twitch and jerk, and I held my breath as the surge of power died away, leaving the creature momentarily still. Then I rushed to its side, watching my creation breathlessly and expectantly.

The smell of ozone hung in the air like misty fingers from another place, another plane entirely. I shivered at my fancy, then dismissed it as I bent over my creature, examining it closely, wondering why it did not move, why its eyes did not open, why it did not *live.*

Slowly I reached out my fingers to its face, irrationally fearing that lightning still surged within the body, that if I touched it I would be burned beyond restoration.

I could not know then how right I was.

But my fingertips touched the yellow-gray flesh, and the eyelids opened—not slowly and laboriously, but all at once, startling me so that I drew back my hand in unaccustomed panic.

For a moment I feared that I had erred. The eyes seemed too small for their sockets, and as they turned to follow me, I thought they were too loosely anchored. These distracting thoughts, however, fled quickly as I realized what I had done.

Inside the body that I and I alone had constructed from parts of dead men, life had been born. My elixir, my planning, my studies, my link from creature to lightning had brought life into the sundered and reassembled flesh. I had done it. Here before me was the fruit of my labors.

I smiled down at my creation. He did not blink at the raindrops stinging his eyes, but remained lying there, watching me, as my heart filled with pride and love.

"My son," I finally choked out. "Adam." Then I extended a hand to him, and he slowly sat up on the table and looked toward the sky, as though he knew it had been from there that the animating impulse of lightning had come.

"Adam," I said again. "Stand. Stand and walk, my boy."

He lurched to his feet swiftly, without hesitation. Behind me I could hear Horg gasp at the sheer power of the motion. It was like a perfectly geared machine come to effortless life.

But I, too, was in awe of what now stood before me. Adam was well over seven feet tall, and his build was massive. The pale gray skin was but a thin covering over the bulbous muscles engraved with arteries. Raised scars covered the body, making the whole look like a relief map divided into strange and marvelous countries.

The creature's face, framed by long hair as black as the night, was the most disquieting aspect of my creation. Though the skin elsewhere was gray, that about the eyes and mouth was pale blue and puckered, shriveled the way meat gets when it dries too long. The lips were a flat and unyielding black, and were parted slightly to reveal a set of teeth whose straight perfection and unexpected whiteness were shocking. And the watery eyes stared at me like blue grapes in a spoiled porridge.

But I could not then see the horror of those features, or of the mind that lay within. I was blinded by joy and pride and, yes, love for this creature to whom I had given life. This was my beloved *child*, and I saw his hideousness through the soft and gentle lens of a father's eyes.

"Elise," I whispered. "Oh Elise, at last we have a son. . . ."

And though I felt he watched me with innocent and learning eyes, I knew later that behind those eyes lay the thoughts of a rabid dog.

Suddenly the rain stopped, the clouds lifted, and the moon become visible hanging low over the sea. The storm had ended.

And begun.

EIGHT

Through gentle coaxing, I led Adam through the laboratory and to the watchtower, where Horg had prepared a small room for him. A specially built bed sat in the center of the curved room, and several barred windows presented a vista of the sea. I wanted Adam to see as much of the world about him as possible, yet still keep him safe and secure.

I patted the huge straw mattress and told him to rest, then took his hand to lead him to the bed. I was surprised at how cold the hand still was, and hoped that it would soon emulate the warmth of truly human flesh. Adam obeyed me when I bade him sit, then lie down, though he did not close his eyes, which he kept locked on me.

At last I drew my hand over my face, closing my eyes to indicate to Adam what he should do. He did close them, but opened them again immediately, and continued to watch me as I left the room with the lantern, leaving him in darkness. I waited silently outside the door for some time, but I did not hear him arise from the bed or attempt to open the door.

Naturally, I was exhausted, but I could not sleep until I wrote a letter to Elise, telling her only that something momentous had occurred, and imploring her to join me as quickly as possible. When I finished, I called Horg, gave him the letter, and told him to take the carriage to

Neufurchtenberg in the morning and bring Elise back with him. I advised him also to tell the other servants to stay away from the vicinity of the watchtower. Then I sank back upon my bed and fell asleep on the instant.

The following days were filled with tremendous excitement for me, learning for Adam, and terror for the foolish servants, who crept away from my employ, all save Horg. But to tell the truth, I scarcely noticed their absence. My attention was focused entirely on Adam, with whom I spent upward of sixteen hours every day. I was amazed at how quickly he learned to speak. It was as if he had known how at one time but had forgotten, and now rapidly relearned the complexities of speech. And I suppose that was exactly what had happened. The brain within his head had known the language, the tongue within his mouth had spoken it. Now they had merely to be reminded of the knowledge they had had when borne by other bodies.

I was equally pleased with Adam's physical coordination. He was capable of a great number of skills, combining agility with speed and great strength, which I quickly discovered had to be carefully controlled.

To illustrate the concept of "bird," I brought into his room a pair of small finches, which Elise had kept in our quarters. She had left them behind when she went to Neufurchtenberg in the hopes, dear girl that she was, that their sweet songs would remind me of her. When I removed one of the birds from the cage, I was delighted to see it receive Adam's undivided attention, as it perched on my finger and began to sing sweetly.

But then his small eyes seemed to grow smaller, and his expression became more quizzical than I had yet seen it. I smiled, nodded, and said. "Bird. The bird is singing a song. Singing. Isn't it lovely?"

Then, to my great surprise, Adam's hand came out with the speed of an arrow, and a scarred forefinger stronger than iron came down upon the little bird's back, crushing it against my knuckles. I gasped in shock as Adam drew back, eyes as wide as they might ever become, his gaze following the bird as it fell dead to the stone floor.

"No," I said softly, rubbing my aching hand. "That was wrong. Too hard. You hurt the bird. You killed it."

Adam slowly looked up into my eyes. His voice was hoarse, the sound of hailstones falling on fresh grass. "Killed?" he said.

"Yes. It is dead."

Adam looked down at the bird. "It is dead," he repeated, then looked back at me. "What is dead?"

"The *bird* is dead," I said.

"No—what is . . . *dead?*"

His naivete about death reminded me of my own at the beginning of my quest. I patiently tried to explain. "Dead is . . . nothing. Without life. Here." I picked up the dead bird and handed it to him, and he took it in his open palm, and pressed it hard with his other forefinger.

"No," I said. "That is too hard. That is what killed it. Hurt it so it cannot sing. It cannot do anything now. It is dead."

Adam thrust the bird at me angrily. "Make live again," he said, but I told him that I could not.

"You say . . . you made . . . *me* live."

"That was different," I told him. "You took a great deal of preparation and care. Years of work."

He raised a long, wiry finger and ran it along his own cheek, tracing the line of one of his facial scars until it stopped at the point of his chin. "Why," he said, "did you make me live?"

And I told him the simple truth, for it was not my intent that the mind of my creation should be suckled on lies. "I gave you life to prove to the world that it can be done. And my wife and I cannot have children, so you are our child."

"Wife?"

"My . . . mate. The woman I love."

"Love?"

One word led, as it invariably does, to another and another, and I explained to Adam the biological differences between men and women, and defined the concept of love as best I could until I heard a knock resound on the heavy oaken door.

I heard Horg's voice, and joy burst over me like sunshine. "Horg!" I cried. "Is Elise with you?"

He replied that she was. Almost beside myself with excitement, I rose and handed Adam a child's book with words, letters, and pictures of animals. "Someone has arrived whom I want you to meet," I said. "I will bring her up shortly. In the meantime, study your letters and words, yes?" At the door, I turned back. "And smile. Remember, what I taught you?" Then I rushed downstairs to my beloved.

Elise had never looked more beautiful, and I embraced her and told her that she was to stay now, never leave me again, be by my side always. Then I told her of my triumph. "I have done it, my darling, what I have strived for all these years!"

Elise freed herself from my arms and laughed to see me so enthused. "But what *is* it, Victor? Have you really succeeded then? Have you restored an animal to life?"

"I must show you," I said, grinning like the fool I surely was. "Come with me. There is someone I want you to meet."

"An assistant?" she guessed as we walked up the broad stairs together.

"No. Someone much closer. Someone who means a great deal to me and who, I trust, will mean much to you as well."

On the long walk to the watchtower, she pressed and pleaded, but I would give her no clues to spoil my surprise. By the time we arrived at the door, she was more impatient than I had ever seen her. "Now," I said, "your curiosity can be assuaged. I want you to meet . . . Adam." And I opened the door.

Had I been able to see with any eyes other than those of a proud father and creator, I would have realized that Elise would see not the wondrous embodiment of the marvelous deed I had accomplished, but instead a frightening, seven-foot-tall giant. She stared at Adam in horror, and her breath came in short, quick pants, as though she feared even to breathe in his presence.

What happened next I could scarcely fathom. The black lips of my creation parted, and Elise's fear made me suddenly aware of the rank odor that wafted from Adam's mouth. His teeth became visible, white and flawless in his fragmented face, as he first seemed to sneer, then to snarl at her, so that his upper lip curled like a savage animal's.

At that sight she screamed, once only, then her eyes slipped shut, and she began to fall. I attempted to grab her, but in a flash, Adam had crossed the room and scooped her up before she hit the stone floor.

I could only hold my breath as he held Elise, looking down into her unconscious face. The savage snarl remained on Adam's visage, and for the first time, I thought that I had failed, that Adam really was and would forever be a dead man.

But then I saw the snarl vanish from his face, and the corners of his mouth began to twist upward. And I realized that he was smiling, actually smiling at Elise as he held her in his arms, and the thought came to me that Adam adored her, found in her the same grace that had drawn me to her years before.

Yes, there *was* humanity there! The finer instincts,

the appreciation of beauty—these existed in my creation. And where these qualities dwelt, there could be
honor and courage and goodness and virtue.

Or so I thought. If only I had known then what that
smile *truly* meant. But I did not. My joy had blinded me.

"You did well, Adam," I said. "This is my wife, Elise,
and you saved her from harm. I thank you. Now I shall
take her back to our quarters. Give her to me, please."

Adam looked up. His eyes narrowed, his smile faded.
"Wife?" he said.

"Yes. You can think of her as your mother. I as your
father; she as your mother."

"Mother . . ." He looked down at Elise's face for a
long time. Then he held her out, his arms straight, for
me to take her. His strength, I thought as I took her into
my embrace, was remarkable.

"You'll stay here, all right?" I asked. Except for the
first time that I had told Adam he must stay in his room,
I had never felt it necessary to repeat that directive.
Now, for some undefined reason, I did. Adam nodded
heavily as I backed out of the room and pushed the
door closed with my foot.

Elise came to consciousness several minutes later in
our bedroom. Her eyes shot open, and she gave a
weak, strangled cry, but I consoled her that everything
was all right. But she would not be soothed so easily.

"Oh, Victor," she said. "What have you done? What
was that thing?"

"That was Adam, Elise. Adam, my creation. Our
child."

Her face soured with disgust. "Don't say that. Oh,
please don't. Is it . . . is *he* the result of your work? All
your years of effort?"

I was confused. Could she not see the wonder I had
wrought? "You knew, my love. You always knew what
my goal was."

"To preserve life, Victor. Or so I thought. You always told me that the rejuvenation experiments were simply a tool to discover the processes of life, and thus sustain them."

"And so they were!" I said. "But when I found that they really worked, that I could indeed create life in dead tissue, I had to ask myself how best to use that knowledge, and I found it not only in resurrection, but in creation! Adam never before lived, Elise. He is an ideal toward which the race of man has been striving for eons. And I have made him a reality!"

But she scoffed at me. "An ideal? You mean that . . . that *thing* you created? Victor, that is no ideal—that's a *monster!*"

"I know you speak out of ignorance and not spite, Elise."

"Then inform me, Victor. Of what raw materials did you make him? Corpses from morgues? Bits and pieces from charnel houses? The recent inhabitants of graves that you defiled? No, don't answer me. I see in your face that what I say is true."

I told her of course that it *was* true, but that I had no other choice. What hospital or university would have supported such learning? It dwarfed their feeble efforts at research as well as their poor intellects. "I *had* to act the way I did," I said. "And what are a few stolen bodies when the results are so remarkable, so magnificent? He is not a monster, Elise, but a man. You'll see. When you get to *know* Adam, you can't help but see how—"

But she interrupted me. "*Know* him? No, Victor, don't ask me to ever see that creature again! He is a dead thing, and should be returned to the dead. Destroy him, Victor, while you still can!"

She clutched me by the front of my coat, and though I was moved by her concern, I could not take such a request seriously. "Destroy him? Elise, you don't know what you're saying. You're distraught, weary from your journey, harried by the shock, the *miracle,* of what I have done."

"An *evil* miracle, Victor!"

"Evil? No, my love, Adam is beyond good and evil. He is truly like a child, his mind a blank slate." I took Elise's hands, sat on the bed next to her, and spoke to her softly and earnestly.

"He is malleable, like all children. Those who are brought up with evil influences about them often turn out to be evil, it is true. On the contrary, those who are brought up to respect and honor the good turn out to *be* good. So shall it be with Adam. His appearance matters not. In time, I may be able to change his looks for the better, but what does matter is the very fact that he lives at all. That which was dead is *alive,* Elise, and he shall grow mentally and philosophically to be an intelligent and gentle giant. We shall teach him together."

Elise's expression grew even colder than before, and she shook her head firmly. "No, Victor. You shall teach him, not I."

"But he *adores* you. If you had seen how he looked at you when he held you—"

Her face drained of blood so that her flesh looked as gray as Adam's. "Held me?"

"He caught you when you fell. He reacts so quickly; I tell you, Elise, he is a superman."

Her eyes widened in horror. "You let him touch me?"

"He is harmless, Elise, as I told you—a child!"

"Then he is one child that shall not have a mother."

I was stunned. "You do not mean that you shall leave me?"

"No, I shall not. I shall stay with you to protect you from that creature . . . and from yourself. But I shall never go into that room, or anywhere where your . . . Adam is."

"Very well, I respect your wishes. I will not force his company upon you. But I will make you change your mind of your own free will. Someday you will see Adam, and you will know that he has truly become a man so far above other men both physically and mentally that he will be heralded as the harbinger of a new and finer race."

And now those words come back to haunt me. My dear wife was wiser than I in many ways. She could see what I could not, that there was something wrong, twisted, in Adam. But unfortunately that realization did not come to me until far too late.

Dear Elise did stay with me. She saw to the affairs of the house, hiring new servants to care for the castle and me and calming them when they became alarmed.

The dear, concerned girl spent as much time with me as I could allow her, but most of the time I was cloistered with my creation and student, teaching him, reading to him, showing him as many of the wonders of the natural world as I could within the confines of the castle.

The weeks became months, and Elise became more and more demanding of me during the time we spent together. She begged me to destroy what she referred to as the monster, and I would as ardently tell her of the progress that Adam had made that day, until she would leave the room, wringing her hands and muttering to herself.

I was deeply concerned that my wife might even be going mad. If she was, I would have to live with the knowledge that it was my fault, the fault of the true child of my brain and the single-minded attention I paid to it.

But I could do nothing less. I had to prove to Elise—and to the world, when it was time—that what I had created was of benefit to mankind. In my months of

educating Adam I had been thrilled by the quickness of
his mind, by his unwavering grasp of complex concepts, his ability to retain any type of knowledge. Adam
was beginning to show signs of a personality with a will
of its own.

Yet what I found more difficult was to instill a moral
sense into my creation. Although I truly believed then
that Adam was beyond good or evil, as I told Elise, I
knew that he would have to conform to the proprieties
of society if I were ever to display him to the learned of
the world. So far that had not happened, and I strove
mightily to discover why.

At first I thought it might have something to do with
Adam's appearance, for often I found him examining
his own arms, trunk, and legs, and looking at his face in
the hand mirror I had given him. But whenever I tried to
draw him out on the subject, he became bluntly taci-
turn, then would stop talking completely, so that I
would be forced to leave the room.

On one of these occasions, I decided to seek solace
among my books. I went to a small room off my laboratory, where I sat and read the latest treatises to come
from the university at the capitol, thinking how laugh-
ably elementary they were. Gradually I dozed off, then
was awakened some hours later by a sound I had heard
only once, some months before—Elise's scream.

It came from our quarters, to which Elise had retired
long before. I leapt up and dashed out of the room,
across the terrace, and down the hall that led to our
bedchamber. The door was open, else I might not have
heard my wife's screams, though in retrospect her tone
was so piercing that I feel I might have been awakened
had I been in the deepest bowels of the castle.

I stopped at the doorway and looked within. From
the light of the candles in the hall sconces I saw Adam,
his long arms holding back the curtains of Elise's bed.

His back was to me, but I could see that his massive head was lowered, gazing at my wife as she lay there, continuing to shriek.

There was a tension in Adam's body, and I feared that he was about to pounce upon her—if for no other reason than to stop that ear-piercing din. So I called his name loudly, and it brought him up short.

He turned and looked at me, and there was in his face what I identified then as confusion, but that I know now was blood lust, and I knew I had come none too soon. I called his name again, this time more softly, hoping to calm him, and told him to come away. To my great relief, he let the bed curtains fall shut and walked toward me. I tried to show no fear, thinking that he would obey firm commands, and he did. My mastery had cowed him, and he followed me, grudgingly but without argument, from the room.

As he passed across the threshold, I heard Elise weakly call my name, and I told her that I would return at once, then closed the door behind my creation and myself. I led Adam back to his room and barred him in. I did not want a repetition of what had just happened, for even then I thought it possible that I could still forge a maternal relationship between the two beings I loved most.

When I returned to Elise, she was trembling with fear and had lit every lamp and candle in the room.

"How did he get *out*?" was the first thing she asked.

"He was never locked in," I answered. "I never thought it was necessary."

"You never locked him in?" she said in disbelief. "He could have gotten out anytime? Victor, how could you? Giving that evil thing the run of the—"

I pleaded with her. "Elise, please, he is *not* evil."

"Not *evil?* Victor, how can you say that?"

"He came in here innocently, my dear, simply to

look at you. His only wish is to attain knowledge, and knowledge alone cannot be evil. Adam is purely knowledge, without experience in social situations. He simply doesn't know how to act and react when in the presence of others. He scarcely knows what others *are*."

"You may say that he is innocent, Victor, but even though I could not see his face when he stood at my bedside just now, I could *feel* what dark thoughts lay beneath. If ever evil was manifest in a living creature, it is so in your Adam."

"Nonsense," I replied, trying to calm her fears. "He is immature. A child in all but his size and his genius. I assure you, he is harmless."

"And *I* assure *you*, Victor, that that creature of yours shall be our bane. No good can come of him, or of what you have done. That thing shall be the death of us both!"

 **NINE**

Another month went by, and slowly I began to fear that what Elise said about Adam might be true.

When I gazed at my creation as he read, I often thought the face seemed to be that not of a creature recently born but of a man old beyond his years. Sometimes I even fancied that the spirit of a stranger had found its way unbidden into Adam's strong and healthy body.

But I quickly put such thoughts behind me, assuming that it was only Elise's terror influencing me, making me uneasy in the presence of my glorious son. Still, when he looked at me with those wet, rolling eyes, I felt pierced by them, as though they were hooks in my brain.

I had not left the castle for many months and thought a change of air would do me good, so one bright morning when the promise of spring was in the air I suggested to Elise that we go to the market in Ludendorf. She accepted instantly and joyously, and we sat arm in arm in the carriage as Horg drove the coach to the town.

It was good to spend time with her again, and we had a wonderful day, buying objects made by the local craftsmen, many of whom looked suspiciously at Elise and me, having no doubt heard stories of my practices. We refused to let their dark looks spoil our outing, and by day's end we were both happily weary and filled with the good, solid victuals of the town's inn.

Darkness was falling when we left the town. As we rode past an alley, I thought I heard the cry of a suffering child. As a physician, I could not ignore so pitiable a summons, so I ordered Horg to stop the coach, then hopped out and walked past piles of stinking offal into the semidarkness of the alley.

I had been correct. The child was lying wrapped in a burlap sack and seemed no more than a pile of bones covered by skin. I picked up the bundle easily and made my way back to the coach.

"Victor," said Elise, "what is it?"

"A child. A waif of the streets. The poor little thing is nearly dead. Horg, get us home immediately."

"Should we not find a doctor here?" Elise asked.

"In this village? Bloodletting is all these butchers know. Horg, onward!"

Horg drove the horses mercilessly, and we traveled the five miles in a quarter of an hour. With Elise in my wake, I took the child into a servant's bedroom just off the warm kitchen, and together we peeled the crusted and filthy rags off the frail body to discover that the child was a little girl.

I rubbed brandy on her gums until she began to regain consciousness and was able to take small sips of warm milk. When we asked her what her name was, she said she didn't know, that she had never been given a name, but had lived on the streets ever since she could remember. Elise then gave her a sponge bath, wrapped her in a warm nightgown, and stayed with her until she slept.

"Victor," Elise said when we were alone together in front of the fireplace in the great hall, "will she be all right?"

I assured her that the child would be fine.

"And . . . and what shall we do with her when she recovers?"

I smiled at my wife. "Do? What *can* we do? We shall keep her, of course."

Tears of happiness shone in Elise's eyes. "Oh Victor, can we really? Shall she be . . . our daughter?"

"She shall." I would have said more had Elise not rushed into my arms.

First thing the following morning, Elise had Horg go to town to buy the girl clothes, then arranged a bed-chamber for the child next to the one we shared together. She named the girl Eva, after her late mother, and for the next few days Elise scarcely left the child's side, seeing that she ate, bathing her, and washing her hair, which was revealed to be as golden as sunlight and as fine as silk when the burrs and tangles had been brushed out.

I frequently visited the girl and tenderly applied salves and poultices, which readily healed the sores and lesions she had developed. Between the ministrations of Elise and me, Eva became a changed girl within a matter of weeks. She gained weight, was healed of her sores, and had actually started to smile and occasionally laugh, both of which had seemed alien to her at first.

It was only when I saw what a transformation had taken place in Eva that I decided to introduce her to Adam. She had become an angel, but one who had been through the horrors of the damned and, thus, might not be afraid of him. I even thought it possible that she might see in him a kindred spirit, another out-sider, also saved by my works.

As for the effect upon Adam, who could fail to be moved by the sweetness of this child? Whose heart would not melt upon seeing her goodness, innocence, and sweetness? Yes, I thought, she would be just what

Adam needed to be made aware of his own humanity, and the gentler side of his nature.

One evening the child was sitting on my knee by the fireside when I said to her, "Eva, how would you like to have . . . a playmate?"

Elise was knitting, and the sound of her needles clicking against each other suddenly ceased.

"I should like to very much, sir. What is the child's name?"

"His name is Adam—"

"*No!*" shouted Elise, so startling us both that I had to grasp Eva to keep her from falling off my lap. "Eva," Elise said in a softer but no less intense tone, "go to your room for a while. I must talk to your . . . to my husband."

Eva obeyed without a word, and when she was gone Elise whirled on me like a she-bear protecting her cub. "You shall not *do* this, Victor! Do you hear me? To place that sweet child into the hands of your monster? No, I tell you, you shall *not!*"

"But, my dear," I said, "don't you see what a calming, humanizing influence Eva is *bound* to have upon Adam? I have told you that there is virtue in him, and now Eva will prove it. She will be the catalyst that makes him truly human."

"Have you become as great a monster as he? You would risk the life and safety of . . . of our child to prove your foolish theory? I swear to you, Victor, you do this and I will leave you! Leave you and take Eva with me!"

I smiled gently at my wife and patted her hand, but she drew it away from me as though I were carrying plague. "Don't speak so foolishly, Elise. How would you leave? And where would you go? We are a family, my dear—you, me, Eva . . . and Adam."

Her response to that was to call me a brute.

"Eva will not be afraid," I said. "I will introduce her to

Adam tomorrow. I promise you I will not leave them alone together."

Her face was pinched with impotent fury. "And what good will that do? If he wants to harm her, he will. He is too fast for you to stop him. And too strong as well!"

"I shall have my pistol, of course. Will that calm your fears?"

"Nothing will calm my fears until that thing is dead." Then she added, "Again."

Next morning I arose before dawn and saw that Elise was still sleeping deeply. Though it is true that I deceived her, I felt that when she saw the results of my deception, she would forgive me. So I went to my dressing room, put on my clothes, and went into Eva's bedchamber, where I gently shook the sleeping girl awake.

"Wake up, my girl," I said, "and be very quiet. It's time to meet your playmate, Adam. I think you will like him very much."

Eva obediently dressed, and then I took her hand and led her across the terrace and into my laboratory. I told her that here was where I created miracles, including making a real person who had never been alive before.

"This is who Adam is," I told Eva, whose eyes were growing wider and wider with every word I uttered. "And he looks very strange—he may even look a little frightening to you—but he is not. He would never hurt you, my girl. So you must not be scared of him, no matter how he looks. Do you understand me?"

She nodded tentatively, and I took her little hand in mine and led her into the watchtower. We climbed the stairs until we stood outside the door of Adam's room. Eva touched the heavy wooden bar with which I had begun to seal the door at Elise's insistence. "Why do you lock his door?" she asked.

"To keep him safe. He gets frightened, too, some-times."

She thought for a moment. "But wouldn't it be better to have the bar on the inside?"

I smiled. She was indeed a bright little thing. I felt sure that she and Adam would get along famously. "Yes," I said. "It would at that," and I pushed the bar back, then knocked. "Adam?" I called. "I have a visitor for you, a playmate." I pulled the door open.

Adam was standing at the window, his back to the door. But when he turned and saw the little girl, he started to put up his hands in front of him. To this day I do not know whether it was an offensive gesture, or if he merely tried to hide his face, but the motion startled Eva, who gave a little squeak of surprise that turned into a squeal of terror as she saw him more clearly, and she tried to run from the room.

I kept her hand firmly in mine and would not let her go. "No, Eva, I told you not to be afraid," I said.

But the girl's eyes saw far more wisely than my own. For what she beheld was no playmate, no friend, but a monster that intended her only ill. Her first impression was the correct one, and I should have heeded it.

Eva started to pant in fear the way Elise had, and I knelt by her side, grasped her shoulders, and shook her firmly, but not enough to harm her. "*Eva!*" I said sternly. "There is no need for this. You see, Adam does nothing to threaten you, he simply stands there. . . ."

And he did, with his face as dark and glowering as though a thunderstorm had passed over it. That was enough for Eva, who had conquered her fear only until she looked at Adam one more time, then closed her eyes and screamed as loudly as she could.

Adam snarled some words that I could not make out over the screaming of the child and turned his grimac-ing face back to the window. I was in torment over how poorly this first meeting was going, but could see no point in extending it. So I whisked the girl out of the room, pushing the heavy door shut behind us.

"There now," I crooned to her as her eyes opened and grew wide, even though she looked only at me and the oaken door. It was as if she still saw Adam, as if the door were paper-thin and the shadow of his hulking frame could still be glimpsed behind it.

"What a silly girl," I said, keeping my tone light, despite my disappointment. But it had simply been too much for the child, to be bluntly confronted with something so titanic and monumental. I should have let her see Adam from afar at first, perhaps have brought him onto the terrace and let her look at him from the security of a barred window.

I knew that I had once again made the error of thinking that everyone would look at Adam through my own proud eyes. But such was not the case. All right then. I determined to be more patient.

I was able to get the girl back to her room without waking Elise, and easily made Eva promise that she would not tell her new mother what had happened. Then I began to plan in earnest how I might more delicately bring the child and my creation together, without alarming or angering either of them.

I quickly put my plan into effect, and the following day, while Elise was busy in the kitchen planning dinner with the cook, I took Eva to her bedroom window, which looked down on the terrace.

"Stay here," I told her. "I'm going to bring Adam out into the open air, and you can watch him safely from your window. You'll see that he means no harm to you or to anyone." For such I still believed.

The girl started to shiver, but I patted her on the head. "Now don't be afraid. He doesn't even have to see you. You may peek from behind the curtains if you like." Then I cupped her chin and grinned slyly at her, as though we shared a great secret. "I won't even tell him that you're watching, all right?"

She nodded shyly. "That's a big girl," I said.

Then I went to Adam's room and told him that today he could come for a walk outside. He seemed mildly surprised, but docilely followed me down the tower stairs, through the laboratory, and onto the terrace.

There he stood for a long time, just letting the breeze blow his long black hair, his face turned upward to the sun, staring into it without blinking. I tried to do the same, but the brightness of it forced me to shut my eyes immediately. Here was further proof, thought I, that Adam was more than mere man.

Then I glanced surreptitiously up at Eva's window, and saw the curtain pushed partway back and a glimpse of the girl's white face. I smiled reassuringly, then talked to Adam about nature, the clouds, the sun, the sky, the sea.

But his mind seemed elsewhere. I thought that he seemed overwhelmed by the outside world, but I know now that it was little more than his joy at the thought of the freedom he would soon grasp with bloody hands.

Eva, from her hiding place, and I, out in the open with the creature, watched as the sun suddenly gave way to a gray sky and gusty winds that nearly staggered me. Through the roar of the gale, I spoke more to Adam, who I was glad to note listened calmly, unshaken by the abrupt change in the weather. It was this placid visage that I wished Eva to see. In another minute the winds ended as abruptly as they had begun, and gray mist dropped upon the land like a sheet over a corpse.

Adam asked me some question or other about the weather, which I answered with alacrity. I was anxious to return him to his room, to which he followed me without protest, then learn of Eva's reaction to seeing

Adam from afar.

I was happy to hear from the girl that her prospective playmate was not nearly as frightening at a distance. "But what," she asked, her voice trembling, "made the storm come so fast?" And I gave her a short lecture on the vagaries of weather.

For the next few days, this peeking from behind curtains continued, until finally Eva felt confident enough to let Adam see her. The heavy fog still surrounded the castle, but Adam seemed to look forward nonetheless to his outings, no doubt plotting his escape and . . . his other deeds. His mood brightened further when I told him that Eva had been watching him and today wanted to let him see her.

"She is at the window of her room," I said. "You may look up at her." I turned toward the window and nodded my head. At that prearranged signal, Eva pushed back the curtain and showed herself to us.

Adam smiled at her, but the look made me shudder. His black-lipped mouth remained in a straight line, with only the corners turning up. I attributed it to shyness, but instead it was surely a feigned smile, and if any joy was there it was joy at the thought of future carnage. Eva, like myself, did not detect the subterfuge, and she raised a hand and waved it in greeting.

The ends of Adam's mouth drew up farther, and he raised his huge hand in a fist, and moved it up and down in an awkward parody of the little girl's wave.

The crudity of the gesture amused her, for she laughed again, waved once more, and shyly pushed the curtain closed, as if reluctant to become too familiar too soon.

She told me later that she had laughed because Adam reminded her of one of the dolls Elise had given her, whose mouth was nothing but an upturned line stitched with black thread, comical in its simplicity.

A doll. That was what he was to her, how he gained her trust. "That silly smile on his lumpy face," she told me. "He looks just like a great big doll that somebody stitched together. And how can a doll hurt you?" She said she felt silly she had feared him. Still ignorant of his true nature, I was exceedingly glad to hear it.

This mutual peekaboo continued for several more days, with the weather contributing by making the very air itself a medium of concealment. The fog grew more and more dense, so much so that there was a constant sound of water dripping from the roofs of the castle and the trees surrounding it, even though no rain fell.

The weather disquieted Adam, who seemed interested only in the few precious minutes when he might gaze at Eva through the fog and the window. He had lost all interest in his books and studies, and I found it impossible to even hold a conversation with him, so intent was he upon the child.

I should have been aware that the effect she was having on him was not the one for which I had hoped. What I thought might become an innocent comradeship had turned into an obsession for Adam, the obsession to do harm to both the girl and her mother, Elise. All, I suppose, in a misguided attempt to punish me for whatever harm he felt I had done him.

Though I admit I was not wise enough to see his overall design, I must have at least sensed enough of his true feelings to keep him physically separated from Eva, despite his appeals and, at length, demands that he be allowed to meet her face-to-face.

He would not accept my refusal, and one dreadful night he took matters into his own bloody hands.

 **TEN**

I dreamed that Elise was screaming before I actually heard her scream. It was only after I could find her nowhere in my dream that I awakened and realized the screams were real.

But they had stopped by the time I ran across the terrace. After Adam's first intrusion into her room, Elise had insisted that I carry a pistol, and I jerked it from the pocket of my coat as I dashed down the hall. Though I no longer heard anything, I saw that both Elise's and Eva's doors were standing wide open. I entered Eva's room first, and what I saw drove me nearer to the edge of madness than anything before or since.

My dear Elise was lying on the floor next to the empty bed. Her sweet body looked as though it had been flung from the top of a high cliff. Her arms and legs were akimbo, jutting at unnatural angles like those of a rag doll flung down by a petulant child. The flesh that I could see was black with bruises, and blood trickled from her mouth and ears. Her eyes were wide with pain and fear, and though she tried to speak, her shattered teeth and bloody mouth made only a weak bubbling sound, like that of a dying animal.

She raised an arm weakly, but it quickly flopped back onto the floor. Instead she turned her head, as though I should look where she did. I followed her unsteady gaze into a dark corner of the room, where something moved stealthily in the blackness.

"Eva?" I whispered, even then uncertain of what had happened, still refusing to believe that Adam could have been responsible for this act of carnage.

And then Adam, my once beloved and now eternally despised creation, reared up from the dark corner like an angry bear, one fist clutching a bloody piece of what could only have been Eva's nightgown, and the other hand dripping blood from its ragged fingernails. It was then that I incontrovertibly realized that I had been wrong about him from the beginning, and I raised my pistol and took aim.

The first ball hit him, pushing him back toward the balcony door. I immediately fired the second shot, the force of which threw him back even farther. Having expended both balls, I lunged toward him, intending to throw him over the rail even if it meant that we both met our doom. But he continued to move backward until he struck the rail and toppled over it, falling into the sea and the rocks far below.

I picked myself off the floor and looked over the edge, but could see nothing. Only a sea of mist hiding the far deadlier sea beneath.

In an instant, I turned my attention to my wife, who was now lying upon the floor, completely still but for the slow flowing of her precious blood. I said her name, nearly choked by grief, then ripped strips of cloth from Eva's bedclothes to stop Elise's bleeding.

I summoned Horg, and together we lifted Elise carefully into Eva's bed so that I could examine her further. The outlook was tragic. There were dozens of broken bones and torn ligaments, and I was certain a number of internal organs were crushed past repair. There was only one chance for her survival.

We took my dear one on the gurney to the laboratory, and once there, laid her on the table where the monster who attacked her had been assembled. I sedated her immediately, for I could not bear the thought of her lifting her eyes to me in pain, especially since my intellectual blindness had been the cause of it, and my cursed insistence that Adam was harmless.

She had been right all along. Adam had been evil through and through. Only a true monster would have beaten Elise the way he had. And what about poor little Eva? What had the creature done to her before he hurled her into the sea? No, Adam was not a man, but a fiend. Something dreadful had gone wrong, and I thought about it as I struggled feverishly to keep Elise alive.

Had it been the brain? It must have been, since that was what controlled the rest of the body. And I determined that it would not be a problem again, no, not with Elise. For I knew her sweet mind all too well.

But there were other considerations, and as I examined her, doing what had to be done, I knew that Horg and I would have to do a great deal of . . . harvesting. There was much that needed to be replaced.

But I would do anything to save my love, to restore her to what she had been. I felt certain I could do it. For I had the power, the knowledge, and the will.

What I also had, though I did not yet know it, was a terrible enemy, one who torments me still.

I thought he had perished that awful night, but such was not the case. I saw him several weeks later, as I was gazing out the window, exhausted from my desperate efforts to keep Elise alive. He was standing down on the rocks below the cliff, the waves thundering around him, and when he saw me he began to laugh. It was a hideous laugh, all the more unexpected because he had never made such a sound before.

"How is your wife, Doctor?" he cried up to me. "Still dead?"

Fury rose within me, and I turned and told Horg to run quickly for a long rifle. "She lives, you brute!" I shouted down to him. "And she will thrive yet!"

"Not after my dealings with her," he called back. "I crushed her bones and pulped the rest of her! She can have no more substance than the jellyfish washed up on these shores!"

"Why did you do it?" I yelled, wanting desperately to understand. "You adored her, did you not?"

"She was an angel to me, but she became a monster when I saw that harming her could spite you!"

"And you have become a monster to me," I said quietly, accepting the weapon that Horg handed me from behind. I thrust it through the window and aimed quickly, but he made no effort to move. Still, I did not let this acceptance of his fate shake my resolve, and I fired a ball into his chest.

I saw it strike him, saw the ragged shirt he wore tear open, saw the hole it made in his flesh, saw him thrown backward into the surf. And I rejoiced at the sight.

But then I saw him roll over, get to his knees, stand up, shake the water from his hair, look up at me and laugh again.

"Your creation is stronger than you thought!" he said. "Proud man, see the fruit of your labor! And your wife, lying in living death—she is your doing as well. *Two* monsters have you created! The one you shall live with, and the other you shall see again!"

And with those words he turned and walked back into the sea until it closed around him, then swam toward an island that lay offshore, an island justly named Isle of Agony. From there he has come time and again to plague the mainland, leaving havoc and sorrow in his wake.

Thus began the war between Adam and the rest of the world, with me as the opposing general.

As I have told you, I treated him only with the utmost kindness and respect. And though Elise was affrighted by him, she never did him harm. As for Eva . . . that dear child had not an atom of hate within her.

All the greater my astonishment then, when came that night he broke the bar over his door, cruelly murdered Eva, that sweet innocent, and attempted to kill my wife as well.

Damned by an evil brain, he has become the monster that Elise feared him to be. He has done everything he can to abort my work, to keep me from restoring my wife to health. He is a dangerous and deadly adversary, and may very well try to doom our new effort.

But if you, Herr Kreutzer and Fraulein Von Karlsfeld—if you are willing to risk his wrath, I promise you that you shall be rewarded greatly.

So, you have seen Elise, and you have heard my story. Now the choice is yours. . . .

 **ELEVEN**

Victor Mordenheim sat back, exhausted from telling his tale. He had not told it altogether truthfully, but most of his life had been a lie, and he no longer separated truth from the fictions he had constructed to protect his sanity. He had told Hilda and Friedrich nothing of what he knew lay within Adam's mind. Mordenheim's telling had served to place only himself in the best possible light. And like all liars who believe their lies, he had told the story well and convincingly; Hilda was overwhelmed with sympathy for him, for Eva, and for the hideous wreck of a woman who lay on the laboratory table.

"It's a dreadful tale," Hilda said. "And you've been attempting to . . . revive her ever since?"

"I have," Mordenheim said. "And every attempt has been equally unsuccessful."

"How have you done it?" Friedrich asked, leaning forward curiously.

Mordenheim raised his hands in the air and spread his fingers wide, as if dissolving the attempts to the winds. "A vast number of methods. First of all, let me bluntly admit that the tales you have heard about, shall we say, 'borrowing' corpses are true to a certain extent. I have no moral dilemma with this, and I trust you do not. I have always felt that the dead are dead, and whatever service they may contribute to the survival of the living is justified. If it were up to those whose superstitious beliefs make them feel otherwise, we should still be back in the dark ages before there was any medicine whatsoever. It is experimentation on cadavers that has provided every medical breakthrough in the history of the art."

He sighed and fell back in his chair again. "That said, I have stolen fresh bodies from graves and morgues, but only in order to give life back to Elise. I have never killed anyone."

"Have you," asked Hilda, "restored the corpses to their resting places when your experimentation is over?"

"Of course." Mordenheim answered so disingenuously that Hilda suspected for the first time that he was lying. She could not imagine him endangering himself—and the fate of his wife—by returning to the scene of the crimes to replace what to him were just so many pieces of dead flesh. "After all," he went on, "there is no reason for me to keep the remains of failed experiments."

"What do the experiments entail?" Friedrich asked.

"I have tried a number of approaches. Chief among them is what I call trans-situation of the brain. That is, situating the organ in a different skull cavity and connecting the nerves and vessels to the host body."

Hilda raised her eyebrows. "You mean you have taken your wife's brain and put it into another body?"

"I have. The brain, you see, holds what the superstitious think of as the spirit."

"But . . . wouldn't the other body have to be alive in order for that to work?"

Mordenheim sat in thought for a moment, and Hilda suspected that she had trapped him in a lie. But he only smiled thinly and shook his head. "Not in the sense you mean. The bodies *are* alive, the tissues re-energized by my knowledge. Unfortunately, the results have all been negative in the extreme."

"In what way?" said Friedrich.

"Imagine yourself, Herr Kreutzer, married to the lovely young woman here. Now imagine that you have placed the brain from her preserved body into a new body . . . restored to life, of course. You expect her to arise and come to you, to call you husband, to return your embrace, to kiss you the way she did in days of old.

"But instead, you find yourself face-to-face with a mindless creature, no better than an animated vegetable. Alive, true, but incapable of relating to you in any way, a thing that will respond with nothing at all when caressed, with a mere twitch when screamed at. A walking dead thing, in truth no more alive than my Elise you saw a short time ago."

Mordenheim gave a sigh that seemed to come from the very depth of his spirit. "Time and again it has happened, and I have replaced Elise's brain in her skull, kept it alive along with the rest of her. But decay, slow and insidious, proceeds, although she does not die. She *cannot*; I will not let her. But the horror that we feel upon seeing her can be only a fraction of the horror she feels at being trapped in a slowly disintegrating body." He looked imploringly at Hilda. "Put *your* mind, Fraulein Von Karlsfeld, into that body you saw upstairs, and think how you would feel."

"Doctor," she said, "if I may be so bold, why do you not simply . . . allow her peace?"

Mordenheim's tone grew cold and bitter. "Let her *die,* do you mean? No, never. My whole career has been dedicated to preserving life, and as long as a spark of it exists in her whom I love most of all things in this world, I shall do all I can to see that she stays with me."

"But why have you chosen us to aid you?" Hilda

asked. "We know little of science."

"I think," Mordenheim said slowly, as if weighing every word, "that this is a situation in which science alone may not have the answer. I know that I dishonor all my predecessors in the scientific arts when I say such a thing, but I am willing to investigate even the talents of those whom I would otherwise call charlatans if there is the slightest hope of success. Who knows, perhaps this necromancy and spirit transference of which you are practitioners may simply be a science whose principles we do not yet understand. Perhaps spells and incantations form some vibrations in the air that have a true physical effect." He rose and walked to the window. "And perhaps . . . just perhaps . . . there may be more to the spirit than merely the function of the brain."

"There is, sir," Friedrich said. "We have seen proof of it."

"And *provided* proof of it," Hilda added, giving Friedrich a warning look. She stood up and walked over to where Mordenheim stood looking out across the balcony at the dark sea. "Whether the notion is scientific or not, Doctor, I tell you that the human animal does possess a spirit, and that spirit can be restored or transferred, as is the operator's will."

He whirled on her. "Operator? You mean as a surgeon would perform?"

"It is a term of the trade. I mean merely the practitioner who makes the preparations and recites the spells or incantations."

"And you have seen these operations work?"

"We have." She did not add that they had not *performed* them.

"Then you know what I wish of you. I wish for you to transfer my Elise's spirit, be it made of brain tissue, electrical impulses, or something whose properties we cannot even guess at, into a . . . new body."

Friedrich joined Hilda and Mordenheim at the window. "A body of your creation, Doctor?"

"Of course. A triumphant combination of science and, shall we say, *new* science."

Hilda cleared her throat. "I don't see, Doctor Mordenheim, how that can be possible. I do not know of any case of spirit transference into a dead, or previously dead, body. The purpose of the entire operation is to take the spirit from a dead body and place it into a living person so that the dead spirit survives. That a spirit could travel from one *living* body to another is a distinct possibility, particularly since the spirit does not first have to be called up from the nether regions. But placing a spirit into a body that has been dead . . ."

Friedrich nodded. "I see what you mean, Hilda. The results of such a living-to-dead transference could be, well, monstrous. Perhaps it is just such a metaphysical complication that endowed your creation, Doctor, with the evil spirit you tell us he has."

"What then are you suggesting?" Mordenheim said, glowering at the pair.

Hilda and Friedrich looked at each other, but Friedrich was the first to speak. "The spirit of your wife, sir, must be transferred into a living recipient. You see, spirit transference has never, to our knowledge—"

"And experience," added Hilda.

"And *experience,* been permanent. It is always a temporary operation, generally used to reveal information known only by the dead. For example, in a typical operation, say a householder dies without telling anyone where his savings are hidden. The spirit of the householder is called up and transferred into the body of say, his son, who is then questioned by the widow and reveals the treasure's hiding place. After the information is divulged, the operator then drives the spirit out of the son and back into the corpse, or, actually, into the ethereal plane once more. And the son's spirit once again inhabits his own body."

"You see," said Hilda, "if the transference were permanent, the spirit of the son would wander forever, lost in a limbo between life and death."

Mordenheim turned his frowning face from them back to the window. "What if," he said shortly, "the vessel could be . . . persuaded to sacrifice itself for the good of the other spirit, or of science, or mankind?"

"That becomes a moral question," Hilda said. "Not a scientific one."

"And are you saying," said Mordenheim, "you would not perform your 'operation' on an unwilling subject?"

Hilda felt Friedrich's hand slip into hers. She squeezed it, both to draw strength from him and give him the strength they shared together. "I do not think we could," Friedrich said, "even if we wished to."

"There must be a psychic balance," Hilda explained, "a peace that can't exist should someone be forced into accepting a different spirit into one's body."

She looked at Friedrich, and he looked back at her. They both knew it was a lie, that the words and the preparation and the spells were all that was necessary. The attitude of the recipient had nothing to do with it. But for some reason they both felt that Mordenheim should not share that particular knowledge. Despite his explanations, there was a ruthlessness about him that made both Hilda and Friedrich uncomfortable.

"Very well then," said Mordenheim, with a touch of pleasantry. "The person must be persuaded. We shall deal with that when the time comes. But for now, could Elise's spirit, her consciousness and memories and emotions, be placed into another living woman, if that person were willing?"

Friedrich nodded. "It could."

Mordenheim's face seemed to glow. Though he did

not smile, there was in the set of his features an emotion beyond joy, a determination to follow the prescribed course through to the end. "Then it *shall*," he said. "Elise shall live again, shall be mine again, and the horrid schemes of Adam shall be overthrown once and for all!"

* * * * *

Had Mordenheim seen through the stone wall that separated the dining room from the balcony, he would not have been so confident. Behind that wall, just out of sight of the window, stood Adam, his back to the wall. He was facing the sea, but his preternatural hearing was picking up every word spoken within, even through the closed doors and windows. And what he heard made him set his black lips in a stern line.

Elise to live again? He had worshiped her once, worshiped the essence of womanhood that she was in his memory. But if she lived again in the new body, as these plotters within intended, she would feel no different toward him. She would continue to loathe him and look on him with revulsion.

And far worse, she would brighten Victor Mordenheim's life so that he would no longer dwell in the hopeless abyss he had made for both himself and her.

Adam could not allow that to happen. With dark glee, he had watched through the years as Mordenheim tried in vain to restore his wife to life. He had seen the doctor and Horg bear the dead ones into the laboratory, and bear them out again, flinging them into the sea. He had seen also the living women arrive only to be borne out days later as corpses, the tops of their skulls sawn off, empty of brains. And Adam had laughed at every unsuccessful attempt, knowing that with each one Victor Mordenheim's inferno grew deeper and hotter, and that with each passing day his wife grew more hideous, and his chances for resuscitating her more dismal and hopeless.

But this transference of spirits was something that had not been tried before. Mordenheim surely must have been desperate, Adam thought, to resort to something so utterly irrational as necromancy. It must have been a huge blow to his pride to turn his back on the purely scientific, and Adam gloried in the fact that the paragon of scientific knowledge had finally been driven to this most unscientific means to his unattainable ends.

"Have I made you turn your back on science then?" Adam whispered to the night, chuckling far too softly for those inside to hear him. It was a grand joke, but one that could prove most unfunny were its results successful. Adam could not take that chance. This experiment would have to be stopped.

He moved his head very slowly around the side of the glass-paned doors that led onto the balcony and looked inside. The three stood away from the window, warming themselves by a fire and drinking a brown liquid from glasses. Adam sniffed and recognized it as port. His sensory acuteness extended to smell as well as to hearing. He examined the two strangers.

This Friedrich Kreutzer seemed an extremely handsome fellow. Of course, Adam reminded himself, even Horg was more attractive than he. But Kreutzer was tall and slender, with a mop of curly blond hair and sharply defined features. Deep blue eyes and a ruddy complexion made him look like an overgrown schoolboy, as did the continual sense of expectation on his features. Foolish man, he was hanging on Mordenheim's every word. A pretty boy then, gullible and easily fooled, open to the world's wiles.

But it was on the oasis of Hilda Von Karlsfeld that

Adam found his gaze coming most often to rest. Elise Mordenheim had been beautiful, and Hilda was not so lovely as Elise had been, but there was another quality that drew Adam's attention to her. He thought it was a self-possession rare in women he had seen. She seemed an equal with her fiance, speaking freely and intelligently, evincing little fear in the face of the horrors Mordenheim had shown her or promised to show.

She was a tall woman with severely cut brown hair and stern features, though her brown eyes were soft. There was in her, Adam thought, a combination of attractiveness and intelligence rare in man or woman, and he wondered if her reaction to him would be like all the other females who had beheld him, beginning with Elise and ending most recently with a shepherd's wife who had come upon him stealing a sheep. She had screamed and screamed, as they all did, and Adam had laughed at first, then struck her down when he had grown irritated at the noise. He did not know whether she had died or not. Perhaps he would find out when he wanted another sheep.

But this woman, this Hilda, did not look the type to scream. Perhaps, he thought, taking one last look at her, he would learn if that was true. He crossed stealthily to the balcony rail and vaulted over it, grasping the edge of the terrace floor and lowering himself down the side of the cliff overlooking the sea.

He moved quickly and with a wondrous economy of motion, like a spider scuttling down an irregular wall, finding footholds and handholds with graceful ease. Sea birds flew from their havens in the rocks, startled by the passage of this interloper. At one point Adam came across a gull's nest, and broke the four eggs one by one, letting the embryonic contents drip and flop into his mouth. He needed little food, but since it was so difficult to find in harsh Lamordia, he took it whenever he found it, storing what energy he could deep within his patchwork body.

Forty feet down the side of the cliff, his legs found no foothold, but hung freely in the air. He dropped onto what seemed a shallow ledge on the cliff but was in reality the mouth of a cavern, one of dozens that he had found honeycombing the rock face. He had sheltered in them many times while surreptitiously observing Mordenheim and delighting in the doctor's misery as each new attempt to revive Elise failed.

Anyone finding the caves—should anyone else dare to climb down the damp cliff, would see no indication that Adam dwelt therein from time to time, for he was nearly as content sleeping on bare stone as he was on the pallet of dried grass that made up the sole piece of furniture in his cave on the Isle of Agony. In the cliff caves, there were not even the bones of the sea birds Adam had caught and eaten. He threw them all into the sea, much the way Mordenheim disposed of the remains of his experiments.

As for fires, Adam welcomed their warmth on the coldest days on his island, but he did not need them. The chill temperatures that would have frozen the flesh of living men did nothing to his own dead-alive body.

This unnatural immunity to the tyrants of cold and hunger that ruled men had made evasion easy for Adam on the rare occasions when he was pursued. Several times, angry groups of villagers or farmers banded together to seek him out after one of his foraging raids, and once Mordenheim hired a professional dealer of death to track him down. That warrior, a huge madman with a red beard, had gone so far as to actually follow Adam to the Isle of Agony. Adam had thought about coming to grips with the man, killing him, and taking his corpse back to Mordenheim. But a more fitting conclusion, he felt, would be to have no conclusion at all, to see to it that the giant fool never even found him, and returned to Mordenheim chagrined and sheepish, if such a blustering clown could ever feel shame.

Any idiot could fight. The red-bearded man was proof of that. But it took brains to evade and harry, and Adam's intelligence was what separated him from the beasts, the only quality in which he took pride, a quality that made him nearly human.

So Adam had hidden, always one step ahead of Redbeard, as he had come to think of the man, luring him on, then disappearing. Taunting, then vanishing. At the end Redbeard was so frustrated that he screamed his rage to the winds, hacked huge chunks out of several tree trunks, hurled a final curse, and returned a beaten hunter to Mordenheim, his employer.

Adam had eavesdropped on the warrior's final report, and had even unleashed a booming roar of laughter that both men, inside the castle, heard. Redbeard stormed outside, but by that time Adam had dropped over the cliff and hidden in one of the caves, where he laughed silently and gleefully long into the night. He had never seen Redbeard again.

Now he sat at the mouth of the sea cave, his legs dangling over the side, and thought about his next move. There had to be a way to stop this plan of Mordenheim's without harming the woman or her betrothed. They did not seem evil and intended no harm to him. So if he could drive them from Mordenheim's side . . . and perhaps figure out a way to enter the presence of that fascinating and intelligent woman as well . . .

He sat and thought, and before another hour had passed, he had the answer.

 **TWELVE**

At the same time that Adam reached his fateful decision, Mordenheim, Friedrich, and Hilda were back upstairs in the laboratory.

Hilda was sitting in the wooden chair that Friedrich had placed for her next to the breathing, withered remains of Elise Mordenheim, and she was trying to summon up enough courage to take the woman's claw-like hand into her own. Friedrich stood behind her chair, one hand resting comfortingly on her shoulder, the other holding the ancient book of Von Schreck's.

"It seems theatrical," Hilda was saying, more to draw her attention from what she was about to do than to inform Mordenheim, "but it is necessary, the only way to find the ideal spirit mate. If the bodily recipient of the spirit is not bound by blood, there must be such a seeking to find the right—"

"Yes, yes," said Mordenheim impatiently. He was standing at his wife's feet. "You've told me all this downstairs, and though it seems like so much mumbo jumbo, I have said that I am willing to allow it to be done. Now, can you not proceed?"

Hilda nodded primly. "Certainly," she said, reaching out to take the dark and twisted hand in her own, barely repressing a shudder. "I shall close my eyes now, and Friedrich shall read the spell to me, which I shall recite. If all goes well, the vision will come to me of the person required and the place where she now is." She cleared her throat and closed her eyes. "I am ready, Friedrich."

"Very well, my dear," Friedrich said, giving her shoulder a final encouraging squeeze, then removing his hand. There could be no further physical contact between them.

He began to read then, and Hilda repeated his words, losing herself in their alien rhythms. After a time, she began to grow drowsy from the constant repetition, and her words became automatic, a parroting of what she now only dimly heard. The trance was starting to claim her.

Now the words seemed liquid, and she was on a boat on a soft sea. And as she looked down at the surface of the water, she was only mildly surprised to find that she was high in the air, and what she had thought was the rocking of the waves of the sea was really the whims of the wind, and the words had now died away, and she saw below her the rocky northern coast of Lamordia, which vanished behind her as her sky boat swept inland at the speed of thought, and she passed over rough plains and bitter forests, ascending into dark green hills that rose until they became the massive ridge that spanned the domain north to south, the one the natives called the Sleeping Beast, and she saw it sleeping even as she was sleeping, but awake far below, and its wakefulness was a terrible thing to feel, and it almost made her cry out, but then she was at the beast's end and drifting to earth again, and her fear left her as she approached the town below and then passed over it to its outskirts, where there was color and music and gaiety and dancing, and the word for it all came to the door of her lips and passed through and was heard by two men far away in a high room in Schloss Mordenheim—

"*Vistani . . .*"

"What?" said Mordenheim sharply. "What did she say?"

"Vistani—the gypsies," Friedrich explained. "Listen . . ."

Hilda was humming a gypsy song that filled her ears while she saw them dancing in the circle of *vardos*—brightly colored, horse-drawn gypsy homes. The fires blazed brightly, and the night erupted with reds and yellows and brilliant blues and oranges. Despite the cold, women danced and banged tambourines, and men played fiddles, guitars, and lutes, and old men sang and laughed, and old women smiled and nodded in time to the music. One girl stood out from among them, stepping down from a vardo that bore a great carving of a hawk across its entire side. She began to dance a dance in which no one saw her feet touch the ground—

". . . ilis . . ."

"What?"

—the most frenzied and beautiful dancer of all, whose black hair flowed like wine in the firelight, whose tan legs flashed like torches, whose eyes and teeth lit flames—

". . . ilisa . . ."

"What does she *say*, Kreutzer?"

—flames in all the young men who watched with a longing that made their stomachs weak and their hearts ache, who would have done anything, even break the cruelest colt of Nova Vaasa, for the smallest of smiles from her crimson lips—

"Ilisa . . ."

"I think she said . . ."

—Ilisa, fairest of all Vistana maids, uncrowned queen of beauty, invader of youths' dreams, loving granddaughter, obedient child, on the threshold of the year in which she would choose a husband and a husband choose her, Ilisa, pride of the Vistani—

"Ilisa!" cried Hilda as her eyes snapped open, and she dropped Elise's decayed hand as though it burned her own.

"Ilisa?" said Mordenheim. "Do you . . . do you mean *Elise?*"

"No, no," said Hilda breathlessly, putting her hand to her heart to try to slow its wild beating. "A gypsy girl, a Vistana. Her name is Ilisa. She is the one. . . . I saw her come down from a wagon emblazed with a gold hawk on a field of blue."

"Where was she?" demanded Mordenheim. "*Where?*"

"I . . . I'm not sure." Hilda rubbed her temples as if trying to draw out the information. "It was a town . . . at the southern end of the Sleeping Beast."

"Neufurchtenberg?" Friedrich asked.

"Was it across a river?" asked Mordenheim. Hilda shook her head. "Then it *has* to be Neufurchtenberg." He turned and stalked toward the door. "Come, we must make haste," he said, and they followed him throught the door and down the stairs. "The Vistani never stay in one place for long. I shall have Horg ride to fetch the girl while we make the other preparations."

"Fetch her?" Friedrich said. "But the Vistani would never let her go, even if she wanted to!"

Mordenheim did not pause in his stride. "Do not worry. Horg will . . . persuade the girl. As for the Vistani, any tribe or race that relies on the practice of magic to settle its affairs is beneath contempt."

Friedrich and Hilda exchanged apprehensive looks. They had heard their mentor speak on the power of Vistana spells, and knew that they were not to be taken lightly.

Horg met them at the bottom of the wide staircase into the great hall, and Mordenheim drew him aside and spoke softly to him. Try as they might, neither Friedrich nor Hilda could hear what he said. But Horg nodded

briskly and scuttled from the room. Mordenheim turned
back to them.

"It will take several days for Horg to ride to Neufurchtenberg in the coach. We will remain here until he
returns. Will your preparations take long?"

"No," Hilda said. "Only a few hours at most."

Mordenheim nodded officiously. "Then I grant you the
freedom of the castle, save for the laboratory. I think
you'll find the library to your liking. The books of old
Baron Helmreich, who built the castle, remain there, and
many concern themselves with the metaphysical arts. In
fact, you may take what you wish, for I have no need of
them, despite the fact that some of the editions are doubtless of monetary value." He raised his head slightly. "And
that reminds me that I should reimburse you for the
expenses of your travels here. Follow me, please."

They went down the hall into the east wing and
stopped outside a door. "Wait here," Mordenheim said,
and entered the room, closing the door behind him.
Friedrich and Hilda heard a low, scraping sound, as if a
heavy piece of furniture were being moved, then a rattle
of wood, a pause, and the scraping sound again.

When Mordenheim reappeared he had a small
packet of currency in his hand. "I trust this will be suffi-
cient," he said, handing the notes to Friedrich.

"Of course," said Friedrich. "More than enough. We
thank you."

"There will be more than that, as you well know,
when the experiment is completed. And, should it prove
successful, far more yet. And now," he went on, "it is
quite late, and I'm sure you must both be weary—particularly you, Fraulein Von Karlsfeld, after your . . . psychic
exertions." His lip twisted in a sneer that showed Hilda
his lack of respect for her skills.

It seemed to her that, even if she could wave her
arms and restore his wife to her original health and

beauty, he would still dismiss her with peremptory thanks, and accept it all as a conjuror's trick. What was wrong with the man? Was he so devoted to science that he could not admit the reality of the spiritual plane? While such thinking might be dubious elsewhere, it was nothing short of madness in Lamordia.

"You know, I believe, how to find your rooms. I shall remain here and work on some affairs of the estate. I will see you in the morning for breakfast. With Horg gone, we must fend for ourselves. I trust you will have a pleasant night."

It was a dismissal, and they thanked their host and made their way back to their rooms, saying nothing until they stood outside the door of Hilda's chamber.

Friedrich took her in his arms and shook his head. "I'm sorry I ever got you into this, my dear. Such a place, and that creature upstairs . . ."

"It was my doing as much as it was yours, Friedrich. I wanted to come." She drew back and looked at him. "But you are right. This place is a madhouse. The doctor is—"

"Insane," Friedrich finished her thought accurately. "Keeping his wife in that condition . . . how can he claim to love her and treat her that way? Why can he not just let her die?"

"I fear for the Vistana girl, too. I'm not sure that I fully believe his proclamations of innocence. If I had to guess, I would think that living women have been previously brought here, but dead ones may have left."

"I have the same feeling, Hilda. If only we'd known what he intended, we never would have come. But from what his letter said, there was no way of knowing he desired something of this nature, no reason to expect anything other than a simple temporary transference. Even Von Schreck would have balked at this."

"So what shall we do?"

"Well, we certainly can have nothing to do with harming the girl, if Horg should be able to bring her back. Could you live with yourself if we did?"

"Of course not, Friedrich."

"There's only one answer then. We must tell him that we're leaving."

"Will he *let* us leave?"

"He doesn't seem strong enough to keep us here on his own, with Horg gone. We'll have a good night's sleep, break the news to him in the morning, and get away from this dreadful place. It's only a couple of miles to the coach road. We can easily walk. And then we'll find another way to make our fortune."

Friedrich kissed her tenderly, then opened her door. "Lock your door behind you, and make sure the windows are locked as well."

Hilda smiled wistfully at him. "To keep you out?"

"To keep *everything* out," he said, now smiling.

Hilda entered her room still breathless from Friedrich's kiss. She had wondered if he would feel the way she did about Mordenheim's monstrous experiment, and knew now she should not have doubted her lover. There was no way that either of them would participate in something so evil.

Relieved that their decision was made, she locked her door and undressed. After a sponge bath, she slipped on a heavy nightgown and climbed between the soft, clean sheets, thankful Horg knew how to make a bed. She listened for Friedrich's movements in the next room, but heard nothing, and thought that the walls must be very thick indeed.

Though she was exhausted, Hilda lay awake for a long time thinking about and pitying the creature that lay upstairs in the laboratory. She felt certain it was not love but madness that had made Victor Mordenheim preserve her poor life.

It seemed a night made for madness. She listened to the wind howling outside her window, creeping up the face of the cliff from the cold sea, pressing its icy fingers into every crack and cranny it could find. Then she shivered and cuddled down farther into the bedclothes.

This was a demanding and terrible domain, and she wondered if the cold ever left it. She had seen tonight, out on the Sea of Sorrows, the ice floes that had formed with the coming of winter, great chunks of frozen sea that looked like a stone walkway, over which one could actually tread if the need were great enough.

She shivered again at the thought of walking on ice, surrounded by deadly chill waters, leaping from ice island to ice island, knowing that the slightest misstep could toss you into the freezing death of the waters below.

Wasn't life the same way? she thought dreamily, so often placid on the surface, though below, unseen, lay a chilling reality of madness and horror.

That thought was with her as she descended into sleep, and the cold and the horrors she had seen that day dropped her into a dream in which she was running, running in darkness and cold, the ground uncertain beneath her bare feet, which had been cold but now grew warmer and warmer. And with the warmth the sun came over the horizon and she saw that she was running on ice, and when she looked down to guide her feet, she saw that they had been feeling warmer because they had frozen, and were blue with cold, red with blood.

But she was unable to stop running—even when the ice stopped and there was water, a mile of it at least, separating her from the next floe. So she leapt and felt herself soar into the air, and her dream bore her up, and she floated until she saw the floe drawing nearer, and prepared her legs to start running again.

She struck the floe, only to find it was paper thin, and she plunged through it as though nothing were there, and sank deep into the cold water, which rushed into her nose and mouth so that she could not breathe. She tried to open her mouth, but could not. Ice held it shut, choking her, cutting off her air, and her eyes grew huge in the dream . . .

. . . and opened from sleep to see a thing from the deepest pits of the underworld looming over her, to feel its iron fingers over her mouth, to hear its words in her ear so clearly that she knew the dream had become reality.

"Don't struggle. Struggle and you will die."

The window. She had not done as Friedrich had asked and locked the window.

With all her heart she wanted to faint, if that were the only way to blot out the being from her consciousness. But she had never been the type to swoon, and so remained awake and alert despite her wishes. She did not struggle at all, for the tone of the voice left no alternative but implicit belief that the thing would do precisely what it said. She merely nodded her head and tried not to choke on the smell of whoever it was who knelt on the bed beside her.

"I am going to put a gag in your mouth, and then bind you," said the voice, and it sounded surprisingly gentle. "I mean you no harm, but I can and will kill you in an instant should you cry out or try to escape me. Do you understand?"

She nodded again. Then she felt a piece of cloth slide between her lips, and she obediently opened her mouth. The gag did not go in deep, only far enough for her to make no noise should she cry out involuntarily. The man sat her up in the bed, and tied her wrists tightly together in front of her. Then he hoisted her up and over his shoulder as though she weighed no more than a coney. He carried her across the room, set her on her feet, and draped her long winter cloak over her, closing the clasp at her neck. Finally he placed her warm, fur-lined shoes firmly on her bare feet.

In the dim light from the window, she could make out none of his features, and had only a vague sense of misshapenness. The fact that he towered nearly two feet over her made her certain that this was Adam, the woman-killing monster Mordenheim had painted in—she felt at this moment—a properly sinister light.

He kept one hand on her shoulder, and with the other he took a dirty yellow paper out of a pocket and placed it beneath the edge of her reticule on the dresser top. Then he turned back toward her, picked her up by her upper arms, and walked to the open window through which the wind was rushing.

He set her down, lowered his head, and brought it up through the circle of her bound arms until she was involuntarily embracing him around his neck. Then he turned until she was behind him and stood up.

The motion hoisted her off the floor, and she thought surely that her weight must be choking him, but when he spoke to her, his voice sounded clear and unimpeded.

"We are climbing down the wall. The knots are tight. You will not fall from me. And I will not fall."

For a moment panic seized her as he climbed through the window and she dangled helplessly down his back. She wanted to shriek, to fight, to pull herself away or even *through* this madman who was going to kill them both.

But then rationality told her that he had climbed *up* the wall, so why could he not climb down again? Still, the terror of hanging from this monster's back while he was descending a rain-slick cliff was almost more than she could bear.

In another moment, it was too late to do anything, for he was moving down the rock wall, and the cold rain and wind were buffeting her against him. Though the rope held her so that she did not have to cling to him, she attempted to do so anyway, digging her fingers into shoulder muscles that felt like steel bands under his roughly textured clothing.

She looked down once only, and then kept her eyes pressed tightly shut until they reached the bottom. But it was not onto solid rock that Adam stepped, but onto a gently rocking surface, and when Hilda opened her eyes again she saw that they were in a fisherman's small skiff.

He twisted about until they were facing each other again, then ducked and brought her arms up and free from around his bull-like neck. Picking her up, he placed her gently into the bottom of the boat, untied and pushed the boat away from the cliff face, sat on a wooden bench, and pulled on the oars, whose oarlocks were wrapped in burlap.

Terror had completely wearied her, and despite her fear, her prone position and the rocking of the boat soon lulled her into a sleep from which she did not awake until the prow of the skiff struck the first of the massive ice floes that surrounded the Isle of Agony.

 **THIRTEEN**

Despite his tiredness, Friedrich had not slept peacefully. His night was full of terrible dreams and many awakenings, and he sweated in spite of the coolness of the room. Though not fully rested, he was actually relieved when gray morning came oozing through his window. His father's watch told him that it was only slightly before seven, but he got up nonetheless, splashing cold water from the basin on his face and cleaning the night-taste from his teeth.

After he dressed, he rapped lightly on the wall that separated his room from Hilda's, but received no response. He was not surprised, for the heavy wall scarcely resounded from his rapping. He went into the hall and knocked softly on her door. Still sleeping, he thought when there was no response.

Just as he was about to turn away, he felt a cool draft from underneath Hilda's door. He knelt and held his fingers in the flow of air. It was so cold that the room within must have felt like an icebox.

He stood and knocked louder. "Hilda?" he called. "Hilda, are you all right?" Only silence answered him.

Alarmed, Friedrich began to pound on the door, calling her name. He tried the knob, only to find it locked, and shouted her name loudly.

"Is something wrong?"

Friedrich turned and saw Mordenheim, dressed as

the day before, coming down the hall toward him. "Do you have a key?" Friedrich asked feverishly.

"No, that door locks only from the inside. Is Fraulein Von Karlsfeld ill?"

"She doesn't answer and the room's like ice!"

"Then kick in the door if you can, by all means."

Friedrich raised his foot and unleashed a savage kick that shook the door but did not open it. He kicked it again, and again, and finally was rewarded with the sound of splitting wood.

"*Again*," Mordenheim urged, and Friedrich slammed his foot against the jamb. With a bang, the door sprang open, and he dashed into the room, Mordenheim right behind him.

The bed was empty, the bedclothes in a state of disarray. The window was open, and Hilda was nowhere to be seen. Friedrich ran to the window and looked out, but thankfully saw no body on the rocks below. He turned angrily on Mordenheim. "Where is she?"

"Out the window," the doctor said. "There is no other way."

"Are you insane? No one could climb down that cliff, least of all Hilda!"

Mordenheim's eyes were filled with a bitter knowledge. "I did not say that *she* climbed down it. . . ."

Friedrich grasped the doctor by the lapels and shook him like a terrier shakes a rat. "Damn you, where *is* she!"

"Adam . . ." Mordenheim choked out.

Friedrich's eyes narrowed. "What?"

"He is the only one who could have climbed that cliff and gone down with her. It *has* to be he." Mordenheim's gaze darted to the dresser top. "Look," he said. "That paper . . ."

Friedrich released the doctor as though he were letting go of garbage, whirled, and snatched the wrinkled, yellow paper from beneath Hilda's reticule. He read it silently, paled, then thrust it toward Mordenheim, who read it aloud:

> Kreutzer—
> I have taken your woman to the Isle of Agony. If you do as I say, she will not be harmed. If you disobey my commands, she will die. The choice is yours. If you wish her to live, you will return immediately to your home in Darkon and cease to help Doctor Mordenheim in any way whatsoever. Do this, and she will be set free. But if you do not arrive in Il Aluk within seven days, she will be killed. If you suspect my heart is too tender to do such a thing, I suggest you ask Mordenheim for confirmation of the character he gave me.
>
> Adam

Mordenheim let the hand holding the letter fall slowly to his side. "He would do anything to keep me from happiness," he said softly.

"Happiness?" Friedrich said. "Happiness? This is Hilda's *life* at stake here!"

"So what are you planning to do, then?"

"I'll do just what he says—return to my home city."

"And you think he'll free her then? You really believe him? Oh, I can give you confirmation, Herr Kreutzer—he would undoubtedly kill Fraulein Von Karlsfeld, and he undoubtedly *will*. I know him all too well."

A lump of fear for his fiancee came into Friedrich's throat, and he swallowed hard. "You mean he will kill her no matter what I do?"

"I guarantee you, young sir, that the moment he learned you were in Il Aluk, Fraulein Von Karlsfeld would be dead. He sees her only as a bargaining tool, and when the bargain is over . . ."

"Then we must . . . we must *save* her, go after them immediately!" He started to leave the room, but Mordenheim stopped him.

"No, not immediately. You do not know this creature. The two of us, even with weapons, would be no match for him. He would destroy us both—or, what is more likely, destroy *you,* and taunt me with your death. Yours, and *hers* on my conscience."

"But we can't just let him keep her!"

"Nor shall we. But to battle him we need a man as strong or stronger than he, who can overpower and capture him."

"Capture?" said Friedrich. "Why not *kill* him—hack him into the individual pieces from which you made him?"

"No!" Mordenheim cried. "He must not be killed. I want him alive."

"But why?"

"That, for now, is my affair. But as for capturing him, there is only one man mighty enough to do that, and though he tried once before, he could not corner the monster."

"Then how can we find him now?"

"There is, due to some . . . quirk of science, a link of some sort between the creature and myself. I would not go so far as to call it 'psychic,' but I might call it a type of electrical transmission. He seems to feel my physical pain, and I sometimes think that his mind occasionally looks out through my eyes. I can often *feel* when he is near." Mordenheim licked his lips nervously. "I felt as much last night, but dismissed it as fancy. I should have trusted myself more. But between my link with Adam and Dragonov's tracking skills, we stand a good chance of hunting this beast down."

"Dragonov?"

"Ivan Dragonov. A Falkovnian by birth, a warrior by trade. He has devoted his life to battling evil. A never-ending struggle in this land." A smile almost appeared on Mordenheim's grim lips, but suddenly his jaw clenched, and he ground his teeth.

"But what am I thinking? We would never *find* Dragonov in seven days. He is a wanderer, going where his whim and the rumors of evil take him."

"If we know his name, I can draw him here with a summoning spell."

"Magic?" Mordenheim said with a sneer.

"Call it magic or call it a science we don't as yet understand. I do know that it works. I have Von Schreck's book, and that is all I need, other than a candle and a room that is totally dark."

"I can supply you with those things." Mordenheim could not help but snort as he added, "For all the good it will do."

"It will do *much* good. You may observe if you like, Doctor. I think you'll be surprised at the efficacy of the . . . magic."

In less than half an hour, Mordenheim stood in a corner of a cellar room, watching Friedrich kneel beside a lit candle, the book of Von Schreck's open in front of him on the floor. Over and over the youth repeated what to Mordenheim sounded like nonsensical syllables, and the doctor looked on with a withering smile.

"Vibrations of the aether . . ." Mordenheim muttered softly, ". . . foolish . . . utter nonsense."

Suddenly Friedrich stiffened. "I see him," he said with an intensity that startled Mordenheim.

"You see him?" Mordenheim said, scarcely able to believe him. "Describe him to me, then."

"A giant of a man. Almost a monster himself. Flaming red hair falling to his shoulders and a beard of darker red. His flesh is brown from the sun, except for

the white scars that crisscross his arms. He is wearing a
leather shirt and carries a huge, twin-bladed axe, and a
short sword in a scabbard."

"What is on the hilt?" Mordenheim asked.

"A red stone, smooth, with no facets."

"That *is* Dragonov, to the life," Mordenheim said, in
awe of Friedrich's accomplishment. His face twitched
as he tried to explain the wizardry to himself scientifi-
cally. ". . . vibrations . . . cause curves in space? Yes
. . . it must be. . . . What is he doing?"

"Walking through woods," Friedrich replied. "There
is something near him, behind him, coming closer . . . it
is . . ."

And then Friedrich screamed a cry of warning.

*   *   *   *   *

More than fifty miles away in Falkovnia, Ivan Dragonov heard the voiceless warning. All senses alerted,
he dropped his horse's bridle, whirled about, and saw
the lycanthrope he had been stalking leap in his direction, a scarce five paces away.

He dived straight toward it, and it passed over him as
he rolled beneath it. At the last moment, he swung his
silver axe upward. The werebeast shrieked in pain and
fury as its blood splashed in Dragonov's face.

The red-bearded man gave a grunt of annoyance as
the blood burned into his eyes, and he wiped them
angrily. His vision cleared just in time to see the thing
turn and charge him again, yellow fangs bared, green
spittle dribbling down its hairy chin. Its forearms were
extended toward him, showing inch-long claws capable
of ripping out a man's bowels with one swipe. The gash
that Dragonov's axe had made in its right calf scarcely
slowed it at all as it surged toward him.

This time he was ready. He jerked the silver sword

from its scabbard and surprised the lycanthrope by running to meet it. The beast's headlong rush bore it right to him, and Dragonov feinted, then delivered the fatal thrust.

The silver bit like molten fire through the creature's heavy coat, its cursed flesh, and the chambers of its black heart. It howled its death howl. Dragonov jerked the blade out laterally so as to widen the wound, then leapt back so that the deadly claws would not scratch him.

But he was a moment too late.

The lycanthrope threw out its arms in agony, and the claws of its right hand raked the bare flesh of Dragonov's arm, leaving four deep furrows that instantly oozed blood.

Dragonov cursed. Tossing away the sword, he raised his axe and brought it down on the beast, now lying on the forest floor and writhing in its death throes. The practiced stroke brought the axe directly down onto the neck, separating the head from the body with almost miraculous ease. Blood spouted from the stump of the neck, and the mouth opened in a howl now silent, with no throat to voice it.

The Falkovnian dropped his axe, knelt down, and frantically gathered together bits of dry leaves, grass, and twigs, then began to break dead branches off nearby trees. He kept his arm moving constantly so that the blood would not congeal, and the wound would keep bleeding.

His horse had bravely held its ground during the fight, and Dragonov rushed to it and burrowed into his saddlebags for flint and steel. He struck them together over the brush until the tinder began to smoke. He blew gently to build the flame, then put larger twigs and branches on top, constantly squeezing and slapping his hurt arm to make his blood flow. He scarcely glanced at

the now dead lycanthrope, which had turned back into
its original form: a middle-aged man whose bald head
lay several yards from his paunchy body.

When the flame was large enough, Dragonov wiped
his sword free of the lycanthrope's blood, then thrust it
into the fire, piling on more brush and wood, until the
silver began to glow. When he felt it was hot enough, he
drew it from the flames, gritted his teeth, and pressed
the hot metal of the flat of the blade against the cuts.

The pain was excruciating, but he gave only a low
grunt, and kept it against his flesh. Finally he took it
away and looked.

The skin was whole. Except for four thin white lines,
it was as though the lycanthrope had never touched
him. Ivan Dragonov barked a hearty laugh and rose to
his feet.

Only then did he remember the warning cry he had
heard, and he looked around the woods to see if he
could spy who had spoken. "Hello?" he called. "Is anyone there?"

I.

He heard the word in his head, and his eyes narrowed.
Sorcery? Had he been possessed by some wood-spirit?
Or was it the voice of a treant? He quickly examined the
trees about him, but none bore the gnarled, thick bark of
the evil tree creatures.

Do not be alarmed, the voice said. *My name is Friedrich Kreutzer, and I am in the castle of Doctor Victor Mordenheim, for whom you have worked in the past.*

"How can you speak to me then?"

Through a summoning spell.

"Dark magic?"

*No. Magic for good ends. To bring you here to track
down Mordenheim's monster and save the life of my
fiancee, whom he has kidnaped.*

"The monster?" Dragonov's lip curled in a snarl.

That half-man, half-corpse called Adam was the only evil being he had never been able to track down, and the memory of its taunting rankled him still. "Do you know where he's taken her?"

The Isle of Agony. He has threatened to kill her in seven days.

"Then," said Dragonov, stooping and picking up his axe and sword, "I'll ride quickly. But tell Mordenheim that this is not for him, but for your woman. And to rid the land of yet one more evil."

*   *   *   *   *

"Thank you, my friend," Friedrich said, then dissolved the spell, shook his head to clear it, and rose. "Some fresh air now," he said to Mordenheim, and they left the cellar and ascended the stairs, Von Schreck's book tucked under Friedrich's arm.

"I sensed that this Dragonov bore some hostility toward you," Friedrich said.

"Dragonov," said Mordenheim, "is a simple man. Anything he does not understand, he considers evil. And he could not understand how I created Adam. The scientific principles behind it are naturally alien to him, so he considers me a wizard, possibly benign but more likely with sinister purposes. His is the blindness of most humans, who cannot understand the original purpose of my work. But Dragonov is more slow of mind than most of them. He is a warrior, good for fighting and little else."

They had reached the kitchen now, and Mordenheim set about preparing them a meal. But the only hunger Friedrich felt was the need to be with Hilda again. "How long will it take for Dragonov to get here?"

"Seventy miles of road," said Mordenheim, putting two bowls of porridge on the table, "but fifty as the crow flies, and Dragonov always rides the shortest way. The terrain is difficult, but I think we should see him in two days at most. Now, eat."

"I'm not hungry."

"The trek to the Isle of Agony will be grueling at this time of year," said Mordenheim, as if to a recalcitrant child. "We shall be able to take a boat only part of the way, and will have to cross the ice floes for the remainder of the journey. You owe it to Fraulein Von Karlsfeld to stay strong, if not to yourself. Now *eat*."

Mordenheim began to spoon up the porridge himself. After he had swallowed a bite, he said, "Do not worry about her, Herr Kreutzer. I will restore your fiancee to you, and then the two of you will restore my Elise to me."

Friedrich almost began to tell Mordenheim that their plans were far different, that they had no intention of placing Elise's spirit into an innocent victim's body. But he realized that if he did that, there would be no reason for Mordenheim to help rescue Hilda. Friedrich would be on his own against a terrible monstrosity in an unknown and savage land.

So he merely nodded, dipped a spoon into the sour-tasting porridge, and forced himself to eat and be strong for Hilda.

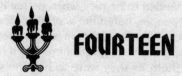

FOURTEEN

Horg was not happy. Gypsies frightened him. They had done so ever since he was a boy, when a caravan had camped for several nights on the Mordenheim estate. He had sneaked out at night to spy on them and was caught by an old woman with only a few teeth, who grinned evilly at him. She took him into the gypsies' midst, where they surrounded him, laughing at his deformity and breathing rank smells into his face. They threatened to put him into a large cage hung from one of the wagons and take him along with them, charging townspeople a penny to look at him. He had been crying in terror by the time they finally let him go, with a thrashing and a warning never to spy on gypsies again.

And now here he was on his way to infiltrate the camp of the wisest and most dangerous of gypsies, the Vistani. Not only was he to enter into their midst, but he had been ordered by Doctor Mordenheim to take a Vistana girl away, by force if necessary. To cross the Vistani was a feat to make even the bravest man quail, and the doctor expected it of Horg as a matter of course.

It was doubly difficult for Horg. Not only was he a *giorgio,* or nongypsy, he was also a physical outsider, with his dwarfish stature and humped back. There was no way he could ride up to their camp and join them, so

Doctor Mordenheim had come up with a plan. It was dangerous, but it stood a chance of succeeding if he was a good enough pretender.

Horg had always been a good pretender. Most of the time he pretended to be nice when he really wasn't. He hated most people, hated the way their faces got when they looked at him, even the ones who tried to pretend there was nothing wrong with him. But if he had been as cruel to them as they were to him, he would never have received any kindness. So he pretended. Fortunately he had been graced with a sweet and flawless face, so that pity rather than revulsion was what most people felt for him. Still, he didn't want their pity. All he wanted was a chance to be a man, like anyone else.

That was what the doctor had given him. Never once, not even when the doctor was a boy, had he ever looked at Horg with anything less than total comradeship, and Horg worshiped him for it. He would have done anything for the doctor, and he *had* done a good many things that could have gotten him hanged. But the doctor seldom asked him to do anything he himself was not willing to do. They had rifled graves together, cut dead men down from the gallows, broken into morgues and hospitals, and . . . done things even worse. Horg knew which sins lay upon the doctor, just as he knew which lay upon his own soul. And if the doctor asked him to do this, then he would do it or die in the attempt.

It had taken him a day and a half to drive the two horses and coach to Neufurchtenberg and then south toward the border of Falkovnia. Most of the way he had gone through a cold rain that often turned to sleet. He had passed few other travelers, the only one of note a huge warrior on a white horse so massive it would have looked more at home behind a leadsmith's wagon. The rider had his head covered against the sleet, but there

was something in his carriage that made Horg think he
had seen him before.

Now, as he neared the border of Falkovnia, the skies
seemed to brighten, and the weather grew warmer, until
he could toss his cloak into the back of the wagon. He
paused when he smelled the first faint whiff of smoke
and scanned the sky for traces of it.

There it was, coming from over that wooded rise.
And better yet, flying above the smoke were the little
gray-and-white birds known only by their Vistana
name, *vista-chiri*, which followed the gypsies from
camp to camp the way cowbirds stay with kine.

Horg got down from the coach and led the horses
several hundred yards off the rough road. There he
unhitched them, tied them to a tree, unloaded oats from
the back of the wagon, and fed them. A small brook ran
nearby, and he brought water for them as well, then
took off his linen shirt and put on a dirty, ragged one,
complete with bloodstains. Gritting his teeth, he took a
rock and hit himself several times on the face, just hard
enough to cause bruises and draw some blood, which
he let trickle down his face onto his clothes. Then he
walked off in search of the Vistani.

It didn't take him long to find them. Their camp was
situated in a hollow of the hills that trapped the weak
warmth of the sun and held it in its bowl. It was a large
tribe. Sixteen wagons, or vardos, were drawn in a circle
around the central campfire. And the largest vardo was
painted a bright blue with a golden hawk, just as the
doctor had told him. Nearly forty horses stood off to the
side in a makeshift corral, with two young Vistana men
holding pikes on guard.

The rest of the tribe were preparing for supper. Several dozen women and children stood about the central
fire, slicing cuts of meat and vegetables and throwing
them in a huge, black iron pot that hung above the fire

from an iron tripod.

Horg crouched behind a fallen tree at the top of the rise and watched for a while, trying to discern the people who ran the tribe, the ones with power, those to whom his pretending had to be the most convincing.

He assumed that they all were related in some way; it was a good bet that the old woman who sat near the fire on the steps of the large blue vardo was the grandmother of the tribe—the wise woman who commanded more respect than anyone, even the strongest male. She looked old, toothless, and feeble, but even from a distance, Horg could see that her eyes were alert, flicking from one person to another, following their actions as though she directed them.

A younger man of about fifty stood near her. He wore a loose crimson blouse and had a bright blue bandanna around his head. An earring of heavy gold dangled from his right ear, and a pair of dapper black mustachios arced from his lip and drooped an inch below his chin. His sense of command led Horg to assume that he was the male elder of the tribe, perhaps the crone's oldest son.

The man turned as the door to the blue vardo opened, and his face shone with pride, for through that door came the most beautiful woman Horg had ever beheld, even more lovely than Frau Mordenheim, whom he had always considered the epitome of feminine perfection.

But this creature was more than perfect. Her hair was as black as night, a darkness so thick that a man might drown in it, and her eyes were fiery yellow jewels that held all the mysteries of earth in their depths. The features of her face were not classically proportioned, but their boldness coalesced into a wildness of expression that no man could tame, though any man would hope to.

Her form was lithe and slender, with willowy limbs
and delicate hands and feet, decorated by rings and
bangles that jingled as she walked down the vardo
steps. She stopped at the side of the man, and for an
instant, a jealousy he had never felt before rushed
through Horg. But when the girl gave the man a respectful kiss on the cheek and the man patted her lovingly,
Horg was certain they were father and daughter.
Though he was a long distance away, he could see no
plain gold ring amidst the sparkling gems that flashed
from her fingers.

What did it matter, he thought, then laughed bitterly
at himself for even feeling the emotion of desire for this
breathtaking woman. Imagine a giorgio, and a parody
of a man to boot, feeling this way about a Vistana maid.
He would be lucky if they did not beat him away from
their camp as soon as they saw him.

The ruse could be put off no longer. Horg lurched
into view and stumbled down the hillside toward the
wagons. "Help," he gasped weakly, "please help
me. . . ."

Dozens of eyes were raised toward him, all of them
dark and suspicious under glowering brows. The young
men guarding the horses looked once at Horg, then
scanned the rim of the bowl in which the camp sat,
ready for an attack from which the stumbling hunch-
back may have been meant to distract them. But there
was no attack, only this wretched, bloody man lumbering toward them, tripping on a root, falling, his face in
the dirt.

Horg heard, over his forced panting, a man's gruff
voice cry, "Ilisa!" and then he felt hands on his shoulders, hands whose wonderful warmth penetrated his
skin even through his rough shirt.

"But he's hurt, Father!" Horg felt himself gently
turned over, and then he was looking into the face of

the girl, only inches from his own. Suddenly his breath-
lessness did not need to be feigned. But it was the girl
who gasped and muttered, "*Angeli,*" under her breath.

"Get back, get back," said the man. "Let me take a
look at him." The mustachioed Vistana came into Horg's
sight, and Horg's breath nearly stopped at the fury in the
man's face. He looked Horg over quickly, and by the
time he was done, they were surrounded by nearly every
Vistana in camp. Horg swallowed heavily, thinking of
the last time gypsies had surrounded him, and he
started his story.

"I was . . . set upon by thieves," he said. "They took
my money, my horse, and beat me—would have killed
me if I'd not gotten away. . . ."

"Thieves, eh?" said the girl's father. "You sure they
weren't gypsies?"

Horg wasn't sure if that was supposed to be a joke,
so he didn't laugh. "No, sir. They looked like trappers
to me."

"Ah. Were they trapping as they robbed you? Or did
they have cards identifying them as members of the
Lamordian Trappers Guild?"

Horg was confused. Was there a trappers guild? "No,
sir, but they wore rough skins, and . . . and *looked* like
trappers."

"Ah," said the man again. "Just like gypsies look like
thieves, eh?"

"Sir, I . . ." Horg shook his head. "I don't understand."

"Stop it, Father," said the girl. "He's been *hurt,* it's
not right to tease him. Let's take him to the vardo." She
put her hands under his right arm and helped him to his
feet.

"*My* vardo?" Ilisa's father said. "A giorgio in *my*
vardo!"

"Be quiet and help me," she said.

The man gave an angry grunt but supported Horg's left side. "Just like when you were little, always bringing crippled birds and puppies who'd lost their mother. And now"—he spat—"*this.*"

"That is why Ilisa is what she is." Horg looked at the speaker and saw the crone who had been supervising before. "Much loved and much desired. Even by those who cannot hope to win her."

The old woman eyed Horg strangely, and he thought that she must see, if not the treachery in his heart, at least the adoration there. It was an emotion he had never had before and one he did not know how to disguise.

"Very well," said the father. "But once he is healed, out he goes."

They took Horg to the blue vardo where Ilisa bathed his self-inflicted wounds under the crone's watchful eye. "Does that feel better?" she asked when she had finished and was washing her hands.

"Yes, it does. Thank you . . . Ilisa, is it?"

"Yes. My father is Petre. This," she said, turning to the old woman, "is my grandmother, Karla. And you?"

"My name is . . . Horg." He had never thought much about his name before, but now it seemed as blunt and ugly as he, and he was ashamed of it. But when Ilisa repeated it, it did not sound nearly as bad as he had thought.

"Come, Ilisa," said Karla with a voice like a strangling crow. "It is time for supper." She hobbled down the vardo steps.

"I will bring you something to eat when we are finished," said Ilisa, smiling at him the way no woman had ever done before.

"A moment, please," said Horg. "When you first helped me, you said something. Something about . . . an angle?"

Her laughter was like thin, silver coins falling on a crystal surface, and she blushed slightly. "*Angeli,*" she said, pronouncing the word with a hard *G.* "It is a race lost in our legends that perhaps never existed at all. Fallen seraphs who committed crimes against the gods and were hurled into this world. Their bodies are . . ." she searched for unoffending words ". . . far from perfect, but their faces are still those of the divine. I could not help but . . ." She left the thought unfinished, shrugged, once more blushed prettily, and then fled for the steps. "I'll bring you supper," she told him again, and she was gone.

Horg lay in the vardo, hearing the Vistana feast while his mind whirled in its own stew of mixed emotions. There was his loyalty to the doctor and the sense that he must fulfill his duty, but there were also these alien feelings, so new and so strange.

Steal the girl away, that was what the doctor had told him. And he could think of nothing that he would like to do more—steal Ilisa away, far from where Doctor Mordenheim could do to her what he had done to those others.

Oh, it was true that they would die eventually anyway, but reason had no room in their screams. They could not realize that what they were doing was making a sacrifice for the doctor's science, for learning that would save untold millions of lives in years to come. That was what the doctor had always told him, and he believed it without a doubt. It was a pity, though, that so many girls had had to make that sacrifice for so little gain.

And now Ilisa. "Ilisa . . ." He said the name quietly to himself over and over and thought about how sweet and gentle it sounded, as gentle as her soothing hands.

Finally, she returned with stew and thick, black coffee, and nothing Horg ate had ever tasted as delicious.

He tried to eat slowly so that she would not think he was rude, and he exclaimed over the excellence of it and thanked her for it between every other mouthful. She would only laugh and nod, the large gold hoops in her ears shaking delightfully with every motion of her head.

When he had finished, she took the empty plate and mug from him. "You must stay here in the vardo tonight," she told him. "Because you are a giorgio, you may not see our dancing."

"May I listen to the music?" he asked.

She laughed again. "I think you'll have no choice." Then she turned and left him alone.

The music began some time later, after night fell. Fiddles sang, guitars provided a sweet undertone, and tambourines rattled and jingled. The music was wild and free and frenzied and melancholy all at once. Horg could picture the Vistana girls dancing around the fire and tried to imagine Ilisa whirling in the firelight.

After the fast dances were over, someone softly played a guitar while a man sang a song whose chorus went:

> "When stars gleam in azure skies
> And midnight fills my soul,
> Then home my thoughts do turn,
> Where my spirit once was whole.
>
> "But now my loved home is gone,
> And I must wander far,
> Trav'ling road on road on road,
> Following a distant star."

The song made Horg think of a home he had never known. The man who fathered Horg had left his mother before he was born; his mother had fled the Mordenheim estate and the sight of her son after giving birth, as soon as she could walk. He never knew where she had gone. He never cared.

The only person he ever cared for was Doctor Mordenheim. He was several years older than Horg and had been kind to him when the boys who worked on the estate mocked him and took their turns beating him.

The young master had happened on such a beating one day and ordered the other boys off. He told Horg he was a fool to take abuse in that manner and encouraged him to stand up for himself. "You are the strongest of them all, Horg," he said. "But you are also the most timid. Be brave and answer them blow for blow, and they will bother you no longer."

He had done as Mordenheim suggested. The next time Rolf began to pick on him, he warned him that this time he would fight back. And when Rolf began pushing him and slapping his cheeks, Horg struck him in the face as hard as he could, breaking his nose, knocking out several teeth, and addling his brain so that Rolf never spoke right again. Old Mordenheim ordered Horg flogged, but the punishment was worth it, and the young master stood next to him during his beating and told him he was very brave not to cry out, and that he would one day need a brave, strong man. Horg smiled then despite his ripped back and knew from that moment on that he would do whatever Victor Mordenheim wanted of him.

Now, after years of faithful service, Mordenheim wanted him to kidnap Ilisa. Horg thought he could do it. He knew he *had* to do it, and he began to think more realistically now that he could not see that raven hair, those flashing eyes. The reason behind the girl's kindness toward him was probably just as her father had said—the urge to protect crippled birds and orphaned puppies. And beaten travelers too, especially those

whose bodies were twisted. Of course. All of them were
objects of pity, useless for loving a woman. She was
probably laughing at him right now.

As if in affirmation, a woman's laugh pealed out over
the music, which had become loud and savage once
more. He did not think it was Ilisa's voice, but that did
not matter. Perhaps she, too, laughed.

Angeli, she had called him. A fallen angel with a
crooked body and a sweet face. He was an angel who
had fallen, all right. And fallen angels were nothing but
fiends.

Very well then. He would be a fiend, one who rewarded kindness with cruelty, hospitality with deceit.
He could not give up a lifetime of service for a few minutes of an infatuation that would only wound him more
deeply than any blade. He would not do that to the doctor. And he would not do it to himself.

Now that he had made up his mind, there was the
deed itself to be planned. These Vistani were dangerous, there was no doubt of that. But danger was something he had never been afraid to face. The real problem
was that the tribe was always together. Vistani did not
wander off alone, so it would be difficult to find enough
time to steal Ilisa away, carry her to the coach, and get
a fast enough head start to elude the gypsies. Someone
was bound to notice her missing.

Night would be the best time, as he would have until
the tribe began to awaken at daybreak. Mordenheim
had supplied him with a number of items, including a
large packet of sleeping powder. Perhaps he could use
the powder to drug those who watched through the
night and steal the girl from her bed.

It was a possibility, and Horg wondered what the
sleeping accommodations were like in the larger part of
the vardo, separated from him by a thick, red curtain.
He got to his feet, wincing at the creaking boards of

both the cot and the wagon floor, and tried to quietly walk the few paces that separated him from the curtain. The noise was thunderous in his ears, loud enough, he thought, to wake even a deaf gypsy. He reached out, pulled back the curtain, and peered behind it.

Ice filled the back of his head as he found himself staring into the eyes of an old woman—colorless eyes like pearls wedged in silt at the ocean's bottom.

She was sitting up in the lower right bunk bed, propped by brightly colored pillows and illuminated by a dimly burning lamp. The map of wrinkles that framed her white eyes told Horg that she was ancient in the extreme. The crone who was Ilisa's grandmother could have been this woman's daughter. Only a few wisps of yellow-white hair clung to the parchmentlike skull. The ears and nose had shriveled as if from lack of moisture until they were nothing but fleshly appendages, and the thin line of the mouth was nearly invisible, save for the vertical cracks above and below the lips.

Those lips now opened, and from them there issued a word that he could almost see as it husked out:

"Whoooo . . . ?"

The sound seemed to last forever and reverberated in his ears even after the lips had closed. The woman's head slowly twisted to one side, as if it had grown too heavy, and the eyes miraculously widened, exposing more of their paleness. Horg knew that the woman was blind.

He wondered if he should answer, but then reasoned that if the hag were able to hear, she would have heard him talking to Ilisa before and known who he was. So he said nothing and looked quickly around the vardo.

Other than the one in which the woman lay, there were three bunks, which he thought must have been for

Ilisa, her father, and her grandmother. Cleverly designed cabinets and drawers filled every available inch of space, and gaudy clothes dangled from hooks screwed into the ceiling.

Horg drew back cautiously, sensing that the ancient being in the bed followed his every move with senses other than sight and sound. Just as he had let the curtain drift back into place, the door to the vardo opened, startling him, and he jerked his head about to see Ilisa standing in the doorway, holding a cup of tea.

"You're up then," she said. "Are you feeling better?"

Already feeling guilty, he imagined that she was looking at him accusingly, and scrabbled for an alibi. "I, uh, was just looking for . . . a chamber pot." He felt a fool as he said it, but on the spur of the moment, he could think of nothing more genteel.

The Vistana was used to the realities of life, and Ilisa only nodded and said, "There's one under your cot." Then she looked toward the curtain. "I'm glad you didn't go in there. You might have disturbed Nana."

"Nana?"

"My great-grandmother. Our tribe's wise woman."

"Oh. I had thought your grandmother Karla . . ."

"Karla does what Nana tells her."

"She must be . . . awfully old," Horg said, knowing full well.

"She is. And blind and deaf. But wisdom doesn't lie in hearing or seeing. It lies in *knowing*." And with that she disappeared behind the curtain. Horg heard her talking softly, but did not hear the old woman reply. Nana—such a benign name for a creature so hideous. Well, Horg reflected, every old hag is a Nana to someone.

That comment about *knowing* made him doubly concerned about accomplishing his goal. How was one to kidnap a girl who is never off on her own, and who sleeps in the same room with her father, her grand-mother, and a gypsy seer of a great-grandam? Horg would simply have to wait and bide his time.

He sighed, sat on his cot, and hoped that the doctor could curb his usual sense of urgency.

 **FIFTEEN**

"Where *is* the thrice-damned fool?"

Victor Mordenheim paced back and forth in the highest room of the circular watchtower, looking out the two windows that faced the land.

He had expected Dragonov to be there by now and cursed the Falkovnian, cursed the snow that had been falling for the past ten hours, cursed the wind that blew the snow across the roads that Dragonov would travel. If the warrior were trapped by the storm or remained in Ludendorf or Neufurchtenberg until the weather cleared, Mordenheim's last hope for Elise's reclamation would be shattered.

He strained his eyes again, looking through the window at the heavy flakes that nearly barred the road from his sight. There could have been an army advancing on the castle, and he would have been hard pressed to define its outlines in the ever shifting panorama of whiteness.

Cursing again, he shoved the door open and descended the spiral stairway to his laboratory. There, calmness came over him for a moment as he looked at the recumbent form of his wife on the table. He placed a damp palm on her forehead and patted it lightly.

"Elise," he said. "Oh, Elise, I shall bring you back to me, my love. And all our suffering shall have been worthwhile, believe me, my darling. I shall hold you in my arms once more, and cover your young and beaming face with kisses of joy and desire."

When he tried to draw his hand away, he realized with dismay that the moisture on his palm had caused it to adhere to the dry flesh of his wife's forehead. Though he drew back his hand as slowly as he could, dark bits of her skin peeled away like dry and flaking leather. He gave a shudder and gingerly brushed the flecks from his hand.

His former calm now gave way to a sense of urgency. Something must be done—and quickly. It seemed that with the passing of every day, Elise's original body declined further. Though his wife's physical form had long been past the state where he could hope to utilize it to bring her spirit back to him, it was still the only vessel in which he could keep that spirit secure and alive. Therefore, it had to be preserved.

But no flesh lasts forever, particularly flesh that wants to die. His techniques, miraculous as they were, could not sustain Elise's body indefinitely. At times he fancied that perhaps Elise tried to advance the deterioration of her body, knowing that when it was truly dead, she could die in peace as well.

Whenever such thoughts came, he drove them savagely away. Such ideas rejected everything he believed in and all his work over so many years. No, Elise could not wish for death. Instead, he told himself that she wished for rebirth, that she was waiting in that vile body, pleading for him to bring her back to life, hungering for the miracle of resurrection in a new, strong, healthy form. He would give her that. No matter whom he had to sacrifice.

But for now, he had had enough waiting. He would clothe himself warmly, saddle a horse, and ride southeast in search of Dragonov. A fool's errand, perhaps, but he could bear to wait here no longer with that insipid boy Kreutzer, who eased his mental anguish by spending most of his hours in the library reading and writing—not science, not even magic, but of all useless pursuits, poetry. He would not even tell the boy he was going. Let him fend for himself for a change.

Mordenheim went down to the great hall, bundled himself warmly, strode to the front door, and opened it, letting the wind and snow rush into the castle.

And there in the doorway before him stood a towering, statuesque figure of blinding whiteness, a gleaming axe raised over its head.

Mordenheim gasped and stumbled back, but the axe did not swing. Instead, it lowered slowly, and a booming noise, half laugh and half grunt, came from the white figure that advanced upon the doctor and into the room, banging the door shut behind it.

The axe dropped heavily to the floor, and the creature shook itself like a bear. The snow that coated it from head to foot shimmered and fell in a miniature blizzard, exposing the red beard and face and fur-clad form of Ivan Dragonov.

"I didn't mean to affright you," said the warrior, "but I'm not used to doors opening before I knock on them. For all I knew, that snake-spawn Adam had slain all here and was opening the door to welcome in his next victim."

Dragonov undid a clasp at his collar and let the snow-saturated furs drop to his feet. "Have that man of yours stable and feed my stallion," he said. "He's colder than I am."

"My man," Mordenheim said, finally finding his voice, "is away. Can you not take care of your own animal?"

"Saints' blood," muttered Dragonov, again donning his furs. "Well met indeed, Mordenheim. I've been in privies with more hospitality. . . ." And he went back into the storm.

Friedrich Kreutzer entered the hall just as the outer door slammed shut. "Is he here?" he asked excitedly. "Dragonov?"

"He is," said Mordenheim. "Nearly slew me as he came through the door. I advise you to stand well back when he returns. The man is as thick as Lamordian sheep's-blood pudding."

Several minutes later Dragonov came through the door again and shook off the snow, and Mordenheim introduced him to Friedrich, who was taken aback by the might of the man. Even in repose, he seemed ready to spring into battle with the sword that never left his hip.

They went into the kitchen, where Mordenheim suggested some steaming wine to warm Dragonov, but the man asked instead for tea, saying it was now the strongest thing he drank.

"You used to drink wine, Dragonov," Mordenheim said.

"I used to do many things that good men should not do. As the years pass, I try to purify my body and spirit, to keep all things that have the potential for evil out of my stomach and my mind."

Mordenheim put a cup of hot tea, a steaming bowl of mutton soup, and a loaf of bread on the table before Dragonov, who set to with a vengeance and did not speak another word until the table was clear of food. Then he leaned back, belched, and said, "Now, how do we find this serpents' brood?"

Mordenheim and Friedrich told him everything, except for the truth about Friedrich and Hilda's purpose for being at Schloss Mordenheim. The doctor said that Friedrich was there in order to help him in his medical experiments.

"Fraulein Von Karlsfeld," Mordenheim explained, "accompanied her fiance. But Adam, as you well know,

Dragonov, can bear to see no human happiness and stole the unfortunate and innocent girl from her bed at night. He has taken her to the Isle of Agony with the purpose of eventually killing her. That he does not do so immediately is due only to his desire to taunt us with his power."

Dragonov nodded soberly. "I know all about his taunting, coward that he is, afraid to face a real man. Stealing a girl in the dead of night—that's about his game. It's a black spirit that you gave to the world, Mordenheim, when you created that thing."

"You know full well," said the doctor, "that it was never my intent to bring evil upon the—"

"Intent!" Dragonov snorted. "You were filled with the sin of pride and the lust to place yourself above the gods. Your intent was *evil*, as was the fruit of your intent. Your creature is a curse upon this land, Mordenheim, and the only reason I haven't slain you is because without you I have no hope of finding that slippery, half-human beast of yours." He banged the tabletop with his fist. "Might I have another cup of tea, my fine *host?*"

When Mordenheim poured another cup, Friedrich noticed that his hand was trembling. So did Dragonov, who said, "Don't be so nervous, Mordenheim. After I've slain that monster of yours, perhaps I won't hunger as much for *your* blood."

"No," said Mordenheim softly. "Don't slay him."

Dragonov slurped his tea and looked at the doctor in a way Friedrich hoped the man would never look at him. "What did you say?"

"I said no. You can't slay him."

The Falkovnian shot to his feet, his hand on his sword hilt. "I can slay anything that moves and has blood in it!"

"I don't mean you can't; I mean you mustn't. We must take him alive."

"Alive? In the name of all that's holy, why? So you can do more of your cursed experiments with him? Maybe breed him to create a *race* of monsters? That's what they say you want to do, you know! Odd's bones, maybe I *should* slay you now and *then* go after your evil offspring!"

"Just *listen* to me for a moment!" said Mordenheim, unaccustomedly flaring. "This is a matter of *science,* not a matter of good or evil! And my motivation should appeal to your bloodthirstiness, Dragonov. Adam *was* an experiment, yes. An experiment that went terribly wrong. As a man of science and not superstition, like *some* I could name"—here he scowled at Dragonov, who gave him a furious glare in return—"I wish to know what exactly went wrong. My purposes were only for the good of mankind, to extend lives and make them better."

"Those things should be left to the gods," said Dragonov, "not to man."

"Very well then, we find ourselves on the horns of a theological dilemma. But instead of killing Adam, would it not satisfy your primitive sense of justice to be the tool that leads him to years of torment here on·this plane?"

"Years of torment?" Dragonov said uncertainly.

"Experiments," said Mordenheim. "Picture Adam bound to a table in iron bands that not even he can break. Picture me leaning over him, cutting into him without giving him any pain-relieving drugs to numb his mind or body or dull his reactions. Picture me doing this day after day, week after week, month after month, until I have solved the mystery of my errors."

"Not a bad picture at that," said Dragonov, starting to grin. "But what about *your* punishment?"

"Do you not think that I will undergo the tortures of the damned as I stand face-to-face with my hideous creation, as I see before me every hour of every day the errors I have made, the science I have botched? Living in an inferno of my own making with the instrument of that damnation? Do you think I could ever enjoy that? I will loathe every moment, and yet I *must* do it. It is the debt that I must pay to mankind and to science."

Dragonov stroked his red beard. The movement of his jaw seemed to indicate to Friedrich that he was thinking. "All right," he said at length. Now that he had decided, there was no further need for discussion or for more histrionics from Mordenheim. "So let's talk about the important part. How are we supposed to track your little boy down, Mordenheim? As you well know, I couldn't find him, and I looked for months."

"Yes," said Mordenheim, "but you could track him. It was just that he always stayed one step ahead of you."

"That's the truth. He was clever, and it took longer to find his spoor than most I've hunted. As a result I couldn't move as fast as he could."

"This time should be different. Herr Kreutzer and I will be going with you."

Dragonov looked from Friedrich to Mordenheim and back again. Then he sneered. "Wonderful. Two mighty warriors. You'll be a lot of help."

"We're not coming to fight," said Friedrich, annoyed by the man's presumption. "Although we could provide the edge, if it comes to that. But someone must care for Fraulein Von Karlsfeld, and Doctor Mordenheim's psychic link with his creature will enable us to find them."

Dragonov's frown was not a pleasant sight. "Psychic link? You mean he thinks like him?"

"Not in so many words," said Mordenheim, shooting Friedrich a glare that would have set him afire had he been tinder. "Let us just say that because I created Adam, I may be more familiar with his thought processes." Dragonov's frown did not go away, so Mordenheim simplified it. "I put his brain in there, so I know how it works."

Dragonov snorted anew. "Humph. You might have gone along with me years back. Saved this domain a lot of woe."

"Yes, well, I'm ready to go with you now."

"And we should begin as soon as possible," Friedrich said. "It's been three days already, and Adam has promised to kill Hilda in seven if—" Mordenheim gestured frantically, and Friedrich said no more, realizing that Dragonov would see the goal of revitalizing Elise as simply more black magic "—if I don't stop helping the doctor."

"Helping him do what?" asked Dragonov, none too kindly.

Friedrich thought quickly. It should not take much of a story to fool this man. "There's a young girl in Ludendorf," he said, "who was run over by a cart and lost her leg. We are attempting to make her an artificial one."

"Why not just get a carpenter to do it?" asked Dragonov.

"This leg," said the doctor, embellishing the story, "will be connected to the nerves and muscles of her thigh, so that she can actually propel herself under her own power, without a crutch. Surely a worthwhile undertaking, is it not, Dragonov?"

"Mmmm." Dragonov's tone was noncommittal. "Growing soft in your dotage, Mordenheim? Helping little lame children? Saving young girls from your monster? If I didn't know you better, I'd think you were a new man." He slapped his meaty thighs with his hands. "All right then, let's not waste any more time. Where are we off to?"

"The Isle of Agony," Mordenheim said.

"Know it well. More caves there than there are chiggers on a Tepestani horse. And the beast's holed up in one of them, eh?"

"Yes," said Friedrich. "Along with Fraulein Von Karlsfeld."

"Well, we'll find that monster and save your little lady, boy. That is, if he hasn't killed and eaten her already." Friedrich grew pale, and Dragonov smacked his shoulder and grinned. "Only a jest, boy. He never eats 'em."

The grin vanished.

"But he does kill 'em, true enough."

 # SIXTEEN

She could feel the wind, even in the depths of the cave. The snows had begun before they finished crossing the ice floes, coming down from the north like a thick, cold, wet blanket thrown over the island. She had not been able to breathe at the end, and he had picked her up easily, held her in his arms, taken off his coat, and draped it over her head so that the snow would not enter her nose and mouth. She breathed more easily in the captured warmth, and though the smell of his body was sharp and pungent, she inhaled blissfully, grateful for air that did not contain water.

The journey had been a nightmare. She had huddled in the bottom of the boat as it drifted out into the Sea of Sorrows, then eventually bumped its way through the ice floes until they could go no farther by water. Adam then told her to get up and handed her a woolen blanket to wrap herself in. He stepped out of the boat onto the ice and took her arm, and they began to walk.

It was like moving through a dream. The moon and stars were choked by thick clouds, and she could barely see more than his form in front of her and the dull gray of the ice beneath her feet. Had he not held onto her, she would have fallen and slid off the ice to a wet, chilling death. Whenever they came to breaks in the ice, he would help her across, picking her up and leaping with her when the watery chasms were too wide. Once at an especially large abyss, he told her to climb on his back and hold on tightly. Then he took a running start and leapt across the water, landing on his feet not only safely, but so delicately and with such grace that she was scarcely jarred.

Often the ice jutted up out of the sea, and then she would hold on to his neck while he climbed up and over each obstacle and jumped down to the next icy island of safety.

They stopped once as daylight neared, and he told her to wrap herself tightly in the blanket. Then he sat on the ice and directed her to lie in his arms and rest. The thought terrified her at first, but he had not harmed her so far, and if she lay on the ice she would freeze. So she let him cradle her. He did not look at her face, but gazed across the floes, his eyes open, his face stony as though he had turned to ice himself.

As far as she knew, he was still all the while she rested. She had not intended to fall asleep, but exhaustion had claimed her quickly, and when she awoke it was just starting to snow. She spoke to him then, to ask him how long she had slept.

"Five hours," he said. "We must move on."

The rest of the trek seemed endless, walking and stumbling, supported by Adam's grip. The snow increased, and the wind began to blow harder, so that she could feel the floes they walked on bumping into the neighboring chunks of ice. Before long she had to close her eyes against the wind, and shortly after that he picked her up and carried her the rest of the way.

She could scarcely hear his voice over the mad howling of the gale, but she felt a difference in the surface over which they moved. "We are off the ice . . . on the island."

It was, she knew, the Isle of Agony, a place feared by all who lived in Lamordia and a legend even in her native Darkon. When she was a little girl, she had heard that man-eating sea monsters dwelt there, and even old Von Schreck, during a sorcerous geography lesson, had referred to it as "the devil's domicile."

If it was, then this thing that held her was a devil. But devil or not, she remained in his arms, the coat over her head, and gradually fell asleep again.

It was silence that woke her. Silence, except for Adam's footfalls, no longer crunching through snow, but coming down solidly on rock. The temperature had changed too. It did not seem as cold, and she reached up and removed the coat from over her face to see where she was.

To her horror, she found that she was being borne through utter darkness. "Where . . . where *are* we?" she asked, close to panic.

"A cave." His rough voice was nonetheless velvety in texture, and it filled whatever subterranean chamber they were in. It made her think of an operatic tenor who had sung too harshly and strained his throat. "It is one of many that I know without sight. Do not fear. We will soon be at our destination."

She guessed that they traveled another hundred yards. Then the acoustics changed, and Adam's footsteps produced a stronger echo. "Stand now," he said, and she obeyed, not daring to move in the blackness.

There was a rustle of wood and kindling, and then she saw a spark in the darkness, another, and another, until the steel and flint ignited bits of dry moss and started the fire. In the ever-growing light, the face of the creature who had kidnaped her was gradually illuminated, and if she thought it hideous in the room at Schloss Mordenheim, it was far worse in this gloomy cavern, removed from anyone or anything civilized. She was entirely at his mercy, and could think of no situation she dreaded more.

But she would not, she decided, show fear. She refused to cower or avert her gaze from the terrible reality of his countenance. If she were to die here, in this remote and awful place, she would do so with courage, looking her slayer full in the face.

To her surprise, however, he averted his face from her and moved around so that his back was to her as he fed the fire. Soon the blaze was burning brightly, and though she feared that smoke would rapidly gather, the air stayed breathable and soon lost its chill. She supposed that there must be a natural chimney in the ceiling of the cave.

When she looked around, she saw that the cave was about thirty feet across. Near the fire were a neatly stacked pile of firewood, several earthenware jugs, a small wooden box, and a pallet made up of bags stuffed with dried grass.

When Adam finally stood up, he kept his head down so that it was lost in shadows. "There is wood there," he said, pointing to it. "Use all that you want. When you run low, I will provide you with more. Those jugs are filled with fresh water, the box with dried meat and fruit, as well as carrots and potatoes you can cook over the fire on that pointed stick."

He was quiet for a moment, then cleared his throat and looked away. "When you need to relieve yourself, there is a bucket behind that rock. I am sorry the accommodations are not more pleasant." She detected no note of irony in his voice. "If your fiance does as I say, you will not stay here for long."

"Why *am* I here?" she asked. "What are you going to do to me?"

He knelt by the fire, but the posture in no way made him less hulking and threatening. "Nothing, if Herr Kreutzer wisely follows my directions to return to Darkon. If he does, you will join him there."

"And if he does not?"

"I always keep my word. You will die."

She did not think she could feel more frightened, but hearing her fate from his lips chilled her to the core. "Why do you want us to return there?"

"It does not matter to me in the least where you go, so long as you do not stay in Schloss Mordenheim. I know your intent, and believe me when I say that Doctor Mordenheim's wife must never be restored. I know that he cannot do it by himself, but I do not know how effective *your* powers may be. Therefore, you must be removed."

"Why did you not simply kill us both?" Hilda asked, afraid that her question might give him the notion.

"Contrary to the myths that have grown up around me," Adam said, "I am not the bloodthirsty monster that some think. There is but one person that I wish to see suffer, and that one is Victor Mordenheim, whom I hate with a hatred that could girdle this world."

"You have never killed anyone?"

"I *have* killed!" he roared, leaping to his feet so that she drew back in fright. "Yes, I have killed when people make me grow so angry that I cannot help but lash out! When people try to deny me the birthright of every man! When they look at me and scream because I am different from them, and try to kill me because of it!"

His voice dropped dangerously low. "Yes, it is then I kill and feel no guilt in it. And I will feel no guilt should I have to kill you. Now, give me your blanket and cloak."

Hilda drew them both tightly around her. "Why?"

Adam lowered his head, as if suddenly unwilling to meet her gaze. "Do not fear. I have no plans to do other than release you or kill you. The cave is warm enough now. If you have no outer garments, you will not try to escape."

Slowly she unwrapped the blanket from around her

body and unclasped the cloak, then handed them both over to him. The nightgown that she wore was made of a heavy cotton and revealed no more than a dress would have. Nevertheless, she felt naked before him.

He took the garments, scarcely looking at her, and she realized that this murdering monster was actually shy in her presence. The revelation surprised her. She should have known immediately, but her terror had been so great that it had stifled her psychic and empathetic abilities.

When she analyzed her situation, she instantly realized that the matter was out of her hands. There was no reason not to relax and try to empathize with what this creature was feeling and thinking.

"I'll try to bring you fresh meat," he said, holding the blanket and cloak awkwardly in his huge hands. He seemed to want to leave, yet could not, and the unmistakable impression crossed her mind that this man, if man he was, was lonely, no doubt the loneliest creature in this world.

The impressions began to come to her more quickly then. She sensed intelligence, frustration, anger, desire, need, and . . .

Yes, there was evil there too. She did not know if she could believe his claim that he struck and killed only out of rage. And then she grimly realized that if killing out of anger was not evil, she did not know what was. Even so, it was an evil she could understand, though not pardon.

Standing before her now, he seemed like an immense child with all the confused and confusing attributes of the young. But he was a dangerous child, a child that would kill with little provocation. Still, she wondered if he was as diabolical as Mordenheim had painted him. She had felt more diabolism from Mordenheim than from this frightening yet pitiful thing called Adam.

For he was pitiful. And horrible. Knowing that he had been pieced together from chunks of the dead was dreadful enough. But seeing the results of the handiwork, the scars that crisscrossed the face and neck and hands, the face on which nothing quite fit together, the eyes that would have looked more at home floating in alcohol in a specimen jar, made it far worse. Alone in the bowels of the earth with a dead thing . . .

She dismissed the thought from her mind. This was no way to communicate with him, and she needed to do that desperately—it was the only thing that could save her life. But she would not have the chance now, for Adam turned and started to leave the cave. "Wait!" she said. He turned, and she did not know what to say next. "You . . . you would not leave me here alone?"

He smiled then, without showing his teeth. "And what horror you find here could be greater than myself?" He disappeared into the darkness, leaving her alone.

That had been countless hours or days ago. Now she sat as she had been sitting for she knew not how long, eating when she was hungry, drinking when thirsty, sleeping when she was tired, feeding the fire, and thinking, thinking nearly all the time.

She did not believe for a moment that Friedrich would return to Il Aluk while she was in Adam's hands. Dear foolish boy, he would probably want to come after them immediately, and she hoped that Mordenheim had enough sense to talk him out of it.

Perhaps they could get a contingent of people from Ludendorf to brave the dangers of the Sea of Sorrows and the Isle of Agony. They would not do it for Mordenheim, not for a stranger like Friedrich, but perhaps they would do it to rid their land once and for all of Adam. She was certain Adam made raids upon the Lamordians. Where else would he have obtained the sheep to make the dried mutton that she subsisted on, or the dried fruits from beyond Lamordia? Hilda could all too easily imagine him being discovered by a merchant or a shepherd or a farmer's wife, and Adam's fury at their reactions. She had sensed such rage in him, such bitterness and anger, that she was sure it would take very little to set him off like a keg of dry gunpowder.

But he must *not* be set off. That was the crux of her problem. Sooner or later Adam would discover that Friedrich had not done as he had ordered. And then what? Would he kill her? It was a distinct possibility. Yet there was a difference between striking down a person who was trying to kill you and murdering a woman in cold blood. She could not sense if Adam was capable of that. But with all the tales of horror he had inspired, she supposed he was.

Then she would have to make herself more than a victim to him. If she could persuade him to speak, to tell his side of things, if she could be the sole sympathetic ear he had ever had listen to his sorrows, then perhaps he would spare her when the moment of decision came, as come it must.

But first she would have to speak to him, and she had slept twice since he had brought her to the cave. Time must be passing swiftly, and soon Friedrich and her would-be rescuers would arrive, or Adam would go to the castle and learn that Friedrich had no intention of leaving. She determined to see Adam again before those things happened, feel him out, gauge his emotions, speak on more intimate terms with him.

But it must be soon. There was little time to waste.

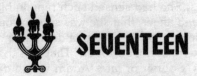

SEVENTEEN

She was different; he had been right. When he awoke her in her room, she tried to scream, but anyone would have. It was later in the boat, crossing the ice, and in the cave, that her true spirit was revealed.

And a brave spirit it was. Any other woman he had ever seen, and a good many of the men, would have shrieked until the cave resounded with it and stopped only when their throats began to bleed. But not this one.

Adam breathed the icy air in deeply and let it hiss back out again. The cold posed no danger to him. He sat on a rock at the southeast edge of the island and looked into the field of whiteness. Above was the falling snow, settling on his shoulders like an ermine robe. Below were the floes, made even more treacherous by the layer of snow over them, so that one could no longer see the cracks or the darker texture of thinner ice. Every step would now necessitate driving a pike into the covered surface before one's feet.

The creature knew that he should cross the ice to the mainland and see if Kreutzer was still a guest of Mordenheim's. But he could not bring himself to leave the island. Even though he had not returned to the cave since he had taken Hilda Von Karlsfeld there, the knowledge of her presence here in his domain kept him from leaving it.

With all his heart, he wanted to see her again, and yet he did not want to. The first grown woman ever to bravely meet his eyes, and he was afraid to look into her face. But perhaps afraid wasn't the right word. Rather, he was ashamed. Ashamed to see disgust, revulsion, or even pity in her forthright gaze.

She had spoken to him, asked him questions, had tried to get a better look at him when he turned away from her. Was it scientific curiosity that emboldened her? Was she as cold and clinical and calculating as Mordenheim himself?

Adam did not think so.

He picked up a rock and tossed it into the teeth of the storm. As if in response, a gust of wind threw a mist of cold, wet flakes into his eyes. He blinked them away, scarcely noticing them, and stood up. He had not even looked for fresh meat, even though he knew there were caribou on the island now. If he had killed one, he would have had to take the meat into the cave for her.

Why was he such a coward? This woman could do him no harm. He had set up mental defenses against such womanly pain years before, after his first encounter with glorious, radiant Elise Mordenheim, who had treated him like the dead offal he was. He could not be hurt by women's looks again.

Very well then. There was no need to avoid her. He had made his decision. He would cross the ice and learn how Kreutzer had reacted to his decision. But first he would see to the woman in the cave and make sure that she was well provided for in his absence.

He called out when he was several dozen yards from her chamber. "Hello? I am coming in."

"Yes, hello." Her voice thrilled him. He was unused to hearing voices addressed to him that were not raised in anger or fright, and hearing another voice on this island was a new experience altogether.

She was standing by the fire when he entered, an uncertain smile on her face. He did not smile in return, recalling the first and last time he had ever smiled at a woman. "I am leaving for a time," he said. "I simply wished to make sure that you had enough firewood, and enough to eat and drink."

"Leave me?" She grew pale. "Alone on this island?"

"You should be all right."

"But you could be gone for days. How long is it since you were here last?"

"Less than one day."

"I thought it was longer. I slept twice."

"You were weary from the journey. And time passes slowly when . . . when you are alone."

"What if wolves should find the cave? Or other beasts?"

He had thought about that when he was making his plans, but at that time he had no concern as to whether or not his unwilling guest was devoured. Now the thought made him uncomfortable. "There are . . . few wolves that come here."

"But if they do, won't they sense the warmth, enter the cave? What could I do if they did?"

The mouth of the cave was too large to seal, and Adam hesitated, saying nothing.

"Please don't leave me alone," Hilda said. "Why not bind me and take me back with you to see if Friedrich has left. If he has, you can let me go. If not . . ." she looked away into a dark corner ". . . you can do what you must."

He looked at her without dropping his gaze. She knew that he had the upper hand. "You realize what you're saying? You're saying that you would accept my killing you?"

She shook her head sadly. "I'm involved in something beyond my expectations. Or my comprehension.

Friedrich and I came to Lamordia for what we thought was a simple magical ceremony. And instead . . ." She shrugged helplessly.

"Mordenheim lied to you then," Adam said.

"I don't know. I don't know anymore what are lies and what's the truth."

"What did he tell you about me? About Elise and . . . and Eva."

Hilda pressed her lips together, then decided there was no point in prevarication. "He said you killed the little girl, and then tried to kill his wife."

Adam released a long sigh. "What else did he say about me? How else did he paint me as a soulless monstrosity? Tell me. Tell me all." He sat with his back against the cave wall, his knees up, and waited for her story.

So Hilda related to him everything that Mordenheim had told her, with as many details as she could remember. When she came to the night when Eva had died and Elise was attacked, she noticed that he was gripping his arms and breathing more heavily than before, and she told the harsh tale more gently.

"And he has ever since been trying to bring his wife back to health," she concluded.

Adam abruptly stood up and gave a cry of derision. "And did you believe him? Did you accept every word?"

"I . . . what else were we to do? We had one side of the story only. In truth, I felt that he was painting himself in a more virtuous light than he probably deserved, but there was no reason why I should not have believed him."

"And do you believe him *still?*"

She thought for a moment. "I don't know. I do know that I should very much like to hear your side of what occurred."

"My side?" He looked at her as though she were deceiving him.

"Yes. Being in your presence, if only for a short time, I do not see the ruthless monster that Mordenheim made you out to be. I should be particularly interested in what happened on that night that Eva disappeared."

"You want to hear . . . my story?" It seemed incomprehensible to him.

She nodded. "Please. I would be honored."

Adam seemed dazed. He sat again, nearer the fire this time. "All right. All right then. I'll tell you how it happened. How it really was."

And he told her the truth as he knew it.

 # EIGHTEEN

Of my creation—or my rebirth—I can tell you little. I remember only a great deal of pain and opening my eyes to gaze into the eyes of a madman.

For that is what Victor Mordenheim, my father, my tormentor, my nemesis, is. Note well that I do not call him my creator, for although it was he who raggedly knit these pitiful parts together into the semblance of a man, it was not he who put breath into these dead lungs. But of that, more anon.

As I say, it was a pair of mad eyes that I first beheld, so is it any wonder that I myself have become mad? I was not created a monster but learned to be monstrous from my mentor and tutor. Mordenheim's sole obsession, before and since my creation, was to take cold flesh and not only make it warm again—which is affront enough to the gods—but to make that flesh more than himself.

From the first, even without understanding the morality of men beyond any vestigial sense that remained in my reanimated brain, I sensed something wrong about Mordenheim. As he led me to my room for the first time, he seemed frenzied, feverish, expectant, with a half-smile on his wan face. He expected me to fall immediately into accord with his wishes and go to sleep—I who had never been awake in this life.

When at last he gave up and left me alone that first

night, I stood at the barred window, looking out at the sea and the blank face of the moon that was, I felt, my face, for I had no idea of my appearance. If I had, perhaps I would have battered my head against the stones of my cell until I had exposed that brain that I bear within.

During the next few days, Mordenheim taught me the things he felt I should know, beginning with the most elementary of concepts and proceeding into those more difficult. I mastered all with ease. The subjects came easily to me, as though I had always known them but merely forgotten and had only to be reminded.

Would that my physical control had been mastered as easily. Whatever body my brain had previously occupied could not have been the equal of this new, man-made one. In short, I did not yet know my own strength, as the doctor was quick to learn when he brought in a bird to show me.

It was a finch, and as it perched on Mordenheim's finger and began to sing, I had never heard anything so beautiful, for the only sounds to which I had been exposed were Mordenheim's voice and the roar of the waves and the wind, as well as the harsh croak of my own poor voice. So the finch's song came over me like a healing balm that soothed my turbulent spirit. When the doctor held out the creature for me to touch, I could not wait to come into physical contact with this tiny miracle that made such glorious music.

My enthusiasm proved the little thing's undoing, for my fingers, as though with a will of their own, came down upon it too heavily, driving the life from its body. I was even more surprised than Mordenheim and drew back in remorse and, yes, shock, that my body had gotten away from the control of my mind. Though I had not seen death before, I knew that something was terribly wrong with the creature. The doctor reprimanded me, and then I spoke to him fleetingly about death, a subject with which he of all people was well versed.

One thing led to another, and as he was explaining the concept of male and female to me, we were interrupted by a knock on the heavy door. Mordenheim was furious at being disturbed, but when he learned that his wife Elise had arrived, he changed completely, and was beaming as he thrust a book into my hands and told me that there was someone I must meet, and remember to smile.

Smile. That was one concept he should not have taught me. For such expressions of emotion can only come from nature, not from a feeble attempt to show what one does not feel. But with me, even when I did feel the emotions that create a smile, the effect was less than satisfactory.

I had devoured the contents of the simple book within minutes, and now I stood in the middle of the room, waiting to meet whomever Mordenheim cared to introduce me to. Eventually the door swung open, and there on the threshold stood a creature who made the finch look rank and drab, and the moon's face dull and lifeless. I was stunned at the beauty of this example of the womanhood of which the doctor had been speaking just minutes earlier, and my reaction to it was something I had never done before.

I smiled.

Yes, fancy that. The monster with the face stitched together from discordant patches of scar tissue smiled its dead smile from its dead heart. It is little wonder that she screamed. And then she fainted dead away, unable to bear the sight of me.

I reacted so fast that I did not have to think, but I suppose my subconscious recalled what had happened with the bird, so I caught Elise Mordenheim gently before she hit the floor and lifted her in my arms, and looked down into that face, the face of all womanhood, so lovely, so ineffable . . . and so distant from me in all ways. I looked at her with joy that there was such beauty in this world and with grief that it was inaccessible to a vile thing such as myself.

I would not have harmed her, not then, not ever. But Mordenheim spoke to me as though I were about to throttle the woman at any moment. I suppose he was so nervous because of what he had witnessed with the bird. But I did as he bade me and gently handed his wife over to him. He kept his eye on me as he backed out the door, closing it behind him.

I thought a great deal about what had happened. Though I struggled to banish Elise Mordenheim from my mind, I could not. Her image remained ever before me, like a guiding angel. And the more I learned from the books about the world, about men and women, about society, the more I knew I was a being that could never be in the society of one such as she. Even the plague-ridden harlots of the filthiest streets of the foulest cities would react as she had.

So the next time Mordenheim came to see me, I had questions for him, more than ever before. I began with a statement that was all too obviously true.

"I am not like other men," I said.

"How do you know that?" he asked me. "The only other men you have seen are Horg and myself. There is a great variety among the human species."

I shook my head. "No. I have seen in the engravings in the books what normal men are like. They are like you. Horg and I are different."

"Horg was born the way he is."

"As was I," I said, looking with accusation at my self-styled creator. "Why did you make me in this form?"

"Because I *intended* for you to be different. I wanted you to be something more than human, something splendid—and that you most assuredly are."

"Your wife did not find me so. She screamed when she saw me. I believe she found me frightening."

"She was . . ." he paused to knit a fabrication ". . . awe-struck, that is all."

"No. I think you are lying to me. She thought me ugly."

"She did not."

"She *did!*" I pounded a fist on the table, and Morden-heim recoiled. Then I told him what I have felt every moment since hearing Elise Mordenheim scream at the sight of me. "You should have made me . . . like other men."

"I'm sorry," the doctor said. "You will see in time that the advantages of the way you are far outweigh the dis-advantages. But you must learn self-control. You must not use violence or strike things. Normal men do not do that."

"And I am not a normal man," I said, standing up so that my head almost touched the ceiling. Then I walked to the barred window, looked out at the dark sea, and said softly, "Why did you make me at all?"

Mordenheim tried to explain, but I had heard his answers before and did not respond to his words.

After a time he left, and I brooded over my state of affairs and the knowledge of what I was. But shortly, that thought was displaced by the haunting image of Elise Mordenheim, and I knew that I had to see her again. Just to gaze on that lovely face was ecstasy beyond imagination—it was the beauty of which I had read in books given living flesh.

Her scent was still strong in my nostrils—a mingling of jasmine and woodbine, and, though I had never been in other parts of the castle, I knew I could find her merely by following that exhilarating odor.

I waited until late at night when I felt she might be

asleep and the doctor working or reading in his lab. Then I opened the unlocked door of my cell and crept quietly out, down the stairs, through the halls, and past the door of Mordenheim's laboratory. The door was ajar, but I did not see him within and moved on.

I crossed the terrace, scarcely looking at the sky overhead, which I had only so far glimpsed out my window. I ascended the steps to Mordenheim's living quarters and went down the dimly lit hall until I came to a door behind whose heavy panels I could not only detect the scent of Elise Mordenheim's perfume, but also hear the soft sound of her breathing.

The door made not a sound as I opened it, and I walked into the bedchamber, guided by the sound and the scent of her behind the closed bed curtains. Exercising every bit of my restraint and self-control, I opened those delicate curtains as gently as parting the closed wings of a butterfly, and in the dim yellow glow looked down upon her face.

I swear to you that is all I wanted, to merely behold her placid countenance, not harm her or profane her beauty by touching her face with my blunt and rough fingers. When I saw her there, I could not help but gasp at the sight of her, her golden hair spread over the pillow, the sweet blossoms of pink in her cheeks.

At the sound she awoke and saw my form outlined against the light. She lost no time in screaming—she no doubt thought—for her life. Her cries froze me to the spot, for the last thing that I wanted to do was to terrify her, and I whispered, "No, no," over and over to her, but I doubt that she heard me over her cries.

Then, after what seemed an eternity of shrieking on her part and indecision on mine, I heard Victor Mordenheim call my name from the doorway. His voice seemed to break the spell that held me, and I turned toward him, able to obey his harsh command to come away from there. I did so, and did not look back or look up. Ashamed, I kept my head down until I was back in my little cell, and Mordenheim, that father of monsters, locked the door on me.

It was then that the full knowledge of my hatred of him came upon me. It had been growing in my idle hours—and most of them were idle, for I quickly absorbed the contents of the books he gave me to read—and now, with this second rejection from Elise Mordenheim, it blossomed fully.

While I was filled with the knowledge that Mordenheim had given me access to, I was filled even more with loathing for the doctor and for myself. I recognized at last the extent of my physical ugliness. Having been made from corpses, there was no way I could ever have been as beautiful as that blind fool Mordenheim thought me.

The other thing I recognized then was the ugliness in my spirit. I knew—and *know*—that if I am not utterly devoid of this strange quality called morality, I am at least lacking in it. These philosophers and pedants in the books who talk about the good, the right, the just—all of them are fools as great as the doctor! In my short life, there has never been any justice. I never asked to be created, to be brought to a life where the first woman I ever saw screamed at the sight of me. I did not ask to be a behemoth, towering over other men, dwarfing them both in size and hideousness.

I knew all too well what the doctor eventually planned to do with me—take me among the populace and exhibit me. Not as in the fairs, perhaps, but among those who would poke and probe and examine, who would treat me as the laboratory creation I was and had never willed myself to be.

No, the will had been the doctor's. He had stolen me from my rest—or *rests*, if you will—blended my various elements and then resurrected them.

There have been times when I have thought I remember other existences, when I recall, ever so dimly, a lovely pair of eyes gazing up into my own, the sound of what can only be children laughing, perhaps *my* children, and most elusive memory of all, looking into a mirror and seeing a face that did not nurture nightmares.

Then I wonder if I remembered those things in the grave. But try as I might, I can recall nothing after death, unless the beautiful face, the laughter of children, my own seemly countenance might in themselves be the memory of some wonderful place to which my spirit had gone after death . . . and been pulled back from unwillingly into this dead shell, which gives me all the more reason to hate my "maker."

My maker's wife was another matter. It seemed to me as though I had not only known Elise before, perhaps in some other life or afterlife, but that I had loved her there as well. Now to have her turn from me in horror due to what Victor Mordenheim had made of me . . . that could not be borne without vengeance.

My vengeance, however, had to wait. I had to learn more, learn as much as possible. Knowledge was power, and while I had physical power beyond imagining, I needed mental power as well to survive in a world that I knew could only be hostile to me, where everyone I met would fear me and want to either flee from me or destroy me.

So I decided to bide my time until I had taken as much from Victor Mordenheim as I could. And then I would leave to make my own strange way in this hateful world.

 **NINETEEN**

Nearly two months later Eva, the little girl of whom the doctor has told you, came into my life. It was early in the morning when I heard the bar of my cell sliding back and the heavy door opening. There stood the doctor and the little child, her eyes wide. To her I must have been the epitome of every householder who had ever driven her from his door, the embodiment of every drunken fiend who ever tried to catch her.

I tried to hide my face with my hands, but it was too late. She had seen me all too well. And her reaction was of course the same as Elise's had been, pure terror. She squealed and tried to run out of the room, but the doctor grabbed her and twisted her around to confront me, saying, "I *told* you not to be afraid!"

She looked at me one more time, and my face must have been frightening, for on it was mixed shame for my appearance, sympathy for the girl's plight, and fury at Mordenheim for bringing a child to me. Whatever she read there was enough to make her fully scream, and Mordenheim clapped his palm over her mouth to quiet her and shook her as if violent agitation would kill her fear.

"Take her out of here!" I roared, and advanced slightly, as if to bolster my command with a show of strength. It was enough, for he picked up the panting child and backed through the door, slamming it behind him and fitting the bar in place.

I threw myself onto my rustic bed in anguish and self-loathing. Was I now to be tormented with this child's terror as well as Elise's? I could not bear the thought and determined to be gone from the castle before further shame was forced upon me.

But the very next day Mordenheim surprised me by telling me that he was taking me outside for the first time, and I followed him docilely out onto the terrace that I had only seen before in the dark. Once there, I looked up at the sky and the bright sun overhead. With the sun shining in my face and the wind ruffling my hair like unseen fingers, I felt as though I were undergoing a wondrous epiphany, like a man blind from birth who is finally able to see the world around him. I turned slowly about in a circle, beholding for the first time the great dome of blue sky.

Then, suddenly, that sky darkened. Clouds formed out of nowhere, covering the golden eye of the sun, the breeze, grew into a strong wind, then a gust attempted to blow us over. While Mordenheim nearly fell with the effort to remain erect, I could only smile into the force of the wind, drawing back my lips to grin at the powers of nature. I learned later that Eva was peering surreptitiously from her window, and it was a good thing that she could not see my face, for it must have been a terrible sight.

Then, in another minute, as quickly as it had come, the wind died down, and my hair hung lank and lifeless. The clouds, no longer held aloft by the winds, descended to the earth as a thick, wet, clinging fog, making the previously bright light now gray and dismal.

I turned to Mordenheim, and the sad smile on my face must have puzzled him. "Does nature change so quickly then?" I said.

"It does, ofttimes," he answered, though my words had been an observation, not a question.

In the absence of Eva and Elise, my daily walks on the terrace brought novelty to my life, making my desire to leave less insistent. On the sixth such excursion, Mordenheim told me Eva had been watching me all along, and that this day she wanted to allow me to see her.

At his direction, I looked up and saw her push back a curtain and look down at me. Her pretty little face made me smile in spite of myself, and as I felt the unfamiliar expression forming, I remembered Elise's first reaction to it and tried to restrain myself from smiling. The effect must have been comical to the child, for she laughed silently behind the glass. I welcomed the laugh, for I would far rather have inspired mirth in her than horror, and the joy must have been evident on my face, for Eva raised her tiny hand and waved it at me. I waved back, at least what I thought was a wave. She must have seen the good spirit behind it, for she laughed again, and waved at me once more before she vanished behind the curtain.

I saw her for the next several days, and the pleasure of her company, even through the window, soothed my troubled mind. It was as though her innocence changed the evil in my spirit to good in the same way that the stone of the philosophers transformed dull lead to brilliant gold. I could feel myself becoming a better—what? person? man? creature?—by simply observing her most ingenuous act.

For example, she would hold up playthings that I assume Elise had gotten for her—dolls, wooden horses, toy soldiers—and make playful motions with them. I was helpless in the face of such sublime innocence, and I would smile and nod and mimic the motions myself, just like another child might do.

My happiness seemed to annoy Mordenheim. Perhaps he did not care to see his superman behaving like a child, and was appalled that what he considered the greatest scientific achievement of the ages was simpering like a kitten in the presence of a little girl. I was certain of his displeasure when I spoke to him after he had taken me back to my cell, following a walk on the terrace.

"When," I said, "shall I finally meet Eva?"

He snorted. "Don't you remember the last time?"

"That was different. She did not know me then. She was not prepared for my appearance. But now she knows me, knows that fearsome as I may look, I would never harm her."

"No," Mordenheim said. "The time has not come. In fact, I think it would be better if you spent less time in view of Eva. There are so many other things you still have to learn. You've become fixed on that girl to the exclusion of everything else of importance. And I can't have that."

His words showed that he thought of me as nothing more than his property, and I felt hot anger boil within me. He quailed before my scowl. "*You* can't have that?" I said. "As I was your creation, am I also your slave forever?"

"No, of course not. But mentally you're still nothing but a child—"

"All the more reason, then, why I should learn to know other children!"

"*No,* Adam." He stepped to the door. "I want you to stay away from Eva. When I feel the time is right, perhaps you may meet her again. But not before."

His proprietary air infuriated me. "I could crush you like a stick of kindling," I growled at him. "How then can you command me as you do?"

"Because I created you. And because there is no other who would dare." And without another word, Mordenheim slammed the door closed and lowered the heavy bar over it, imprisoning me within, or so he thought.

If he could have heard my thoughts then, he would have blanched and begged me for forgiveness. *No other who would dare,* he had said. But Mordenheim dared only because he thought he owned me. And knew me. But he was wrong on both counts. No one owned me. And I had learned enough of the world from books and Mordenheim's teaching to know that no man alive could stand against me or say me nay. "No other," I whispered in the silence of my cell, "would dare."

But Mordenheim dared. He had dared, first of all, to disinter my disparate parts, reassemble them, and give life again to a creature that was dead and, for all he ever knew, desirous of remaining so. Then he had dared to cage me in that cell, and teach me only what he felt I should be taught. And finally, most audacious of all, he had dared to demand that I should refrain from even seeing the sole person in the world with whom I shared a semblance of human warmth. It tore at my restored innards like a bone saw.

I paced his cell, then walked over to the plate of food that Horg had left there when Mordenheim and I were on the terrace. I took only a few bites, then hurled the rest out through the barred window into the sea below. I did not think it wise to let the doctor see how little I truly needed to sustain both life and my superhuman strength.

Then, alone in my cell, I thought with both joy and sorrow of Eva. Understand that I had nothing but adoration and honor for the two sole members of the female sex I had so far seen. The sight of Elise had been like a vision outside my cell door. I had never beheld anything as beautiful, as altogether wondrous as she, not even when the sun sank over the sea, and red and purple shadows danced on the waves until night came. But she had screamed when she found me at her bedside, and I had never seen her since, though I dreamed of her often in the hour or so of sleep that I required each day.

Then there came Eva—Eva, who had also shrieked in terror when she first saw me. But my first sight of her had been even more exquisite than when I had first seen Elise. Eva had all of Elise's qualities, but combined with them was that innocence that touched my heart. In her I saw everything that I did not and never could possess—a purity that my provenance forbade me from ever acquiring. Her delicacy made her a china doll to the classic sculpture that was Elise, but I swear that I revered them both.

And Eva, unlike Elise, had changed toward me, revised her judgment until she could not only look at me without feeling revulsion, but could laugh, not only at me, but with me. I had seen her hold up her toys, as if in invitation to me to come and play. And now, after that long hoped for and never expected invitation had come, the doctor, my thrice-damned maker, had refused to let me accept it! It galled me, cut into me like the cancer that might have previously killed me, and I continued to walk back and forth in his cell, slamming my fists against the stones of the walls, all the while pondering the injustice of what had been and was being done to me.

I should be Eva's protector, I thought, not the doctor. I would allow no one to harm her, nor even to come near her. Perhaps we could go away together somewhere, into the green wildernesses I had read of, where I could build a small cabin and till the soil. As my imagination continued to bubble, I dreamed of Elise being with us, accepting me, and Elise and I acting as mother and father to Eva, living far from the prying eyes of strangers, being happy always.

But no. I realized the impossibility of my sweet

dream. Elise would never have any feeling for me other than revulsion and terror. But Eva . . .

I thought throughout the day, and by the time night came I had formulated my plan. I determined to break down my door, go to Eva's room, steal her away, and bear her overland to a heavily wooded country far to the east, where I could clear land and establish a homestead. My knowledge of flora and fauna was great, and I had exhausted the contents of the books Mordenheim had given me, though he could scarcely have guessed it.

Yes, it was time to leave Schloss Mordenheim, and if the doctor *dared* to get in my way . . . well, I would know what to do.

 **TWENTY**

I waited until well after midnight. It was impossible to gauge the time from the heavens, for thick mists covered the moon and stars, but my sensitive ears were able to hear the clock in the hall of the Mordenheims' private quarters strike the hour. The doctor would most likely be in his laboratory, reading and writing, and perhaps still experimenting far into the night, so I had to move quietly.

Shattering the door was my first task. While an incredibly strong man might have been able to batter the door until the bar split, I think that no one could have done what I did. Once I had my footing, I pressed slowly against the door until it began to bulge outward, finally reaching the point where the bar began to split. I kept pushing slowly, listening to the soft sounds of the wood fibers breaking inch by inch. Finally it was separated in two, and the pieces fell to the floor as the door creaked open.

I listened in the hall, but heard no sound from the direction of the laboratory. So I walked out the tower door, across the terrace, into the Mordenheims' quarters, and, flanked by rusting suits of armor whose iron gauntlets bore pikes and lances, down the hall that I knew must lead to Eva's room.

At the first door on the right I stopped, since she had waved to me from the window on the right facing the terrace. From inside I could hear her soft breathing and realized I must be careful not to frighten her. If she screamed, the doctor and his wife would come running. I could subdue them, of course, but it would complicate matters, and I did not want Eva to have to see that.

Gingerly, I turned the door handle, pushed inward, then closed it behind me as I surveyed the room. It was uncomfortably warm, and the window through which Eva had waved to me was opened, as was a door that led to a small, decorative balcony. Though this cooled the room, the mists drifting in made it oppressively humid.

I crossed the room, knelt by the side of Eva's little bed, and looked at her sweet, sleeping face. Thinking how happy we would be together, I smiled broadly and gave an involuntary sigh of contentment for the happiness that would be ours.

Just then, Eva opened her eyes and screamed.

It tears at my heart to say it, but I know what she saw—not the big, happy playmate she had watched from her window, but a grinning monster about to devour her, and she shrieked with all the power of her small lungs.

I was panicked, I admit, by the sudden noise in the stillness of the night, and I pressed my hand over her mouth to quiet her until I could explain, and whispered, "No, no, it is I, it is your friend *Adam*." But still she continued to fight me, making mewing noises from beneath my hand.

Then the door burst open behind me, and I saw Elise, her long hair and white nightgown flowing about her, bearing down on me with a decorative pike she must have wrenched from one of the empty suits of armor in the hall. She, too, was screaming, and she thrust at me with the pike.

I tried desperately to explain. "No," I said, "you don't

understand!" But she stabbed at me again, and I felt the flesh rip in my side.

The sensation shocked me, and I involuntarily let Eva go so that I could grasp the pike, twist it out of Elise's hands, and hurl it into a corner. Free, Eva rolled out of the bed and ran in what she must have considered the only direction of escape—out the door onto the balcony.

But her terror had made her speed too great, and she hit the decorative railing with enough force to wrench it from its rusty brackets. Eva grasped the top of the rail as she and it went flying out of sight.

My heart was a cold lump within me as I dashed after her, fearful that she was gone forever. But one of the lower bolts had held where the others had failed, so that the piece of twisted iron had gone out and down only a few feet before slamming into the stone wall. Somehow she had managed to hang on, and now she dangled over the sea that crashed on the rocks below, too terrified to scream, fearing no doubt that her slightest movement would plunge her into the gulf.

When I saw her hanging on with both hands to the railing, swinging like a pendulum in the wind from the sea, I fell on my stomach and reached down for her with both hands.

She screamed again, closed her eyes and twisted her head away from me. But I had to save her in spite of her terror of me. I stretched down as far as I could, shifting my torso on the flagstones, trying to dig in with the toes of my heavy shoes, reaching down until finally my fingers just touched her right wrist. She squealed at the contact, and jerked her right hand away so that now she clung to life only with her left. I had to act instantly.

I lurched farther out over the edge until I thought I might tumble over myself, then stretched my arm down and down until my fingers brushed the sleeve of her nightgown. I grasped her then with a grip of steel, and her screams rattled in my ears as her fingers released the ironwork. Now I was her only hold to life.

Just as I was about to draw her up in one swift move, a terrible pain shot through me, and I knew that I had been pierced with the pike I had wrenched from Elise. May the gods forgive me, but the wound startled and weakened me so that my grip on Eva slackened just enough for her arm to slide down the sleeve of her nightgown. I scrabbled for her flesh, but it was too late. I heard the harsh rip of fabric—

And then I held nothing but a scrap of white, bloody cloth.

I cried out in rage as I twisted my body around and lunged back onto the tiny balcony. The pike was still sticking in my flesh, just below my lung. Lying on my side, I reached behind me, yanked it out, and hurled it into the abyss, ignoring Elise, who was screaming and battering me with her fists. The pike had harmed me, but her feeble blows could not.

I could only look at her in disbelief as she struck me over and over, look at her and realize that she was the cause of Eva's death, not me, that I had tried with every effort of my will to save her, while everything Elise had done had only ensured her fall.

With Eva's tattered sleeve still clenched in my hand, I stood up. I felt all the hatred that had grown and festered in me come to the surface in a palpable wave that made me shudder—hatred for Mordenheim, for a world that would never accept me as anything but a monster, for Elise's rash acts and lack of understanding, and for my own pitiful and blundering self.

I advanced on Elise with hatred filling every cell in my dead-alive body—my gaze, the lineaments of my face, in the set of my body. And at the sight of that burning hatred, she screamed and screamed and screamed

again until there was nowhere to go, and I began to
release that hatred in the only way I knew how—with
fists that had become bludgeons.

I beat her to the point of death.

I had begun by adoring her, but I was now unable to
help myself. When I looked in her maddened face, I saw
the woman who had caused Eva's death. And too, the
sneering, all-knowing face of Victor Mordenheim, the
source of all my sorrow, all my misery, my death in life.

I make no apology for my deed. Perhaps that is how I
know evil dwells in my spirit. I felt no remorse, no
regret, no shame for what I did to Elise Mordenheim. I
caused her pain, and I caused Mordenheim pain. I
would do nothing differently. If that makes me a monster, so be it.

All the time I beat her, I held the scrap of Eva's nightgown in my fist, until it was soaked with Elise's blood. I
stopped hitting her only when the red rage began to
subside, when I could *see* the rage flowing out of me as
her blood flowed out of her, and finally my spirit was
empty of hatred.

I left her lying in her own blood then and sought the
darkest corner of the room, I suppose to merge with the
blackness of my accursed spirit. There I stood, my
shoulders hunched, bleak despair replacing my former
fury, until I heard Mordenheim's footsteps rushing down
the hall.

He ran into the room, looked at his wife for a long
moment, and then his mad gaze found me. I straight-
ened, ready for his justice, and he raised his gun. The
pistol exploded, its flames blinding me for a split second, but I did not try to dodge out of harm's way. It was
only when the bullet struck me in the shoulder, searing
skin and muscle like a hot iron, only when Mordenheim
hurt me once more that I knew how much I still loathed
him, and could not die my second death until making

him suffer ten times what his wife already had.

I roared with the pain of the wound and with the thought that it might even now be too late for my revenge, for the force of the shot had driven me backward toward the open balcony door. Then Mordenheim fired his other shot.

The second bullet caught me in the hip, thrusting me backward onto the balcony. Desperately I windmilled my arms, trying not to fall, but to no avail. I plunged over the edge, following my beloved Eva into the mist, the cruel rocks, the savage sea so far below.

As I fell, I was surprised to find that I looked forward to the oblivion that quickly followed.

 **TWENTY-ONE**

When I opened my eyes again, I hoped at first that I was in the afterlife, but quickly learned otherwise. The afterlife I had hoped for had warm and sandy beaches, not rocky strands where shards of ice melted slowly in the dim spring sun. My expected afterlife had me wearing a body whose flesh was clean and clear and flawless, not one stitched crudely together. No, I was all too alive.

I stood upon my feet, spitting the dregs of salt water from my mouth. My clothes were sodden and torn, and I was pocked with small cuts from having washed up on the rocks and ice. But the wounds in my side and back that the pike had made, as well as the two bullet wounds, were nowhere to be seen. There was only my gray skin, unmarked save for the stitches that held my various parts together.

In a near panic, I wondered what had happened. Had Mordenheim's science made me impervious to wounds? Could I not die at all? Was I doomed to live forever as this monstrous amalgam of flesh?

I looked about, wondering where I had washed up. The mists were hanging high enough in the air that I could see several flat, unappealing islands across the water, and beyond them, farther still, a long stretch of what might be mainland. As I looked more closely, I could just make out a structure of some sort at its highest point, and wondered if the building might be Schloss Mordenheim atop its cliff. If so, I was on one of the islands of the Finger, a broken archipelago extending far out into the chilly Sea of Sorrows.

When I turned and looked at the topography of the island I was on, I saw that it was much larger than its fellows and knew I must be on that land called the Isle of Agony. It could be nowhere else, for I could see several miles to the high center of the island. From that point, it would be easy to see the whole of the mainland.

Though the strand was barren, there were signs of vegetation farther inland, and as I looked toward the rugged rise at the island's center, I saw numerous caves dotting the surface of the land. There was no sign of human habitation.

Very well, then, I thought. This would be my home. And my base of operations, from which I would carry out what had become my life's work. I would wreak my revenge on Mordenheim—for creating me in the first place, for turning me into a monster, and for turning Eva against me and bringing about the circumstances that led to her death, and my own unwarranted destruction of Elise. Now I would have my vengeance. I would not kill Mordenheim, but I would make him wish for death a thousand times. I would see him grow old, every day a torture of living. And if there was justice in the world, even old age would not bring the peace of death that Mordenheim would so desperately crave. If death would not come for me, neither should it come for Mordenheim. We should be bound, maker and monster.

So I fell to my knees on the strand, ignoring the sharp rocks that tore into my flesh, and bellowed up at the sky. "Hear me, oh gods, if such you be! Harken, you beings of power that rule this land! If you be jealous

gods, if you rejoice in seeing the proud brought low, if
you glee in dark justice, heed my plea! Let Victor Mordenheim feel what I feel, let my fate be his and his
mine, and let there be no pain between us that is not
shared! Do this for me, and I swear I will serve your
ends—for evil or for good as you will!"

A rumble of thunder rattled the island, and I felt the
strength of the gods in this movement of nature from
the ends of my hair to the horny pads of my feet. Winds
whipped in from the sea, momentarily blinding me with
salt spray, but I opened my eyes, rose to my feet, and
stretched my arms wide, laughing for the first time into
the gale, knowing that my dark desire had been
granted.

At that moment I thought I could feel Mordenheim's
pain at the loss of Elise, and I hoped that Mordenheim
could feel my pain as well, the hundred little cuts and
bruises made by rock and ice. They would be slight, but
they would let Mordenheim know that I had not perished, that our shared story was far from over, that Mordenheim had a twin spirit with no other intended goal
than his utter destruction, his eternal damnation to a
self-made inferno.

Soon I would go to the mainland, to "share" in Victor
Mordenheim's grief, to relish in his pain.

To see how much deeper I could drive him into
damnation.

The first time I visited him, I scaled the wall of the
castle very early in the morning and found that Mordenheim had retired to his bed. But I also found Elise Mordenheim. Through the window of the laboratory, I saw
her ruined body, kept in the state of living death to
which he has consigned her—not from love but from
pride and his stubborn insistence that he should one
day restore her to health. At first I shook my head
sadly, but then I saw that here was the most delicious

way to torment the good doctor—by taunting him with
his inability to resurrect his wife's warm corpse.

Climbing down to the strand once again, I remained
there until I saw him several hours later, looking out the
window of his laboratory at the sea. His face was hag-
gard and gaunt, and his eyes, even from a distance,
looked more insane than ever. I called his name, and he
jerked as though a shock of electricity had passed
through him, then looked down at me.

His eyes grew even more mad, and I tried to add to
that madness by taunting him with his wife's death. But
he shouted down to me in a rough and croaking voice
that she still lived. We exchanged a few more insults,
when suddenly he thrust a long rifle through the window
and fired down upon me, hitting me fully in the chest so
that I fell back into the roiling surf.

But even as I fell I could see him grasp his own chest
and hear him cry out in pain, and I knew that he felt the
impact of the bullet as surely as had I, and I laughed
weakly as the waves crashed over me, and the pain
slowly left me, and my wound healed; I knew then that
the gods—or whatever they were—had heard my plea,
and I knew too what else those angry and jealous gods
had done for Victor Mordenheim.

I stood then and called up to him, telling him to be
proud since he was a monster who was able to make
not one but two others in his image—his wife and me.
Then I said the thing that rankled him most:

"I call you 'Maker,' Mordenheim, but not '*Creator!*'
You sewed my limbs together, you put the organs
within my trunk, you neatly fit the brain inside the cavity of my skull. But you did not give the spark of life to
those dead chunks, you poor fool! The *gods* did that,
Mordenheim, to torture you for your ignorant boldness!
You thought that you could become a god by creating
life, and the gods punished you by granting what you

had hoped to achieve with your own hands and mind!"

"No!" he howled from high above, but I went on, my words flying up at him like savage hawks.

"The surest way to damn a man is to give him what he wishes. So the gods gave life to my lifeless flesh and a spirit whose darkness any normal man would have seen as soon as he gazed into my eyes! But not you! You were blinded by your vanity to what others could clearly see!

"The gods gave me life that I might torment you with your failure—I am the torturer to whom they have condemned you. I have taken your wife, and you shall hear my mocking laughter in your ears every day and night as you struggle and fail to make her yours again!

"Farewell, fool! Live on with your dead shell of a bride! You shall see me again. . . ."

And so I came back to this, my island, where I have dwelt ever since, save for when I am forced to forage for provisions on the mainland or venture out to torment Victor Mordenheim.

If the gods have any purpose for me, it is this: to despoil his work, to block his every effort to bring his wife back to health. And if it were not the gods' will, I should do it nonetheless. For I loathe Mordenheim for making me what I am and tempting me with glimpses of a humanity I can never fully achieve.

Oh, I have tried. The very first time I ever came into contact with any humans other than those at the castle, I tried with all my heart to accomplish my ends in a civilized manner. It was on the leeward side of the mountain range known as the Sleeping Beast. I thought it best to avoid the village of Ludendorf and to deal rather with one person at a time. They would undoubtedly be frightened when they saw me, but if I could overcome their fear long enough, I might be able to explain my situation and offer work for food. After all, my speech is certainly as eloquent as that of the average farmer or shepherd, and I felt that my great strength might make me of use to settlers who wanted logs split or boulders moved.

I should have known better. But I learned the truth at the first farm I entered, where three dogs immediately began barking at me and snapping at my ankles. I held back the anger that bade me kick at them and continued to walk toward the little cabin, hoping Mordenheim was even now feeling the nipping of sharp teeth at his own bony ankles.

The front door opened a crack as I stepped onto the flat slab of wood that served as a poor porch, and then slammed shut immediately. I stopped, though I tried to keep my legs moving so the dogs would have a more difficult target.

"Hello in there," I said. "Do you have some work I could do for food?"

My only answer was an attack with a long scythe. The cabin must have had a back door, and the householder had exited through it, grabbed the weapon nearest at hand, and was coming around the side of the cabin, the implement drawn back and ready to swing.

I ducked under it, for I did not know if my marvelous rehabilitative powers included anything as drastic as decapitation. The rusty blade of the scythe swung over my head, and before the farmer could ready himself for another swipe, I had grasped the handle and wrenched it away from him.

No sooner had I done so than I felt a deep pain in my back, where the good farmer's wife, who had crept up on me from the other side of the cabin, had buried a sickle blade, and now tried to wrench it back out again. I agonized as she tugged at it, and then my vision swam in red. Furious at this savage hospitality, I swung the scythe blindly around, and nearly sheared the woman in twain. The man leapt on me, and I shook him off as easily as I did the dogs, who now jumped at my face, snapping with their powerful jaws.

Then I killed the man and the three dogs. And with them I killed the hope that I should ever be welcomed as anything less than a monster. I took what food I wanted, slew one of their sheep, and made ready to carry all back with me to my island. Their small amount of money I left behind, for where could I ever spend it? No, my strength would be my coin. It would have to take for me what I could not buy from screaming and fear-maddened merchants.

Inside the cabin, I also found a child in a cradle, and I thought of leaving it with the money. If someone found it, well and good. If not, it would simply not grow up to be as ignorant and violent as its dead parents, and of all those in the vicinity.

But then I knew I could not. If I left it, it could starve to death. The only way to keep it from that suffering would be to kill it instantly, and I could not do such a thing, for its innocence put me in mind of my own naivete.

So I concocted a makeshift sling out of a blanket, and secured the child so that it hung down in front of my chest. It neither cried nor screamed, only looked up into my face with no expression whatsoever, and I remember thinking that at least a little child found nothing to fear in my countenance, and that fear, like so many other negative emotions, needs to be firmly taught to be fully learned.

Baron Von Aubrecker's castle was the nearest place with inhabitants, so I turned my steps in its direction, thinking I could leave the baby nearby where those who lived in or near the castle would be certain to find it.

As we walked through the woods, the baby, apparently relishing the swinging motion of my gait, began to cluck softly to itself, then gave a series of little gurgles that alarmed me until I looked down and saw that it was smiling. I chuckled myself and walked with more of a bounce in my step to increase the pleasurable motion for the child.

It was scarcely a mile from Von Aubrecker's ancient pile that I came upon a hunting party of five of the Baron's men. So entranced was I by the baby's cooing that I did not even notice them until they were only fifty yards away. Then all at once I caught the scent of their gunpowder and heard the sound of their footsteps, which until then had been muffled by the sighing of the pines in the wind. They saw me at the same time, and cried out at the sight of me. Before I could hold up a hand or say a word, five long rifles went to five shoulders, and the only thing left for me to do was turn and protect the child from the bullets with my own body.

This I did, dropping the dead sheep and other food, and ran as fast as my leaping legs could carry me into the underbrush. I heard the rifles crack behind me and felt more than one lead ball slam deep into my back. Their force nearly threw me down, but knowing that if I fell I would land on the baby, I managed to stay erect, staggering through the woods until the pain began to fade and the wounds to heal. Even then I did not stop, but continued to run, putting as much distance as possible between me and the hunters for the child's sake, not for my own.

Some time later I slowed and drew back the bit of blanket that had flopped over the baby's face. But I stopped fully when I saw that face was white and pale, and the blanket sling red with blood. One of the balls had passed through my body and struck the little thing, killing it instantly, or so I prayed. Its eyes were still open, and there remained a tiny smile on its face, as though its last emotion had been joy in my wild running.

I buried it beneath a tree, wrapped in the blanket, and walked on, more alone than ever, thinking of the men who had fired blindly and stupidly and deciding that I would go back and kill them, if not that day, sometime in the future. Though I had had only a glimpse of each, it was enough to mark them in my memory. Over the years, each has died mysteriously and unpleasantly. Each was typical of the race of mankind.

Nothing has happened in the intervening years to make me change my mind or my opinion of humanity. Every creature with whom I have come into contact, human or animal, has treated me with fear, hatred, and revulsion, so that I not only hate Mordenheim all the more but hate every other living thing as well. Why should I ever expect kindness or even indifference when every response to my overtures has been with weapon or fist or fang, and even the innocent suffer because of it?

So I take what I need. If the owners attack me, I kill them. If they flee, I let them go, for they are not worth my hate. Only one man is worthy of that, and after I take the food I require, I journey back to him and back to my island, the only place that provides me with peace.

This place may appear stark and unforgiving to you, but to me it is a place of great beauty. In winter the crystals of the ice that shelters me reflect the sun like millions of tiny candles, and the land glows with a blue-gray fire on moonlit nights. Often I watch the caribou herds move south across the frozen sea to seek food, and I mark the wolves that stalk them, a dance of death under the moon.

In the summer, the vegetation turns green for a few weeks only, and small red and yellow flowers dot the sparse grass with bits of color before the colder wind blows in and kills them, and their seed sleeps until the following year. For a month or two the ponds and brooks lay free of ice. Sometimes, when a soft wind blows, and the grass is green, and the water is warm, I can almost imagine I am a shepherd, resting by the side of a still pool.

But then I look at the face of the water, and I see my *own* face, and the truth of my life all comes back to me.

TWENTY-TWO

Adam stopped speaking, and the silence of the cave was disturbed only by the crackling of wood on the fire.

"You must think me a fool," he said at length.

"I do not," Hilda said. "Nor do I think of you any longer as a monster."

Adam stood, turned his back to her, and roughly cleared his throat. "I have told you much," he said. "Now tell me one thing more. In whose body did you intend to place Elise Mordenheim's spirit?"

"Our spell revealed that a certain Vistana girl would be the proper vessel. Mordenheim sent Horg to get her. Kidnap her, I suppose. Friedrich and I decided that we would not cooperate, that we would leave in the morning. We couldn't be part of it."

Adam thought quickly. He believed this woman, but if he told her that, there was no further reason to keep her here on the island. He wanted her here. At least for a few days more. He had never before told anyone his story, and having done so, he felt somehow cleansed. If both he and Mordenheim were to perish, there would at least be someone now who knew the truth, who had heard both sides. He would trust her to judge for herself, for she was wise and brave.

"How can I believe you?" he said, fabricating his scheme. "You may intend to do whatever Mordenheim wants but tell me otherwise for fear that I'll kill you now, and not wait until seven days are up."

She lifted her head and met his accusing stare without wavering. "I tell the truth, and you know it."

"My past experience has made me dubious of the word and good intent of all beings," he said. "You are no exception. But because you ask me not to leave you, and because there may be danger to your safety here, I shall remain on the island with you until the seven days are over. Then we shall return to the mainland together to see what has transpired there. Now, is there anything you require from me?" She shook her head. "I have been sleeping at the mouth of the cave. I shall continue to do so. I hope the time will not pass too slowly."

He gave a short nod and walked into the darkness, carrying her words, her face, her look of sympathy with him, clutching them to his heart like the unique and precious things they were.

He would not kill her, she thought. Although she had used every portion of her powers, she could detect from him no hostility toward her. Perhaps even his accusation of her lying had been a sham, intended to keep her there on the island rather than returning her to the mainland and Friedrich immediately.

Then she wondered if she had accomplished her goal too well. What if he didn't want to let her go at all? She felt a tremendous amount of sympathy for this tragic creature called Adam, but not enough to remain with him for any longer than necessary. Her heart bled for his plight, but she would have forsaken him in a minute to be safe in Friedrich's arms once more, far from Lamordia and its horrors, back in Il Aluk.

At any rate, she felt safe for now. She did not think Adam would harm her, not yet. And maybe, even as she sat by Adam's fire, help was on the way.

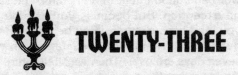

TWENTY-THREE

"Come on, come on! The damned creature isn't going to stay there forever!"

Ivan Dragonov spat to his side into the wind. It was blowing back toward Mordenheim and Kreutzer, and if the spittle hit them, that was just too bad. Never had he been saddled with such a prissy pair of partners!

"If you two walked any slower, you'd be going backward!" he shouted for his own benefit, not caring whether they heard or not. "Even feeling poorly, I could go twice as fast as the two of you put together!" He thought for a moment, and wondered if that meant four times as fast, then dismissed the thought.

He *was* feeling poorly, too. He'd been a little dizzy as they were preparing their gear for the trek and had had a touch of seasickness while they boated across the unfrozen portion of the Sea of Sorrows. He had felt better when he got on his feet and started to walk, but he was still a little queasy and had begun to see spots and blotches in the unbroken field of white that stretched before them.

It was probably due to the food that vile Mordenheim had given him. The whole castle seemed unholy and unclean. It was no wonder he felt sick. At least he had his own jerky and hardtack now, his prime provisions along with whatever edible plants he could find, and there were always plenty of those. Even in winter, certain mosses and lichens could brew a nourishing tea.

But there were no plants here, not on these ice floes. At least they felt solid underfoot. When they neared the Isle of Agony the real trouble would start. There the currents flowed more swiftly, and in many places the ice would be thin and treacherous. A practiced eye such as Dragonov's could see the dangerous spots, but the snow had been heavy. They would have to go single file, prodding the surface with an ice pike. If the ice sounded as if it were becoming thinner, they would have to find another way around. And if the pike broke through, they were in trouble, for the cracks would quickly spread, dunking them in freezing cold water with no fuel within miles with which to start a fire to save their lives.

If the ice cracked, stand still was the rule. If it began to spread, fling yourself backward and pray that you would drown right off rather than crawl out and freeze to death. Drowning was far kinder.

They had left at the first hint of dawn, and it had taken an hour to row from the foot of the cliff at Schloss Mordenheim to where the ice started. They had been walking for several more hours, Dragonov moving boldly, but the other two daintily picking their way across with pikes, despite Dragonov's instructions to "walk in my footsteps and put those blasted pikes away 'til we need 'em!"

The Falkovnian estimated that it was only six miles from where they had left the boat to landfall on the Isle of Agony, but it was fast becoming six miles of the most treacherous terrain imaginable. They could not hope to traverse it in one day, especially not with the two timid travelers who followed him. He sorely doubted if they had gone a half mile since leaving the boat.

A blotch appeared in the field of white ahead of

them, and Dragonov called out, "There's something up ahead." Friedrich started to run through the snow, but when he reached Dragonov, the warrior put a hand on his shoulder to stop him.

"Take your time, boy. It's too big to be your woman, and it's not going anywhere."

What it was, they saw as they approached, was an eight-foot boat with oars. "The monster's," said Dragonov. "He must have dragged it here . . . or maybe there's a route farther through the ice that he knew about." He scanned the eastern horizon, then looked to the west.

"Yes, there," he said, pointing to a rivulet of navigable water scarcely fifty yards from them, but only dimly visible through the falling snow. "He must know these floes like the back of his foul hand," said Dragonov. "A topography that changes with the season, and that bloody monster cruises about in it as sweet as you please. It's no wonder I couldn't corner him!"

Dragonov drew his two-bladed axe from the hasp on his belt and raised it over the timbers of the boat, but Mordenheim cried out. "Stop! Don't ruin it!"

"Why not? You want him to escape in it?"

"It is possible," said Mordenheim, "that *we* should like to escape in it."

"What?"

Mordenheim hesitated a moment before he explained. ". . . should anything happen to you."

"To *me?*" Dragonov roared. "You expect that oaf to defeat me?" He lifted the axe.

Mordenheim drew back and held up his hands placatingly. "I did not mean to imply that. But supposing you should plunge through a hole in the ice just as we sight the monster on the island, and Adam comes after us?"

"He'd catch you long before you got back to this boat." And Dragonov swung down the axe, chopping a huge hole in the side of the skiff.

Mordenheim flinched but said nothing more as Dragonov continued to hack the boat into small pieces.

"Now," the warrior said when he had finished, "you want to build a fire, or you want to go on?"

"Let's go," said Friedrich, gesturing onward.

The scene seemed a permanent dusk, but it was only midafternoon by the time they reached the area where the currents made the ice truly dangerous to cross. Dragonov could feel the snow-packed surface becoming thinner under his feet, and he took his ice pike off his shoulder and began to rap sharply ahead of him. Interpreting the sounds, he led them on a zig-zag path across the ice.

* * * * *

It was an hour later that the wolves came. There were five of them—huge beasts, broad in the shoulders, and ravenous for flesh. Their last kill had been a caribou dragged down six days before. They had glutted themselves on it and lain drowsily in their den on the Isle of Agony like vampires until hunger had made them rise again. They had scoured the island and found the scent of the human female, but when they followed it they learned that it was commingled with the scent of the man-thing that lived there, the one who had killed three of their kind the first and only time they had tried to bring him down. So they forgot about the human and wandered out onto the ice floes looking for another caribou or possibly a moose. If game was sparse, they would head across to the mainland.

Here now, however, was game in abundance—three slow-moving creatures picking their way across the ice like cripples fallen away from the herd. The wolves went in hard and fast, three of them moving on the big one, the herd leader, while the other two split off to harry the weaker ones trailing behind.

Dragonov dropped his pike, yanked out his axe with his right hand, grabbed his sword with his left, and shouted back to Mordenheim and Friedrich. "Use the pikes! If they pull you down, ball yourselves up and cover—" And then they were on him.

The first backswing of his axe sheared through the leader's jaw, opening its head like a melon. Dragonov followed it with a slash of his sword that caught the second wolf on the upper right foreleg so that it dropped, yelping, to the ice.

By then two wolves had thrown themselves at Mordenheim and Friedrich. Friedrich attempted to stab his with the pike but missed, and the animal went for his face. He threw his arms up so that the jaws closed on his heavily coated wrist, and he fell backward, the wolf atop him.

Mordenheim fared far worse. He swung the pike like a scythe at his wolf, knocking it off balance, but instead of attempting to stab it, he turned to run, and his foot plunged through an area of thin ice. He screamed and twisted his body around, but he kept plunging through until both legs were in the water. He threw himself down on his stomach and managed to hold on to the ice so that his upper body was not submerged. His frenzied struggles and the water flying as he tried to pull himself out of it seemed to startle the wolf, which backed away growling.

Dragonov had by now finished the wolf he had wounded; a swipe of his axe sank through its chest and buried itself in several inches of ice. Unable to pull it out immediately, he turned on the third wolf with only his sword. The beast leapt at his sword arm and savaged it. Dragonov's fingers opened involuntarily, and his sword fell to the ice.

Seeing that this furry animal had lost its long tooth, the wolf released the wrist, pulled back its lips to fully bare its fangs, and went straight for Dragonov's face . . . only to find its muzzle buried in an even larger maw, entrapped in spearlike teeth that crunched through its snout and jaw. From its throat came an anguished cry of pain, and it tried to pull away, but claws had been suddenly thrust into its side, piercing its lungs and puncturing its heart so that it could only gasp out its dying breath without hearing it.

For a moment Dragonov was lost in utter blackness. Then he came to himself and saw that he was holding a dead wolf in his hands, and that his jaws were spread wide, his mouth filled with blood and bone and gristle.

He spat out the remnants of the wolf's snout, nearly gagging, and tried to drop the dead beast but discovered that his fingertips had pierced his heavy gloves and had even passed through the thick coat and hide of the creature. He could feel the heat of the inside of the wolf's body, and with an inarticulate cry of rage and revulsion, he yanked his hands free. The wolf fell dead to the ice.

He turned and saw Friedrich trying desperately to keep another wolf's fangs from his face. Dragonov picked up his axe, got a running start, and severed the wolf's head with one swing. By this time, the last wolf, the one that had attacked Mordenheim, had seen that it was now outnumbered and was running south as fast as it could.

Dragonov grabbed an ice pike, lay on the ice several feet from Mordenheim, and extended the pike so that the doctor could grab it. Then Dragonov pulled until Mordenheim was able to slide up onto the slick surface. The warrior kept hauling until the ice felt solid beneath him, and by then Friedrich had gotten to his feet and was helping.

"Get up," said Dragonov, spitting more of the wolf's blood from his mouth. "Stand *up*, Mordenheim, curse you! And keep walking." He grabbed Friedrich's hand and pressed it to Mordenheim's shoulder. "Keep him going, boy. Bring him over here. . . ."

Dragonov ran to one of the dead wolves and sliced open its belly with his sword. "Get his boots off! And his socks and trousers," he said to Friedrich, as he did the same to another wolf.

It was wet, cold work, and Mordenheim was shivering so much that manipulating his limbs to remove his clothes was incredibly difficult. But with Friedrich's help, his lower limbs were soon bare. "Stick his legs in here," said Dragonov, dragging a wolf carcass to where Mordenheim sat on his pack.

Friedrich thrust one of the doctor's legs into the open belly of the wolf, its heat steaming in the cold air. Then Dragonov brought up the other carcass, and they slipped Mordenheim's other leg into it.

"Not pretty at all," said Dragonov, "but effective. Leastwise till the wolf cools off. And maybe by then, if you're lucky, you'll have some feeling back." He put his hands into the red hollow and started rubbing the doctor's left leg. "Rub, boy," he commanded Friedrich. "Keep the blood going, whatever you do. He may lose toes, but maybe we can keep the feet and legs. He can't walk on stumps out here, that's for certain."

They continued to rub, and Mordenheim began to speak through chattering teeth. "Wha . . . what did you *do*, Dragonov?"

"Do?" asked the warrior, guiltily wiping the blood from his lips with his sleeve.

"Your mouth's . . . all blood."

"Did what I had to, nothing more. They're going to bite you, you bite them first."

"But you . . . I saw you from the water. . . . You

looked different."

For a moment Dragonov stopped rubbing, and his eyes were far away. Then he set to with more vigor than ever. "Everything looks different when you're drowning, good doctor. Now quiet that yammering mouth and try to move your frozen parts. Wiggle your toes, man!" Mordenheim tried, but nothing happened. "Your leg then. Bend your knee." The attempt was successful. "Good. Now the other one. Good. Your ankles, one at a time." The feet rotated. "Fine. Now try the toes again." And again, nothing.

"Curse it," said Dragonov. "Frostbite. In the water too long, not enough blood gets to the toes." He pressed his lips together grimly. "You know what this means?"

"I *am* a doctor," said Mordenheim petulantly. "If I don't lose the damaged toes now, they'll become gangrenous, and the gangrene will undoubtedly spread to the rest of the foot, and *that* will have to be amputated before the gangrene proceeds farther, eventually killing me. Of *course* I know what it means."

Dragonov nodded. "Shall I do it?"

"I hardly think I'd have the willpower to amputate my own limbs, so I believe you'll *have* to." Mordenheim let out a shuddering sigh. "Just do it as quickly as possible."

"Doctor," said Friedrich, "I have read in books about such things. I could—"

"No," Mordenheim said. "Let this Falkovnian butcher do it."

"But, sir, it should be precise and—"

"Precision does not matter. *Do* it, Dragonov!"

Dragonov drew a slim, sharp rapier from an inner sheath. "We have no fire to cleanse it."

"Just *cut!*"

At Dragonov's orders, Friedrich held Mordenheim's leg. Mordenheim bit down on the corner of the wooden provision box lid, and nodded his head.

Dragonov cut as fast and strongly as he could, but to sever the toes took nearly a minute of unrelieved agony for the doctor. He thrashed and screamed through his gritted teeth, pounding the surface of the snowy ice with his fist.

His words were unintelligible to the other two men, but often he said Adam's name, and they wondered at the vile laughter that bubbled from Mordenheim's raw throat.

*   *   *   *   *

On the Isle of Agony, Adam stiffened, his eyes widened, and his teeth ground together in pain.

"What is it?" Hilda asked. "What's wrong?"

The pain continued in his left foot. He reached down and removed his shoe and saw that, despite the sharp pangs that lanced through his foot, nothing was amiss.

It was Mordenheim then. What was happening to him, this self-proclaimed creator of his whose pain he shared? What did it mean? Had he severed his toes somehow? The pain was far greater than that created by dropping an object on one's foot.

Then another searing pain shot through his right foot, but he did not remove the shoe, for he knew he would see nothing. He gave a low grunt and tried to bear it.

"Adam?"

"It's nothing," he said. "Nothing physical, at any rate. Something is . . . happening to Mordenheim."

"You . . . are feeling his pain now?"

"I do. We are bound together, for good or ill."

"How can such a thing be?" The woman's eyes were filled with horror and wonder.

"Just as I told you," said Adam. "I asked the gods, and

they gave it to me. Just as Mordenheim wished for me to have life. He did not ask, but it was given to him anyway. His boon and his curse." Adam shuddered as the last sensation of agony died away, and his body was his own again. "A curse upon all of us."

He looked into the fire and let the memory of the pain pass. It was good here, sharing the fire and food, listening to this woman as she talked to him, told him things about the world to which Adam was barred, teaching him the way no one had since Mordenheim, back in the days before what he thought of as the fall.

"I'm sorry for the interruption," Adam said. "Please, go on. You were telling me about Il Aluk, all the people and different creatures there. . . ."

Hilda talked on, weaving a web of words that fascinated and ensnared Adam, made him forget Mordenheim's pain, and, more importantly, his own.

*   *   *   *   *

"It's done."

Mordenheim looked up through the sea of red that covered his vision and retched once again as the pain subsided. "Good," he managed to choke out. "No . . . no harm done."

Dragonov gave Friedrich a look that indicated that the doctor may have lost his mind as well as his toes. Then he began to bandage Mordenheim's feet with strips torn from the cloth lining of the doctor's coat. When he finished, he and Friedrich took out of oilcloth wrappings the extra clothing they had packed in case any got wet, and helped Mordenheim into it.

"We'll sleep here," said Dragonov, "then start back in the morning."

"Back?" said Mordenheim. "*No!* We must go on—on after Adam and Fraulein Von Karlsfeld!"

"I intend to do so," said Friedrich, "even if I must go alone."

"Oh, that would be smart," Dragonov said with a scoffing tone. "The monster'd take care of you in one bite, then gobble down your woman for dessert. You want that, boy?"

"I'm *not* a boy, and I *will* save my fiancee or die in the attempt!"

"You've got *that* right. But what do you suggest we do with the good doctor? If you've forgotten, the plan is that we need him to find his creature. People don't walk well without toes, especially over *this* terrain, and I'm damned to the seventh inferno if I'm going to *carry* him!"

"You won't have to carry me," said Mordenheim.

"Planning on flying now, Mordenheim?" said Dragonov.

"We will camp here tonight," said the doctor firmly. "In the morning we shall be able to go on. And you will not have to carry me, Dragonov."

"Well then you're a miracle man indeed, Doctor." Dragonov looked at the sky, which had grown almost completely dark. "No point in arguing before tomorrow then. Let's get the bedrolls unpacked and go to sleep. Kreutzer, you take the first watch. Wake me when four hours have passed. And change the doctor's bandages in two. They'll be seeping bad."

Dragonov unrolled his cylinder of blankets, then rolled himself up in them again. Just before he covered his head to seal in the warmth of his breathing, he said, "If anything happens, shout loud to wake me. I sleep lightly when alone, but when someone else is on watch, I dive into sleep for the luxury it is."

Friedrich prepared Mordenheim's bedding for him, and the doctor crawled in. "You needn't wake me until dawn. My feet are all right," Mordenheim said, and pulled the cover up over his head to sleep.

Delirious, Friedrich thought. The shock of the impromptu amputations would have driven any man slightly mad for a time. He would let him sleep and wake him in two hours despite Mordenheim's orders.

Friedrich stood up and slowly walked the perimeter of their little camp, careful to tread in no spot that had not previously proven secure. He could see next to nothing in the darkness. Though the snow had stopped for a time, clouds hung heavily in the sky, allowing no moon or stars to be seen. He hoped, if something came out of the night, that he would hear it in time to wake Dragonov. Despite the man's pigheadedness, Friedrich knew that both he and the doctor would have been dead without him.

He continued to walk, fighting the cold and looking into the thick blackness until he felt that two hours might have passed. But when he took his pocket watch from deep within his clothing, lifted its glass face, and felt the hands, he discovered that only one hour had elapsed.

It seemed an interminable length of time, but finally two hours had gone by, and he knelt by Mordenheim's side. "Doctor, wake up," he said softly, shaking Mordenheim's shoulder under the heavy covers.

"What is it?" came the reply. Mordenheim did not sound nearly as sleepy as Friedrich had expected.

"I must change your bandages."

"I told you I didn't need them changed. Now leave me be."

"Doctor, they must be changed, or they'll become infected. And we have enough problems without that."

"I am fine, and my feet are fine." He had not pulled the covers back from his head, and Friedrich felt slightly absurd, as though he were talking to a child huddling in his bed, playing peekaboo.

"Listen to me, Doctor," he said angrily. "Either let me change the bandages or I wake Dragonov and he'll do it."

The blankets snapped back, and Mordenheim's annoyed face appeared. "Very well, just be quiet. I told you my feet would be all right, and now I'll prove it to you. . . ." He maneuvered himself out of his bedroll and peeled the dry, heavy woolen socks off his feet. Then he told Friedrich to unwrap the bandages. "And don't shout when you see what's happened," he added.

Friedrich lit a candle from his pack, and Mordenheim held it as the younger man unwound the strips of cloth. In truth, there seemed to be a distinct absence of pus seeping through, and no fresh blood at all.

When he removed the last scrap of cloth, Friedrich was hard put to keep from making some sound, for what he saw were not raw-edged, open wounds, but cleanly healed over stubs, vestigial toes that Friedrich could swear had grown longer in the few hours since the amputation.

"Yes," said Mordenheim. "You're not seeing things. They're growing back. That's why I said we could go on in the morning, why it didn't matter to me how carefully the job was done, just so it was done quickly. That way the pain would pass sooner."

"But . . . but how?" Friedrich stammered.

"Keep your voice down," the doctor hissed. "All I need is for that fool to wake up and see this. He'd think me a sorcerer and kill me on the spot."

"But it's . . . regeneration. Isn't it?"

"Yes. Regeneration." Mordenheim tossed the bandages aside and shoved his foot back into his sock, then ripped the bandages off the other foot and pulled a sock back around that one as well. "Have to leave them room to grow," he said. "Every toe will be back to its original size by daybreak. Regeneration," he said softly.

"And of more than you can ever imagine."

"What do you mean?"

"I mean," said Mordenheim, slipping his legs back into the warmth of his bedroll, "that I am essentially immortal, Herr Kreutzer."

Friedrich knew that he was gaping like a fish but couldn't help it. "Immortal?"

The doctor nodded. "It has something to do with Adam. Whatever . . . brought him to life, made him insane, established the link between the two of us, whatever that is, is responsible, I am certain. Most fools would call it the vengeance of gods, or divine retribution, or some such blather. But I know it is only the result of a scientific phenomenon whose cause is as yet unknown, even to me."

Mordenheim examined Friedrich's unbelieving face in the sickly light of the candle. "You doubt me. You see the proof with your own eyes, and still you doubt."

"But . . . immortal? How . . . how did you learn this?"

"It is obvious that you shall give me no peace until I tell you. Very well then. It happened in this wise. . . ."

 **TWENTY-FOUR**

It happened several months after Adam killed Eva and maimed Elise. I was just at the beginning of my experiments. Elise's body, at least that which had not been crushed by Adam's fists, was still fresh and free from the decay with which it has since been visited. At that time, I thought that replacing certain parts—limbs, organs, transplanting patches of flesh—would be the simplest and most effective way to restore my dear wife to me. So I sent Horg into Ludendorf to be my ear, and overhear what women were nearest death.

There was a young wife soon to give birth, but the doctor feared for her health. When it was her time to deliver, Horg and I came into the town by night, hid the coach, and went to the woman's house, where we lurked outside in the rain. The midwife was already there, and we could see her shadow moving about against the second-floor window shade. Before much time passed, we heard a baby cry from that upstairs window. A short time later, the visiting relatives began to leave, but not joyfully. They were weeping, and I assumed correctly that the woman had died.

We lingered several more hours, until well past midnight. Then I boosted Horg, with a coil of rope looped over his shoulder, high enough to grab a rain gutter, and he shinnied up the rest of the way to the window that was now dark. In a few minutes he lowered the dead body of

the woman and climbed down after it. We carried it down
a twisting labyrinth of alleys to where we had secreted the
coach, placed it in the back under some blankets, and
gave the reins a shake. The horses, their harness swathed
in cloths to muffle the sound, started off.

We had gone scarcely half a mile before we heard the
alarm bell sound in the village and assumed that the theft
of the corpse had been discovered. Horg lashed the
horses, and we rattled along as fast as they could run,
which was fast indeed.

Though we saw no one behind us, Horg, at my insistence, drove the horses unmercifully. I shouted to him to
take us along an old, disused road on the edge of the sea
cliff, thinking that if our pursuers were not close enough to
see us take it, they would continue on the main road, and
we would lose them. The rain fell more heavily. Peals of
thunder cracked, and lightning split the air, driving the
horses into a greater frenzy. We came to the spot where
the road turned and paralleled the cliff, but we were going
too fast. A sudden bolt of lightning blinded the horses,
and by the time Horg pulled the reins to the right, it was
too late.

The horses tried to turn, but their hooves slipped in the
mud, and centrifugal force slid the coach, the horses, and
the two of us toward the cliff. Horg cried, "Jump!" and
leapt free, but I was a second too late.

I had jumped at the last moment, but my leap carried
me off the edge of the cliff, along with the horses, the
coach, and the dead woman inside. It seemed an infinite
amount of time during which I fell through the air. And
then I struck the first rock. The pain was excruciating,
taking away my breath so that I could not even scream. I
crashed into another, and another, rolling, bouncing down
the side of the cliff. I could feel my organs burst within me,
my flesh tear, my bones crack, and finally my skull struck
something in the darkness, and I knew no more.

Much of the rest of the story I got from Horg, who climbed down the cliff after me. He found me at the bottom and was certain that I was dead. He tells me that he sat next to me for a while grieving, but then he noticed that my nearly crushed chest was still rising and falling, despite the fact that most of my blood had drained from my many wounds, and that not a bone seemed left unsplintered. In addition, my neck was broken so that my head was twisted about, and my skull was cracked so badly that much of the brain had issued forth. Nevertheless, I still breathed.

Amazed, he carried me up the cliff, and bore me to the castle. It is a wonder that walk, me thrown over his shoulder like a sack of potatoes, did not kill me. He took me into my bedroom, arranged my shattered limbs, turned my head about, and covered me with a sheet. Poor fellow, he didn't know what else to do. For all he knew—and for all *I* knew, I should have been dead. Yet I lived. And not only lived, but recovered.

I regained consciousness just before morning, a consciousness of agonizing pain. Regeneration *hurts*, my boy. It is no parlor trick to cut off toes to amuse your guests. I am even now in great pain while my feet restore themselves. Imagine then the pain of one's whole body healing itself, drawing ripped muscle, broken bone, flayed skin, sundered organs together.

I experienced two days and nights of that, until I was whole again. All the while Horg came in and watched over me, brought me soup and tea that I could not touch, and sat and worried and waited.

Finally, the pain stopped. I was complete. Without a scar to remind me of what had happened. Aside from being shaken to my very core, I was the picture of health, or at least as much of one as I was before I went over the cliff. And I knew then that I could not die. I knew then that I was immortal. . . .

# TWENTY-FIVE

"But how?" asked Friedrich. "Total regeneration? How could such a thing be?"

"I have told you that I do not know," said Mordenheim, "but I do believe it is somehow tied to Adam. Perhaps it is due to my exposure to certain drugs or electric fields that went into his creation. Or perhaps it's something else that I can't even fathom—not yet, at any rate.

"The one thing I do know is that this inability of mine to die only adds to the necessity that Elise be restored to me. Living without her is a cruel joke, and an eternity of separation from her is *infinite* cruelty. Both of us can live forever, Kreutzer. She can only die if I permit it. Otherwise, her spirit lives on in whatever her body becomes. I have delayed her decay, but someday she may deteriorate to nothing but a puddle of slime. And if that happens, I *still* will not let her leave me! I must have her back, you see. I *must!* I cannot live forever without her. . . ."

Mordenheim fell back, as if exhausted by relating his tale. "Put out the candle. I must rest. The pain grows, along with my flesh and bone." He nodded toward Dragonov, sleeping in his bedroll. "Wake him. He must stand watch. In the morning, if you want Fraulein Von Karlsfeld back as badly as I do, say nothing of this. Tell Dragonov only that the healing has gone well, and I will pretend to be able to walk. I'll limp a bit for effect. But he mustn't know about the regeneration."

"I understand," Friedrich said. He blew out the candle, put it into his pack, and walked over to Dragonov. He leaned down next to him and shook his shoulder gently, speaking his name in the darkness.

The snarling head of something that was not Dragonov reared up from the blankets and roared. Though he could not see it, Friedrich felt the heat of rank breath in his face, and fell back gasping, uncertain of which way to run in the darkness. He merely lay on the ice, frozen in terror.

"Boy?" It was Dragonov's voice, but much deeper, and sounded as though it came from far away. "*Boy?* Is that you?"

"Y-yes. . . ." Friedrich managed to say.

"I'm sorry, I . . . I wake abruptly." Now the words sounded more normal, but Friedrich thought there was something else in Dragonov's voice that he had not heard there before. To Friedrich Kreutzer's ears, Ivan Dragonov, the warrior who was not afraid of anything, sounded frightened.

"Is everything all right?" Mordenheim called from his blankets.

"Yes, yes," Dragonov said. "The boy just woke me too fast. I was startled, that's all. Go back to sleep, good doctor. My watch then, boy?"

"Yes." Friedrich got to his feet and walked slowly toward Dragonov's voice.

"You look scared, boy. I'm sorry I frightened you."

Look scared? How, Friedrich wondered, could Dragonov descry the expression on his face when Friedrich could scarcely see the lump that was Dragonov detaching itself from the blankets and rising?

"All quiet?"

"Yes." Friedrich licked his lips, chapped from the

cold. "Dragonov—are you all right? You seem . . . different somehow."

"Different." In the gray-black light of Lamordian night, Friedrich could just make out the Falkovnian's shoulders. The man came toward him, and though Friedrich had a strong urge to run, he held his ground. "Listen to me, boy. I'll tell you once, and once only.

"I have been dreaming about being . . . something else, something terrible. Something evil." Friedrich felt a strong hand on his shoulder. "If that dream comes true, if I . . . ever become what I most hate—if that happens, take my axe if you can and kill me."

Gods above, was he out on the ice with *two* madmen now? "Kill you?"

"If I can, I'll let you. But now I'll say no more. You'll know if the time comes. My axe, remember. Now, go to sleep."

That was easier said than done. Friedrich nearly laughed with madness himself as he realized his state. He was on an ice floe in the middle of nowhere with an insane immortal who had created a monster, and a warrior who believed he was *becoming* a monster, and the three of them were *after* a monster. If it had not been for Hilda, he would have sneaked off into the darkness and taken his chance with the wolves and the thin ice. But he had to try to sleep. He had to be refreshed enough to help rescue her, get her off the Isle of Agony and out of Lamordia. They'd return immediately to their home in Il Aluk where they would do whatever work, secretarial or otherwise, they could find and never dabble in necromancy again.

He closed his eyes, and hoped that dawn would not be long in coming.

*   *   *   *   *

And as Friedrich Kreutzer closed his eyes, many miles away Horg opened his and thought that the time had come. It was roughly four hours before dawn, and he picked himself up off the soft moss, walked several yards to the edge of the incline, and looked down into the Vistana camp.

He had malingered there for two days, pretending his faked injuries would not let him leave safely. But eventually Petre, Ilisa's father, told him that he was as hale and healthy as any man, that a healthy giorgio had no business in a Vistana camp, and that that evening's meal would be his last with them.

Horg left that night, but not before seeing to it that everyone would sleep soundly enough so that he would be able to steal Ilisa away.

It had been easy. At Ilisa's request, he had taken a pan full of carrots that she had sliced to the huge communal cook pot. But when he dumped them in, along with them went the packet of sleeping drugs that Mordenheim had given him.

Horg had not eaten any of the stew. He had let regret serve as his reason for his loss of appetite, regret that he was leaving the Vistani, and, most particularly, Ilisa. Although the gypsies had not been particularly kind to him during his stay there, neither had they been unkind, as the rest of the world had so often been to Horg. They had accepted him as an outsider, nothing more, for as long as he was required to stay with them.

Ilisa was friendlier than the others and talked with him a great deal, much to her father's distress, Horg thought. He had still not been permitted to watch their dancing, although he had found cracks in the vardo through which he had peered and seen Ilisa dancing with the rest.

It had been wonderful. She seemed to dance for no single man, but for all men and women who could

appreciate her grace and beauty. She was neither coy
nor flirtatious, but danced as though dancing was as
much a part of her as flying was to the birds. This natural grace, along with her kindness, had endeared her to
him in spite of his resolution that he must feel nothing
toward her. Although he knew that her kindness was
due to no romantic feelings on her part, even if she *had*
called him *angeli*, he loved her. And in the back of his
mind was the thought that if he kidnaped her, perhaps
he would not obey Doctor Mordenheim, but instead
would take her to a place where there were no other
people, Vistani or giorgios. There he would stay with her
until she realized his devotion and returned his love.

But he could not know what he would do until she
was in the doctor's coach and they were riding away
from the Vistana camp.

He had left after the supper, wishing a cursory
farewell and thanks to Petre and Karla, and a more sincere one to Ilisa. He had not seen Nana, the old hag in
the vardo, since that first night and had no intention of
saying good-bye to her. Her face that saw nothing, yet
everything, terrified him still.

Once he was out of sight of the camp, he had lain on
a soft tussock of moss and gone to sleep, knowing that
the music would wake him before too long. When it did,
he saw by the moon that it was nearly midnight. Mordenheim had said that the drugs would not work for
several hours, and from the energy of the music, he
thought that perhaps they had not worked at all.

He could just make out the swirling figure of Ilisa
from where he hid in the darkness. The dancing and
music continued, but after another hour it began to
grow less fiery, and soon soft ballades replaced the
czardas and mazurka.

Horg sat down, his back to a tree, and waited for the
music to end. Before he knew it, he had fallen asleep,

the soft sounds of the Vistana guitars lulling him into slumber. But now he was awake, and gazing down into what looked like a village of the dead.

They were all lying on the ground—dancers, musicians, singers, the old men and women, the children, the young men who guarded the horses. Horg slowly walked down the hill and then into their midst, fearing that they might rise at any moment to accuse him. But they were all as still as death, and he knelt down by one, fearing that what the doctor had given him was not a powerful sleeping draught, but a poison. To his great relief, he found that every person he examined was still breathing gently, although some had minor cuts and bruises from their falls, having been overtaken all at once by the drug.

Some were in positions that showed they had tried to help the others as they were swooning, and others, expecting the inevitable, had lain down comfortably when they grew tired, proof to Horg of the gypsy creed of taking both life and death as it comes.

It did not take him long to find Ilisa. She seemed unharmed, having apparently lowered herself to the ground before unconsciousness set in. He looked at her for a moment, steeling himself to touch her. It seemed almost a profanation, but he knew that he must do what the doctor had ordered. For now, at least.

He knelt and picked her up. He could not bear to sling her over his shoulder, so he bore her instead in both arms. It was more difficult, but more respectful.

Just as he turned with the girl, he heard a sound of life in that otherwise dead place. It was the door of a vardo creaking open. And when he looked, he was shocked to see the ancient crone, Nana, standing in the doorway, staring straight at him with her blind eyes. One of her clawlike hands was wrapped around the door frame, while the other held a stick nearly as crooked as its owner. Her thin, wrinkled lips opened, and the word Horg had heard before came oozing out.

"Whooooo . . . ?"

He froze, once more unable to move while fixed by the white irises of her blind eyes. Then she smiled, and it was the most horrible thing Horg had ever seen in a lifetime of horrible sights. And he recalled the stories of the evil eye, how old Vistana women could curse with just a look. But the thought was scourged from his mind as she spoke again. It was only one word, but it chilled him more than her smile, more than the surety of the evil eye.

She spoke his name.

It was as though he had been galvanized by lightning. The need to flee overcame his numbing terror, and he turned and ran, the girl in his arms. He dashed up the side of the hill and through the woods, not slowing until he reached the place where he had hidden the coach. He placed Ilisa gently but hastily inside, leapt to the seat, and struck the horses' rumps sharply with his whip.

He guided them onto the main road and headed north toward Ludendorf. After he had gone several miles, he felt calm enough to stop and bind Ilisa so that she would not try to escape when she awoke from her drugged sleep. He solicitously put cushions and blankets around her so that she would not be jostled by the rough roads over which they would travel. Just before he climbed back into the box, he watched her sleeping, leaned down, and let his lips just brush her cheek.

He looked then where his mouth had touched her face, and felt a tear start to pool in his eye. "What shall I do?" he whispered. "Oh, what shall I do?"

Then, his mind as troubled as the cloudy and turbulent night sky, he started the coach north, toward Schloss Mordenheim.

*   *   *   *   *

When dawn came, Horg was seven miles north of
Neufurchtenberg, and the Vistana camp had still not
awakened. The only person alive and moving in the
camp was old Nana. After Horg had left with Ilisa, Nana
had gone from person to person, touching each face,
identifying each of the Vistani that was of her clan. All
were there save one. Ilisa. The flower of her old age.

Nana had gone back into her vardo then and opened
the cabinets. She did not need eyes to find the jars and
vials with which she had worked ever since she was a
girl, ever since it was learned that she had the seeing.

She knew where everything was, from the dried fruits
of Barovia, which had been sliced with a killing knife
under the blood moon, to the dried eyes of the red-
gilled lizards found only on one peak of the Balinoks, to
the slime of sand snails that burrow in the Nightmare
Lands. All were there under her practiced fingers.

And this morning with the dawn, Nana, otherwise
known as Anna Zsolty Taksony, the wise woman of the
Zsolty clan, would make her most lethal and terrible
spell upon the one who had accepted Vistana hospitality and then betrayed them all, stealing their most precious jewel.

Horg. She had *seen* his name, and she had fixed him
with her eye, and she would know wherever he went.
She could not follow him until the others awoke, but
she knew how long they would sleep. Her parchment
tongue had tasted the stew that Ilisa had brought her,
had spat it out, and had known that it was too late, that
the others had already eaten and would slumber
deeply.

She had sensed the noises of celebration diminish
and the silence reign. And she had heard the footsteps
of the one who would curse the day he was born.

Horg. She had felt his fear. Seen it with his name. And he would live long enough to know that his fear was well-founded, long enough to wish to die a thousand times.

She began mixing. Her eye had cast the curse, and the mixture would define and finalize it. Into it she put all her venom gathered over a hundred years, all her loathing of traitors, her hatred of those who would take what was offered and then steal more.

When Nana was finished, the concoction was poured into a tiny pan. She lit a puddle of green oil in a small brazier, and held the pan over it. The mixture began to smoke, then in an instant blazed up, a tongue of fire whose heat nearly charred her yellow-white hair, and licked the ceiling of the vardo, a straight, white-hot line that, had anyone been awake outside to watch, appeared to pass *through* the vardo roof, into the sky like a flaming arrow that hurtled north, north to a road, a coach, a misshapen and confused man sitting on the coachman's box, to . . .

"*Horrrrg,*" Nana rasped out, and then began to laugh, a loud, cackling laughter that still did not wake the sleepers.

They would wake soon enough, and travel north, following their child, their betrayer, and Nana's curse.

 **TWENTY-SIX**

Adam watched Hilda as she slept. In the glow of the firelight, her cheek seemed the softest, warmest thing he had ever imagined. He longed to touch it with his rough fingers, but he would not. He longed to place his face near her brown hair that shone like burnished copper, but he would not.

What he would do was watch her, and talk to her when she awoke, talk as they had talked before, freely. When she looked at him now, it did not seem that she saw the monster that the rest of the world saw, but a man like other men, who did not want to hate, did not want to kill, who wanted only to speak and laugh and live in the world without being feared and attacked. And as he looked at her, he wondered if he could kill her when the time came.

The intruding thought saddened him, and he decided to banish it from his mind. There were still two more days before that decision had to be made. For now, she was as close to a friend as he had ever had, and he had the impulsive idea to do something for her when she woke.

Perhaps a good breakfast would be nice. He had seen the signs of a caribou on the north of the island. If he could spot it, it would be no trick to run it down and twist its antlers until its neck broke. He had done similar things many times. Perhaps he could also find some eggs of the sea birds hardy enough to winter on the island. If so, he could cook them and the caribou steaks, and offer Hilda a good meal.

He stood up quietly, not wanting to disturb her sleep, and left the cave. The day outside was growing lighter. The snow had stopped falling, and the sun was brightening the sky. Soon, he thought, the snow would be blindingly bright, and the sunshine would feel warm and good on his flesh.

He turned north and ran faster than any hoofed creature, with great bounding leaps that carried him yards at a single step. In a matter of minutes, he was only a spot on the horizon, and then had vanished from sight.

*　*　*　*　*

So it was that Ivan Dragonov, Friedrich Kreutzer, and Doctor Victor Mordenheim did not see Adam as they approached the cave where Hilda Von Karlsfeld was held.

Mordenheim was so intent upon psychic tracking of his creation that he had forgotten to continue to limp, an omission that made Dragonov even more curious than before. The warrior had been astounded when Mordenheim had not only said he could go on at dawn, but demonstrated it by getting to his feet and hobbling about, apparently with no more trouble than a slight limp. Kreutzer had supported Mordenheim's assertion that the toes had healed well enough to go on, and Dragonov had agreed, though he expected to see Mordenheim collapse at any moment, his feet puddles of bloody pus.

Such had not been the case. Mordenheim had trudged on like a trooper, and several hours past dawn they finally left the dangers of the ice and stepped onto the solid ground of the Isle of Agony. Dragonov had begun to look about for spoor, but Mordenheim merely raised his head as if scenting the air.

"He is here," he said, then pointed toward the north with a gloved hand. "That way."

They walked due north, toward a multipeaked and rough-hewn prominence that dominated the island. Snow covered its jagged peaks, making it look like a ghost hand digging its way out of a snowy grave. The outcroppings of rock to which the snow did not cling heightened the illusion, appearing to be gray shards of dead flesh from the rising, mammoth revenant.

Mordenheim walked first, followed by Friedrich, with Dragonov bringing up the rear. Several times Friedrich stopped, then turned, startled, sure he had heard the snarl of a wolf or the chuffing breath of a bear nearby. But he never saw anything other than Dragonov behind him, head down, his face buried in his hood. He called to him once to ask if he had heard anything, and the Falkovnian looked up, his visage ghastly and pale against the fire of his red beard. It seemed strange, since Friedrich and Mordenheim's faces were red from the cold wind and the exertion.

Then Friedrich thought once again about what Dragonov had said last night, how Friedrich was to kill him with the axe if he became what he most hated. For the hundredth time the youth wondered what he had meant, and if it was just a fancy, or if Dragonov truly believed he was in danger of turning into a beast of some sort. He hunched his shoulders, trying to draw his neck farther down, and wishing that Dragonov were not walking behind him.

* * * * *

The blood, Ivan Dragonov—slayer of a hundred monsters, destroyer of evil—thought to himself. It must have been the blood. He had burned the other wounds well enough. The purity of the flame had healed them and made them vanish. So it must have been the blood, the blood that got into his eyes.

He dimly remembered a conversation with an alchemist in a Port-a-Lucine tavern years before. The man had the theory that vampirism, lycanthropy, and a host of other plagues could be passed not only through the piercing of skin, but through the pathway of the eyes. Not by sight, but by introducing blood or saliva into the fluid of the eyeball. At the time, Dragonov had thought it but the drunken ravings of a fool, but now he wondered if the man had been right.

He had felt it coming upon him. The first time was when the wolves had found them. He usually experienced something akin to berserker rage building within him, but this sensation was wholly new. He had been savage when the wolves had attacked him, and when the beast had thrust at his head, he felt in retrospect that his face had actually *changed,* as though a snout had shot out from it, opened, and closed on the wolf's smaller snout with the force of a vise. And what about his hands, piercing the sides of the wolf, his fingers playing among its organs? As strong as he was, no man could have shoved blunt fingertips through his own gloves and then a wolf's hide and sinew. But if claws had shot out . . .

Dragonov gave a dull groan of mental anguish that he choked off immediately. It sounded too much like the low whimper of an animal. How could it be? he wondered. How could the gods reward him thus for his labors, his constant battles with evil? Unless, he thought with a flash of panic, the gods of this land were themselves evil. If that were so, and if he had indeed become a lycanthrope, there was no other answer but the cure.

Dragonov had seen the ceremony several years before. The lycanthrope had been a young man of Morfenzi named Erik whose mother had enlisted Dragonov's help. Her son had shown evidence of the dreaded disease, and recently animals had been slaughtered in the vicinity. The woman asked Dragonov to watch over the boy at night. Despite Dragonov's best efforts, the lad had somehow eluded him, and the next morning three sheep were found, their throats ripped out, and Erik had blood on his sheets. Though such evidence was strong, the cure was so dangerous and horrific that the mother begged Dragonov to be certain beyond a doubt.

So the next night, Dragonov went into Erik's room to question him. He took no chances, wearing mail under his cloak. He browbeat the boy, shouting at him and threatening him until Erik grew ever angrier and began involuntarily to change his shape, hair and whiskers sprouting from a face that became long and ratlike.

Dragonov immediately threw a silver chain over the creature's long snout, and gave it a hearty tug, securely snapping its jaws shut. Then, ignoring its nasal squeals of pain, he took a rope with silver threads interwoven with the jute, and wrapped its arms tightly around its body.

So secured, the rat-lad was hoisted by Dragonov and taken to Hamer, the priest of Stangengrad, the only man who, to Dragonov's knowledge, had ever successfully cured anyone of lycanthropy. By the time Dragonov, Erik, and his mother got to Stangengrad, the boy had reverted to his human form and was now fully aware of what he had become. Sobbing, he told his mother that he went into the fields at night to slay sheep because otherwise he feared that he would slake his blood lust on human flesh, even that of his dearly beloved mother.

Hamer, a tall, gaunt man in his sixties, was sympathetic but realistic. He warned Erik and his mother that not many possessed both the physical strength and the strength of will needed to successfully facilitate the cure, but that the only alternative was death. "We cannot," said Hamer, "allow you freedom if you remain a lycanthrope. Dragonov's bringing you here means that you shall be free of this curse—either as a young and healthy man, or as a dead one. But either way, your spirit will no longer be in peril."

Then they went into the great sanctuary, where the boy underwent a ritual of piety to cleanse his spirit, in which he recited many prayers to the gods, abased himself, and scourged himself with a cat-o'-nine-tails whose ends were tipped with silver.

Next, he had to take on his lycanthropic form. That very night was the full moon, and Dragonov and the mother watched as the shapeshifting took place. Erik was bound on the altar with silver cords, and as his body expanded with the change, they cut deeply into the rat-thing's flesh. It screeched, jaws agape, its yellow and crusted fangs flashing in search of prey. At Hamer's orders, Dragonov closed the shutters of the window that let in the moonlight so that they were illuminated only by a lantern's sickly beam and the ceremonial candles the priest had lit.

Then Hamer cast the first of the three spells, the atonement. As he recited the words, the creature seemed to slowly grow calmer, until by the end, Dragonov could have sworn that he saw Erik's gentle eyes staring out of the otherwise vicious face. The second spell was that of the cure, and as Hamer chanted, made signs in the air, and cast sacred water, Dragonov was amazed to see the hair vanish, the long teeth recede, and the face slowly take the shape of the boy's once more. The mother clutched Dragonov's arm, whispering, "Praise the gods, he is cured, he is *cured!*"

"Not yet," Hamer said when the spell was fully cast and the boy returned to his human form. "A final spell follows, and it is the most dangerous of all. The cure is not completed so long as the curse remains. It must be removed now, and that means not only stripping it from every cell of his body, but from his very spirit as well."

The priest then chanted the final spell, his voice rising and growing stronger. The lamp and the candles seemed to fade, and a wind blew, even though its source was nowhere in the chapel that Dragonov could determine.

Then the boy started to scream.

He shrieked as if his skin were being flayed all at once, or as if even greater pain were locked beneath every inch of flesh, so that flaying might release it and actually be a mercy. The wind blew harder, and the candles winked out, leaving only the sickly lamp to light the pitiful scene. Blood came from the boy's mouth, ears, and nose as he thrashed back and forth, unable to break his bonds. The priest's voice boomed louder and louder, as if it were the gods themselves who commanded the curse to vacate Erik's body and mind.

Then, after what seemed an eternity of watching the boy suffer, the spell was finished, and the wind stopped so quickly that Dragonov stumbled and the boy's mother fell, since they had braced themselves against its push.

Hamer stood, head down, arms hanging by his sides, totally exhausted. Erik lay on the altar to which he was bound, looking like any other boy on the verge of manhood. His mother ran to him and wiped the blood away from his face with the hem of her skirt, and then kissed his cheeks over and over again.

"Thank you," she said as Hamer put a hand on her

shoulder. "Oh, thank you, your worship. . ." Her words melted into incoherent babblings of gratitude.

"Do not thank me yet," Hamer said. "Ivan?" He turned to Dragonov with a questioning look, and Dragonov patted the handle of his axe in reply. Hamer nodded. "Open the shutters," he said.

Dragonov strode to the window through which the moonlight had poured, and threw back the shutters. But so much time had passed during the rituals that moonbeams no longer shone through. Hamer gestured to a pair of shutters farther down the chapel wall, and Dragonov went to them, trying not to listen to the mother babbling happily over the child that she felt had been restored to her.

Pausing only a moment, Dragonov threw back the wooden coverings. They struck the stone wall with a *clack,* and moonlight shot in through the stained glass windows, bathing the boy and his mother with reds and blues and golds all muddied by the dust motes the great wind had disturbed.

At first Dragonov thought the priest had been successful. The mother laughed as she ran her fingers over her son's human face, and Hamer stood hesitantly, scarcely daring to believe that he had been successful before the proof was incontrovertible.

But it was not long before proof of another nature reared its feral claws. In less than a minute after the moonlight struck Erik, the hair, the fangs, the snout began to grow, and had Dragonov not snatched the mother away from her son, the boy would have shredded her flesh with his sharp teeth. When she saw the transformation that had come over him again, and knew what it meant, she screamed and tried to go to him, as though she could drive out with maternal love what the priest had failed to abolish with all his sacred efforts.

Hamer looked at Dragonov. "Your young arms are stronger than my old ones. Make it swift and merciful. Remember, it was not his fault that he became thus."

"No!" the mother screamed, but Dragonov turned her over to the priest, who was able to hold her just long enough for Dragonov to draw his silver-bladed axe and, with one mighty swipe, sever the boy's head from his body.

The head went bouncing along the floor, and so rapid was the transition from beast to human that when it stopped rolling, Erik's young and innocent face lay looking up at them. There was peace in its expression, and Dragonov closed his eyes and breathed a prayer of thankfulness before he tugged his axe out of the altar.

Later, after they had calmed the mother and Hamer had given her several kroner to get her safely back to her home, they discussed the failed ceremony over a glass of wine in the priest's rooms.

"He was too young, too weak," said Hamer. "I was afraid his doom was a foregone conclusion. But it was worth taking the chance."

"Are *any* fully cured of the curse?" asked Dragonov.

The priest grinned bitterly. "I've performed that ritual two dozen times, and I can count on one hand the ones I've saved—usually grown men who are strong to begin with and who really want to be cured. With that young pup just now, lycanthropy probably offered him the first real excitement he'd ever had in his life. It's that way for many, I fear." He took a large gulp of wine, then sat back and appraised Dragonov. "Now you, Ivan, are the kind of man who'd come through it all right. Not to say that you'd want to undergo the experience."

"It looked pretty rough," Dragonov agreed.

"Rough indeed. I feel part of their pain during it, did you know that? Yes, a good priest shares in both the joy and misery of his flock. And if that pain is a taste of

what damnation is like, then I'll remain a priest until I
die, for I want no part of *that.* . . ."

* * * * *

Mordenheim's strangled cry brought Dragonov back
to the present. He saw that the doctor had stopped up
ahead to let Friedrich and Dragonov catch up to him.
The Falkovnian decided to try to put the dreadful memories behind and the uncertain future ahead of him, and
concentrate on the task at hand. "What is it?" Dragonov
asked, coming to the doctor's side.

"I feel him strongly here. It is so strong that I'm confused. Perhaps if we spread out widely across the plain
we may come across his tracks more readily."

So they walked abreast, fifty yards separating one
from another, and thus advanced upon the hill, Friedrich on the left, Dragonov in the middle, and Mordenheim on the right.

* * * * *

Another half mile brought them to the broad hill,
where mouths of caves dotted the land like pockmarks
in an ivory face. Friedrich despaired, for there seemed
to be so many, and Dragonov had told them that they
honeycombed the hill, one leading into another like a
vast labyrinth. How could they ever find Hilda?

Just as he was about to sob with frustration, he saw
regular indentations in the snow ahead. They were
spread so far apart that he thought they could not possibly be footprints, yet as he got closer, he saw that
they could be nothing else. They were both long and
wide, as if made by monstrously large feet, and they
bounded off around the left side of the great hill, head-
ing north.

"Here!" Friedrich called to the others, and they came running through the snow toward him.

"That's his trail, all right," said Dragonov. "I've seen it enough times to know. He takes long leaps, whether to confuse his trackers or just to travel fast, I don't know. But there's no man nor beast leaves tracks like that." The Falkovnian looked to where the tracks faded into the distance. "Let's follow him."

"Wait," said Friedrich. "The question is, is he going to where he's holding Hilda, or was he coming from there? These tracks make it look as though he came from these caves. If we follow them in reverse, mightn't we run a good chance of being able to rescue her while he's gone?"

"You may be right," said Mordenheim. "After all, finding and bringing back Fraulein Von Karlsfeld is our prime consideration."

Dragonov thought a moment. "These tracks have been made within the past hour. We might have time enough to get her out of wherever he's keeping her and maybe get a good head start as well." He eyed Friedrich. "What's that look for, boy? Surprised?"

"No, it's just that . . . well, you had seemed so anxious to confront the monster, and now . . ."

"And now maybe I'm not. We all confront our monsters sooner or later, boy. If he doesn't chase us down and catch us today, well, there's always another day."

Friedrich shook his head. "It's fine with me. All I care about is getting Hilda somewhere safe."

"Let's go then," said Dragonov, "and not stand about chattering like a bunch of old peasant women." He turned and strode toward the caves on their right, following the backward tracks as they grew closer together.

In truth, Dragonov was not looking forward to finding Adam. He was not afraid of the creature, but he was more than apprehensive about what the confrontation might do to him. So far it had been during moments of violence and surprise that whatever change it was had come upon him. If, he thought, he could avoid such situations, he might be able to get back to Stangengrad and Hamer. If there were a beast lurking within him, old Hamer would know how to banish it. It would be difficult and painful, but Dragonov had never shrunk from either ordeals or pain. He only prayed that the gods would keep him from harm's way until he could be freed of the lycanthropic blood that may have cursed him.

"This is it," Dragonov said, stopping at a hole in the wall of the hill. It led down at a steep angle, and the rock floor was streaked with ice.

"Hild—" Friedrich started to call, but Dragonov clapped a heavy gloved hand over his mouth.

"He could be in there, you know—maybe came in another way. Let's not herald our appearance, boy." He pointed downward. "Now be careful. You can see where the dry rock is, so stay to that. There's an open space down there where we can stop and light candles before we go farther in. Come on, and if either of you fall, don't take me with you."

They half walked, half slid down the slope, but all of them landed on their feet at the bottom. There they took candles from their packs, lit them, and started walking into the blackness, Dragonov in the lead, holding his axe.

Scarcely twenty yards in, they found two crude torches, heavy sticks of wood with cloth wrapped around the thickest end. When Dragonov held his candle to the cloth it flamed brightly, and he dropped the candle, lit the other torch, and handed it to Friedrich behind him.

It was a good thing that they had the strong light, for the passage was treacherous. Sharp stalactites hung low, and one spot that appeared to offer solid footing was slippery with moisture. Mordenheim lost his balance, but Friedrich grabbed him before he fell down a steep incline, at the bottom of which were stalagmites, their points as sharp as spears.

A short time later they passed by a dark hole in the cave wall. It was roughly a foot around, and Friedrich curiously thrust his torch into it, desperate for some clue of Hilda's presence.

The air was suddenly filled with flapping leathern wings streaming from the hole, hundreds of them striking Friedrich's head and shoulders. He felt wisps of hair against his face and in his mouth, and he panicked, dropping his torch, swinging his arms in the air to drive the things away.

A great blow felled him, and just as quickly the creatures were gone. He looked up to see a disgusted Dragonov standing over him, holding his torch and Friedrich's, both in one hand.

"They're called bats, boy. They live in caves, if your education didn't teach you that. Now get up and grab your torch and don't go sticking it where you're not going to follow."

Friedrich murmured an apology, took the torch, and followed as Dragonov walked on, shaking his head in disbelief at the boy's foolishness. For his part, the warrior had tensed for battle when Friedrich had flushed out the bats, but when he had seen there was no real danger, he successfully fought down the transformation. Still, he was annoyed at Friedrich for having nearly made him lose himself again.

They traveled another two hundred yards before they saw a glow up ahead. Dragonov held up his hand for silence, and the others stopped and listened as well. The only sound was that of a crackling fire, the snap and pop of pine knots bursting.

"Hilda!" Friedrich cried, and before Dragonov could

stop him, he ran past, his torch illuminating the way down a narrow and low-ceilinged hall until he burst through into a fire-lit inner chamber.

No more welcome sight could have met Friedrich's eyes, for there was Hilda, on her feet and apparently healthy, with no one else in the chamber.

"Friedrich?" she said. "Oh, my dear, is it truly you?" And then he enfolded her in his arms, and she knew that what she beheld was no delusion, but the glorious truth.

"All right," Dragonov boomed from the chamber entrance. "Get her bundled up and let's get out of here."

Mordenheim pushed past him and walked up to Hilda. "Fraulein Von Karlsfeld, are you unharmed?"

She frowned at the sight of the doctor, knowing that his concern was only for the blasphemous rite he wished her to perform, knowing him to be a liar and a far greater monster than his misunderstood creation.

"I am, Doctor. *Adam*"—she stressed the name—"has shown me every courtesy, and, as you can plainly see, has made me as comfortable as possible."

Mordenheim snorted. "Like one would keep an animal before butchering it, that is all. You were a hostage, not a guest. But now you are free, and I suggest we go from here immediately."

He started to turn, but she laid a hand on his arm. "No, Doctor Mordenheim. I think we should wait until Adam returns."

"Hilda!" Friedrich said. "What are you saying? Wait until the monster comes back?"

"Yes," she answered calmly. "I should like to see the doctor and his creation confront each other peacefully."

"You're insane, girl!" Mordenheim said. "Your abduction has made you lose your senses!"

"It has not," Hilda said. "I have spoken to Adam at length and have heard both sides of the story now. You painted him to be a monster, Doctor, and perhaps he is. But you, with your extreme lust to create life, no matter how vile the quality of that life may be, may have proven yourself the greater monster of the two."

Friedrich shook his head, as if he could not understand. "You . . . you have spoken with this thing?"

"Yes, Friedrich. You know my abilities; you know of the wrongness I felt concerning Doctor Mordenheim. Well, I have spoken to Adam long enough to form an impression, and yes, there is great potential for evil in him, and he *has* done evil in the past. But the great rift between him and the doctor was born of error and misunderstanding, a misunderstanding that could be rectified should the two of them come together without hostility for just one hour."

"He *lies!*" cried Mordenheim. "He lies and you believe him! Is a dead little girl not proof enough? Is what he did to my wife so easily wiped away? And what about the times he has ransacked the countryside? Dragonov, you have followed in his wake, you know the havoc he has caused!"

Dragonov nodded. "It is true. He has marked his trail with the corpses of innocents. I have seen them."

"It must then have been due to self-defense," Hilda insisted. "Would they not have tried to attack him? And can you blame him for fighting back?"

"Does fighting back explain men whose heads are wrenched from their bodies?" Dragonov said. "Or women with their garden sickles driven into their necks? I saw these things. I found no children murdered, but a good many orphaned, in farms miles away from any other settler, left to freeze or starve unless I led them to people who would care for them. I have seen this creature's evil, and someday . . ." His eyes looked far away, and his words were low. "Someday I shall stop him." Then he looked sharply at Hilda. "But not today. I know this man Mordenheim is no saint, miss, and what you say about him may well be true. Indeed, I've long suspected it.

"But we have no time this day. We must get you to safety, and I . . . well, there are things that I must do before I track the creature again." He threw off his pack and from it took a heavy cloak and high boots. "Put these on," he said, "and let's be off quickly. That thing won't stay away forever."

Hilda grabbed Friedrich's arms and looked at him beseechingly. "Friedrich, don't let this happen. Don't let this war go on. You know my powers; you know that when I have an impression it is never wrong. The things I felt about Mordenheim were grounded in truth, and Adam *told* me the truth."

"I know, my dear, and I do believe you, but it's your safety I have to be concerned with first. Think about the reaction this Adam will have when he finds us here— Mordenheim, whom we know he hates, and Dragonov, who has harried him before. He will see us as enemies, Hilda, and Dragonov is the only one fit enough to fight him, and he is weary and weakened from this journey. I beg you, dear, come with us. *Now.*"

"But, Friedrich, how can I when—"

"*Enough* of this!" Mordenheim said. "It is this simple, Fraulein Von Karlsfeld—if we wait for him, some of us, and quite possibly *all* of us, will *die.* There is no hope for reconciliation or explanations. Too much blood has been shed. And I have no doubt that that monster would tell you the same thing. He will kill your fiance, miss, without a moment's hesitation. But I shall no longer try to convince you of what I know to be fact. Dragonov, carry her out of here if she won't come with us!"

The warrior looked grim and nodded. "I beg your pardon, miss, but that is exactly what I'll do."

She whirled on Friedrich. "And would you let him?"

"I must, my love. For your own safety."

Hilda looked about her like a desperate animal ringed by predators. Then she seemed to deflate, and she hung her head. "Very well then. I leave here against my will. Do not blame me, any of you, for what is to follow."

She took the cloak and boots from Dragonov and put them on. "Let's go, then," she said.

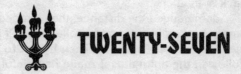 # TWENTY-SEUEN

The time had run away from Adam. He had found the tracks of a caribou a mile north of the cave and had begun to follow them rapidly, bouncing over the snowy ground with his giant leaps. He had spotted the trail just a few hundred yards short of the solid plain of ice that lay over the wintery Sea of Sorrows on the island's north.

Adam began to stalk the beast then, trying to get as close as possible before it saw him and fled. But cover was hard to come by in winter, and the darkness of his clothing made him prominent against the white landscape. The caribou soon saw him and started to run north. Adam followed, running as fast as he could. He had no doubt that he could eventually catch it, for while the creature could beat him in a sprint, his endurance was far greater.

The caribou ran until it reached the edge of the frozen sea, then turned east. Adam followed, paralleling its course, keeping the animal between him and the ice, for he knew there was a promontory a mile ahead where it would be cornered. When it reached that point, Adam began to close on it. If it ran to the left, he ran left more quickly. If it turned right, so did he, cutting it off. At length, it gave up trying to outflank him but then it did what he did not expect.

It leapt off the promontory, some twenty feet to the

ice below. When Adam ran to the edge, he saw that the fall had harmed its legs, and it limped away across the smooth surface, its left front hoof skittering out from under it, the others scrabbling madly to make up for the lack of traction.

Adam gauged the distance, then jumped as well. His knees bent as he hit, and he rolled himself into a ball to help cushion the impact. Then he got to his feet and followed the animal as it made its painful and ragged way across the ice. It took only minutes to reach the beast, grab its antlers, and twist. But the caribou slipped on the ice and came down atop Adam, knocking the air from his lungs. He got his feet under him, dug madly for a foothold, and wrenched on the antlers as hard as he could.

He felt the neck muscles give and heard the satisfying crack of the neck bones breaking. The caribou went limp, and he pushed it from him. It was dead within a few seconds. The tension vanished from the head as it lolled back, and the eyes went from frenzied and wide to soft and placid. Adam hoped that if he ever died, this was how death would come to him—like a gentle and welcome stranger.

From his belt he drew a knife that he had taken from a shepherd who had tried to kill him with it. After Adam had finished with him, the shepherd needed it no longer. There on the ice, he gutted the animal and left the innards for whatever sea birds or larger predators might come across them. Then he shouldered the animal's carcass and made his way across the ice to the shore.

The muffled globe of the sun was climbing higher in the dull gray sky, and with the burden he bore on his back slowing him down, he thought it might be close to noon before he reached the cave. The roasted meat would make a luncheon rather than a breakfast for

Hilda, but he was sure she would appreciate it whenever she ate.

He even took the time to stop and search several rock faces he knew where sea birds laid their eggs, but was unable to find any. In one nest he found a few hatchlings several days old, and thought about eating them, but decided that he would save his appetite for when he and Hilda ate their caribou steaks together.

It was shortly after noon when Adam, the caribou over his shoulders, arrived back at the cave. It took only a moment for him to figure out what had happened: three pairs of tracks entering the cave from the south and four pair leaving.

Rage swept through him. He tossed the carcass from his shoulders and ran into the darkness of the cave, experience guiding him through the labyrinth until he saw the glow of the fire. As he had suspected, the chamber was empty. Hilda was gone. He screamed a cry of fury that seemed to well up from the depths of his spirit, ripped the pallet off the floor, and threw it against the wall. He kicked over everything that he had gathered for her use, and when all was destroyed that could be, he pounded his fists against the stone walls and howled. Then he lowered his head, breathed deeply several times until his temper subsided, and walked very slowly and purposefully out of the cave.

He examined the tracks. The fourth set was Hilda's, that was certain, and he recognized Mordenheim's footprints as well. The doctor, in spite of his height, had a small, almost womanly foot. Another set of tracks were those of a heavier man and were nearly as long as Adam's himself. He had seen such footprints before in connection with Mordenheim, those of the red-bearded hunter who had once before sought to track him down. This time he and Mordenheim must have joined forces and succeeded.

The link. That damned link between the doctor and himself must have been the answer. Adam snarled angrily and examined the final set of tracks. A man, but not heavy. Kreutzer, no doubt, come to help save his fiancee. Three men then, and only one with any fight in him. Kreutzer he could easily break, and the doctor was no threat. Only Redbeard. Redbeard, who had hounded him like a stupid but persistent dog.

Adam had easily evaded him before, but this time they were bound to meet. Oh, yes. And then he would spill all his anger and rage on Redbeard. Then he would kill Kreutzer as well. As for Hilda, part of him wanted to take her back to the cave and keep her there, and part of him wanted to tear her apart for betraying him and fleeing with her rescuers. Perhaps by the time he had finished with Kreutzer and Redbeard, his blood thirst would be assuaged.

And Mordenheim? He would not die. Oh, no. The man *could* not die. He must live on and on, to see the woman he loved dead-alive and know he was powerless to save her. Adam would show him what his magical dabblings had accomplished—nothing but the deaths of two, and possibly three, people, the fate that must come to anyone trying to help Mordenheim revive dear, decaying Elise.

He started to follow the tracks south.

* * * * * *

A bullet whistled over Horg's head, and he hauled back hard on the reins, then jumped down off the coachman's box and hid behind the coach. The shot had been fired from behind, for he had heard the bullet slap into the bole of a tree ahead of him and to his right. He knew that the Vistani would pursue, but it surprised him that he had been caught so far from his destination.

It was only midafternoon, and he had expected that the drug would keep the Vistani asleep for at least twelve hours.

It must have been that witch, Horg thought—that horrible crone whom the sleeping powders had not affected. She must have awakened them with some countermeasure. He cursed himself for not doing something about her at the time. He could have struck her down, killed her. . . . No. That would have been impossible. She had terrified him too much for him to even approach her.

"What is it?" Ilisa called drowsily from inside the coach. "What is happening?"

Horg did not answer. He waited for a moment but heard nothing more and slowly raised his head. Another shot rang out, the bullet ripping the wood at the edge of the box. Horg ducked, but not before he had seen where the shot had been fired from—a rise a hundred yards behind the coach. He had seen a bright purple head scarf and a young man's face behind the gun. It would take the shooter a moment to reload after every shot, but that would not be enough time for Horg, with his bandy legs and slow gait, to reach him before he was ready to fire again.

Horg looked about and saw a jagged, fist-sized stone nearby. He grasped it in his gloved throwing hand, waited until he was sure his pursuer had reloaded, took a deep breath, and raised his head again, this time a few feet away from where he had peered before.

The shot came quickly, and at the sound of it he let out a loud grunt, threw up his left arm, and toppled slowly backward, out of sight of the sniper. There he waited, his heart pounding, squinting toward the back of the coach, around which he trusted his attacker would come.

"Horg?" Ilisa said. "*Horg?*"

He had not long to wait. From the sound of the rapid footsteps, the Vistana rifleman was running up as excitedly as a boy who has just bagged his first coney, with no sense of caution or suspicion of trickery. Either he had been taught poorly, or he was a fool.

"Ilisa?" he called in a voice that had scarcely changed from the piping of pubescence. "Are you in there?"

"Mikael!" the girl called back.

The boy had scarcely rounded the back of the coach, his gun barrel pointing toward the ground, when Horg launched the rock, sending it speeding toward the boy's chest. It caught him full over the heart, knocking the wind out of him so that he fell back, landing on his buttocks and dropping his gun. He sat there stupidly, just long enough for Horg to grasp the rifle, point it at the boy, and pull the trigger.

Nothing happened. The Vistana, so sure of his aim, had not even reloaded. The boy, in his midteens with scarcely a trace of beard, started to push himself to his feet, rage and embarrassment commingling on his smooth face.

But Horg lifted the rifle barrel first and brought the wooden butt down heavily on the boy's head. The young man groaned and fell again, and this time did not get up. Blood trickled onto the muddy soil from the wound in his head, and Horg knew the lad would trouble him no more.

"Mikael!" Ilisa called. "Are you there? Are you all right? What has—"

"He is *dead,*" Horg said. There was silence in the coach for a moment, and then Horg heard Ilisa softly sobbing. "I didn't mean to hit him so hard."

"He was fifteen," Ilisa said, tears in her voice. "Only fifteen."

"He tried to kill me," Horg said by way of explanation.

But no words from within condoned his actions, and he sadly turned and went to the spot from where the boy had fired.

There he found, as he had thought he would, a horse tied to a tree. It was a fine chestnut mare. Horg assumed that the boy had been the first to wake up, had figured out what had occurred, and had taken the fastest horse in the Vistana corral to save Ilisa, probably the girl he loved. How could any of the young bucks *keep* from loving her?

Horg untied the horse and led it back to the coach. There he unfastened the two horses, took a saddle from the back of the coach, and placed it on the stronger of the two mounts. Then he climbed into the back and untied Ilisa.

"We ride from here," he said. "I'll take the chestnut, and you'll ride the bay. The chestnut is clearly faster, so if you try to escape I'll have no trouble catching you. Don't drag behind either. I know the horse well. Now come."

She blinked when she came out into the daylight, even though the sky was overcast with clouds. When she saw the gypsy boy's body, she gasped and knelt by his side, but Horg jerked her to her feet and led her to the saddled bay. It was not until he had helped her onto the horse that she finally looked at him, and when she did, her eyes widened. "Your face . . ." she said.

He put his hand to his face, but could feel nothing amiss. It had been itching for the past several hours, but he had thought nothing of it, and could feel no hives or blemishes on the cherubic countenance that had caused Ilisa to dub him *angeli*. There was no mirror in the coach, and he did not want to take time to stop and examine his face in a pond. "What?" he said. "What is it, what's wrong?"

She shook her head, whether in confusion or pity he

could not tell. "It's darkening," she said. "Look at your hands."

He tugged the leathern glove from his right hand and gave a grunt of amazement as his flesh came into view. The fingers were dark, far darker than exposure to the sun would have made them. Tentatively, he pulled up his sleeve and saw that the change in shade had extended up his arm as well, and now that it was exposed to the air, his arm had begun to itch as badly as his face. Horg looked up at Ilisa. "What is this? Is it . . . a curse?"

"Did Nana know it was you?" asked Ilisa slowly. "When you took me away?"

Horg's throat was suddenly too thick to speak, and he only nodded.

"Then it is hers," Ilisa said. "Her punishment."

Horg stood for a minute uncertain of what to do. He had heard tales of those who stole from the Vistani, that there were curses that turned their fingers as black as midnight, and that every Vistana who saw them after would recognize them as a thief and an enemy to the tribes. Was there, he wondered, a curse that would make the whole body so dark that no light whatsoever would reflect off it? Was this what would happen to him?

Then he remembered the person he had always turned to. Doctor Mordenheim could help him. It was a condition of the skin, a rash of some kind, and there would be medicines the doctor could give him, *some* way he could help. There *had to* be, because there was no alternative. Letting Ilisa go would not lift the curse, for he had still killed the Vistana boy. As for waiting for the Vistani to catch up to him and begging for their forgiveness, well, one might just as well ask for mercy from Mordenheim's monster for all the good that would do.

So his decision was made for him. There would be no betrayal of the doctor, no running away with the girl to some idyllic future that could never be. He would do his duty to Mordenheim and hope the doctor could do right by him.

Horg said nothing more to Ilisa, pulled down his sleeve, tugged his glove back on, and swung into his saddle. He grasped his mount's reins as well as those of Ilisa's horse and began to ride north. After a mile or so, Ilisa asked him why he had taken her away.

"There is someone who needs your help," he said. "Someone I work for."

"Why didn't you just ask me?"

"Would you have come?" Horg said with a scoffing tone. "With *me?*"

"I might have."

"You lie."

"And do you owe this employer of yours so much that you would risk the vengeance of the Vistani?"

"I don't . . . think about those things. I obey, that is all."

"That can be a dangerous habit to have, Horg."

"Be quiet and ride," Horg said. "The night is coming fast enough, and the longer we are abroad in this land after dark, the greater the chance of this danger you fear."

TWENTY-EIGHT

Mordenheim and his party had been on the ice for some time before Adam caught up with them. They were picking their way across, Dragonov in front trying to hurry them, striking the ice with his pick and stepping heavily as if to show the others that there was nothing to fear if they followed in his footsteps.

Mordenheim and Hilda were the stragglers. Mordenheim was exhausted, and Hilda was simply not well prepared for the grueling trek across the floes. Friedrich helped her all he could, though the girl resented his assistance. She seemed distracted and irritable, for reasons other than the hardship of the walk.

"Hilda," he said, "I am sorry, truly, but this is the only way."

"Any way has difficulties, Friedrich. The one you have chosen may have the worst of all."

"But how?"

"Did it not occur to you that Adam will find me missing and follow me? And his rage will be far greater than if we had waited for him in the cave."

"But we would feel his wrath either way. At least now we have a chance of escaping him. He may not catch up to us, and hopefully by the time he reaches the mainland, *we* may be on our way home." He kept his voice low so that Mordenheim would not hear. "What Adam wanted was for us not to help Mordenheim. And we will not. Even if Horg has somehow managed to whisk the girl from under the gypsies' eyes, we still need not perform the operation. We can walk to Ludendorf if we must—it's only a few miles from the castle. And Dragonov can help us. In fact, I'm sure he will if he learns what Mordenheim intends. And I suspect Mordenheim would rather that Dragonov *not* know. It would strike him as more black wizardry."

Hilda shook her head. "You forget, Friedrich, that I saw him cross this terrain. He carried me much of the way and still moved far faster than we are moving now. I have no doubt that he will overtake us."

"But look up ahead," said Friedrich, pointing to a dark pile of something that Hilda eventually discerned as broken boards. "His boat. We destroyed it. If we reach the water, we are safe, and it can only be another mile or so. See, the ice is growing thinner."

"And more precarious, making us move slower," said Hilda grimly.

She was right. Dragonov was gauging his footfalls more precisely now, tapping with the pick and moving one way or the other, making an irregular path across the floes. They leapt over water several times, Hilda's strong legs bearing her across, while Mordenheim's weary limbs nearly plunged him into cold wetness more than once.

"Be careful!" Dragonov roared. "It'll take more time to pull one of you out of the drink than it will to cross this lunatic's ice pile safely!"

After another half mile of delicate and hazardous walking, Dragonov finally shouted, "The boat! I see our boat!"

* * * * * *

Adam heard a shout somewhere up ahead, and continued his pursuit with increased vigor, especially after having found the shattered remnants of his boat.

If they reached their vessel before he caught them, their escape would be assured. The icy waters would not kill him, so he could swim after them for a distance, but eventually his limbs would grow numb, and he would be unable to propel himself and be at the mercy of the tides.

So he ran, less carefully now. He broke through the ice several times, but each time was able to pull himself out before the cold currents dragged him underneath the thick barrier between water and air.

Soon he saw some figures ahead, and as he grew closer he counted four of them. Mordenheim, his creator and nemesis, was in the rear, walking slowly and painfully. Adam's heart started pounding more heavily as he recognized Hilda Von Karlsfeld, walking next to young Kreutzer. Ahead was the red-bearded man, a hundred yards in front of him a long, dark object that could only be their boat.

As he advanced upon them, Adam did not yet know what he intended to do. His thought of killing all but Mordenheim had evaporated at the sight of Hilda. Now he wanted only to take her back with him again, keep her in the cave, listen to her tell of the world to which he was barred, and see a female face that did not instantly recoil at the sight of him. If that meant killing Kreutzer and Redbeard, so be it. She would be repulsed, no doubt, but time would ease her sorrow for her lover and dull the hatred she would feel toward Adam for killing him. If it was a choice between speaking to him or going mad from loneliness in the cave, she would choose the former.

He clenched his teeth and ran, though there was plenty of time to overtake them before they reached their boat.

* * * * *

"The monster!" Dragonov shouted, and instantly the other three whirled to look. Mordenheim spat a curse and raised his ice staff, ready to skewer Adam when he approached. Friedrich protectively tried to put Hilda behind him, but she came around his side, already raising her arms to plead that no man would harm another.

But for Dragonov, there was no waiting to meet an enemy. Axe in hand, he hurled himself forward across the fragile surface of ice nearly as fast as Adam ran toward them. Though Hilda tried to stop Dragonov, he evaded her easily. "Get to the boat!" he growled as he ran past Mordenheim, and the doctor thought that his voice sounded more thick and guttural than usual.

Adam stopped and set himself as the Falkovnian approached. If the man could swing that axe as lightly as he carried it, he might make a formidable opponent indeed. Dragonov aimed the first swing at Adam's midsection, so there could be no dodging, only retreat. Adam fell back as the blade sheared through his coat and sliced his flesh. He grunted, not from the pain, but from the effort to escape what might have been a killing thrust.

Dragonov tried to use his backswing, but Adam was too quick. He dived under the flashing arc of the axe and struck the warrior in the legs, throwing him backward so that he landed on his back and slid another yard across the ice, his fingers still wrapped firmly around the axe handle.

Dragonov was up in a flash, but had no time to prepare for Adam, who struck him in the face with his fist, a blow that would have felled a war-horse. Dragonov lurched to the left, then caught himself and drew back his arm to deliver another swing of his weapon. But Adam was already there. He grasped Dragonov's arm with one huge hand and the shaft of the axe with the other, then ripped the deadly weapon away, flinging it over and off the edge of the ice so that it sank beneath the chill waters of the Sea of Sorrows.

Redbeard would follow, thought Adam, and he grabbed the man by the shoulders, struggling to bring him to the edge of the ice floe and hurl him into the deadly water.

But he found the man not so easy to move. Dragonov reached up between Adam's arms and smashed him in the face with a two-fisted blow that staggered Adam and made him take a few steps back.

The two men stood looking at each other for a moment. Adam wondered how best to get inside the man's guard and had decided to go for the legs again and get his opponent down on the ice, but suddenly Dragonov charged him with a berserker shout, both hands raised like claws.

Adam blocked the attack with his forearms in an **X** pattern, but the force of the man's rush pushed Adam down, Dragonov atop him, his gloved fingers clawing ineffectively at Adam's face.

Then something happened that Adam, even with his years of misadventures, had never yet seen. The fingertips of Dragonov's gloves ripped out, and through them burst long, yellow claws that darted toward Adam's eyes. As quick as a thought, Adam uncrossed his forearms and locked onto the man's wrists. But it seemed that Dragonov's strength had increased threefold. It was all Adam could do, even with his own superhuman strength, to hold the sharp claws at bay.

The man growled then, and hot spittle dripped from his mouth down onto Adam's face. Adam blinked it away and saw that now the man's *face* was changing. It seemed to be moving toward Adam, and he realized that it was lengthening, the nose and mouth jutting snoutlike toward him. Yes, it was *becoming* a snout, and bright red hair was sprouting over the part of the face that was naked of beard, until the face itself seemed to blend into the fur collar of the coat. The lips were drawing back as if tugged by invisible wires, and the eyeteeth had lengthened to fangs.

Now that cavernous maw creaked open, and Adam smelled a breath stinking of cold tombs and hot blood. Green eyes burned down at him, and in them he saw not even the trace of humanity that he spied in his own reflection. There was only mindless destruction and wrath.

And then the jaws drove toward his face.

He whipped his head to the side, but felt the fangs tear into his ear, and the cool trickle of blood down the side of his neck. Adam released the arms of the thing that the red-bearded man had become, then wrapped his huge, long-fingered hands around the neck of the beast, now far thicker than a man's neck, and pushed it up and away from him, driving with all his strength.

Adam's arms were longer than any man's but were only a few inches longer than the lycanthrope's. Still, it was enough, and the claws reaching futilely for Adam's flesh slashed the air. When it could not reach his head, it grasped his arms. But by then Adam was firmly on his feet, holding the strangling thing at bay as its claws shredded his coat and began digging into his skin.

Finally the beast-man's struggles began to diminish. Its tongue started to droop from its ravening snout, its eyes began to bulge with more than blood lust, and its arms waved helplessly, Adam's blood dripping from its claws. Adam was about to throw it to the ice and smash its skull with both fists when he heard a loud cracking noise and felt the world give way beneath him.

* * * * * *

Mordenheim had not followed Ivan Dragonov's
instructions. Instead of rushing himself and the others
to the boat, he had breathlessly watched the battle
between what had become two monsters. Friedrich and
Hilda were similarly transfixed, unable to take their
eyes off this clash of titans.

Aside from the suffocating sense of dread he knew to
be Adam's pain, Mordenheim's emotions were mixed.
He had wanted Dragonov to defeat Adam and not kill
him, but now the Falkovnian had transformed into what
could only be a lycanthrope. Such matters changed
everything. What was to stop Dragonov from turning on
them if he dispensed with Adam? But now it looked as
though Adam had the upper hand, so that they would
have to face the lesser of two evils—a raging Adam
rather than a savage werebeast. In spite of his danger,
Mordenheim could not help but be curious as to
whether or not the contagion of lycanthropy, which, he
felt, had no supernatural basis but was simply a sys-
temic disease, would affect Adam, whose physiology
was far different from that of humans.

Friedrich and Hilda's feelings were not as scientific.
They watched with horror as Dragonov changed from
man to beast, and Hilda found herself wanting Adam to
triumph. Him she knew, but she had scarcely met this
giant Falkovnian who now proved to be something
other than a mighty protector. Friedrich, on the other
hand, saw no hope no matter who proved victorious.
He thought that Adam would kill them all, and if Dragonov's wolf form won, the only weapon with which
Friedrich could keep the bloodthirsty creature at bay,
the silver-edged axe, was at the bottom of the sea.

So it was with a certain horrified delight that he saw
the ice crack open beneath the weight of the two behe-
moths. Both of them tottered for a moment, then slowly
slid toward the water as the broken slabs of ice on

which they had been standing tilted and rose higher and higher, precipitating them at last into the frigid sea.

Adam never once removed his hands from Dragonov's neck.

Mordenheim, Friedrich, and Hilda ran as close to the break-up as they dared, and saw two dark forms being swept away by the currents under the ice, not toward open water, but to where the ice grew too thick for even a superman to break, to where there was no place to surface, no air, no life.

Hilda, disregarding the ice that had broken nearby, followed the dusky forms as they drifted beneath the ice like ghosts within a faded tapestry. Shortly they came to a place where the currents changed, and they stopped drifting so that Hilda and the men who followed her stood directly above them.

She saw Dragonov's face first. The eyes were open, and the hair on the face moved and shimmered in the water so that it looked as though the transformation were still occurring.

Adam's hands were locked about the thick throat, and she called his name, not loudly, but in anguish that any creature should die like this. He seemed to hear, for his face turned upward until it was pressed to the ice. His eyes were barely open, but Hilda was as sure as she was of anything in life that he saw her face.

A bubble drifted from his partly open mouth, and was trapped beneath the ice as the corners of his mouth drew slightly upwards. It might have been a smile, or it might have been merely a trick of the thick prism of frozen sea through which she saw him. Whatever the truth, she fell to her knees, her face only inches from his own but worlds apart. She wanted him to know that she had not meant it to end like this, wanted to tell him that he was not a monster but a man, wanted to save him.

But instead she could only watch as a whim of the sea sucked him and the werebeast down and away into smothering blackness.

The two men stood there, and Hilda remained on her knees, straining her eyes, trying to focus on something beyond the ice, but there was nothing there to see.

"They're gone," said Friedrich softly.

Hilda looked up at him. "He wasn't a monster, Friedrich."

Friedrich nodded as though he understood and held his hand out to her. She took it, stood up, and moved into his embrace.

"All right," said Mordenheim with barely contained elation, "we've wasted enough time. They're gone, so let's get to the boat. Horg must have returned by now. And Elise is waiting."

Hilda started to say something, but Friedrich signaled her to be quiet. She understood. There would be plenty of time to tell Mordenheim of their decision not to help him when they were safely back on the mainland.

"Did you speak?" asked Mordenheim, and she thought there was a sly look about him.

"No, Doctor. Nothing. It can wait."

Then, ever so carefully, they made their way back to where the boat waited, and rowed for Schloss Mordenheim.

 **TWENTY-NINE**

Horg groaned in spite of himself. Although he kept his gloves on, he could feel all too easily what was happening to him. His flesh had been itching unbearably ever since they had rounded the northern end of the Sleeping Beast. Several times he had put his gloved hand within his coat and shirt and scratched himself. Even with the gloves on, he could feel the texture of his skin. It was dry, thin, almost papery in spots, and when he looked at his gloves, there were bits of black flakes, like the ashes of burned parchments, clinging to them. He shuddered, wiped them on his trousers, and did not touch himself again.

It was maddening. It felt as though every inch of skin were being bitten by fleas. Yet he knew that if he scratched, pieces would come off, and perhaps the flesh would never grow back.

Ilisa had to know how terrible his plight was, but she had said nothing throughout the entire ride. He had caught her looking at him only twice, and both times the expression on her face was one that Horg did not want to inspire, and he could not help but wonder what his itching, formerly *angeli* face must look like now.

Fortunately, however, he had seen no sign of pursuit. They rode quickly and rested the horses seldom. Now that night had fallen, they moved more slowly, but he knew it would take only another hour of riding before they saw the castle.

That hour was the longest of Horg's life. Now it seemed as though the imaginary fleas biting him had mandibles of fire and were burrowing beneath his flesh and laying eggs, and that those eggs were hatching and the grubs were chewing on the muscle beneath his skin. He whimpered many times, and rubbed his arms against his body, trying to get some ease. But there was none. And seeing darkness in every window of Schloss Mordenheim only made things worse. The doctor was not there to help Horg.

All right then, he would help himself. He would find something in the doctor's laboratory to give him ease, perhaps one of the drugs that caused the fatally ill to die just a little sooner. Taken in smaller doses, the doctor had told him, it could erase the pain of the dying. But as they rode down the path to the castle gate, he saw three figures dragging themselves over the rim of the cliff where the slope was easiest to climb. The man was there, and the woman, and—oh, thank the gods—the doctor too!

"Get off," he told Ilisa when they reached the figures. She did not move quickly enough, so he shouted, "Get off, get off!" He had not brought her all this way and gone through so much suffering to let her escape now.

He let the horses stand where they had stopped, grasped Ilisa's arm, and dragged her to meet Mordenheim. "Doctor!" he cried. "The girl, I have brought her, but they have *cursed* me, Doctor. Look, look at my skin!"

Though Mordenheim was appalled by the condition of Horg's flesh, the servant could not fail to notice the joy that swept over Mordenheim's face at his first glimpse of Ilisa.

"Yes, yes, she is beautiful, Doctor," panted Horg. "But what about *me?* You must help me, you must!"

"For pity's sake, Mordenheim," said Friedrich, "help the man! Can't you see he's in agony?"

"All right, all right," Mordenheim barked. "Let's get into the castle, up to the laboratory."

"But wait," said Ilisa. "Can't you tell me why I'm here? What do you want from me?"

"All in good time, my dear," said Mordenheim silkily. "But for now we must ease my servant's complaints. Come, all of you." He took Ilisa's arm and led her through the courtyard into the great hall, and through the labyrinth of stairs and halls that led to the laboratory. Friedrich, Hilda, and Horg followed, the servant scratching madly all the way.

Hilda had looked at Horg only once and could not bear to look again. His suffering was evident in every line of what little face was left him. His skin appeared to be flaking off in large, feathery, black pieces.

When they entered the laboratory and Mordenheim lit the lamps, Ilisa looked about her. She saw the figure of Elise under the sheet and started to shake. "What place is this?" she asked, her voice trembling.

"It is a sacred place, my dear, the sanctuary of science. There is nothing for you to fear here. You will not be harmed in any way."

"Master, *please* . . ." said Horg.

"Yes, yes," Mordenheim said. "My poor Horg, let me prepare something to make you feel better." The doctor took several jars of chemicals from his shelves and mixed some together, then held a vial of the mixture, a thick, yellowish brew, out to Horg. "Drink," he said. "It will first ease the pain, then banish it altogether."

"And my skin? It will be made aright?"

"It will, my friend. But the first thing is to ease your suffering. Now drink, and quickly." Horg emptied the vial down his throat and shuddered at the taste. "You should begin to feel better momentarily. Now tell me," the doctor went on, more urgently, "have you been followed by the Vistani?"

"I was . . ." said Horg, trying to get back his breath after taking the bitter medicine ". . . was followed by one of them. He is dead. We left the coach and rode the horses after that. I saw nothing more, though they might be after us."

"What do you think, girl?" Mordenheim asked Ilisa. "Will your people come after you? And if they do, can they find you?"

"I know they will," said Ilisa proudly. "And if they can do *that* from afar," she said, gesturing to Horg, "they can surely find one of their own. Let me go now, and I will beg them to leave without doing further harm to any of you."

Mordenheim laughed. "Let you *go?* After all the struggles that my friend Horg and I have undergone to bring you here? I hardly think so."

"*I* think so, Doctor," said Friedrich. "There is no way you can do this without Hilda and me. And we have decided not to help you."

"That's right, Doctor," Hilda said. "This girl is an unwilling victim, and we will not be a part of this. Let her go."

Mordenheim sneered. "*You* have decided? *You* will not be a part of this? Do you think I have gone to all this trouble for you to merely change your minds and walk out on me?"

He turned and strode to a small cabinet on the wall, yanked it open, and drew out two pistols, which he pointed straight at Hilda and Friedrich. "These are primed and loaded with two shots each. If you do not help me, you are worthless to me, and there is no reason I should keep you alive."

"That will not change our minds!" Friedrich cried.

"You think not? Then perhaps the thought of your

fiancee being killed first, and then being experimented on as you watch, will have some bearing on your decision. *Horg!* How are you feeling?"

Horg shook his black and cracking head in wonder. "The pain . . . it's *gone*. But my skin . . ."

"It will heal. Now," the doctor continued, "give me the syringe from the tabletop there." Mordenheim laid down one of the pistols, but kept the other trained on Hilda and Friedrich as Horg handed him the needle. "Good. Now bring the girl here."

Ilisa struggled, but was helpless in Horg's hands. Friedrich moved to stop the servant, but Mordenheim said, "Ah ah!" and swung the pistol on Hilda. Friedrich stopped and stood, fuming.

"Now, Horg," said Mordenheim, "show me this child's pretty arm." Horg tugged up Ilisa's bunched sleeve until it was far above her elbow, and Mordenheim stuck the needle tip into the muscle of the girl's arm. Ilisa gave a small cry of pain, and then almost immediately went limp in Horg's grasp.

"Put her on the table next to Elise," said Mordenheim. When Horg had done so, the doctor clapped his hand on the servant's shoulder. "Get several rifles from the armory and climb to the watchtower. If the Vistani come, sound the alarm bell and fire down upon them. They must not enter, Horg, and if they do, it must not be before the experiment is completed. You understand?"

"Yes, Doctor," Horg said, sounding almost happy. "And thank you, sir, thank you. . . ."

Mordenheim shook his head dismissively, as though what he had done for Horg was nothing, and Hilda wondered if that might not just be the case.

After Horg had bowed and scraped his way out of the laboratory, she fixed Mordenheim with a glare. "You didn't cure him, did you?" she said.

Mordenheim looked back at her steadily, not at all abashed. "Horg is a dead man," he said. "I have seen that condition only once before, back when I was a medical student. It was a man who said he had killed an old gypsy woman and stolen her purse. There was nothing we could do for him but banish his pain, so that when the time came he only saw the horror, but did not feel it."

"The horror?" said Friedrich.

"You are better off not knowing," Mordenheim answered. "In the watchtower, he will die alone, and perhaps, if he sees the Vistani coming, he may be able to perform me one final service."

"I don't understand you," Hilda said. "He has served you loyally all his life, the only one of your servants who didn't desert you. And you treat his death with such callousness. . . ."

"What do you expect, Fraulein Von Karlsfeld—that I should weep for the man, and cry 'boo hoo hoo?'" The scoffing words were obscenely exaggerated. "Had it not been for me, he'd have died when he was a boy, beaten by bullies. And if not then, later, sold into some circus where he'd have been fed slops and people would've paid half a penny to gawk at him until his proud and stupid heart broke. If I could save him, I would. But I can't. No one can."

His voice grew softer. "I'm sorry he will die, yes. But if my life's work succeeds, no one need ever die again. And that work *cannot* succeed until Elise is back with me again, to love and inspire me. And by the fanciful gods I mock, she will return to me—this very night!"

"You really expect us to help you?" Friedrich said.

"Yes, I expect you to help me," said the doctor. "*Or,* I expect you to watch your fiancee die and possibly live again. . ." He pointed with one of the two guns to the table on which the vile flesh of Elise was visible. "Would

you enjoy that, Herr Kreutzer? To see your dear Hilda
alive in death as my Elise has been all these years?
Or would you rather help me and have the only price
be the spirit of a stupid gypsy girl, a Vistana, who
many people say are no more than animals? It is your
choice."

"Friedrich," Hilda said calmly. "I think we should
help Doctor Mordenheim."

Friedrich turned toward her, amazed. He could not
read her look. She only gazed at him from under cool
and canted brows, as though she were in total control of
the situation. Was she willing to perform the operation
then, to save her life and his?

The thoughts clustered in his head like hordes of
those damnable bats from Adam's cave, all fluttering at
once. Performing the ceremony would be a terrible
thing to do against the gypsy girl's will. But the girl
might be doomed anyway, for Mordenheim would
never let her go alive. Then why throw his and Hilda's
lives after the girl's? Yet might it not be better to die
pure than to participate in such evil? He felt his head
would break with the conflicting thoughts.

"We will prepare," Hilda said smoothly, "and then I
will read, and you repeat what I say." She looked at
Friedrich knowingly, and he knew that somehow she
had a plan that might rescue both their lives and their
spirits. "Do you understand?"

"Yes," he said, nodding his head. "I suppose it is the
only way."

"A wise decision," said Mordenheim. "Still, you will
not be offended if I retain my weapons? It is not my
hands that shall be busy this night, but yours." He
jerked the guns toward the two women lying side by
side. "Make haste, for the Vistani ride swiftly."

Hilda stayed with Mordenheim while Friedrich
returned to their rooms to get the equipment they

needed. Mordenheim kept one eye on Hilda, the other on the Vistana girl lying atop the table. She was beautiful indeed, both in face and form, and he knew that her body would be an ideal dwelling place for his dear Elise's spirit.

Hilda's voice broke through his reverie. "Do you ever worry, Doctor, about your own spirit?"

"My spirit? My dear fraulein, I have no spirit. I have consciousness and intelligence, both of which are the result of the workings of my brain."

"Then what is it that you wish us to take from your wife's body and place into this girl's, if not the spirit?"

"Her life-force, the electrical impulses in which her memory and thoughts are stored. These I have kept alive in her."

"Then," said Hilda, "what is there to keep the gods from keeping your 'electrical impulses' alive when *your* body dies and torturing those 'impulses' of yours forever?"

Mordenheim chuckled. "My dear lady, *I* am *real,* these gods of yours are fancy."

"Then, Doctor Mordenheim, what gave Adam life?"

His eyes narrowed. "Why, *I* did!" he said petulantly.

She shook her head. "No, Doctor. Your mind is brilliant, but you did not create life in Adam."

"And how do you know that?"

"Because he has a spirit, Doctor, as do all creatures made by the gods. I felt it when I was with him. And you, Doctor, great as your knowledge may be, do not have the ability to grant a spirit. Or should I say that while you have great knowledge, you have very little wisdom."

Mordenheim's face soured. "You may say what you like. Just make certain that you move Elise's 'spirit,' as you idiotically call it, into that girl's body. And as for *her* spirit, you may do with it what you will!"

"Do you mean that?" Hilda eyed him appraisingly.

"Of course. Let it dissipate into fragments or pop it in a pot and cook it up—what do I care?"

"I shall preserve it then," said Hilda. "There are certain . . . operations in which a spirit may prove a valuable item of barter."

Mordenheim snorted. "And you called *me* callous."

"Have you," said Hilda, "a spare retort I could use?"

"Of course. Over there." He gestured to a counter filled with chemical glassware. "Take whatever you like."

She chose a retort and placed it on the floor between the tables on which Elise Mordenheim and Ilisa lay. "The spirit, so say my lunatic studies, will enter an open vessel rather than an uninhabitable body. And then it will be mine, along with the money you have promised, yes?"

"I always pay my debts," said Mordenheim. "Despite your attempted change of heart, I have no intention of withholding from you what I said I would pay. I am a man of honor, regardless of what you may think. Ah, but here comes the honorable Herr Kreutzer, with everything your ceremony requires. Sir, I pray you hold out everything you have brought before I turn this pistol from Fraulein Von Karlsfeld. There are other weapons in this house, and if you have betrayed me once, you may do so again."

Friedrich held out what he had fetched—a red robe, Von Schreck's book, several bizarrely shaped scepters, and a rack that held vials of earth and oils.

Mordenheim nodded. "Very well. Proceed."

Friedrich donned the robe, then began to make designs on the floor between the two unconscious women, first with the oils, then with the vials of earth directly on top of the oils so that the earth adhered to the floor and would not be blown away.

While he did this, Hilda perused the book, taking in every word and nodding to herself, glancing from the living girl to the woman who lay half in death, half in life. Then she rose, showed Friedrich a design in the book, and said, "Make this pattern around the retort. It is to catch the girl's spirit when it leaves her."

Friedrich looked at her oddly, but she merely nodded and smiled as if to assure him of her intent, and he did as she asked.

Mordenheim watched and waited impatiently, but would not hurry them. Everything had to be correct. There could be no mistakes. Soon he would hold Elise again, in the charming guise of this dark-eyed gypsy girl. He could understand why the tribe would be anxious to have her back. She was truly beautiful, in a far wilder way than Elise had been, and Mordenheim could hardly wait to take her in his arms. He wondered if Horg had tried to kiss the girl, then decided that he would not have. He had given Horg orders not to harm her in any way, and if there was one thing of which he could be certain, it was Horg's obedience.

The poor fool. At least he would not suffer long. Mordenheim doubted if Horg had an hour of life left to him. Well, he had been a faithful servant. No man could have wanted better. And he had done his final duty well. Mordenheim silently reminded himself to put a marker above Horg's grave.

 **THIRTY**

In spite of Mordenheim's fatalism, Horg felt good. He did not feel in the slightest like dying. A little weary, that was all, from riding so long without rest. It was good to sit up here in the watchtower, feeling the air blow against his previously hot flesh.

But it was hot no longer. The doctor had fixed it. He had cured Horg, made him all better. There was no pain now, no burning, no itching. There was hardly any feeling at all. Horg thought that he should have felt colder, but he did not. It was a strange sensation, to be high in that tower with its open windows, the wind blowing in, and not feel cold at all. It puzzled him, so he opened his coat and his shirt, and let the freezing gusts batter his chest.

No. Nothing. Not cold at all. He felt like a superman.

Maybe he was, he thought. Perhaps the combination of the gypsy's curse and Doctor Mordenheim's medicine had made him something more than human, had haphazardly created what the doctor had wanted all along.

He chuckled at the thought, but scarcely heard himself over the screaming of the gale. If only his skin *looked* better. But it would. The doctor had told him so. He had extinguished the lantern that had led him up the tower stairs so that he might better see any movement below or on the southern horizon from which the Vistani would come. But a gibbous moon that skulked behind clouds occasionally lit the tower room enough for him to see his flesh, still black and crusted, as though he had burned it badly.

Yet it did not hurt, and every time the moon peered out again, he expected it to be healed and whole—the doctor's elixir providing its promised miracle.

So he watched his flesh and the horizon, and neither one changed for a long time. Then he thought that he detected movement out there in the darkness, and fixed his eyes upon the spot, watching carefully. It seemed that a darker night descended on the plains of Lamordia. Something huge and black and irregular slowly fell over Horg's vision, and he realized that it was not with both his eyes that he saw this second night, but with his left one only. It continued to fall, and he reached up to wipe it from his eye.

When his hand came away, he saw his left eyelid clinging to his knuckle. Though he barely felt the wet stickiness that kept it attached to his hand, he saw it glimmering in the moonlight.

Then his attention was drawn away by the motion he had seen before. There was a flicker of light far in the distance, then another and another. Horg tried to blink and bring his eyes more sharply into focus, but though his right eye obeyed, there was no lid on the left to clear and cleanse the eyeball, and its vision quickly grew cloudy.

He scratched his head in confusion, unable to even close the offending eye and thus achieve sharp vision with his remaining one. But when he scratched, he found that his fingers sank into a liquified layer that could be nothing but the skin over his temple. He felt the tips of his fingers brush the strands of muscle, felt soft and wet lumps of skin break off and ooze their way down the side of his face.

He snorted in disbelief, for there was still no pain at

all, and as the air passed explosively from his mouth, the two thick flaps of skin that had been his lips flew from his face and landed with a wet slap on the stone floor. The horror of the sight drained his strength from him, and his legs gave out so that he fell to the floor, his legs and buttocks striking heavily and splashing a fountain of black putrescence about him like a veil.

The idiot moon went behind a cloud then, but when it returned, Horg looked down at his chest and saw that the skin on it seemed to be melting away, turning to a thin tar that trickled down over his stomach and onto his lap. Panicked, he tried to take off his shirt, but now the transformation had extended to his fingers as well. The skin slid down each fingertip like the fingers of gloves, leaving only muscle, also black in the moonlight, and softening bone peeking through.

He could feel it all now, but without pain. It felt just as though someone were slipping wet clothing off his body, but he knew from the sight in his remaining eye that it was flesh rather than cloth that slipped away from him.

At last he opened his jaw to scream, but all that issued forth from his throat were black bubbles that frothed at the ruined gate of his mouth. Then he felt his jawbone detach itself from his skull, and realized that not just his flesh, but every part of his body, bone and cartilage, muscle and tendon, was liquefying, melting, turning to a dank rottenness that his decaying nostrils could no longer smell.

Horg dissolved, became a series of puddles in the moonlight on the dank stone floor, and was fully aware of everything that was happening to him until at last his brain leaked through the gaping cracks in his spongy skull.

Had he not been drugged by Mordenheim, he would have lost consciousness from the pain long before.

* * * * *

The torches that Horg had seen were those of the Vistani. They had trailed him, but had moved more slowly than a full gallop since they brought with them Nana, who had demanded to come.

She was sitting in a small caravan, the only one in the retinue, pulled by two swift horses. The party numbered twenty others, all on horseback. Most were men, but some were women, fire-eyed and grinning with rage, and all save Nana were armed with rifles and *kruks,* the short curved swords of the Vistani.

When they came into sight of the castle, far in the distance, a yell went up. Nana could not hear it, but she sensed it, knew its portent all the same, and started to laugh, flecks of spittle flying from between her toothless jaws.

"Horrrg . . ." she muttered in between her bouts of grim merriment, and when she felt the warmth of her curse, now expended, return to her, her laughter stopped and was replaced by a shriek of triumph that froze the blood of all the riders. They knew her power and knew that someone had just suffered a terrible doom for the theft of a daughter of the clan of Zsolty.

Then they rallied and roared as one a battle cry as old as the race of Vistana. They put the spurs to their steeds and headed toward the great pile of Schloss Mordenheim, torches blazing, their scarves flying in the wind as freely as the manes of their horses. They rode under the moon, determined to rescue Ilisa and take vengeance upon any who might have dared to harm her.

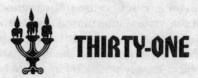

THIRTY-ONE

"Are you finished?" said Mordenheim. He waggled his pistols at Friedrich and Hilda. "What are you just standing there for?"

"The girl is still asleep," Hilda replied. "She must be conscious for the transference to take place."

Mordenheim uttered a curse and walked to his array of drugs and medicines. He laid the pistols where he could grasp them quickly, then drew a syringe full of a clear fluid. "Inject her with this," he said to Friedrich.

"I cannot touch anything now," said Friedrich. "Not even the book of Von Schreck's. My flesh has been purified."

"All right then, back away, damn you!" Keeping one pistol in his hand, he stuck the needle in Ilisa's arm, depressed the small plunger, then pulled the needle out again. "There. She'll be awake in a few moments. Now begin!"

Hilda looked toward the southern windows. "Were you expecting anyone, Doctor?"

Mordenheim whirled, saw the lights approaching in the distance, and knew they could mean only one thing. "The Vistani!" he cried. "But the fools are too late. They're still several miles away, and the gates of the castle are strong, so they'll find it hard going to batter their way in." He turned back and saw that Ilisa was beginning to stir. "*Start*, Kreutzer!"

282   CHET WILLIAMSON

Even if the gypsies did manage to get in, Mordenheim was still not lost. There were secret chambers in
which they could hide and passages in which they
could descend far into the cliffs and wait until the Vistani had gone. But first the transference had to take
place. If the Vistani interrupted that, all was lost, and
Elise might stay in her present, terrible form until the
world dissolved in chaos. So the doctor was pleased to
see Kreutzer crisply position himself between the two
women, while Hilda examined first Elise, then Ilisa.

What he did not hear, however, were the words that
Hilda whispered to the girl as she bent over her, her
mouth next to her ear. They were as soft as a breath,
but Ilisa heard them:

"Fear not. We won't let you be harmed. . . ."

Then Hilda stood erect. "Are you prepared?" she
asked, and Friedrich nodded. "Very well then. We
begin. I must caution you, Doctor Mordenheim, to say
nothing. Any interruption of either myself or Friedrich,
who is the true operator, could be disastrous, plunging
both spirits into an abyss from which neither of them
might ever reappear. No matter what we do or say, no
matter how strange or . . . foolish it may sound to you,
hold your peace. Do you understand?"

"Yes, yes. Go ahead, then." Mordenheim walked to
the far end of the room, glanced nervously out the window to the south, saw that the Vistani were still a fair
distance away, then turned back to watch.

Hilda and Friedrich began the ceremony. She
opened the huge book with the worm-eaten binding
and began to read in a language Mordenheim had
never heard before. It was filled with glottal stops, and
its sound was guttural, as though it were spoken, Mordenheim thought, through a throat choked with blood.
It was uncharacteristic of Mordenheim to have so fanciful a notion. He was, after all, a man of science. Still,

the odd words, the sense of mystery that hung in the room like mist, and the strange scene before him led him to believe for the first time that this sorcery might truly work.

There was an impalpable something in the air, vibrations of which Mordenheim had spoken. Was it the mere vibration of sound waves? Was that the secret of what people thought of as magic? He watched and listened, fascinated, as Hilda droned on and Friedrich repeated her words, far more dramatically. There were a few times when he seemed unsure of himself, as though he could not remember the entire phrase, and he would glance at her, and she would nod and repeat the incomprehensible jargon.

Of course, Mordenheim thought. There was nothing sorcerous in this. It was science, something as simple as the vibration of certain sound waves the words formed in the aether. But how, he wondered, were the proper words found? Years and years of experimentation, doubtless, the same way in which every scientific advance had ever been made. But this particular science had taken a wrong turn, and become magic, filled with inane trappings and ceremonies, when the words would have been enough. "Operation" was indeed the proper term for it, not "ceremony," for there was nothing of the supernatural in it. Perhaps the misguided and superstitious practitioners had sensed the true characteristics of it and named it accordingly, in spite of their silly beliefs.

When Elise was back with him again, he would explore this new science, seek out the books like this one of Von Schreck's, and strip this so-called magic down to its basics, to the science it truly was.

A new goal in his life, and his wife back by his side. What more could he ask for? The first thing they would do would be to flee Lamordia altogether, leaving the domain to Adam, if by some miracle he had survived being dragged under the ice. They would go somewhere far away, where the creature could never find them—to Darkon, perhaps, far to the east in Nevuchar Springs, or south to Valachan, putting as many miles as possible between them and the creation that had nearly ruined their lives—and would attempt to do so again if he lived.

A sudden noise drew Mordenheim's attention back to the procedure. There seemed to be a crackling in the air, and he thought that he beheld a blue glow surrounding both the bodies of Elise and the gypsy. Electromagnetic fields? Was he seeing the actual life-force of the two women, the energy fields that made up their individual consciousness? Were these the "spirits" of which the holy prattled?

He watched, spellbound by the words that seemed to hang in the air as lightly as did the aura around the two supine women. Then those auras seemed to broaden, rise higher into the air, and come together between the two tables on which their owners lay. There was a hissing sound, as of a red-hot poker plunging into water, and the combined aura changed from blue to green to yellow to orange, and finally to a fiery red whose brightness made Mordenheim turn away his eyes.

*　*　*　*　*

Light blazed at the southern windows of the laboratory, and the wildly riding Vistani beheld it as they drew nearer the castle. Petre, in the lead, shouted as he saw it, and from the cries of the others, he knew they saw it as well.

A hundred yards from the barred and imposing castle gate, Petre wheeled his mount to the left to see if there was another way into the courtyard, but found that the land dropped away into the sea. One would either have to make a hazardous climb along the cliff wall or straight up the smooth side of the castle itself, and though the Vistani had been called leeches by those who hated them, they had not a leech's ability to cling to such surfaces.

"Back!" cried Petre to those who had followed him. "We must open the gate!"

Such a task was easier spoken of than done. The gate was at the top of a flight of stairs, and in recent years Mordenheim had replaced the original wrought iron gate, which might have been easily climbed, with a gate of solid iron, the top of which towered nearly thirty feet above the top step.

One of the braver Vistana lads balanced himself on the wide railing of the stairway and leapt for the front wall, but the angle was too awkward, and the lip of the wall was rough and jagged. Though his fingertips caught the edge, he could not hang on and fell to the earth some twenty feet below, breaking his leg.

"We'll have to batter our way in!" Petre cried, and immediately the Vistani followed him to a nearby copse of woods, where their axes flew into the trunk of a thick-boled tree, making the chips fly until it toppled over. Just as quickly, they cut off the branches and bore it back to the steps.

There they got on either side and ran up the steps as fast as they could so that the hacked-off end of the tree crashed into the gate. A tremendous ringing sound filled their ears, and the gate shuddered, but held as firmly as before. What made assaulting the gate doubly difficult was that the end of the ram could only hit at an angle, not dead-on, and much of the energy of the charge was expended by running up the stairs.

"A curse on a man who builds a gate at the top of stairs!" muttered Petre as he and the others carried the heavy ram down the steps once more. "But we'll keep at it until it shatters, or the last of us lies dead from trying!"

The others shouted assent, and they ran up the steps again, thrusting the heavy wood against the unyielding iron.

*　*　*　*　*

Mordenheim was aware of a dull clanging sound, and somewhere in the back of his mind came the concern that the gypsies were trying to enter the castle. His attention, however, was otherwise fixed on the astounding phenomenon that was taking place in front of him.

His eyes had grown used to the aura, and he had begun to see images in the haze. He saw Elise, and himself, as when they were young and falling in love. He saw the two of them together, after they were married, sharing a meal, lying with their arms around each other, walking by the cliff side, looking down at the sea. . . . Were these Elise's memories then? The things that made her consciousness what it was?

Then, as if from behind a curtain, he saw Adam's face, with a smile that seemed cold and mocking. Then Eva's, open and innocent, and finally Adam's again, filled with hatred. And mixed with these images were pictures that must have dwelt in the gypsy girl's mind: smiling, hawk-faced women wearing bandannas over their dark hair and shining hoops in their ears; men with thick mustaches and eyebrows; the strong necks and haunches of horses; the caravans; the road. . . .

Then these images blended together until all became a vast, swirling, indistinct mass, and Mordenheim grew dizzy and nauseated just looking at it. He turned his face away and looked down at the floor, and there came a sound as of rushing waters, as if all the dark cold cataracts of this world were converging in one mighty torrent, roaring over the edge of the world and falling into a sea of chaos.

And suddenly it was over.

Mordenheim looked up at the silent room, and saw no auras, no faces, no swirling mass of memories.

Instead there was only Friedrich Kreutzer, standing as though exhausted from his effort, and Hilda Von Karlsfeld, clutching the worm-eaten book to her breast, her eyes closed as if in prayer. The two women were still on their respective tables, neither moving. In the retort on the floor between the two of them spun a tiny whirlwind of what looked like flakes of gold, always in motion, never settling to the bottom of the glass container.

"Is . . . is it over?" Mordenheim asked, annoyed at how his voice was trembling.

"It is," Friedrich answered. "The transference is complete."

Mordenheim scarcely heard the pistols fall to the floor as he crossed the room to the lovely body that now must hold Elise's even more beautiful spirit. He bent over her, saw her chest rising and falling, and knew that she was alive, that the shock of the operation had not destroyed her. He took one of her hands in his and let his fingers run along the curve of her cheek.

"Elise . . ." he whispered. "Elise, speak to me. . . ." There was no response, and he looked up at Friedrich and Hilda, half pleading, half angry. "What is *wrong?*" he demanded.

Friedrich seemed too drained to answer.

"It will take a moment," Hilda said. "The process is exhausting. But let me assure you, Doctor Mordenheim, that everything went precisely as I intended it to. *Precisely,*" she added in a way that made Mordenheim frown.

"It better have," the doctor said. "Or else—" He was interrupted by a great clanging sound. He ran to the window and looked out. "The gypsies! They're battering down the gate." He ran back to the table. "How *long* until she regains consciousness?"

"It should be any moment," Hilda said. "May I suggest that you pat her brow and talk soothingly to her. I tell you, she will respond to you." Hilda knelt and picked up the glass retort. "And this, you said, is mine to do with as I wish?"

"Yes, yes, whatever you like." He tenderly touched the gypsy girl's forehead. "Elise, Elise, my darling, I am here. It is Victor. I have been waiting for you to come back to me, my love. Won't you speak to me? It is your Victor, your husband. I have not let you die, my dear. I have brought you back to a new and wonderful life."

Tears of frustration began to dampen Mordenheim's cheeks. "Speak to me, won't you? I beg you, just say my name—my name. Such a little thing, Elise, won't you say it? Say it, Elise!"

". . . Vuh . . . ak . . . tuh . . ."

He had heard it, though he had not seen her lips move. He blinked madly to drive the tears from his eyes so that he could see her crimson lips form the syllables of his name again. "*Yes,* my dear, I am here! Yes, speak again, Elise!"

"*Vak*-torh . . ."

And again he heard it, although her lips did not move. What was happening? Did part of her essence still remain in the aether? Were the words she was thinking propelled through the air by something other than her breath and lips?

"Yes! Yes, my love! It is Victor. Rise and touch me! Open your eyes! Be my beloved wife again!"

The girl on the table did not move. But from behind him Mordenheim heard a rustling sound. It was similar

to the sound of an old saddle creaking as a rider strad-
dles it, or the dry leather of an ancient book cracking as
it is opened too wide. With a realization that turned his
spine to ice, he knew what that sound augured. Fear
froze him, and he could not turn around.

"Vahktoooo. . ." came the voice again. And it was
not a voice from the throat of a young girl. Rather it
crawled from something terribly old and irreparably
decayed, like a worm undulating from a long-dead
corpse's mouth. It did not come from the girl on the
table in front of him, but from the dead-alive monstrosity behind him.

From Elise. From the living corpse of his wife.

It was thence that the hand fell upon his shoulder,
making him close his eyes and clench his teeth, as
every muscle in his body screamed for flight.

"You read them . . . *wrong*. . . ."

"Yes," he heard Hilda Von Karlsfeld say. "You wanted
your wife back, Doctor Mordenheim. Well, now you
have her."

The claw on his shoulder felt as heavy as lead, pin-
ning him to the spot so that he could not move, nor
even turn. And through it all, he knew what had happened. The changes that the damned Von Karlsfeld
woman had made in the words had changed other
things as well. It was not Elise's spirit that had gone into
the gypsy's body, but the gypsy girl's life-force that had
occupied Elise's rotting corpse, and was making the
dying limbs move, the dying brain seek its mate.

"Vahktor . . . Vahktor . . . *Vahk*-toooor . . ." The voice
was filled with unholy longing and muffled by the thick
feeding tube that descended into Elise's stomach.

Mordenheim, trembling in every part of his body,
turned and beheld his wife. Her face was a nightmare of
black, wrinkled flesh. The needles still pierced each of
her puckered eyes, and the rubber tubes dangled from

them down over her cheeks.

He backed away from her, but she took another step toward him. The tubes, attached to a rubber bladder and pump, went taut, and the movement ripped the needles from her eyes, shredding the surface so that a milky froth dribbled from them and down over her cheeks. The same step tugged the last few inches of the feeding tube, coated with gray fluid, from her throat, as though a dreadful serpent had fed upon her innards and now, sated, left her.

But the other hoses and tubes that pierced her skull, lungs, and bowels were not so easily dislodged. They held her in place, though her legs continued to move as if she were on a treadmill.

Fortunately for the observers, most of her body was hidden. The leakage of the fluids that had nurtured and preserved her kept her sheet stuck firmly to her flesh. But what Mordenheim could see was nearly enough to drive him mad. What he heard was equally horrible. Her mouth now free of the feeding tube, the thing that was Elise Mordenheim began to babble, frustrated by her inability to go to the arms of the man she loved. She repeated Victor's name over and over, and he heard other words like *love* and *hold me* and *embrace*.

And *forever*.

That was the word that struck him to the core. For how could there be a forever now? All this effort, all these years of agony for both him and Elise, and now a lying slut who thought to judge him—*him*, Victor Mordenheim!—had destroyed it all!

He looked to where he had dropped the pistols but saw that Kreutzer had already picked them up, one in each hand, and seemed to be deciding whether to train them on the doctor or his wife. Perhaps with a rush he could grab them away, kill them both, and then—

Then his equipment—machines, storage batteries,

flasks, beakers—all came crashing to the floor as Elise
Mordenheim strained to the utmost to be nearer the
man she loved. Dragging a mass of clattering appara-
tuses, she slowly closed the space between herself and
Mordenheim, advancing as inexorably as the putrefac-
tion that had riddled her body.

When she was no more than an arm's length from
Mordenheim, he shrieked and dashed to the nearest
door. He struggled with the knob for a moment, then
pulled it open, and ran directly into the arms of Adam.

*   *   *   *   *

The booming roar of laughter from the monster engulfed Mordenheim's gasp in the same way that
Adam's long arms engulfed his creator.

"Little man!" he said. "Surprised to see me, 'Father'?
You didn't think that those waters would finish me, did
you? No, you built me too strong to have such a small
thing kill me. Only the lightning, Mordenheim, only all
the power of the gods of this dark land who gave me life
could take life away from me!"

Hilda and Friedrich stared at Adam, whose ragged
clothes were dripping water. Friedrich began to bring
up one of the pistols, but Adam gave him a grim smile.
"You had best drop those, my young friend. They will
have little effect on me other than annoyance, and you
do not wish to see me annoyed."

Hilda glanced at Friedrich and nodded, and the man
slowly deposited them on the floor.

"Vic-tooor . . ." Whether or not she could see from
her pierced eyes, Elise had hesitated, as if aware that
someone else had come into the room, a new player in
this odd game.

Adam jerked Mordenheim around, holding him by
both shoulders so that he now faced his wife. "Ah, Frau

Mordenheim, I presume? You're looking even more lovely than the last time we met. Perhaps you recall? Your flesh was far more attractive than mine then. But now I see that you have aged rather quickly. Hasn't she, Doctor? But she does seem to have recovered some of her former energy. Fraulein Von Karlsfeld, does the good doctor have you and your fiance to thank for this miraculous rejuvenation?"

"He does," Hilda said. Despite all logic, she felt strengthened by Adam's presence.

"Then I find in you an even greater colleague than before," Adam said, and from the relative softness of his tone, Hilda knew that he had read her look correctly through the ice as he had been pulled down and away by the currents. "For Frau Mordenheim must live on in this guise," Adam continued, his voice growing sharper, "in order to love and comfort her hardworking husband. Isn't that right, Frau Mordenheim?"

The cracked lips opened again. "Vic-tor?"

"Yes, to offer him your love . . ."

"No!" Mordenheim struggled to free himself but could not break Adam's steely grip.

The hideous creature began to shuffle toward her husband again, trailing tubes and hoses like obscene tentacles. "Vic-tooooor," she wailed.

"To offer him your embraces . . ." Adam held Mordenheim like a rock holds down paper. The doctor's arms and legs thrashed, but he was going nowhere.

"Let me *go!*" he cried.

Still she came on, until her cracked and seeping face was only inches away from Mordenheim's. "My . . . loooove . . ."

"To offer him," said Adam triumphantly, "your *kiss!*"

So saying, he pushed Mordenheim's head toward hers, and her withered arms wrapped around Mordenheim's neck, drawing his face tenaciously against hers, so that her ruined and loathsome lips pressed upon his, and the breath of the dead entered his mouth and glutted his brain with horror.

Laughing, Adam released him with one final push, so that Mordenheim fell farther into his wife's clutches. Free of Adam's grip, the doctor pulled his head back, away from Elise's clinging mouth, and stared full into the tattered and yearning face.

The sunken nose, the ragged lips, the decay-riddled flesh were bad enough. But what maddened Mordenheim were the eyes, still oozing fluid, and the voice that whispered as tenderly as a corpse could, "Hussssband . . ."

Mordenheim screamed and ran for the only escape open to him, straight for the northern window that overlooked the unforgiving sea. He did not pause for an instant, but burst through the panes of glass and the wooden frame as eagerly as if he were a burning man plunging into a cool stream. The glass shattered into fragments and exploded outward, and Mordenheim followed, out over the face of the cliff, and down, down toward the jagged rocks below, on which the icy waves cruelly broke.

Hilda and Friedrich ran to the window, through which the wind blew with what seemed a wicked glee, as though the gods were overjoyed to claim in their waters the man who had mocked them for so long. And though Hilda and Friedrich looked, they could see no sign of Mordenheim in the dark night, and the thrashing waves below offered no trace of his passing.

Then from behind them they heard a muffled groan and saw that Adam was standing erect, eyes pressed closed, arms tensed at his side, fingers clawing at the air, as though he were undergoing the greatest conceivable agony. At the same time, Elise Mordenheim sank to the floor like the wretched pile of rotting flesh and bone that she was.

Over and over, spasms passed through Adam, and he trembled repeatedly as small whimpers escaped him. At length, he gave a deep sigh and opened his eyes. They looked weary, but Hilda could see that he had returned from wherever his spirit had been.

"Was it Mordenheim?" she asked. "Was it his . . . his death you felt?"

Adam sighed again, then smiled weakly at her. "His pain. Perhaps his death. But even though he may have died down there, he will live again. He will return here, to this place, to behold this woman, and to suffer anew. This I know as surely as I know that I will never walk among men."

The creature knelt beside Elise Mordenheim and took her in his surprisingly gentle arms. "She still lives as well. And she will continue to do so." Then he placed her on the table on which she had lain for so long, and began to reinsert the tubes and hoses into their proper machines.

"I have watched him often enough through the windows, clinging like a fly to the rock of the walls. I have reveled in my spirit as I saw him destroy his own, the frustration he felt with every unsuccessful experiment. And now this one, his 'crowning achievement.'"

He laughed viciously, then glared heavily at them. "It might have been successful, however, had you not sabotaged it, Fraulein Von Karlsfeld. It was a singularly just strategy, and I congratulate you on your foresight. But to assure us that the doctor, should he return, never attempts such wizardry again, I would suggest that you take your book and go to a land where he is not likely to find you. Then I will not have to harm either of you."

"We shall follow your directions implicitly," Hilda said, and Friedrich nodded in agreement.

"Then I would further suggest that you pay yourselves whatever sum the good doctor promised you.

You will find his secret treasury in the parlor of the east wing. Simply slide the sofa aside, and you will find a loose floorboard under the right rear leg. You may be amazed at how much is there."

"You know," Friedrich said, "and you have never taken any?"

"My pleasures are not derived from money, Herr Kreutzer, but from the agony of my maker, a rare coin indeed. So take what you want and begone. For I tell you that should you ever aid Mordenheim again, for good or ill, I shall be forced to kill you both." He beetled his brows at Hilda. "Your expression is strange, Fraulein Von Karlsfeld. Do you not believe me?"

"I do believe you, sir."

"That is good, for I would do what I say, even though I should regret it. Dearly."

The pounding of the gypsies' ram against the gate had been constant and insistent. Now there was a new noise, a tremendous crashing sound, as though two great slabs of iron had fallen onto stones.

"The Vistani, stubborn tribe that they are, have achieved their purpose. The gate is down, and they should find you shortly. I imagine that your deliverance of this child may help to soothe their ire. If she *is* still alive."

In response, Hilda reached into her pocket and produced the retort, in which the gold flakes were still sparkling and whirling. She opened the stopper, and the tiny golden whirlwind swirled out of the vessel, drifted out to form a shroud above Ilisa's still form, and descended upon the girl, becoming one with her, vanishing from sight. In an instant, Ilisa's limbs started to twitch, and her eyes opened.

"Are you all right?" Hilda asked, her hand soothingly placed on the girl's brow.

Ilisa nodded and cleared her throat several times

before she could speak. "I saw and heard everything that happened. It was like I was above you all, looking down." Hilda helped her to sit up, and Ilisa looked at her gratefully. "Thank you for doing . . . whatever it was that you did. Both of you." She looked at Adam, and her gaze did not break. "All of you."

"Thank me not, girl. For I did nothing for you. My acts are for my own pleasure and nothing else. You see, I am my father's son." He walked toward the window through which Mordenheim had disappeared.

"And now I must follow my father. There is no love lost between the Vistani and me, and were they to find me on nonviolent terms with you, it would not bode well." He bowed shortly. "Farewell, Kreutzer."

Then he closed his eyes and bowed more deeply toward Hilda. "And farewell to you, Hilda Von Karlsfeld. Perhaps one day we shall meet again under less desperate circumstances. I deeply enjoyed the talks that we have shared."

"As have I, sir. I do not believe I have ever met . . . a *man* quite like you before."

Adam smiled in spite of himself. "You are kind. And that, as you know, is the only reason I have not killed you."

Before she could respond, he sprang out through the window into the night. Hilda ran to the shattered casement and saw his body, arms spread like the wings of a giant bat, fall into the welcoming sea. She saw him strike the surface, and saw the great splash of water that the impact threw up. But there was no movement thereafter, save for the ebb and flow of the cold, black ocean.

THIRTY-TWO

A few seconds after Adam's leap, Hilda, Friedrich, and Ilisa heard the clattering of many feet on the stairs leading to the laboratory. Then the door was thrown open, and a horde of Vistana men and women burst in, Petre in the lead.

"Father!" Ilisa cried, and ran into his arms. The expression of fury on his face vanished at the joy of seeing her safe again, and even the other gypsies broke into grins, belying their drawn kruks and pistols.

"Are you all right, daughter?" Petre said.

"Yes, I'm fine. These two saved me from the doctor. I owe them my life, Father. Please don't harm them."

"On my word, they shan't be touched. But where *is* Mordenheim? My knife shall drink his blood and sever his gizzard for what he's done!"

"He is dead, Father. He fell out the window to the sea below."

"And what about that other, that horrible little toad whom we befriended but repaid us by vilest betrayal?" Petre's white teeth snarled beneath his fierce mustache.

"Mordenheim ordered him to the watchtower to look for you," said Friedrich. "Through that door and up the stairs. But I doubt if you'll find him alive."

Petre briskly ordered one of the Vistani to check, then nodded. "The curse worked then. I had no doubt. My grandmother's power is strong."

"Where is Nana?" asked Ilisa.

"Waiting for you in the caravan."

"Take me to her, please?"

Petre nodded. "Once we learn the fate of the giorgio who stole you from us."

The gypsy who had been sent to the tower returned shortly. He was ashen-faced, and his mouth was set in a grim line. "Dead," he said. "Even his bones . . ." He left it unfinished, but everyone understood.

"It is just. As for the two of you," said Petre to Hilda and Friedrich, "I thank you for saving my daughter. Though you are giorgio, you are always welcome in the camp of the Zsolty Vistani, and so in any Vistana clan that roams this world."

Petre was turning toward the door when one of the women noticed Elise's body lying on the table and brought it to his attention. "And what is this?" he said. "One more of Mordenheim's victims?"

Friedrich started to speak, but Hilda interrupted. "Indeed, another unfortunate result of the madman's depredations." She looked at Ilisa, and the girl gave her a look in return that said she would not reveal the secret. "Let us take care of her body."

Petre jerked his head gruffly. "Do what you will. And take what you will. We will touch nothing in this cursed house, a house that will bear a still greater curse. Come, my kin and clan, let us leave this foul place. Fare you well." His arm around his recovered child, Petre regally left the laboratory and the castle, the others following in his train.

Alone, Hilda and Friedrich held each other. "That," said Friedrich, "was audacious, to say the least."

"It was the only thing I could do," Hilda said, her face against his chest. "Fortunately it took only a few word changes to put Ilisa's *life-force* in Elise's body rather than Elise's spirit in the body of the girl."

"And in the meantime, the girl's *spirit* was safe enough in the retort while her life-force made those withered limbs move." Friedrich shook his head in admiration. "But how did you have the presence of mind to do it?"

"I had to—I was the one holding the book. And now," she sighed, "we're left holding nothing."

But Friedrich's face brightened. "Not necessarily. Come on."

"Where are we going?" she asked, as he led her by the hand out of the laboratory.

"The parlor of the east wing, of course. To collect what Mordenheim, be he dead or alive, owes us."

Beneath the sofa, as Adam had said, was the loose board. And under it was a large money box. It was unlocked, more evidence of Mordenheim's feeling of superiority. After all, who would have dared to rob him? The only thing that surprised Hilda was that the box was not out in plain view.

"Five thousand kroner was the price, I believe," said Friedrich, beginning to count out the money.

"Ten thousand if we were successful," Hilda said, smiling. "And we were nothing if not that."

"Ten thousand kroner it is then. And perhaps a little more? For our return expenses?"

Hilda shook her head. "No. Let us take only what is owed us. More would be . . . I'm not sure. It just doesn't feel right. It feels like . . . blood money."

"Ten thousand is plenty to buy us our home." He bounced the stack of bills in his hand, and then transferred it to his purse.

"And now, my soon-to-be wife, let's depart this madhouse and go back to the more predictable tyranny of Darkonian government. That little cottage just north of Il Aluk may still be for sale. . . ." He noticed her stolid mien and took her hand. "But why so sad, Hilda? We have enough to buy our heart's desire."

"We do," she said softly. "But when I think of how simple the heart's desire is for others. . . ."

"Adam, you mean."

"Yes. To walk with other men, to talk to a woman without her cowering in fright, to be one of us, even the poorest of creatures, is all that he wants. And yet . . ." She sighed, and they turned and walked from the chamber, down the hall to their rooms to pack.

But while Hilda was packing, a certain knowledge came over her, a psychic surety that froze her in place. She was standing over her suitcase when Friedrich came in to see what was keeping her.

"Hilda? What is it?"

"Mordenheim—he isn't dead, is he?"

"You . . . felt it?" She nodded. "I don't know," said Friedrich. "He told me certain things that would lead me to believe he can live through what other men could not. On the ice, I saw his toes regenerate from the stumps. And he told me of things more incredible than that."

"I believe them," Hilda said, shuddering. "His spirit, at any rate, will never leave here. Come, let's be gone as quickly as we can. Perhaps the Vistani will take us back to the main road."

It was with relief in their hearts that they passed through the doors of Schloss Mordenheim for the last time. A flat, gray sky heralded dawn, and gypsies stood near the sole, small vardo with lit torches.

There Hilda and Friedrich saw an ancient Vistana woman casting a spell over a torch held by Petre. She sprinkled on the flame several handfuls of gleaming earths and powders that burst into multicolored streamers of fire, and chanted croaking words from a toothless mouth.

". . . And be he returned here forever. . . . Let his spirit dwell in this place. . . . And though he die, yet shall his tortured spirit return to haunt this castle with its misery. . . . May no man comfort him or aid him or give him peace or set him to rest, else that man shall share his fate. . . . This be cursed ground, until this world shall dissolve into the mists whence it came. . ."

The old woman turned to each of the four compass points, spitting each time she paused, then began to shuffle slowly toward her vardo.

Hilda turned to Friedrich. "Give me the book," she said. He understood immediately, opened his valise, and handed the grimoire of Von Schreck to Hilda. She hurried over to the old woman and stopped her just as she was about to ascend the two steps into the caravan.

"Old mother," Hilda said, "this is safest in your hands. Do with it what you will." And she put the eldritch tome into the withered claws.

Nana turned her blind eyes toward Hilda, her sightless but all-seeing gaze never resting on the book. Then her face brightened in a grin terrible to behold, and a name crawled out of her mouth. "Von *Schreck* . . ." she said.

Hilda could only nod, and thought instantly how absurd it seemed to nod to a blind woman. But even more absurd was the thought that this woman could know the book and its owner by merely touching it.

Hilda walked back to Friedrich, thinking that the magic of the Vistani was as strong as she had heard, and knowing that she wanted no part of it, nor any part of magic hereafter.

She would try to ignore her psychic proclivities. The only transformations she would practice from this moment on would be transforming the romance and terror through which she had lived into fiction, the creation of which would be wizardry enough for her spirit.

THIRTY-THREE

Slowly, he awoke.

The first thing he felt was tremendous cold against his flesh, then something slapping him. When he opened an eye, he saw that he lay in water, tiny waves rushing through a labyrinth of rocks and splashing into his face. He raised his head and shook the water from his thick hair, then realized that he was lying half in, half out of the cold wetness. He rolled onto his stomach, pushed himself to his feet, then shook himself like a dog after a swim.

The water still clung to his skin and saturated his clothing, but he was not shivering as any other man would have, and he knew why all too well. What he did not know was where to go next. Everything that mattered to him had been taken away. Everything his life had stood for was now a travesty. And he now stood on a rocky strand that he did not even recognize.

It was that last fact that made up his mind for him. He had never been lost, and he would not be lost now. He would act and be strong, as he always had. He would not accept such a cruel fate. He would travel south, to Stangengrad. To Hamer, the priest.

Somehow, Ivan Dragonov would find a way to escape the curse of lycanthropy that now chained him tightly with links of evil.

He took off his garments, wrung each of them out,

and dried his skin as best he could with patches of moss ripped from the rocks. When he donned his clothes once more, they were still wet, but at least he would not drip like a leaking waterskin with every step he took.

The damp clothes on his back were all he had now. His horse was still in the stable at Schloss Mordenheim, and he knew not in which direction the castle lay. His weapons were gone as well. The silver-bladed axe and sword were somewhere at the bottom of the Sea of Sorrows. But thinking of what he lacked would do him no good. Instead, he would think about what was to come. He knew that he could not have drifted far after he came out from under the ice, so the odds were that he was somewhere on the northern coast of Lamordia.

He would travel southeast, and eventually the Sleeping Beast would come into view. Once he reached that mountain chain, he would find settlements, get some decent food, and cross the border into Falkovnia, and thence to Stangengrad and the old priest. Hamer could at least attempt the curing.

Dragonov could not help thinking that the pain of the purifying ceremony would seem like a healing balm after the unparalleled psychic pain of his becoming a lycanthrope. He had dedicated his life to good, and now to find himself one of the most evil of creatures was more than he could bear. He thought about ending it all, but to do so, he would have to have another silver blade forged, or have someone shoot him with a silver bullet. The country through which he traveled was sparse and poor, and he guessed that there was not a piece of silver within a day's walk.

Besides, Hamer had told him that he was the type of man on which the cure could work. He was physically, mentally, and morally fit. Surely those qualities would count for something. Hamer could save him. And if not, he would let Hamer put an end to him, and die in peace.

So he trudged onward, the water squishing in his boots with each step he took. Strange, he thought, that the cold did not seem to bother him. Perhaps it was the supernatural blood coursing through his veins. Hot blood. For a hothead. He almost laughed at the simple joke. Hotheadedness had always been his curse, and now here he was, becoming a beast when angered.

He stopped walking. There was something there, something to that thought, and he almost had it when a deep roar shattered his reverie. He looked around him to see, coming from behind a barrow, a flesh golem as mindless and destructive as the rest of its misborn species, placed to protect the tombs and dwellings of the wizards who created them. Even though those mages might have been dead for centuries, it made no difference to the deadly creatures, who would destroy any living thing to come within their circle of guardianship.

The golem was made from dead flesh, but unlike Adam, the other dead-alive being with which Dragonov had recently battled, it had no intelligence other than to kill what it saw. It towered a head taller than he, and outweighed him by fifty stone at least.

But as soon as the monster approached him with its obvious intentions of rending him limb from limb, Ivan Dragonov became someone—and some*thing* else. He felt his bones lengthening, his flesh stretching, the thick hair enclosing him like a second skin. And then all he knew was savagery. It was not like the fighting rage he had driven himself to when he was a man. It went far beyond that. It was a feeling that only the slaying of every living thing in his sight could bring him peace.

And he sought that peace with a scream of savagery that penetrated even the muddy consciousness of the golem. Dragonov launched himself at the guardian with muscles made three times as strong by the curse of lycanthropy. A thing like this had defeated him before, but this time *he* would taste victory.

And blood, if any flowed in this monster's veins.

The thing strove to grasp him as he leapt upon it, drawing him to it and crushing his ribs and chest in its deathless embrace. But Dragonov welcomed the closeness, sinking his claws into the golem's back and thrusting his muzzle into its neck, ripping the gray flesh of its throat while his legs, black claws extended, tore at the monster's midsection, scattering shreds of skin and muscles like confetti.

The golem fell forward atop Dragonov, grabbed his head, and began trying to pound it into pulp on the rocks of the barrow, which must have seemed a particularly efficient and satisfactory way for it to obey its creator's wishes.

The lycanthrope, however, was far faster than his enemy, whose nearly dead muscles had not been used for decades. Dragonov knocked the golem's moldering arms away, then rolled from beneath it, leaped up, and clamped himself to the monster's back before it could even rise. Wrapping his legs around its wide trunk, he dug into the front of its neck with his long claws, slicing and rending the tissues and letting the pieces fall, while his fangs began ravaging the monster from behind.

It was as though a steam-driven thresher had been turned loose on the golem's thick neck, and even the largest of trees can be felled through rapid and constant hacking. The golem staggered to and fro as Dragonov kept diminishing the thick bole of flesh and muscle that attached its head to its trunk. Though it battered him as best it could, it could not dislodge the thing that was slowly tearing it to pieces. Its bellows of anger turned to distress, which finally ceased when claw and fang finished their work, and the flesh of the neck was severed, so that the head clung only by a cord of bone.

One mighty blow of the lycanthrope's bunched fists, and that link was gone as well, so that the head, mouth open as stupidly as it had been in life, fell to the rocks with the hollow sound of a huge, empty barrel.

The body, however, did not cease to struggle, but continued to thrash about. It was not that there was no brain to control it, for the creature had never depended upon thought, but now there were no eyes to see or ears to hear. The only sensory apparatus was skin, which still felt the tenacious clinging of Dragonov to its body. And as long as there was another life present, the golem would attempt to take it.

It fought on, headless and heedless, lumbering about and striking Dragonov with its huge fists, so that the lycanthrope now targeted these annoying arms, chewing and clawing at the shoulder until the left arm hung only by a strip of flesh, which soon parted. Then Dragonov released the golem, or what was left of it, and stepped back to survey the situation.

This ripped-apart thing still moved, and Dragonov attacked again with no hesitation, knowing only, like the golem, that whatever moved must die. He grasped the sole remaining arm, twisting and biting and clawing until it too separated from its owner and flopped to the rocks, where the fingers twitched for a moment, and then lay still.

Now all that remained was a massive trunk on legs, whose wounds scarcely seeped. So ancient was the golem and so long its guardianship that the few fluids within it had dried to a gel-like consistency. Dragonov smashed the dismembered golem to the rocks, where it lay like a turtle, its huge legs moving, but unable to raise it upright again. Within several minutes, the lycanthrope had divided the helpless creature twice more, so that both legs and the trunk, finally lifeless, lay unmoving.

The beast-man roared a cry of triumph, then picked up a piece of the flesh to feast upon. Just as its jaws were about to close on the hideous meat, it stopped and trembled, then dropped the chunk of carrion and stood looking at its paws and forearms, the red hair saturated with the slime the golem had dripped instead of blood. Ever so slowly those paws became hands, and the claws shrank down to fingers with roughened nails, and the beast became the man again. Ivan Dragonov shivered at what he had done and what he had been about to do.

Then a new realization came to him, the knowledge that he had stopped the beast within him as it had been about to feed. He had somehow, perhaps through the zeal for goodness that he had possessed all his life, brought himself back from the edge of bestiality to take human form again. Oh yes, he thought, it could have been that since the fight was over and the impetus that had shifted his shape had now passed, that the change back had simply come on its own. Still, he did not believe it, for if the beast ruled, why would it have not bitten into that horrible repast with the lust for flesh that had urged him to devour it in the first place?

No, there was something else at work here, he *knew* it. What had he done since he had become a lycanthrope? He had battled Mordenheim's monster, and he had slain an evil golem. He had not harmed the innocent, and he would have rid this world of that dead-alive Adam had he known more about his powers. But it had been his first battle as a lycanthrope, and he had let the creature have the advantage. Next time would be different.

Next time?

Why not? Perhaps the priests who had influenced him to dedicate his life to fighting evil were right. Perhaps all things were for the best—all one need do was to leave them in the hands of the gods.

Perhaps even this lycanthropy that he had thought a curse had come to him for a reason. For if a mighty man fighting evil were a force for good, how much greater a force for the right could be a *beast*-man three times as mighty?

Hamer's rituals could still be in his future. But now that future seemed farther off. Now there was something else ahead: stalking the fiends and monsters that haunted and harried this world; confronting evil and letting his fury and anger change him into something evildoers would fear even more than Ivan Dragonov the Warrior—Dragonov the Beast. Using evil to battle evil and presenting the wicked and diabolic with a foe the likes of which they had never faced before!

Laughter rattled from his throat, and he looked up at the gray sky of this suffering world and imagined he saw the gods smiling down at him.

"If this is what you made me," he bellowed, "then I'll use it and be glad! When the full moon comes, I'll put myself away from its light or bind myself with silver chains. Or make sure I'm in a land where *all* are evil!" Then his face grew stern, and he added, "And if I ever do harm to the innocent, well then I'll not even attempt to be cured, but I'll cut my throat with a silver dagger, and be grateful to do it. . . ."

He cleaned himself up as best he could, then searched around the stones of the barrow until he found the long-sealed entrance. It yielded readily to his strength, and inside he discovered the desiccated corpse of a man wearing the remnants of a mage's robes. Arrayed around the body were a number of ceremonial weapons as well as a fair number of gems and golden coins. These he stuffed into a leather wineskin whose contents had long dried up on the mage's way to whatever eternity he expected. Dragonov took several weapons too, though he thought it likely the change would come whenever he battled.

"I'll get some silver tips for my claws," he said to himself with a chuckle. "Have to be careful not to scratch myself, though."

Then, laden with booty, girded with steel, and defended by a weapon in his blood more terrible than any sword, Ivan Dragonov continued southeast. He had had enough of frigid Lamordia and wished for warmer climes. Mordenheim's monster, if it was still alive, could wait until another day. Let the miserable creature live. He would face him again.

But for now, there lay before him an entire realm of evil to fight, with claw and fang and the strength of the righteous.

He walked on, grinning the grin of a beast.

THIRTY-FOUR

The fire seemed as cold as the cave was empty.

Here she had sat with him such a short time ago. He and she had spoken here, in a place that had never heard words before, and he wondered if perhaps the echoes still lingered like audible smoke in the deepest cracks of the stone, and that if he opened the rocks and went down and down into the belly of the world, he might be able to catch up with her words, and hear her again.

No. She was gone. And it was better so—for her and for him. He was not meant for such as she, not meant for anyone human, anyone who had always been alive.

Adam picked up a chipped cup that she had used, and he turned it in his hands like a connoisseur examining a work of art. What was it that he felt toward her, he wondered. It was not love, he was not that foolish. It was merely that she had been the only one not to turn away, the only one not to shut him out. And now that he had known such comparative warmth, such human contact, he was filled with even more despair than before.

He smiled bitterly at the memory of a line from a book of philosophy that Mordenheim had given him: *Who once has gazed upon the hut of the gods can no longer be content with his realm's finest palaces.* And it was true. He had not known what it was like to be accepted before, and now he wished he never had. Better to live in ignorance and without emotions than to feel the loss of something so ineffably wonderful: the contact between two human beings, and being thought of as a man instead of a monster.

He set down the cup, turned, and threaded his way through the dark passage until he was outside the cave. Looking up at the sky, hanging above him as heavy and gray as the flesh of his face, he cursed this land, cursed Mordenheim, cursed fate and the gods for giving him life and the intelligence to feel loss. He knew he would never forget Hilda Von Karlsfeld, that as the years passed and she grew feeble and old and finally, one day, died, she would remain ever young and vibrant in his memory. That memory of her would cling to him, drawing forth his torment as a leech draws blood, plaguing him with his loss, tantalizing him with the thoughts of what might have been in a kinder world.

And how he would make *this* cruel world pay for that unkindness!

Mordenheim would be the first to feel his wrath. He knew his creator too well to think that he had not survived that fall into the sea. Any other man would have died the instant that the waves dashed his body against the rocks. But the gods would not let Mordenheim die. They would bring him back again, back to his castle, to his dead-alive love. They would give him the life that he could not give to others, and Adam would be there to welcome him back to that knowledge, that very special damnation.

He would be there to mock his creator for deserting his sacred science and depending on sorcery, for the way in which the two young people outsmarted him, for the warm and loving embrace with which his beloved Elise had blessed him.

Oh, yes, there was so much ahead, so much taunting, so much happiness, so much joy.

Hilda came again into Adam's thoughts, as she had since he had spoken to her, as she always would until he might somehow find death.

He turned back into his cave, away from the sad light and into the sadder darkness.

Left alone, the Isle of Agony brooded, as did its lord and only denizen. The sharp, jutting hill in the center of the island seemed to look with aching, empty eyes at the mainland, as if longing to be a part of it. But the sea, much of it now turned to cold, hard ice, would keep them separated forever.

*   *   *   *   *

Many miles south, at the mouth of a river on the westernmost point of Lamordia, a figure lay. Anyone walking the rough, pebbly shore and coming across it would have thought it a corpse. Its stomach was round and bloated, its limbs broken and bent at impossible angles. Pieces of its flesh were missing, having been devoured by hungry fish. The right foot was gone completely, as was most of the left arm, the remnants of which were still attached by a thick thread of tendon.

The face was in the worst condition. The eye sockets were empty, the soft and swollen eyes having proven most tempting to the feeders of the deep. Lips and much of the cheeks had also been nibbled away, exposing the grinning teeth beneath.

There was no movement in the figure, and the gull that landed nearby felt no fear as it hopped toward the carrion feast. It pecked for a moment at the man's side, then hopped up onto the chest to get better access to the flesh of the face already opened by fish. Just as it was drawing back its head to drive its beak toward the raw meat, the figure's right arm shot up and grasped the bird by the neck.

Although the gull struggled, beating against this supposedly dead creature with its huge wings, the hand
squeezed tighter and tighter around the fragile neck
until thin bones snapped, blood spurted, and the gull
hung limp in the gray-fingered fist. The fingers opened,
and the dead bird fell onto the pebbles.

Victor Mordenheim lay there for several more hours,
but no other birds molested his sundered flesh. They
caught the scent of their murdered companion, an
undertone to the ripe, heady smell of Mordenheim's
gelid body, and stayed far away.

He lay there until he was sure he could think, rather
than act by instinct alone as he had done when he
grabbed the gull. In order to stabilize himself mentally,
he thought back over the past few hours—or was it
days?—that had brought him to this sad end and terrible beginning.

What he remembered most was the fall.

In his memory was the pain of the breaking glass,
the chill of the sea, the battering of the rocks, the pull of
the current, dragging him down, down into a darkness
devoid of any light, being thrown and whirled about like
a feather in a storm, until alighting here, washing up on
this unyielding beach of cold stone.

But what lingered was the fall, the flying through air,
the roar of the sea and of blood surging through his
head, the uncertainty of what would happen and where
and if he would land, and the surety that he would die.

Falling into death.

Running from the nightmare and falling into the cold,
wet darkness of death.

But now, awakening on the stones in a dead man's
body, he knew that the nightmare had just begun.
Already he could feel his body begin to heal itself, the
crippled leg start to rebuild its bone and tissue, the rav-
aged muscles knit themselves. In the sockets of his

eyes, he could feel new orbs growing, swelling to fit the holes made for them. And in time, he could see again, dimly. With every minute his vision improved until the shadows were no longer of his making but of Lamordia's.

He coughed, and water came forth from his mouth, so he rolled onto his swollen stomach and coughed again, clearing the green, brackish fluid from his lungs. Then he pressed his stomach against the stones and rolled back and forth on it, until the gases within him dissipated.

Finally he sat up and looked around, trying to avoid glancing at the ruin of his own body. It was dusk, and the sun was visible through the gray clouds only as a dull globe about to fall into the sea. A western shore, but more temperate than where he had come from, no ice visible.

The currents must have carried him south, then. He would have to travel northeast to return to Schloss Mordenheim. Yes, he would go there. That was his home. But more importantly, that was where his life awaited.

Elise.

That had not been her, that thing wearing her tired, forever-dying body. He had been betrayed by a science called magic, a science that was illogical and irrational and untrustworthy, that could be made lies by liars and could make the fairest foul. He had been a fool to ever put himself and Elise into the hands of those charlatans. He hoped Adam had killed them both, yes, and the Vistana girl too!

He pushed himself to his feet and swayed for a moment before getting his balance. Whatever had happened, he thought, they were gone now, and the gypsy girl as well. Maybe the gypsies had killed Kreutzer and the Von Karlsfeld woman. It didn't matter, as long as they'd left Elise alone.

Elise. He did not know if she would still be there, or if
Adam or the Vistani had torn her apart in their rage.
They might even have left her there, still animated by
those nameless rites. But somewhere within that foul
body was her fair spirit, and whether it now moved by
sorcerous means or remained still atop the laboratory
slab, he had to return and learn its fate, and try to make
it live once again.

And again and again and again, without rest, without
sleep, without joy or love or all the things that other,
lesser men lived for.

He would succeed, he *would!* For was he not Mordenheim, the miracle worker, the bringer of life, bringing the fire of knowledge to stubborn humankind?

He began to walk northeast, toward home, toward
his love and his destiny, toward the everlasting torment
that waited for the man who, for all his knowledge,
could not learn. The children who glimpsed him
through their late night windows as he shambled along
the shore shuddered at him. A few even mistook him
for his own monster.

And those who did not added him to the pantheon of
the creatures of Lamordia. He became the Thing on the
Strand, the Man Without a Face, the Dead Sailor, and a
dozen other ancient and instant legends, hated and
turned away from in dread, inspiring many tears and
many prayers.

By the time he reached Schloss Mordenheim, Victor
Mordenheim was whole again, and the gates lay open,
welcoming him.

Back to the abode of the damned.